FANTASY MASTERWORKS

The books are chests full of wonders; full of images like jewels, of words a reader can get drunk on, of people and incidents that will linger long in memory. For years and years to come, I think, we'll see inferior imitations of Wolfe's masterpiece decked out with the phrase "In the tradition of Wolfe", for that is the tribute all great originals are inevitably paid' George R. R. Martin

An accomplishment which must justify itself by nothing less than total success . . . What results is a . . . page-turningly tense and ominously dark narrative' Algis Budrys

A masterpiece. Gene Wolfe is a wizard, a torturer, frightening, delightful. Beware! This is magic stuff! . . . Totally original, new, incomparable' Ursula K. Le Guin

One expects any book from Gene Wolfe to be a classic – and here it is . . . Dark, daunting, and thoroughly believable.' Thomas M. Disch

'In fantasy, as in SF, Gene Wolfe's originality lies in the sense that – more thoroughly than almost any of his contemporaries – he is in the process of finishing the stories he tells. His work signals the late maturity of the genres he faces' *The Encyclopedia of Fantasy*

ALSO BY GENE WOLFE

Novels

Operation Ares (1970)

The Fifth Head of Cerberus (1972)

Peace (1975)

The Shadow of the Torturer (1980)

The Claw of the Conciliator (1981)

The Sword of the Lictor (1982)

The Citadel of the Autarch (1983)

The Castle of the Otter (1983)

Free Live Free (1984)

The Boy Who Hooked the Sun: A Tale From the Book of Wonders of Urth and Sky (1985)

Soldier of the Mist (1986)

Empires of Foliage and Flower: A Tale From the Book of Wonders of Urth and Sky (1987)

The Urth of the New Sun (1987)

There are Doors (1988)

Soldier of Arete (1989)

Castleview (1990)

Pandora by Holly Hollander (1990)

Nightside of the Long Sun (1993)

Lake of the Long Sun (1994)

Caldé of the Long Sun (1994)

Exodus From the Long Sun (1996)

On Blue's Waters (1999)

In Green's Jungles (2000)

Short Story Collections

The Island of Doctor Death and Other Stories and Other Stories (1980)

Gene Wolfe's Book of Days (1981)

Bibliomen: Twenty Characters Waiting For a Book (1984)

The Wolfe Archipelago (1983)

Plan[e]t Engineering (1984)

Storeys from the Old Hotel (1988)

Endangered Species (1989)

Castle of Days (1992)

Strange Travellers (1999)

Non Fiction

Letters Home (1991)

Fantasy Masterworks

THE BOOK OF
THE NEW SUN

VOLUME 2

Sword and Citadel

The Sword of the Lictor
The Citadel of the Autarch

GENE WOLFE

www.orionbooks.co.uk

The right of Gene Wolfe to be identified as the author of this work has been
asserted by him in accordance with the
Copyright, Designs and Patents Act 1988.

First published in Great Britain in 2000 by
Millennium
An imprint of Victor Gollancz
Orion House, 5 Upper St Martin's Lane, London WC2H 9EA
An Hachette Livre UK company

This edition reprinted in 2004 by
Gollancz
An imprint of the Orion publishing Group

10 9 8

A CIP catalogue record for this book is available
from the British Library

ISBN 978-1-85798-700-3

Printed in Great Britain by
Clays Ltd, St Ives plc

The Orion Publishing Group's policy is to use papers that
are natural, renewable and recyclable products and
made from wood grown in sustainable forests. The logging
and manufacturing processes are expected to conform to
the environmental regulations of the country of origin.

Into the distance disappear the mound of human heads.
I dwindle – go unnoticed now.
But in affectionate books, in children's games,
I will rise from the dead to say; the sun!

Osip Mandelstam

THE SWORD OF
THE LICTOR

I

Master of the House of Chains

"IT WAS IN my hair, Severian," Dorcas said. "So I stood under the waterfall in the hot stone room—I don't know if the men's side is arranged in the same way. And every time I stepped out, I could hear them talking about me. They called you the black butcher, and other things I don't want to tell you about."

"That's natural enough," I said. "You were probably the first stranger to enter the place in a month, so it's only to be expected that they would chatter about you, and that the few women who knew who you were would be proud of it and perhaps tell some tales. As for me, I'm used to it, and you must have heard such expressions on the way here many times; I know I did."

"Yes," she admitted, and sat down on the sill of the embrasure. In the city below, the lamps of the swarming shops were beginning to fill the valley of the Acis with a yellow radiance like the petals of a jonquil, but she did not seem to see them.

"Now you understand why the regulations of the guild forbid me from taking a wife—although I will break them for you, as I have told you many times, whenever you want me to."

"You mean that it would be better for me to live somewhere else, and only come to see you once or twice a week, or wait till you came to see me."

"That's the way it's usually done. And eventually the women who talked about us today will realize that sometime they, or their sons or husbands, may find themselves beneath my hand."

"But don't you see, this is all beside the point. The thing is . . ." Here Dorcas fell silent, and then, when neither of us had spoken for some time, she rose and began to pace the room, one arm clasping the other. It was something I had never seen her do before, and I found it disturbing.

"What is the point, then?" I asked.

"That it wasn't true then. That it is now."

"I practiced the Art whenever there was work to be had. Hired myself out to towns and country justices. Several times you watched me from a window, though you never liked to stand in the crowd—for which I hardly blame you."

"I didn't watch," she said.

"I recall seeing you."

"I didn't. Not when it was actually going on. You were intent on what you were doing, and didn't see me when I went inside or covered my eyes. I used to watch, and wave to you, when you first vaulted onto the scaffold. You were so proud then, and stood just as straight as your sword, and looked so fine. You were honest. I remember watching once when there was an official of some sort up there with you, and the condemned man and a hieromonach. And yours was the only honest face."

"You couldn't possibly have seen it. I must surely have been wearing my mask."

"Severian, I didn't have to see it. I know what you look like."

"Don't I look the same now?"

"Yes," she said reluctantly. "But I have been down below. I've seen the people chained in the tunnels. When we sleep tonight, you and I in our soft bed, we will be sleeping on top of them. How many did you say there were when you took me down?"

"About sixteen hundred. Do you honestly believe those sixteen hundred would be free if I were no longer present to guard them? They were here, remember, when we came."

Dorcas would not look at me. "It's like a mass grave," she said. I could see her shoulders shake.

"It should be," I told her. "The archon could release them, but who could resurrect those they've killed? You've never lost anyone, have you?"

She did not reply.

"Ask the wives and the mothers and the sisters of the men our prisoners have left rotting in the high country whether Abdiesus should let them go."

"Only myself," Dorcas said, and blew out the candle.

Thrax is a crooked dagger entering the heart of the mountains. It lies in a narrow defile of the valley of the Acis, and extends up it to Acies Castle. The harena, the pantheon, and the other public buildings occupy all the level land between the castle and the wall (called the Capulus) that closes the lower end of the narrow section of the valley. The private buildings of the city climb the cliffs to either side, and many are in large measure dug into the rock itself, from which practice Thrax gains one of its sobriquets—the City of Windowless Rooms.

Its prosperity it owes to its position at the head of the navigable part of the river. At Thrax, all goods shipped north on the Acis (many of which have traversed nine tenths of the length of Gyoll before entering the mouth of the smaller river, which may indeed be Gyoll's true source) must be unloaded and carried on the backs of animals if they are to travel farther. Conversely, the hetmans of the mountain tribes and the landowners of the region who wish to ship their wool and corn to the southern towns bring them to take boat at Thrax, below the cataract that roars through the arched spillway of Acies Castle.

As must always be the case when a stronghold imposes the rule of law over a turbulent region, the administration of justice was the chief concern of the archon of the city. To impose his will on those without the walls who might otherwise have opposed it, he could call upon seven squadrons of dimarchi, each under its own commander. Court convened each month, from the first appearance of the new moon to the full, beginning with the second morning watch and continuing as long as necessary to clear the day's docket. As chief executor of the archon's sentences, I was required to attend these sessions, so that he might be assured that the punishments he decreed should be made neither softer nor more severe by those who might otherwise have been charged with transmitting them to me; and to oversee the operation of the Vincula, in which the prisoners were detained, in all its details. It was a responsibility equivalent on a lesser scale to that of Master Gurloes in our Citadel, and during the first few weeks I spent in Thrax it weighed heavily upon me.

It was a maxim of Master Gurloes's that no prison is ideally situated. Like most of the wise tags put forward for the edification of young men, it was inarguable and unhelpful. All escapes fall into three categories—that is, they are achieved by stealth, by violence, or by the treachery of those set as guards. A remote place does most to render escapes by stealth difficult, and for that reason has been favored by the majority of those who have thought long upon the subject.

Unfortunately, deserts, mountaintops, and lone isles offer the most fertile fields for violent escape—if they are besieged by the prisoners' friends, it is difficult to learn of the fact before it is too late, and next to impossible to reinforce their garrisons; and similarly, if the prisoners rise in rebellion, it is highly unlikely that troops can be rushed to the spot before the issue is decided.

A facility in a well-populated and well-defended district avoids these difficulties, but incurs even more severe ones. In such places a prisoner needs, not a thousand friends, but one or two; and these need not be fighting men—a scrubwoman and a street vendor will do, if they possess intelligence and resolution. Furthermore, once the prisoner has escaped the walls, he mingles immediately with the faceless mob, so that his reapprehension is not a matter for huntsmen and dogs but for agents and informers.

In our own case, a detached prison in a remote location would have been out of the question. Even if it had been provided with a sufficient number of troops, in addition to its clavigers, to fend off the attacks of the autochthons, zoanthrops, and cultellarii who roamed the countryside, not to mention the armed retinues of the petty exultants (who could never be relied upon), it would still have been impossible to provision without the services of an army to escort the supply trains. The Vincula of Thrax is therefore located by necessity within the city—specifically, about halfway up the cliffside on the west bank, and a half league or so from the Capulus.

It is of ancient design, and always appeared to me to have been intended as a prison from the beginning, though there is a legend to the effect that it was originally a tomb, and was only a few hundred years ago enlarged and converted to its new purpose. To an observer on the more commodious east bank, it appears to be a rectangular bartizan jutting from the rock, a bartizan four stories high at the side he sees, whose flat, merloned roof terminates against the cliff. This visible portion of the structure—which many visitors to the city must take for the whole of it—is in fact the smallest and least important part. At the time I was lictor, it held no more than our administrative offices, a barracks for the clavigers, and my own living quarters.

The prisoners were lodged in a slanted shaft bored into the rock. The arrangement used was neither one of individual cells such as we had for our clients in the oubliette at home, nor the common room I had encountered while I was myself confined in the House Absolute. Instead, the prisoners were chained along the walls of the shaft, each with a stout iron collar about his neck, in such a way as to leave a path down the center wide enough that two clavigers could walk it abreast without danger that their keys might be snatched away.

This shaft was about five hundred paces long, and had over a thousand positions for prisoners. Its water supply came from a cistern sunk into the stone at the top of the cliff, and sanitary wastes were disposed of by flushing the shaft whenever this cistern threatened to overflow. A sewer drilled at the lower end of the shaft conveyed the wastewater to a conduit at the cliff base that ran through the wall of the Capulus to empty into the Acis below the city.

The rectangular bartizan clinging to the cliff, and the shaft itself, must originally have constituted the whole of the Vincula. It had subsequently been complicated by a confusion of branching galleries and parallel shafts resulting from past attempts to free prisoners by tunneling from one or another of the private residences in the cliff face, and from countermines excavated to frustrate such attempts—all now pressed into service to provide additional accommodations.

The existence of these unplanned or poorly planned additions rendered my task much more difficult than it would otherwise have been, and one of my first acts was to begin a program of closing unwanted and unnecessary passages by filling them with a mixture of river stones, sand, water, burned lime, and gravel, and to start widening and uniting those passages that remained in such a way as to eventually achieve a rational structure. Necessary though it was, this work could be carried forward only very slowly, since no more than a few hundred prisoners could be freed to work at a time, and they were for the most part in poor condition.

For the first few weeks after Dorcas and I arrived in the city, my duties left me time for nothing else. She explored it for us both, and I charged her strictly to inquire about the Pelerines for me. On the long journey from Nessus the knowledge that I carried the Claw of the Conciliator had been a heavy burden. Now, when I was no longer traveling and could no longer attempt to trace the Pelerines along the way or even reassure myself that I was walking in a direction that might eventually bring me in contact with them, it became an almost unbearable weight. While we were traveling I had slept under the stars with the gem in the top of my boot, and with it concealed in the toe on those few occasions when we were able to stop beneath a roof. Now I found that I could not sleep at all unless I had it with me, so I could assure myself, whenever I woke in the night, that I retained possession of it. Dorcas sewed a little sack of doeskin for me to hold it, and I wore it about my neck day and night. A dozen times during those first weeks I dreamed I saw the gem aflame, hanging in the air above me like its own burning cathedral, and woke to find it blazing so brightly that a faint radiance showed through the thin leather. And once or twice each night I awakened to discover that I was lying on my back with the sack on my chest seemingly grown so heavy (though I could lift it with my hand without effort) that it was crushing out my life.

Dorcas did everything in her power to comfort and assist me; yet I could see she was conscious of the abrupt change in our relationship and disturbed by it even more than I. Such changes are always, in my experience, unpleasant—if only because they imply the likelihood of further change. While we had been journeying together (and we had been traveling with greater or lesser expedition from the moment in the Garden of Endless Sleep when Dorcas helped me clamber, half-drowned, onto the floating walkway of sedge) it had been as equals and companions, each of us walking every league we covered on our own feet or riding our own mount. If I had supplied a measure of physical protection to Dorcas, she had equally supplied a certain moral shelter to me, in that few could pretend for long to despise her innocent beauty, or profess horror at my office when in looking at me they could not help but see her as well. She had been my counselor in perplexity and my comrade in a hundred desert places.

When we at last entered Thrax and I presented Master Palaemon's letter to the archon, all that was by necessity ended. In my fuligin habit I no longer had to fear the crowd—rather, they feared me as the highest official of the most dreaded arm of the state. Dorcas lived now, not as an equal but as the paramour the Cumaean had once called her, in the quarters in the Vincula set aside for me. Her counsel had become useless or nearly so because the difficulties that oppressed me were the legal and administrative ones I had been trained for years to wrestle with and about which she knew nothing; and moreover because I seldom had the time or the energy to explain them to her so that we might discuss them.

Thus, while I stood for watch after watch in the archon's court, Dorcas fell into the habit of wandering the city, and we, who had been incessantly together throughout the latter part of the spring, came now in summer to see each other hardly at all, sharing a meal in the evening and climbing exhausted into a bed where we seldom did more than fall asleep in each other's arms.

At last the full moon shone. With what joy I beheld it from the roof of the bartizan, green as an emerald in its mantle of forest and round as the lip of a cup! I was not yet free, since all the details of excruciations and administration that had been accumulating during my attendance on the archon remained to be dealt with; but I was now at least free to devote my full attention to them, which seemed then nearly as good a thing as freedom itself. I had invited Dorcas to go with me on the next day, when I made an inspection of the subterranean parts of the Vincula.

It was an error. She grew ill in the foul air, surrounded by the misery of the prisoners. That night, as I have already recounted, she told me she had gone to the public baths (a rare thing for her, whose fear of water was so great that she washed herself bit by bit with a sponge dipped in a bowl no deeper than a dish of soup) to free her hair and skin from the odor of the shaft, and that she had heard the bath attendants pointing her out to the other patrons.

II

Upon the Cataract

THE FOLLOWING MORNING, before she left the bartizan, Dorcas cut her hair until she almost seemed a boy, and thrust a white peony through the circulet that confined it. I labored over documents until afternoon, then borrowed a layman's jelab from the sergeant of my clavigers and went out hoping to encounter her.

The brown book I carry says there is nothing stranger than to explore a city wholly different from all those one knows, since to do so is to explore a second and unsuspected self. I have found a thing stranger: to explore such a city only after one has lived in it for some time without learning anything of it.

I did not know where the baths Dorcas had mentioned stood, though I had surmised from talk I had heard in court that they existed. I did not know where the bazaar where she bought her cloth and cosmetics was located, or even if there were more than one. I knew nothing, in short, beyond what I could see from the embrasure, and the brief route from the Vincula to the archon's palace. I had, perhaps, a too-ready confidence in my own ability to find my way about in a city so much smaller than Nessus; even so I took the precaution of making certain from time to time, as I trod the crooked streets that straggled down the cliff between cave-houses excavated from the rock and swallow-houses jutting out from it, that I could still see the familiar shape of the bartizan, with its barricaded gate and black gonfalon.

In Nessus the rich live toward the north where the waters of Gyoll are purer, and the poor to the south where they are foul. Here in Thrax that custom no longer held, both because the Acis flowed so swiftly that the excrement of those upstream (who were, of course, but a thousandth part as numerous as those who lived about the northern reaches of Gyoll) hardly affected its flood, and because water taken from above the cataract was conveyed to the public fountains and the homes of the wealthy by aqueducts, so that no reliance had to be put upon the river save when the largest quantities of water—as for manufacturing or wholesale washing—were required.

Thus in Thrax the separation was by elevation. The wealthiest lived on the lowest slopes near the river, within easy reach of the shops and public offices, where a brief walk brought them to piers from which they could travel the length of the city in slave-rowed caiques. Those somewhat less well off had their houses higher, the middle class in general had theirs higher still, and so on until the very poorest dwelt just below the fortifications at the cliff tops, often in jacals of mud and reeds that could be reached only by long ladders.

I was to see something of those miserable hovels, but for the present I remained in the commercial quarter near the water. There the narrow streets were so thronged with people that I at first thought a festival was in progress, or perhaps that the war—which had seemed so remote while I remained in Nessus but had become progressively more immediate as Dorcas and I journeyed north—was now near enough to fill the city with those who fled before it.

Nessus is so extensive that it has, as I have heard said, five buildings for each living inhabitant. In Thrax that ratio is surely reversed, and on that day it seemed to me at times that there must have been fifty for each roof. Too, Nessus is a cosmopolitan city, so that although one saw many foreigners there, and occasionally even cacogens come by ship from other worlds, one was always conscious that they *were* foreigners, far from their homes. Here the streets swarmed with diverse humanity, but they merely reflected the diverse nature of the mountain setting, so that when I saw, for example, a man whose hat was made from a bird's pelt with the wings used for ear flaps, or a man in a shaggy coat of kaberu skin, or a man with a tattooed face, I might see a hundred more such tribesmen around the next corner.

These men were eclectics, the descendants of settlers from the south who had mixed their blood with that of the squat, dark autochthons, adopted certain of their customs, and mingled these with still others acquired from the amphitryons farther north and those, in some instances, of even less-known peoples, traders and parochial races.

Many of these eclectics favor knives that are curved—or as they are sometimes called, bent—having two relatively straight sections, with an elbow a little toward the point. This shape is said to make it easier to pierce the heart by stabbing beneath the breastbone; the blades are stiffened with a central rib, are sharpened on both sides, and are kept very sharp; there is no guard, and their hafts are commonly of bone. (I have described these knives in detail because they are as characteristic of the region as anything can be said to be, and because it is from them that Thrax takes another of its names: the City of Crooked Knives. There is also the resemblance of the plan of the city to the blade of such a knife, the curve of the defile corresponding to the curve of the blade, the River Acis to the central rib, Acies Castle to the point, and the Capulus to the line at which the steel vanishes into the haft.)

One of the keepers of the Bear Tower once told me that there is no animal so dangerous or so savage and unmanageable as the hybrid resulting when a fighting dog mounts a she-wolf. We are accustomed to think of the beasts of the forest and mountain as wild, and to think of the men who spring up, as it seems, from their soil as savage. But the truth is that there is a wildness more vicious (as we would know better if we were not so habituated to it) in certain domestic animals, despite their understanding so much human speech and sometimes even speaking a few words; and there is a more profound savagery in men and women whose ancestors have lived in cities and towns since the dawn of humanity. Vodalus, in whose veins flowed the undefiled blood of a thousand exultants—exarchs, ethnarchs, and starosts—was capable of violence unimaginable to the autochthons that stalked the streets of Thrax, naked beneath their huanaco cloaks.

Like the dog-wolves (which I never saw, because they were too vicious to be useful), these eclectics took all that was most cruel and ungovernable from their mixed parentage; as friends or followers they were sullen, disloyal, and contentious; as enemies, fierce, deceitful, and vindictive. So at least I had heard from my subordinates at the Vincula, for eclectics made up more than half the prisoners there.

I have never encountered men whose language, costume, or customs are foreign without speculating on the nature of the women of their race. There is always a connection, since the two are the growths of a single culture, just as the leaves of a tree, which one sees, and the fruit, which one does not see because it is hidden by the leaves, are the growths of a single organism. But the observer who would venture to predict the appearance and flavor of the fruit from the outline of a few leafy boughs seen (as it were) from a distance, must know a great deal about leaves and fruit if he is not to make himself ridiculous.

Warlike men may be born of languishing women, or they

may have sisters nearly as strong as themselves and more reso-
lute. And so I, walking among crowds composed largely of
these eclectics and the townsmen (who seemed to me not
much different from the citizens of Nessus, save that their
clothing and their manners were somewhat rougher) found
myself speculating on dark-eyed, dark-skinned women, women
with glossy black hair as thick as the tails of the skewbald
mounts of their brothers, women whose faces I imagined as
strong yet delicate, women given to ferocious resistance and
swift surrender, women who could be won but not bought—if
such women exist in this world.

From their arms I traveled in imagination to the places
where they might be found, the lonely huts crouched by
mountain springs, the hide yurts standing alone in the high
pastures. Soon I was as intoxicated with the thought of the
mountains as I had been once, before Master Palaemon had
told me the correct location of Thrax, with the idea of the
sea. How glorious are they, the immovable idols of Urth,
carved with unaccountable tools in a time inconceivably ancient, still lifting above the rim of the world grim heads
crowned with mitres, tiaras, and diadems spangled with snow,
heads whose eyes are as large as towns, figures whose shoulders
are wrapped in forests.

Thus, disguised in the dull jelab of a townsman, I elbowed
my way down streets packed with humanity and reeking with
the odors of ordure and cookery, with my imagination filled
with visions of hanging stone, and crystal streams like car-
canets.

Thecla must, I think, have been taken at least into the
foothills of these heights, no doubt to escape the heat of
some particularly torrid summer; for many of the scenes that
rose in my mind (as it seemed, of their own accord) were
noticeably childlike. I saw rock-loving plants whose virginal
flowers I beheld with an immediacy of vision no adult
achieves without kneeling; abysses that seemed not only

frightening but shocking, as though their existence were an affront to the laws of nature; peaks so high they appeared to be literally without summit, as though the whole world had been falling forever from some unimaginable Heaven, which yet retained its hold on these mountains.

Eventually I reached Acies Castle, having walked almost the entire length of the city. I made my identity known to the postern guards there and was permitted to enter and climb to the top of the donjon, as I had once climbed our Matachin Tower before taking my leave of Master Palaemon.

When I had gone there to make my farewell to the only place I had known, I had stood at one of the loftiest points of the Citadel, which was itself poised atop one of the highest elevations in the whole area of Nessus. The city had been spread before me to the limits of vision, with Gyoll traced across it like the green slime of a slug across a map; even the Wall had been visible on the horizon at some points, and nowhere was I beneath the shadow of a summit much superior to my own.

Here the impression was far different. I bestrode the Acis, which leaped toward me down a succession of rocky steps each twice or three times the height of a tall tree. Beaten to a foaming whiteness that glittered in the sunlight, it disappeared beneath me and reappeared as a ribbon of silver racing through a city as neatly contained in its declivity as one of those toy villages in a box that I (but it was Thecla) recalled receiving on a birthday.

Yet I stood, as it were, at the bottom of a bowl. On every side the walls of stone ascended, so that to look at any one of them was to believe, for a moment at least, that gravity had been twisted until it stood at right angles to its proper self by some sorcerer's multiplication with imaginary numbers, and the height I saw was properly the level surface of the world.

For a watch or more, I think, I stared up at those walls, and traced the spidery lines of the waterfalls that dashed down them in thunder and clean romance to join the Acis, and watched the clouds trapped among them that seemed to press softly against their unyielding sides like sheep bewildered and dismayed among pens of stone.

Then I grew weary at last of the magnificence of the mountains and my mountain dreams—or rather, not weary, but dizzied by them until my head reeled with vertigo, and I seemed to see those merciless heights even when I closed my eyes, and felt that in my dreams, that night and for many nights, I would fall from their precipices, or cling with bloody fingers to their hopeless walls.

Then I turned in earnest to the city and reassured myself with the sight of the bartizan of the Vincula, a very modest little cube now, cemented to a cliff that was hardly more than a ripple among the incalculable waves of stone around it. I plotted the courses of the principal streets, seeking (as in a game, to sober myself from my long gazing on the mountains) to identify those I had walked in reaching the castle, and to observe from this new perspective the buildings and market squares I had seen on the way. By eye I looted the bazaars, finding that there were two, one on either side of the river; and I marked afresh the familiar landmarks I had learned to know from the embrasure of the Vincula—the harena, the pantheon, and the archon's palace. Then, when everything I had seen from the ground had been confirmed from my new vantage point, and I felt I understood the spatial relationship of the place at which I stood to what I had known earlier of the plan of the city, I began to explore the lesser streets, peering along the twisted paths that climbed the upper cliffs and probing narrow alleys that often seemed no more than mere bands of darkness between buildings.

In seeking them out, my gaze came at last to the margins of the river again, and I began to study the landings there, and the storehouses, and even the pyramids of barrels and boxes and bales that waited there to be carried aboard some vessel.

Now the water no longer foamed, save when it was obstructed by the piers. Its color was nearly indigo, and like the indigo shadows seen at evening on a snowy day, it seemed to slip silently along, sinuous and freezing; but the motion of the hurrying caiques and laden feluccas showed how much turbulence lay concealed beneath that smooth surface, for the larger craft swung their long bowsprits like fencers, and both yawed crabwise at times while their oars threshed the racing eddies.

When I had exhausted all that lay farther downstream, I leaned from the parapet to observe the closest reach of the river and a wharf that was no more than a hundred strides from the postern gate. Looking down at the stevedores there who toiled to unburden one of the narrow river boats, I saw near them, unmoving, a tiny figure with bright hair. At first I thought her a child because she seemed so small beside the burly, nearly naked laborers; but it was Dorcas, sitting at the very edge of the water with her face in her hands.

III

Outside the Jacal

WHEN I REACHED Dorcas I could not make her speak. It was not simply that she was angry with me, although I thought so at the time. Silence had come upon her like a disease, not injuring her tongue and lips but disabling her will to use them and perhaps even her desire to, just as certain infections destroy our desire for pleasure and even our comprehension of joy in others. If I did not lift her face to mine, she would look at nothing, staring at the ground beneath her feet without, I think, seeing even that, or covering her face with her hands, as she had been covering it when I found her.

I wanted to talk to her, believing—then—that I could say something, though I was not certain what, that would restore her to herself. But I could not do so there on the wharf, with stevedores staring at us, and for a time I could find no place to which I could lead her. On a little street nearby that had begun to climb the slope east of the river, I saw the board of an inn. There were patrons eating in its narrow common room, but for a few aes I was able to rent a chamber on the floor above it, a plaçe with no furniture but a bed and little space for any, with a ceiling so low that at one end I could not stand erect. The hostess thought we were renting her chamber for a tryst, naturally enough under the circumstances—but thought too, because of Dorcas's despairing expression, that I had some hold on her or had bought her from a procurer, and so gave her a look of melting sympathy that I do not believe she noticed in the least, and me one of recrimination.

I shut and bolted the door and made Dorcas lie on the bed; then I sat beside her and tried to cajole her into conversation, asking her what was wrong, and what I might do to right whatever it was that troubled her, and so on. When I found that had no effect, I began to talk about myself, supposing that it was only her horror of the conditions in the Vincula that had moved her to sever herself from discourse with me.

"We are despised by everyone," I said. "And so there is no reason why I should not be despised by you. The surprising thing is not that you should have come to hate me now, but that you could go this long before coming to feel as the rest do. But because I love you, I am going to try to state the case for our guild, and thus for myself, hoping that perhaps afterward you won't feel so badly about having loved a torturer, even though you don't love me any longer.

"We are not cruel. We take no delight in what we do, except in doing it well, which means doing it quickly and doing it neither more nor less than the law instructs us. We obey the judges, who hold their offices because the people consent to it. Some individuals tell us we should do nothing of what we do, and that no one should do it. They say that punishment inflicted with cold blood is a greater crime than any crime our clients could have committed.

"There may be justice in that, but it is a justice that would destroy the whole Commonwealth. No one could feel safe and no one could be safe, and in the end the people would rise up—at first against the thieves and the murderers, and then against anyone who offended the popular ideas of propriety, and at last against mere strangers and outcasts. Then they would be back to the old horrors of stoning and burning, in which every man seeks to outdo his neighbor for fear he will be thought tomorrow to hold some sympathy for the wretch dying today.

"There are others who tell us that certain clients are deserving of the most severe punishment, but that others are not, and that we should refuse to perform our office upon those others. It certainly must be that some are more guilty than the rest, and it may even be that some of these who are handed over to us have done no wrong at all, neither in the matter in which they are accused, nor in any other.

"But the people who urge these arguments are doing no more than setting themselves up as judges over the judges appointed by the Autarch, judges with less training in the law and without the authority to call witnesses. They demand that we disobey the real judges and listen to them, but they cannot show that they are more deserving of our obedience.

"Others yet hold that our clients should not be tortured or executed, but should be made to labor for the Commonwealth, digging canals, building watchtowers, and the like. But with the cost of their guards and chains, honest workers might be hired, who otherwise would want for bread. Why should these loyal workers starve so that murderers shall not die, nor thieves feel any pain? Furthermore, these murderers and thieves, being without loyalty to the law and without hope of reward, would not work save under the lash. What is that lash but torture again, going under a new name?

"Still others say that all those judged guilty should be confined, in comfort and without pain, for many years—and often for as long as they will live. But those who have comfort and no pain live long, and every orichalk spent to maintain them so would have to be taken from better purposes. I know little of the war, but I know enough to understand how much money is needed to buy weapons and pay soldiers. The fighting is in the mountains to the north now, so that we fight as if behind a hundred walls. But what if it should reach the pam-

pas? Would it be possible to hold back the Ascians when
there was so much room to maneuver? And how would
Nessus be fed if the herds there were to fall into their hands?

"If the guilty are not to be locked away in comfort, and are
not to be tortured, what remains? If they are all killed, and all
killed alike, then a poor woman who steals will be thought as
bad as a mother who poisons her own child, as Morwenna of
Saltus did. Would you wish that? In time of peace, many
might be banished. But to banish them now would only be to
deliver a corps of spies to the Ascians, to be trained and supplied with funds and sent back among us. Soon no one could
be trusted, though he spoke our own tongue. Would you wish
that?"

Dorcas lay so silent upon the bed that I thought for a moment she had fallen asleep. But her eyes, those enormous eyes
of perfect blue, were open; and when I leaned over to look at
her, they moved, and seemed for a time to watch me as they
might have watched the spreading ripples in a pond.

"All right, we are devils," I said. "If you would have it so.
But we are necessary. Even the powers of Heaven find it necessary to employ devils."

Tears came into her eyes, though I could not tell whether
she wept because she had hurt me or because she found that I
was still present. In the hope of winning her back to her old
affection for me, I began to talk of the times when we were
still on the way to Thrax, reminding her of how we had met in
the clearing after we had fled the grounds of the House Absolute, and of how we had talked in those great gardens before
Dr. Talos's play, walking through the blossoming orchard to
sit on an old bench beside a broken fountain, and of all she
had said to me there, and of all that I had said to her.

And it seemed to me that she became a trifle less sorrowful
until I mentioned the fountain, whose waters had run from its
cracked basin to form a little stream that some gardener had
sent wandering among the trees to refresh them, and there to
end by soaking the ground; but then a darkness that was no-

where in the room but on Dorcas's face came to settle there like one of those strange things that had pursued Jonas and me through the cedars. Then she would no longer look at me, and after a time she truly slept.

I got up as silently as I could, unbolted the door, and went down the crooked stair. The hostess was still working in the common room below, but the patrons who had been there were gone. I explained to her that the woman I had brought was ill, paid the rent of the room for several days, and promising to return and take care of any other expenses, asked her to look in on her from time to time, and to feed her if she would eat.

"Ah, it will be a blessing to us to have someone sleeping in the room," the hostess said. "But if your darling's sick, is the Duck's Nest the best place you can find for her? Can't you take her home?"

"I'm afraid living in my house is what has made her ill. At least, I don't want to risk the chance that returning there will make her worse."

"Poor darling!" The hostess shook her head. "So pretty too, and doesn't look more than a child. How old is she?"

I told her I did not know.

"Well, I'll have a visit with her and give her some soup when she's ready for it." She looked at me as if to say that the time would come soon enough once I was away. "But I want you to know that I won't hold her a prisoner for you. If she wants to leave, she'll be free to go."

When I stepped out of the little inn, I wished to return to the Vincula by the most direct route; but I made the mistake of supposing that since the narrow street on which the Duck's Nest stood ran almost due south, it would be quicker to continue along it and cross the Acis lower down than to retrace the steps Dorcas and I had already taken and go back to the foot of the postern wall of Acies Castle.

The narrow street betrayed me, as I would have expected if I had been more familiar with the ways of Thrax. For all those crooked streets that snake along the slopes, though they may cross one another, on the whole run up and down; so that to reach one cliff-hugging house from another (unless they are quite close together or one above the other) it is necessary to walk down to the central strip near the river, and then back up again. Thus before long I found myself as high up the eastern cliff as the Vincula was on the western one, with less prospect of reaching it than I had when I left the inn.

To be truthful, it was not a wholly unpleasant discovery. I had work to do there, and no particular desire to do it, my mind being still full of thoughts of Dorcas. It felt better to wear out my frustrations by the use of my legs, and so I resolved to follow the capering street to the top if need be and see the Vincula and Acies Castle from that height, and then to show my badge of office to the guards at the fortifications there and walk along them to the Capulus and so cross the river by the lowest way.

But after half a watch of strenuous effort, I found I could go no farther. The street ended against a precipice three or four chains high, and perhaps had properly ended sooner, for the last few score paces I had walked had been on what was probably no more than a private path to the miserable jacal of mud and sticks before which I stood.

After making certain there was no way around it, and no way to the top for some distance from where I stood, I was about to turn away in disgust when a child slipped out of the jacal, and sidling toward me in a half bold, half fearful way, watching me with its right eye only, extended a small and very dirty hand in the universal gesture of beggars. Perhaps I would have laughed at the poor little creature, so timid and so importunate, if I had felt in a better mood; as it was, I dropped a few aes into the soiled palm.

Encouraged, the child ventured to say, "My sister is sick.

Very sick, sieur." From the timbre of its voice I decided it was
a boy; and because he turned his head almost toward me
when he spoke, I could see that his left eye was swollen shut
by some infection. Tears of pus had run from it to dry on the
cheek below. "Very, very sick."

"I see," I told him.

"Oh, no, sieur. You cannot, not from here. But if you wish
you can look in through the door—you will not bother her."

Just then a man wearing the scuffed leather apron of a
mason called, "What is it, Jader? What does he want?" He
was toiling up the path in our direction.

As anyone might have anticipated, the boy was only frightened into silence by the question. I said, "I was asking the
best way to the lower city."

The mason answered nothing, but stopped about four
strides from me and folded arms that looked harder than the
stones they broke. He seemed angry and distrustful, though I
could not be sure why. Perhaps my accent had betrayed that
I came from the south; perhaps it was only because of the way
I was dressed, which though it was by no means rich or fantastic, indicated that I belonged to a social class higher than his
own.

"Am I trespassing?" I asked. "Do you own this place?"

There was no reply. Whatever he felt about me, it was
plain that in his opinion there could be no communication
between us. When I spoke to him, it could only be as a man
speaks to a beast, and not even to intelligent beasts at that,
but only as a drover shouts at kine. And on his side, when I
spoke it was only as beasts speak to a man, a sound made in
the throat.

I have noticed that in books this sort of stalemate never
seems to occur; the authors are so anxious to move their stories forward (however wooden they may be, advancing like
market carts with squeaking wheels that are never still,
though they go only to dusty villages where the charm of the

country is lost and the pleasures of the city will never be found) that there are no such misunderstandings, no refusals to negotiate. The assassin who holds a dagger to his victim's neck is eager to discuss the whole matter, and at any length the victim or the author may wish. The passionate pair in love's embrace are at least equally willing to postpone the stabbing, if not more so.

In life it is not the same. I stared at the mason, and he at me. I felt I could have killed him, but I could not be sure of it, both because he looked unusually strong and because I could not be certain he did not have some concealed weapon, or friends in the miserable dwellings close by. I felt he was about to spit onto the path between us, and if he had I would have flung my jelab over his head and pinned him. But he did not, and when we had stared at each other for several moments, the boy, who perhaps had no idea of what was taking place said again, "You can look through the door, sieur. You won't bother my sister." He even dared to tug a little at my sleeve in his eagerness to show he had not lied, not seeming to realize that his own appearance justified any amount of begging.

"I believe you," I said. But then I understood that to say I believed him was to insult him by showing that I did not have faith enough in what he said to put it to the test. I bent and peered, though at first I could see little, looking as I was from the bright sunshine into the shadowy interior of the jacal.

The light was almost squarely behind me. I felt its pressure on the nape of my neck, and I was conscious that the mason could attack me with impunity now that my back was toward him.

Tiny as it was, the room inside was not cluttered. Some straw had been heaped against the wall farthest from the door, and the girl lay upon it. She was in that state of disease in which we no longer feel pity for the sick person, who has instead become an object of horror. Her face was a death's head over which was stretched skin as thin and translucent as the head of a drum. Her lips could no longer cover her teeth even in sleep, and under the scythe of fever, her hair had fallen away until only wisps remained.

I braced my hands on the mud and wattle wall beside the door and straightened up. The boy said, "You see she is very sick, sieur. My sister." He held out his hand again.

I saw it—I see it before me now—but it made no immediate impression on my mind. I could think only of the Claw; and it seemed to me that it was pressing against my breastbone, not so much like a weight as like the knuckles of an invisible fist. I remembered the uhlan who had appeared dead until I touched his lips with the Claw, and who now seemed to me to belong to the remote past; and I remembered the man-ape, with his stump of arm, and the way Jonas's burns had faded when I ran the Claw along their length. I had not used it or even considered using it since it had failed to save Jolenta.

Now I had kept its secret so long that I was afraid to try it again. I would have touched the dying girl with it, perhaps, if it had not been for her brother looking on; I would have touched the brother's diseased eye with it if it had not been for the surly mason. As it was, I only labored to breathe against the force that strained my ribs, and did nothing, walking away downhill without noticing in what direction I walked. I heard the mason's saliva fly from his mouth and smack the eroded stone of the path behind me; but I did not know what the sound was until I was almost back at the Vincula and had more or less returned to myself.

IV

In the Bartizan of the Vincula

"YOU HAVE COMPANY, Lictor," the sentry told me, and when I only nodded to acknowledge the information, he added, "It might be best for you to change first, Lictor." I did not need then to ask who my guest was; only the presence of the archon would have drawn that tone from him.

It was not difficult to reach my private quarters without passing through the study where I conducted the business of the Vincula and kept its accounts. I spent the time it took to divest myself of my borrowed jelab and put on my fuligin cloak in speculating as to why the archon, who had never come to me before, and whom, for that matter, I had seldom even seen outside his court, should find it necessary to visit the Vincula—so far as I could see, without an entourage.

The speculation was welcome because it kept certain other thoughts at a distance. There was a large silvered glass in our bedroom, a much more effective mirror than the small plates of polished metal to which I was accustomed; and on it, as I saw for the first time when I stood before it to examine my appearance, Dorcas had scrawled in soap four lines from a song she had once sung for me:

33

> Horns of Urth, you fling notes to the sky,
> Green and good, green and good.
> Sing at my step; a sweeter glade have I.
> Lift, oh, lift me to the fallen wood!

There were several large chairs in the study, and I had anticipated finding the archon in one of them (though it had also crossed my mind that he might be availing himself of the opportunity to go through my papers—something he had every right to do if he chose). He was standing at the embrasure instead, looking out over his city much as I myself had looked out at it from the ramparts of Acies Castle earlier that afternoon. His hands were clasped behind him, and as I watched I saw them move as if each possessed a life of its own, engendered by his thoughts. It was some time before he turned and caught sight of me.

"You are here, Master Torturer. I did not hear you come in."

"I am only a journeyman, Archon."

He smiled and seated himself on the sill, his back to the drop. His face was coarse, with a hook nose and large eyes rimmed with dark flesh, but it was not a masculine face; it might almost have been the face of an ugly woman. "Charged by me with the responsibility for this place, you remain a mere journeyman?"

"I can be elevated only by the masters of our guild, Archon."

"But you are the best of their journeymen, judging from the letter you carried, from their choosing you to send here, and from the work you've done since you arrived. Anyway, no one here would know the difference if you chose to put on airs. How many masters are there?"

"I would know, Archon. Only two, unless someone has been elevated since I've been gone."

"I'll write them and ask them to elevate you *in absentia*."

"I thank you, Archon."

"It's nothing," he said, and turned to stare out the embrasure as though the situation embarrassed him. "You should have word of it, I suppose, in a month."

"They will not elevate me, Archon. But it will make Master Palaemon happy to hear you think so well of me."

He swung around again to look at me. "We need not be so formal, surely. My name is Abdiesus, and there is no reason you should not use it when we're alone. You're Severian, I believe?"

I nodded.

He turned away again. "This is a very low opening. I was examining it before you came in, and the wall hardly reaches above my knees. It would be easy, I'm afraid, for someone to fall out of it."

"Only for someone as tall as yourself, Abdiesus."

"In the past, were not executions performed, occasionally, by casting the victim from a high window or from the edge of a precipice?"

"Yes, both those methods have been employed."

"Not by you, I suppose." Once more he faced me.

"Not within living memory, so far as I know, Abdiesus. I have performed decollations—both with the block and with the chair—but that is all."

"But you would have no objection to the use of other means? If you were instructed to employ them?"

"I am here to carry out the archon's sentences."

"There are times, Severian, when public executions serve the public good. There are others when they would only do harm by inciting public unrest."

"That is understood, Abdiesus," I said. As sometimes I have seen in the eyes of a boy the worry of the man he will be, I could see the future guilt that had already come (perhaps without his being aware of it) to settle on the archon's face.

"There will be a few guests at the palace tonight. I hope that you will be among them, Severian."

I bowed. "Among the divisions of administration, Abdiesus, it has long been customary to exclude one—my own—from the society of the others."

"And you feel that is unjust, which is wholly natural. Tonight, if you wish to think of it in that way, we will be making some restitution."

"We of the guild have never complained of injustice. Indeed, we have gloried in our unique isolation. Tonight, however, the others may feel they have reason to protest to you."

A smile twitched at his mouth. "I'm not concerned about that. Here, this will get you onto the grounds." He extended his hand, holding delicately, as though he feared it would flutter from his fingers, one of those disks of stiff paper, no bigger than a chrisos and lettered in gold leaf with ornate characters, of which I had often heard Thecla speak (she stirred in my mind at the touch of it), but which I had never before seen.

"Thank you, Archon. Tonight, you said? I will try to find suitable clothing."

"Come dressed as you are. It's to be a ridotto—your habit will be your costume." He stood and stretched himself with the air, I thought, of one who nears the completion of a long and disagreeable task. "A moment ago we spoke of some of the less elaborate ways that you might perform your function. It might be well for you to bring whatever equipment you will require tonight."

I understood. I would need nothing beyond my hands, and told him so; then, feeling I had already been remiss in my duties as his host, I invited him to take what refreshment we had.

"No," he said. "If you knew how much I am forced to eat and drink for courtesy's sake, you'd know how much I relish the company of someone whose hospitable offers I can refuse. I don't suppose your fraternity has ever considered using food as a torment, instead of starvation?"

"It is called planteration, Archon."

"You must tell me about it sometime. I can see your guild is far ahead of my imagination—no doubt by a dozen centuries. After hunting, yours must be the oldest science of them all. But I cannot stay longer. We will see you at evening?"

"It is nearly evening now, Archon."

"At the end of the next watch then."

He went out; it was not until the door closed behind him that I detected the faint odor of the musk that had perfumed his robe.

I looked at the little circle of paper I held, turning it over in my hand. Pictured on the back were a falsity of masks, in which I recognized one of the horrors—a face that was no more than a mouth ringed with fangs—I had seen in the Autarch's garden when the cacogens tore away their disguises, and a man-ape's face from the abandoned mine near Saltus.

I was tired from my long walk as well as from the work (almost a full day's, for I had risen early) that had preceded it; and so before going out again I undressed and washed myself, ate some fruit and cold meat, and sipped a glass of the spicy northern tea. When a problem troubles me deeply, it remains in my mind even when I am unaware of it. So it was with me then; though I was not conscious of them, the thought of Dorcas lying in her narrow, slant-ceilinged room in the inn and the memory of the dying girl on her straw bound my eyes and stopped my ears. It was because of them, I think, that I did not hear my sergeant, and did not know, until he entered, that I had been taking up kindling from its box beside the fireplace and breaking the sticks with my hands. He asked if I were going out again, and since he was responsible for the operation of the Vincula in my absence I told him I was, and that I could not say when I would return. Then I thanked him for the loan of his jelab, which I said I would not need again.

"You are welcome to it anytime, Lictor. But that was not

what concerned me. I wanted to suggest that you take a couple of our clavigers when you go down to the city."

"Thank you," I said. "But it is well policed, and I will be in no danger."

He cleared his throat. "It's a matter of the prestige of the Vincula, Lictor. As our commander, you should have an escort."

I could see he was lying, but I could also see that he was lying for what he believed to be my good, and so I said, "I will consider it, assuming you have two presentable men you can spare."

He brightened at once.

"However," I continued, "I don't want them to carry weapons. I'm going to the palace, and it would be insulting to our master the archon if I were to arrive with an armed guard."

At that he began to stammer, and I turned on him as though I were furious, throwing down the splintered wood so that it crashed against the floor. "Out with it! You think I am threatened. What is it?"

"Nothing, Lictor. Nothing that concerns you, particularly. It is just . . ."

"Just what?" Knowing he was going to speak now, I went to the sideboard and poured us two cups of rosolio.

"There have been several murders in the city, Lictor. Three last night, two the night before. Thank you, Lictor. To your health."

"To yours. But murders are nothing unusual, are they? The eclectics are forever stabbing one another."

"These men were burned to death, Lictor. I really don't know much about it—no one seems to. Possibly you know more yourself." The sergeant's face was as expressionless as a carving of coarse, brown stone; but I saw him look quickly at the cold fireplace as he spoke, and I knew he attributed my breaking of the sticks (the sticks that had been so hard and dry in my hands but that I had not felt there until long after he entered, just as Abdiesus had not, perhaps, realized he was contemplating his own death until long after I had come to watch him) to something, some dark secret, the archon had imparted to me, when in fact it was nothing more than the memory of Dorcas and her despair, and of the beggar girl, whom I confused with her. He said, "I have two good fellows waiting outside, Lictor. They're ready to go whenever you are, and they will wait for you until you're ready to come back."

I told him that was very good, and he turned away at once so I would not guess he knew, or believed he knew, more than he had reported to me; but his stiff shoulders and corded neck, and the quick steps he took toward the door, conveyed more information than his stony eyes ever could.

My escorts were beefy men chosen for their strength. Flourishing their big, iron claves, they accompanied me as I shouldered *Terminus Est* down the winding streets, walking to either side when the way was wide enough, before and behind me when it was not. At the edge of the Acis I dismissed them, making them the more eager to leave me by telling them they had my permission to spend the remainder of the evening as they saw fit, and hired a narrow little caique (with a gaily painted canopy I had no need of now that the day's last watch was over) to carry me upriver to the palace.

It was the first time I had actually ridden on the Acis. As I sat in the stern, between the steersman-owner and his four oarsmen, with the clear, icy river rushing by so near that I could have trailed both hands in it if I wished, it seemed impossible that this frail wooden shell, which from the embrasure of our bartizan must have appeared no more than a dancing insect, could hope to gain a span against the current. Then the steersman spoke and we were off—hugging the bank to be sure, but seeming almost to skip over the river like a thrown stone, so rapid and perfectly timed were the strokes of our eight oars and so light and narrow and smooth were we, traveling more in the air above the water than in the water itself. A pentagonal lantern set with panes of amethyst glass

hung from the sternpost; just at the moment when I, in my
ignorance, thought we were at the point of being caught
amidships by the current, capsized, and swept sinking down to
the Capulus, the steersman let the tiller hang by its lashings
while he lit the wick.

He was right, of course, and I wrong. As the little door of
the lantern shut upon the butter-yellow flame within and
the violet beams leaped forth, an eddy caught us, spun us
about, whirled us upstream a hundred strides or more while
the rowers shipped their oars, and left us in a miniature bay as
quiet as a millpond and half-filled with gaudy pleasure boats.
Water stairs, very similar to the steps from which I had swum
in Gyoll as a boy though much cleaner, marched out of the
depths of the river and up to the brilliant torches and elaborate gates of the palace grounds.

I had often seen this palace from the Vincula, and thus I
knew that it was not the subterranean structure modeled on
the House Absolute that I might otherwise have expected.
No more was it any such grim fortress as our Citadel—apparently the archon and his predecessors had considered the
strongpoints of Acies Castle and the Capulus, doubly linked
as they were by the walls and forts strung along the crests of
the cliffs, sufficient security for the safety of the city. Here the
ramparts were mere box hedges intended to exclude the gaze
of the curious and perhaps to give a check to casual thieves.
Buildings with gilded domes were scattered over a pleasance
that seemed intimate and colorful; from my embrasure they
had looked much like peridots broken from their string and
dropped upon a figured carpet.

There were sentries at the filigree gates, dismounted troopers in steel corselets and helmets, with blazing lances and
long-bladed cavalry spathae; but they had the air of minor
and amateur actors, good-natured, hard-bitten men enjoying a
respite from running fights and wind-swept patrols. The pair
to whom I showed my circle of painted paper no more than
glanced at it before waving me inside.

V

Cyriaca

I WAS ONE of the first guests to arrive. There were more bus-
tling servants still than masquers, servants who seemed to
have begun their work only a moment before, and to be determined to complete it at once. They lit candelabra with crystal
lenses and coronas lucis suspended from the upper limbs of
the trees, carried out trays of food and drink, positioned
them, shifted them, then carried them back to one of the
domed buildings again—the three acts being performed by
three servants, but occasionally (no doubt because the others
were busy elsewhere) by one.

For a time I wandered about the grounds, admiring the
flowers by the fast fading twilight. Then, glimpsing people in
costume between the pillars of a pavilion, I strolled inside to
join them.

What such a gathering could be in the House Absolute, I
have already described. Here, where the society was entirely
provincial, it had, rather, the atmosphere of children playing
dress-up in their parents' old clothing; I saw men and women
costumed as autochthons, with their faces stained russet and
dabbed with white, and even one man who was an autochthon and yet was dressed like one, in a costume no more and

no less authentic than the others, so that I was inclined to laugh at him until I realized that though he and I might be the only ones who knew it, he was in fact costumed more originally than any of the rest, as a citizen of Thrax in cos-tume. Around all these autochthons, real and self-imagined, were a score of other figures not less absurd—officers dressed as women and women dressed as soldiers, eclectics as fraudulent as the autochthons, gymnosophists, ablegates and their aco-lytes, eremites, eidolons, zoanthrops half beast and half hu-man, and deodands and remontados in picturesque rags, with eyes painted wild.

I found myself thinking how strange it would be if the New Sun, the Daystar himself, were to appear now as suddenly as he had appeared so long ago when he was called the Concilia-tor, appearing here because it was an inappropriate place and he had always preferred the least appropriate places, seeing these people through fresher eyes than we ever could; and if he, thus appearing here, were to decree by theurgy that all of them (none of whom I knew and none of whom knew me) should forever after live the roles they had taken up tonight, the autochthons hunching over smoky fires in mountain huts of stone, the real autochthon forever a townsman at a ridotto, the women spurring toward the enemies of the Common-wealth with sword in hand, the officers doing needlepoint at north windows and looking up to sigh over empty roads, the deodands mourning their unspeakable abominations in the wilderness, the remontados burning their own homes and set-ting their eyes upon the mountains; and only I unchanged, as it is said the velocity of light is unchanged by mathematical transformations.

Then, while I was grinning to myself behind my mask, it seemed that the Claw, in its soft leathern sack, drove against my breastbone to remind me that the Conciliator had been no jest, and that I bore some fragment of his power with me. At that moment, as I looked across the room over all the feathered and helmeted and wild-haired heads, I saw a Pelerine.

I made my way across to her as quickly as I could, pushing aside those who did not stand aside for me. (They were but few, for though not one of them thought I was what I seemed, my height made them take me for an exultant, with no true exultants near.)

The Pelerine was neither young nor old; beneath her narrow domino her face seemed a smooth oval, refined and remote like the face of the chief priestess who had permitted me to pass in the tent cathedral after Agia and I had destroyed the altar. She held a little glass of wine as if to toy with it, and when I knelt at her feet she set it on a table so she could give me her fingers to kiss.

"Shrive me, Domnicellae," I begged her. "I have done you and all your sisters the greatest harm."

"Death does us all harm," she answered.

"I am not he." I looked up at her then, and the first doubt struck me.

Over the chatter of the crowd I heard the hiss of her indrawn breath. "You are not?"

"No, Domnicellae." And though I doubted her already, I feared she would flee from me, and I reached out to catch the cincture that dangled from her waist. "Domnicellae, forgive me, but are you a true member of the order?"

Without speaking she shook her head, then fell to the floor.

It is not uncommon for a client in our oubliette to feign unconsciousness, but the imposture is easily detected. The false fainter deliberately closes his eyes and keeps them closed. In a true faint, the victim, who is almost as likely to be a man as a woman, first loses control of his eyes, so that for an instant they no longer look in precisely the same direction; sometimes they tend to roll up under their lids. These lids, in turn, seldom entirely close, since their closing is not a deliberate action but a mere relaxation of their muscles. One can usually see a slender crescent of the sclera between the upper and lower lids, as I did when this woman fell.

Several men helped me carry her to an alcove, and there was a good deal of foolish talk about heat and excitement, neither of which had been present. For a time it was impossible to drive the onlookers away—then the novelty was gone, and it would have been almost equally impossible for me to have kept them there had I desired to do so. By then the woman in scarlet was beginning to stir, and I had learned from a woman of about the same age who was dressed as a child that she was the wife of an armiger whose villa stood at no great distance from Thrax, but who had gone to Nessus on some business or other. I went back to the table then and fetched her little glass and touched her lips with the red liquid it contained.

"No," she said weakly. "I don't want it . . . It's sangaree and I hate it—I—I only chose it because the color matches my costume."

"Why did you faint? Was it because I thought you were a real conventual?"

"No, because I guessed who you are," she said, and we were silent for a moment, she still half-reclining on the divan to which I had helped carry her, I sitting at her feet.

I brought the moment when I had knelt before her to life again in my mind; I have, as I have said, the power to so reconstruct every instant of my life. And at last I had to say, "How did you know?"

"Anyone else in those clothes, asked if he were Death, would have said he was . . . because he would be in costume. I sat in the archon's court a week ago, when my husband charged one of our peons with theft. That day I saw you standing to one side, with your arms folded on the guard of the sword you carry now, and when I heard you say what you did, when you had just kissed my fingers, I recognized you, and I thought . . . Oh, I don't know what I thought! I suppose I thought you had knelt to me because you intended to kill me. Just from the way you stood, you always looked, when I saw you in court, like someone who would be gallant to the poor people whose heads he was going to lop off, and particularly to women."

"I only knelt to you because I am anxious to locate the Pelerines, and your costume, like my own, did not seem to be a costume."

"It isn't. That is to say, I'm not entitled to wear it, but it isn't just something I had my maids run up for me. It's a real investiture." She paused. "Do you know I don't even know your name?"

"Severian. Yours is Cyriaca—one of the women mentioned it while we were taking care of you. May I ask how you came to have those clothes, and if you know where the Pelerines are now?"

"This isn't a part of your duty, is it?" For a moment she stared into my eyes, then she shook her head. "Something private. I was nurtured by them. I was a postulant, you know. We traveled up and down the continent, and I used to have wonderful botany lessons just looking at the trees and flowers as we passed. Sometimes when I think back on it, it feels as if we went from palms to pines in a week, though I know that can't be true.

"I was going to take final vows, and the year before you're to be invested they make the investiture so you can try it on and get the fit right, and then so that you'll see it among your ordinary clothes each time you unpack. It's like a girl's looking at her mother's wedding dress, when it was her grandmother's too and she knows she'll be married in it, if she is ever married. Only I never wore my investiture, and when I went home, after a long time of waiting until we passed close by since there would be no one to escort me, I took it with me.

"I hadn't thought of it for a long time. Then when I got the archon's invitation I got it out again and decided to wear it tonight. I'm proud of my figure, and we only had to let it out a little here and there. It becomes me, I think, and I have the face for a Pelerine, though I don't have their eyes. Actually I never had the eyes, though I used to think I'd get them when I took my vows, or afterward. Our director of postulants had that look. She could sit sewing, and to look at her eyes you would believe they were seeing to the ends of Urth where the perischii live, staring right through the old, torn skirt and the walls of the tent, staring through everything. No, I don't know where the Pelerines are now—I doubt if they do themselves, though perhaps the Mother does."

I said, "You must have had some friends among them. Didn't some of your fellow postulants stay?"

Cyriaca shrugged. "None of them ever wrote to me. I really don't know."

"Do you feel well enough to go back to the dance?" Music was beginning to filter into our alcove.

Her head did not move, but I saw her eyes, which had been tracing the corridors of the years when she talked of the Pelerines, swing around to look at me sidelong. "Is that what you want to do?"

"I suppose not. I'm never completely at ease among crowds, unless the people are my friends."

"You have some, then?" She seemed genuinely astonished.

"Not here—well, one friend here. In Nessus I used to have the brothers of our guild."

"I understand." She hesitated. "There's no reason we have to go. This affair will wear out the night, and at dawn, if the archon is still enjoying himself, they'll let down the curtains to exclude the light, and perhaps even raise the celure over the garden. We can sit here as long as we wish, and every time one of the servers comes around we'll get what we like to eat and drink. When someone we want to talk with goes by, we'll make him stop and entertain us."

"I'm afraid I would begin to bore you before the night was much worn," I said.

"Not at all, because I have no intention of allowing you to talk much. I'm going to talk myself, and make you listen to me. To begin—do you know you are very handsome?"

"I know that I am not. But since you've never seen me without this mask, you can't possibly know what I look like."

"On the contrary."

She leaned forward as though to examine my face through the eyeholes. Her own mask, which was the color of her gown, was so small that it was hardly more than a convention, two almond-shaped loops of fabric about her eyes; yet it lent her an exotic air she would not otherwise have possessed, and lent her too, I think, a feeling of mystery, of a concealment that lifted from her the weight of responsibility.

"You are a very intelligent man I am sure, but you haven't been to as many of these things as I have, or you would have learned the art of judging faces without seeing them. It's hardest, of course, when the person you're looking at has on a wooden vizard that doesn't conform to the face, but even then you can tell a great deal. You have a sharp chin, don't you? With a little cleft."

"Yes to the sharp chin," I said. "No to the cleft."

"You're lying to throw me off, or else you've never noticed it. I can judge chins by looking at waists, particularly in men, which is where my chief interest lies. A narrow waist means a sharp chin, and that leather mask leaves just enough showing to confirm it. Even though your eyes are deeply set, they're large and mobile, and that means a cleft chin in a man, particularly when the face is thin. You have high cheekbones—their outlines show a trifle through the mask, and your flat cheeks will make them look higher. Black hair, because I can see it on the backs of your hands, and thin lips that show through the mouth of the mask. Since I can't see all of them, they curve and curl about, which is a most desirable thing in a man's lips."

I did not know what to say, and to tell the truth I would have given a great deal to leave her just then; at last I asked, "Do you want me to take my mask off so you can check the accuracy of your assessments?"

"Oh, no, you mustn't. Not until they play the aubade. Besides, you should consider my feelings. If you did and I found you weren't handsome after all, I should be deprived of an interesting night." She had been sitting up. Now she smiled and leaned back on the divan again, her hair spreading about her in a dark aureole. "No, Severian, instead of unmasking your face, you must unmask your spirit. Later you will do that by showing me everything you would do were you free to do whatever you wished, and now by telling me everything I want to know about you. You come from Nessus—I've learned that much. Why are you so eager to find the Pelerines?"

VI

The Library of the Citadel

AS I WAS about to answer her question, a couple strolled by our alcove, the man robed in a sanbenito, the woman dressed as a midinette. They only glanced at us as they passed, but something—the inclination, perhaps, of the two heads together, or some expression of the eyes—told me that they knew, or at least suspected, I was not in masquerade. I pretended I had noticed nothing, however, and said, "Something that belongs to the Pelerines came into my hands by accident. I want to return it to them."

"You're not going to do them harm then?" Cyriaca asked. "Can you tell me what it is?"

I did not dare to tell the truth, and I knew I would be asked to produce whatever object I named, and so I said, "A book—an old book, beautifully illustrated. I don't pretend to know anything about books, but I feel sure it's of religious importance and quite valuable," and from my sabretache I drew the brown book from Master Ultan's library that I had carried away when I left Thecla's cell.

"Old, yes," Cyriaca said. "And more than a little water-stained, I see. May I look at it?"

49

I handed it to her and she fanned the pages, then stopped at a picture of the sikinnis, holding it up until it caught the gleam of a lamp burning in a niche above our divan. The horned men seemed to leap in the flickering light, the sylphs to writhe.

"I don't know anything about books either," she said, handing it back. "But I have an uncle who does, and I think he might give a great deal for this one. I wish he were here tonight so he could see it—though perhaps it's all for the best, because I'd probably try to get it from you in some way. In every pentad he travels as far as I ever did when I was with the Pelerines, just to seek out old books. He's even gone to the lost archives. Have you heard about those?"

I shook my head.

"All I know is what he told me once when he had drunk a little more of our estate cuvee than he usually takes, and it may be that he didn't tell me everything, because as I talked to him I had the feeling he was a bit afraid I might try to go myself. I never have, though I've regretted it sometimes. Anyway, in Nessus, a long way south of the city most people visit, so far down the great river in fact that most people think the city would have ended long before, there stands an ancient fortress. Everyone save perhaps for the Autarch himself—may his spirit live in a thousand successors—has forgotten it long ago, and it's supposed to be haunted. It stands upon a hill overlooking Gyoll, my uncle told me, staring out over a field of ruined sepulchers, guarding nothing."

She paused and moved her hands, shaping the hill and its stronghold in the air before her. I had the feeling that she had told the story many times, perhaps to her children. It made me conscious that she was indeed old enough to have them, children old enough themselves to have listened to this and other tales many times. No years had marked her smooth, sensuous face; but the candle of youth that burned so brightly still in Dorcas and had shed its clear, unworldly light even about Jolenta, that had shone so hard and bright behind Thecla's strength and had lit the mist-shrouded paths of the necropolis when her sister Thea took Vodalus's pistol at the grave side, had in her been extinguished so long that not even the perfume of its flame remained. I pitied her.

"You must know the story of how the race of ancient days reached the stars, and how they bargained away all the wild half of themselves to do so, so that they no longer cared for the taste of the pale wind, nor for love or lust, nor to make new songs nor to sing old ones, nor for any of the other animal things they believed they had brought with them out of the rain forests at the bottom of time—though in fact, so my uncle told me, those things brought them. And you know, or you should know, that those to whom they sold those things, who were the creations of their own hands, hated them in their hearts. And truly they had hearts, though the men who had made them never reckoned with that. Anyway, they resolved to ruin their makers, and they did it by returning, when mankind had spread to a thousand suns, all that had been left with them long before.

"So much, at least, you should know. My uncle once told it to me as I have told it to you, and he found all that and more recorded in a book in his collection. It was a book no one had opened, as he believed, for a chiliad.

"But how they did what they did is less well known. I remember that when I was a child, I imagined the bad machines digging—digging by night until they had cleared away the twisted roots of old trees and laid bare an iron chest they had buried when the world was very young, and that when they struck off the lock of that chest, all the things we've spoken of came flying out like a swarm of golden bees. That's foolish, but even now I can hardly imagine what the reality of those thinking engines can have been like."

I recalled Jonas, with the light, bright metal where the skin of his loins ought to have been, but I could not picture Jonas setting free a plague to trouble mankind, and shook my head.

"But my uncle's book, he said, made clear what it was they did, and the things they let go free were no swarm of insects but a flood of artifacts of every kind, calculated by them to revive all those thoughts that people had put behind them because they could not be written in numbers. The building of everything from cities to cream pitchers was in the hands of the machines, and after a thousand lifetimes of building cities that were like great mechanisms, they turned to building cities that were like banks of cloud before a storm, and others like the skeletons of dragons."

"When was this?" I asked.

"A very long time ago—long before the first stones of Nessus were laid."

I had put an arm about her shoulders, and now she let her hand creep into my lap; I felt its heat and slow search.

"And they followed the same principle in all they did. In the shaping of furniture, for example, and the cutting of clothing. And because the leaders who had decided so long before that all the thoughts symbolized by the clothes and furniture, and by the cities, should be put behind mankind forever were long dead, and the people had forgotten their faces and their maxims, they were delighted with the new things. Thus all that empire, which had been built only upon order, passed away.

"But though the empire dissolved, the worlds were a long time dying. At first, so that the things they were returning to humans would not be rejected again, the machines conceived of pageants and phantasmagoria, whose performances inspired those who watched them to think on fortune or revenge or the invisible world. Later they gave each man and woman a companion, unseen by all other eyes, as an advisor. The children had such companions long before.

"When the powers of the machines had weakened further— as the machines themselves wished—they could no longer maintain these phantoms in the minds of their owners, nor could they build more cities, because the cities that remained were already nearly empty.

"They had reached, so my uncle told me, that point at which they had hoped mankind would turn on them and destroy them, yet no such thing had occurred, because by this time they who had been despised as slaves or worshiped as devils before were greatly loved.

"And so they called all who loved them best around them, and for long years taught them all the things their race had put away, and in time they died.

"Then all those whom they had loved, and who had loved them, took counsel together as to how their teachings could be preserved, for they well knew their kind would not come again upon Urth. But bitter quarrels broke out among them. They had not learned together, but rather each of them, man or woman, had listened to one of the machines as if there were no one in the world but those two. And because there was so much knowledge and only a few to learn it, the machines had taught each differently.

"Thus they divided into parties, and each party into two, and each of those two into two again, until at last every individual stood alone, misunderstood and reviled by all the others and reviling them. Then each went away, out of the cities that had held the machines or deeper into them, save for a very few who by habit remained in the palaces of the machines to watch beside their bodies."

A sommelier brought us cups of wine almost as clear as water, and as still as water until some motion of the cup woke it. It perfumed the air like those flowers no man can see, the flowers that can be found only by the blind; and to drink it was like drinking strength from the heart of a bull. Cyriaca took her cup eagerly, and draining it cast it ringing into a corner.

"Tell me more," I said to her, "of this story of the lost archives."

"When the last machine was cold and still and each of

those who had learned from them the forbidden lore mankind had cast aside was separated from all the rest, there
came dread into the heart of each. For each knew himself to
be only mortal, and most, no longer young. And each saw that
with his own death the knowledge he loved best would die.
Then each of them—each supposing himself the only one to
do so—began to write down what he had learned in the long
years when he had harkened to the teachings of the machines
that spilled forth all the hidden knowledge of wild things.
Much perished but much more survived, sometimes falling
into the hands of those who copied it enlivened by their own
additions or weakened by omissions . . . Kiss me, Severian."

Though my mask hampered us, our lips met. As she drew
away, the shadow memories of Thecla's old bantering love
affairs, played out among the pseudothyrums and catachto-
nian boudoirs of the House Absolute welled up within me,
and I said, "Don't you know this kind of thing requires a
man's undivided attention?"

Cyriaca smiled. "That's why I did it—I wanted to see if you
were listening.

"Anyway, for a long time—no one knows quite how long, I
suppose, and anyway the world was not as near the sun's failing then and its years were longer—these writings circulated or
else lay moldering in cenotaphs where their authors had concealed them for safekeeping. They were fragmentary, contra-
dictory, and eisegesistic. Then when some autarch (though
they were not called autarchs then) hoped to recapture the
dominion exercised by the first empire, they were gathered up
by his servants, white-robed men who ransacked cocklofts and
threw down the androsphinxes erected to memorialize the
machines and entered the cubicula of moiraic women long
dead. Their spoil was gathered into a great heap in the city of
Nessus, which was then newly built, to be burned.

"But on the night before the burning was to begin, the
autarch of that time, who had never dreamed before the
wild dreams of sleep but only waking dreams of dominion,

dreamed at last. And in his dream he saw all the untamed worlds of life and death, stone and river, beast and tree slipping away from his hands forever.

"When morning came, he ordered that the torches not be kindled, but that there should be a great vault built to house all the volumes and scrolls the white-robed men had gathered. For he thought that if the new empire he planned should fail him at last, he would retire to that vault and enter the worlds that, in imitation of the ancients, he was determined to cast aside.

"His empire did fail him, as it had to. The past cannot be found in the future where it is not—not until the metaphysical world, which is so much larger and so much slower than the physical world, completes its revolution and the New Sun comes. But he did not retire as he had planned into that vault and the curtain wall he had caused to be built about it, for when once the wild things have been put behind a man for good and all, they are trap-wise and cannot be recaptured.

"Nevertheless, it is said that before all he gathered was sealed away, he set a guardian over it. And when that guardian's time on Urth was done, he found another, and he another, so that they continue ever faithful to the commands of that autarch, for they are saturated in the wild thoughts sprung from the lore saved by the machines, and such faith is one of those wild things."

I had been disrobing her as she spoke, and kissing her breasts; but I said, "Did all those thoughts of which you spoke go out of the world when the autarch locked them away? Haven't I ever heard of them?"

"No, because they had been passed from hand to hand for a long time, and had entered into the blood of all the peoples. Besides, it is said that the guardian sometimes sends them out, and though they always return to him at last, they are read, whether by one or many, before they sink once more into his dark."

"It is a wonderful story," I said. "I think that perhaps I

know more of it than you, but I had never heard it before." I found that her legs were long, and smoothly tapered from thighs like cushions of silk to slender ankles; all her body, indeed, was shaped for delight.

Her fingers touched the clasp that held my cloak about my shoulders. "Need you take this off?" she asked. "Can't it cover us?"

"It can," I said.

VII

Attractions

ALMOST I DROWNED in the delight she gave me, for though I did not love her as I had once loved Thecla, nor as I loved Dorcas even then, and she was not beautiful as Jolenta had once been beautiful, I felt a tenderness for her that was no more than in part born of the unquiet wine, and she was such a woman as I had dreamed of as a ragged boy in the Matachin Tower, before I had ever beheld Thea's heart-shaped face by the side of the opened grave; and she knew far more of the arts of love than any of the three.

When we rose we went to a flowing basin of silver to wash. There were two women there who had been lovers as we had been, and they stared at us and laughed; but when they saw I would not spare them because they were women, they fled shrieking.

Then we cleansed each other. I know Cyriaca believed that I would leave her then, as I believed that she would leave me; but we did not separate (though it would, perhaps, have been better if we had), but went out into the silent little garden, which was full of night, and stood beside a lonely fountain.

She held my hand, and I held hers as children do. "Have

you ever visited the House Absolute?" she asked. She was watching our reflections in the moon-drenched water, and her voice was so low I could scarcely hear her.

I told her that I had, and at the words her hand tightened on mine.

"Did you visit the Well of Orchids there?"

I shook my head.

"I have been to the House Absolute also, but I have never seen the Well of Orchids. It is said that when the Autarch has a consort—as ours does not—she holds her court there, in the most beautiful place in the world. Even now, only the loveliest are permitted to walk in that spot. When I was there we stayed, my lord and I, in a certain small room appropriate to our armigerial rank. One evening when my lord was gone and I did not know where, I went out into the corridor, and as I stood there looking up and down, a high functionary of the court passed by. I did not know his name or his office, but I stopped him and asked if I might go to the Well of Orchids."

She paused. For the space of three or four breaths there was no sound but the music from the pavilions and the tinkling of the fountain.

"And he stopped and looked at me, I think in some surprise. You cannot know how it feels to be a little armigette from the north, in a gown sewn by your own maids, and provincial jewels, and be looked at so by someone who has spent all his life among the exultants of the House Absolute. Then he smiled."

She gripped my hand very tightly now.

"And he told me. Down such and such a corridor and turn at such a statue, up certain steps and along the ivory path. Oh, Severian, my lover!"

Her face was radiant as the moon itself. I knew the moment she had described had been the crown of her life, and that she now treasured the love I had given her partially, and perhaps largely, because it had recalled to her that moment, when her beauty had been weighed by one she felt fit to rule upon it, and had not been found wanting. My reason told me I should take offense at that, but I could find no resentment in me.

"He went away, and I began to walk as he had said—a score of strides, perhaps two score. Then I met my lord, and he ordered me to return to our little room."

"I see," I said, and shifted my sword.

"I think you do. Is it wrong then for me to betray him like this? What do you think?"

"I am no magistrate."

"Everyone judges me . . . all my friends . . . all my lovers, of whom you are neither the first nor the last; even those women in the caldarium just now."

"We are trained from childhood not to judge, but only to carry out the sentences handed down by the courts of the Commonwealth. I will not judge you or him."

"I judge," she said, and turned her face toward the bright, hard light of the stars. For the first time since I had glimpsed her across the crowded ballroom I understood how I could have mistaken her for a monial of the order whose habit she wore. "Or at least, I tell myself I judge. And I find myself guilty, but I can't stop. I think I draw men like you to myself. Were you drawn? There were women there lovelier than I am now, I know."

"I'm not certain," I said. "While we were coming here to Thrax . . ."

"You have a story too, don't you? Tell me, Severian. I've already told you almost the only interesting thing that has ever happened to me."

"On the way here, we—I'll explain some other time who I was traveling with—fell in with a witch and her famula and her client, who had come to a certain place to reinspirit the body of a man long dead."

"Really?" Cyriaca's eyes sparkled. "How wonderful! I've

heard of such things but I've never seen them. Tell me all about it, but make sure you tell me the truth."

"There really isn't anything much to tell. Our path lay through a deserted city, and when we saw their fire, we went to it because we had someone with us who was ill. When the witch brought back the man she had come to revive, I thought at first that she was restoring the whole city. It wasn't until several days afterward that I understood . . ."

I found I could not say what it was I understood; that it was in fact on the level of meaning above language, a level we like to believe scarcely exists, though if it were not for the constant discipline we have learned to exercise upon our thoughts, they would always be climbing to it unaware.

"Go on."

"I didn't really understand, of course. I still think about it, and I still don't. But I know somehow that she was bringing him back, and *he* was bringing the stone town back with him, as a setting for himself. Sometimes I have thought that perhaps it had never had any reality apart from him, so that when we rode over its pavements and the rubble of its walls, we were actually riding among his bones."

"And did he come?" she asked. "Tell me!"

"Yes, he returned. And then the client was dead, and the sick woman who had been with us also. And Apu-Punchau— that was the dead man's name—was gone again. The witches ran away, I think, though perhaps they flew. But what I wanted to say was that we went on the next day on foot, and stayed the next night in the hut of a poor family. And that night while the woman who was with me slept, I talked to the man, who seemed to know a great deal about the stone town, though he did not know its original name. And I spoke with his mother, who I think knew something more than he, though she would not tell me as much."

I hesitated, finding it hard to speak of such things to this woman. "At first I supposed their ancestors might have come from that town, but they said it had been destroyed long before the coming of their race. Still, they knew much lore of it, because the man had sought for treasures there since he had been a boy, though he had never found anything, he said, save for broken stones and broken pots, and the tracks of other searchers who had been there long before him.

" 'In ancient days,' his mother told me, 'they believed that you could draw buried gold by putting a few coins of your own in the ground, with this spell or that. Many a one did it, and some forgot the place, or were kept from digging their own up again. That's what my son finds. That is the bread we eat.' "

I remembered her as she had been that night, old and stooped as she warmed her hands at a little fire of turf. Perhaps she resembled one of Thecla's old nurses, for something about her brought Thecla closer to the surface of my mind than she had been since Jonas and I had been imprisoned in the House Absolute, so that once or twice when I caught sight of my hands, I was startled to see the thickness of the fingers, and their brown color, and to see them bare of rings.

"Go on, Severian," Cyriaca said again.

"Then the old woman told me there was something in the stone town that truly drew its like to it. 'You have heard tales of necromancers,' she said, 'who fish for the spirits of the dead. Do you know there are vivimancers among the dead, who call to them those who can make them live again? There is such a one in the stone town, and once or twice in each saros one of those he has called to him will sup with us.' And then she said to her son, 'You will recall the silent man who slept beside his staff. You were only a child, but you will remember him, I think. He was the last until now.' Then I knew that I, too, had been drawn by the vivimancer Apu-Punchau, though I had felt nothing."

Cyriaca gave me a sidelong look. "Am I dead then? Is that what you're saying? You told me there was a witch who was the necromancer, and that you only stumbled upon her fire. I think that you yourself were the witch you spoke of, and no doubt the sick person you mentioned was your client, and the woman your servant."

"That's because I have neglected to tell you all the parts of the story that have any importance," I said. I would have laughed at being thought a witch; but the Claw pressed against my breastbone, telling me that by its stolen power I was a witch indeed in everything except knowledge; and I understood—in the same sense that I had "understood" before—that though Apu-Punchau had brought it to his hand, he could not (or would not?) take it from me. "Most importantly," I went on, "when the revenant vanished, one of the scarlet capes of the Pelerines, like the one you're wearing now, was left behind in the mud. I have it in my sabretache. Do the Pelerines dabble in necromancy?"

I never heard the answer to my question, for just as I spoke, the tall figure of the archon came up the narrow path that led to the fountain. He was masked, and costumed as a barghest, so that I would not have known him if I had seen him in a good light; but the dimness of the garden stripped his disguise from him as effectively as human hands could have, so that as soon as I saw the loom of his height, and his walk, I knew him at once.

"Ah," he said. "You have found her. I ought to have anticipated that."

"I thought so," I told him, "but I wasn't sure."

VIII

Upon the Cliff

I LEFT THE palace grounds by one of the landward gates. There were six troopers on guard there, with nothing of the air of relaxation that had characterized the two at the river stairs a few watches before. One, politely but unmistakably barring the way, asked me if I had to leave so early. I identified myself and said that I was afraid I must—that I still had work to do that night (as indeed I did) and would have a hard day facing me the next morning as well (as indeed I would).

"You're a hero then." The soldier sounded slightly more friendly. "Don't you have an escort, Lictor?"

"I had two clavigers, but I dismissed them. There's no reason I can't find my way back to the Vincula alone."

Another trooper, who had not spoken previously, said, "You can stay inside until morning. They'll find you a quiet place to bunk down."

"Yes, but my work wouldn't get done. I'm afraid I must leave now."

The soldier who had been blocking my way stood aside. "I'd like to send a couple of men with you. If you'll wait a moment, I'll do it. I have to get permission from the officer of the guard."

"That won't be necessary," I told him, and left before they could say more. Something—presumably the committer of the murders my sergeant had told me of—was clearly stirring in the city; it seemed almost certain that another death had occurred while I was in the archon's palace. The thought filled me with a pleasant excitement—not because I was such a fool as to imagine myself superior to any attack, but because the idea of being attacked, of risking death that night in the dark streets of Thrax, lifted some part of the depression I would otherwise have felt. This unfocused terror, this faceless menace of the night, was the earliest of all my childhood fears; and as such, now that childhood was behind me, it had the homey quality of all childhood things when we are fully grown.

I was already on the same side of the river as the jacal I had visited that afternoon, and had no need to take boat again; but the streets were strange to me and in the dark seemed almost a labyrinth built to confound me. I made several false starts before I found the narrow way I wanted, leading up the cliff.

The dwellings to either side of it, which had stood silent while they waited for the mighty wall of stone opposite them to rise and cover the sun, were murmurous with voices now, and a few windows glowed with the light of grease lamps. While Abdiesus reveled in his palace below, the humble folk of the high cliff celebrated too, with a gaiety that differed from his chiefly in that it was less riotous. I heard the sounds of love as I passed, just as I had heard them in his garden after leaving Cyriaca for the last time, and the voices of men and women in quiet talk, and bantering too, here as there. The palace garden had been scented by its flowers, and its air was washed by its own fountains and by the great fountain of cold Acis, which rushed by just outside. Here those odors were no more; but a breeze stirred among the jacals and the caves with their stoppered mouths, bringing sometimes the stench of or-

dure, and sometimes the aroma of brewing tea or some humble stew, and sometimes only the clean air of the mountains.

When I was high up the cliff face, where no one dwelt who
was rich enough to afford more light than a cooking fire would
give, I turned and looked back at the city much as I had
looked down upon it—though with an entirely different
spirit—from the ramparts of Acies Castle that afternoon. It is
said that there are crevices in the mountains so deep that one
can see stars at their bottoms—crevices that pass, then, entirely through the world. Now I felt I had found one. It was
like looking into a constellation, as though all of Urth had
fallen away, and I was staring into the starry gulf.

It seemed likely that by this time they were searching for
me. I thought of the archon's dimarchi cantering down the
silent streets, perhaps carrying flambeaux snatched up in the
garden. Far worse was the thought of the clavigers I had until
now commanded fanning out from the Vincula. Yet I saw no
moving lights and heard no faint, hoarse cries, and if the Vincula was disturbed, it was not a disturbance that affected the
dim streets webbing the cliff across the river. There should
have been a winking gleam too where the great gate opened
to let out the freshly roused men, closed, then opened again;
but there was none. I turned at last and began to climb once
more. The alarm had not yet been given. Still, it would soon
sound.

There was no light in the jacal and no noise of speech. I
took the Claw from its little bag before I entered, for fear I
would lack the nerve to do so once I was inside. Sometimes it
blazed like a firework, as it had in the inn at Saltus. Sometimes it possessed no more light than a bit of glass. That night
in the jacal it was not brilliant, but it glowed with so deep a
blue that the light itself seemed almost a clearer darkness. Of
all the names of the Conciliator, the one that is, I believe,
least used, and which has always seemed the most puzzling to

me, is that of Black Sun. Since that night, I have felt myself almost to comprehend it. I could not hold the gem in my fingers as I had done often before and was yet to do afterward; I laid it flat on the palm of my right hand so that my touch would commit no more sacrilege than was strictly necessary. With it held thus before me, I stooped and entered the jacal.

The girl lay where she had lain that afternoon. If she still breathed I could not hear her, and she did not move. The boy with the infected eye slept on the bare earth at her feet. He must have bought food with the money I had given him; corn husks and fruit peels were scattered over the floor. For a moment I dared to hope that neither of them would wake.

The deep light of the Claw showed the girl's face to be a weaker and more horrible thing than I had seen it by day, accentuating the hollows under her eyes, and her sunken cheeks. I felt I should say something, invoke the Increate and his messengers by some formula, but my mouth was dry and more empty of words than any beast's. Slowly I lowered my hand toward her until the shadow of it cut off all the light that had bathed her. When I lifted my hand again there had been no change, and remembering that the Claw had not helped Jolenta, I wondered if it were possible that it could have no good effect on women, or if it were necessary that a woman hold it. Then I touched the girl's forehead with it, so that for a moment it seemed a third eye in that deathlike face.

Of all the uses I made of it, that was the most astounding, and perhaps the only one in which it was not possible that any self-deception on my part, or any coincidence no matter how farfetched, could account for what occurred. It may have been that the man-ape's bleeding was staunched by his own belief, that the uhlan on the road by the House Absolute was merely stunned and would have revived in any event, that the apparent healing of Jonas's wounds had been no more than a trick of the light.

But now it was as though some unimaginable power had acted in the interval between one chronon and the next to wrench the universe from its track. The girl's real eyes, dark as pools, opened. Her face was no longer the skull mask it had been, but only the worn face of a young woman. "Who are you in those bright clothes?" she asked. And then, "Oh, I am dreaming."

I told her I was a friend, and that there was no reason for her to be afraid.

"I am not afraid," she said. "I would be if I were awake, but I am not now. You look as if you have fallen from the sky, but I know you are only the wing of some poor bird. Did Jader catch you? Sing for me . . ."

Her eyes closed again; this time I could hear the slow sighing of her breath. Her face remained as it had been while they were open—thin and drawn, but with the stamp of death rubbed away.

I took the gem from her forehead and touched the boy's eye with it as I had touched his sister's face, but I am not sure it was necessary that I do so. It appeared normal before it ever felt the kiss of the Claw, and it may be that the infection was already vanquished. He stirred in his sleep and cried out as though in some dream he were running ahead of slower boys and urging them to follow him.

I put the Claw back into its little bag and sat on the earthen floor among the husks and peels, listening to him. After a time he grew quiet again. Starlight made a dim pattern near the door; other than that, the jacal was utterly dark. I could hear the sister's regular breathing, and the boy's own.

She had said that I, who had worn fuligin since my elevation to journeyman, and gray rags before that, was dressed in bright clothing. I knew she had been dazzled by the light at her forehead—anything, any clothing, would have appeared bright to her then. And yet, I felt that in some sense she was correct. It was not that (as I have been tempted to write) I came to hate my cloak and trousers and boots after that moment; but rather that I came in some sense to feel they were indeed the disguise they had been taken to be when I was at the archon's palace, or the costume they had appeared to be when I took part in Dr. Talos's play. Even a torturer is a man, and it is not natural for a man to dress always and exclusively in that hue that is darker than black. I had despised my own hypocrisy when I had worn the brown mantle from Agilus's shop; perhaps the fuligin beneath it was a hypocrisy as great or greater.

Then the truth began to force itself upon my mind. If I had ever truly been a torturer, a torturer in the sense that Master Gurloes and even Master Palaemon were torturers, I was one no longer. I had been given a second chance here in Thrax. I had failed in that second chance as well, and there would be no third. I might gain employment by my skills and my clothing, but that was all; and no doubt it would be better for me to destroy them when I could, and try to make a place for myself among the soldiers who fought the northern war, once I had succeeded—if I ever succeeded—in returning the Claw.

The boy stirred and called a name that must have been his sister's. She murmured something still in sleep. I stood and watched them for a moment more, then slipped out, fearful that the sight of my hard face and long sword would frighten them.

IX

The Salamander

OUTSIDE, THE STARS seemed brighter, and for the first time in many weeks the Claw had ceased to drive itself against my chest.

When I descended the narrow path, it was no longer necessary to turn and halt to see the city. It spread itself before me in ten thousand twinkling lights, from the watchfire of Acies Castle to the reflection of the guard-room windows in the water that rushed through the Capulus.

By now all the gates would be closed against me. If the dimarchi had not already ridden forth, they would do so before I reached the level land beside the river; but I was determined to see Dorcas once more before I left the city, and, somehow, I had no doubt of my ability to do so. I was just beginning to turn over plans for escaping the walls afterward when a new light flared out far below.

It was small at that distance, no more than a pinprick like all the others; yet it was not like them at all, and perhaps my mind only registered it as light because I knew nothing else to liken it to. I had seen a pistol fired at full potential that night in the necropolis when Vodalus resurrected the dead woman—a coherent beam of energy that had split the mists like lightning. This fire was not like that, but it was more nearly like that than like anything else I could call to mind. It flared briefly and died, and a heartbeat afterward I felt the wash of heat upon my face.

Somehow I missed the little inn called the Duck's Nest in the dark. I have never known if I took a wrong turning or merely walked past the shuttered windows without glimpsing the sign hanging overhead. However it happened, I soon found myself farther from the river than I should have been, striding along a street that ran for a time at least parallel to the cliff, with the smell of scorched flesh in my nostrils as at a branding. I was about to retrace my steps when I collided in the dark with a woman. So hard and unexpectedly did we strike each other that I nearly fell, and as I went reeling back, I heard the thud of her body on the stone.

"I didn't see you," I said as I reached down for her.

"Run! Run!" she gasped. And then, "Oh, help me up." Her voice was faintly familiar.

"Why should I run?" I pulled her to her feet. In the faint light I could see the blur of her face, and even, I thought, something of the fear there.

"It killed Jurmin. He burned alive. His staff was still on fire when we found him. He . . ." Whatever she had begun to say after that trailed off into sobs.

"What burned Jurmin?" When she did not answer, I shook her, but that only made her weep the harder. "Don't I know you? Talk, woman! You're the mistress of the Duck's Nest. Take me there!"

"I can't," she said. "I'm afraid. Give me your arm, please, sieur. We ought to get inside."

"Fine. We'll go to the Duck's Nest. It can't be far—now what is this?"

"Too far!" She wept. "Too far!"

There was something in the street with us. I do not know whether I had failed to detect its approach, or it had been undetectable until then; but it was suddenly present. I have heard people who have a horror of rats say they are aware of them the moment they enter a house, even if the animals are not visible. It was so now. There was a feeling of heat without warmth; and though the air held no odor, I sensed that its power to support life was being drained away.

The woman seemed still unaware of it. She said, "It burned three last night near the harena, and one tonight, they said, close by the Vincula. And now Jurmin. It's looking for some-body—that's what they say."

I recalled the notules and the thing that had snuffled along the walls of the antechamber of the House Absolute, and I said, "I think it has found him."

I let her go and turned, then turned again, trying to discover where it was. The heat grew, but no light showed. I was tempted to take out the Claw so as to see by its glow; then I recalled how it had waked whatever slept beneath the mine of the man-apes, and I feared the light would only permit this thing—whatever it might be—to locate me. I was not sure my sword would be more effective against it than it had been against the notules when Jonas and I had fled them through the cedar wood; nevertheless, I drew it.

Almost at once there was a clatter of hooves and a yell as two dimarchi thundered round a corner no more than a hundred strides away. Had there been more time I would have smiled to see how closely they corresponded to the figures I had imagined. As it was, the firework glare of their lances outlined something dark and crooked and stooped that stood between us.

It turned toward the light, whatever it was, and seemed to open as a flower might, growing tall more swiftly, almost, than the eye could follow it, thinning until it had become a crea-ture of glowing gauze, hot yet somehow reptilian, as those many-colored serpents we see brought from the jungles of the north are reptilian still, though they seem works of colored enamel. The mounts of the soldiers reared and screamed, but one of the men, with more presence of mind than I would have shown, fired his lance into the heart of the thing that faced him. There was a flare of light.

The hostess of the Duck's Nest slumped against me, and I, not wishing to lose her, supported her with my free arm. "I think it's seeking living heat," I told her. "It should go for the destriers. We'll get away."

Just as I spoke, it turned toward us.

I have already said that from behind, when it opened itself toward the dimarchi, it seemed a reptilian flower. That impression persisted now when we saw it in its full terror and glory, but it was joined by two others. The first was the sensation of intense and otherworldly heat; it seemed a reptile still, but a reptile that burned in a way never known on Urth, as though some desert asp had dropped into a sphere of snow. The second was of raggedness fluttering in a wind that was not of air. It seemed a blossom still, but it was a blossom whose petals of white and pale yellow and flame had been tattered by some monstrous tempest born in its own heart.

In all these impressions, surrounding them and infusing them, was a horror I cannot describe. It drew all resolution and strength from me, so that for that moment I could neither flee nor attack it. The creature and I seemed fixed in a matrix of time that had nothing to do with anything that had gone before or since, and that, since it held us who were its only occupants immobile, could be altered by nothing.

A shout broke the spell. A second party of dimarchi had galloped into the street behind us, and seeing the creature were lashing their mounts to the charge. In less than the space of a breath they were boiling around us, and it was only by the intercession of Holy Katharine that we were not ridden down. If I had ever doubted the courage of the Autarch's soldiery I lost those doubts then, for both parties hurled themselves upon the monster like hounds upon a stag.

It was useless. There came a blinding flash and the sensation of fearful heat. Still holding the half-unconscious woman, I sprinted down the street.

I meant to turn where the dimarchi had entered it, but in my panic (and it was panic, not only my own, but that of Thecla screaming in my mind) I rounded the corner too late or too soon. Instead of the steep descent to the lower city I expected, I found myself in a little, stub-end court built on a spur of rock jutting from the cliff. By the time I realized what was wrong, the creature, now again a twisted, dwarfish thing but radiating a terrible and invisible energy, was at the mouth of the court.

In the starlight it might have been only an old, hunched man in a black coat, but I have never felt more terror than I did at the sight of it. There was a jacal at the back of the court: a larger structure than the hovel in which the sick girl and her brother had suffered, but built of sticks and mud in the same fashion. I kicked its door in and ran into a little warren of odious rooms, bolting through the first and into another, through that into a third where a half dozen men and women lay sleeping, through that into a fourth—only to see a window that looked out over the city much as my own embrasure in the Vincula did. It was the end, the farthest room of the house, hanging like a swallow's nest over a drop that seemed at that moment to go down forever.

From the room we had just left I could hear the angry voices of the people I had wakened. The door flew open, but whoever had come to expel the intruder must have seen the gleam of *Terminus Est*; he stopped short, swore, and turned away. A moment later someone screamed and I knew the creature of fire was in the jacal.

I tried to set the woman upright, but she fell in a heap at my feet. Outside the window there was nothing—the wattled wall ended a few cubits down, and the supports of the floor did not extend beyond it. Above, an overhanging roof of rotten thatch offered no more purchase to my hand than gossamer. As I struggled to grasp it, there came a flood of light that destroyed all color and cast shadows as dark as fuligin itself, shadows like fissures in the cosmos. I knew then that I must fight and die as the dimarchi had, or jump, and I swung about to face the thing that had come to kill me.

It was still in the room beyond, but I could see it through the doorway, opened again now as it had been in the street. The half-consumed corpse of some wretched crone lay before it on the stone floor, and while I watched, it seemed to bend over her in what was, I would almost swear, an attitude of inquiry. Her flesh blistered and cracked like the fat of a roast, then fell away. In a moment even her bones were no more than pale ashes the creature scattered as it advanced.

Terminus Est I believe to have been the best blade ever forged, but I knew she could accomplish nothing against the power that had routed so many cavalrymen; I cast her to one side in the vague hope that she might be found and eventually returned to Master Palaemon, and took the Claw from its little bag at my throat.

It was my last, faint chance, and I saw at once that it had failed me. However the creature sensed the world about it (and I had guessed from its movements that it was nearly blind on our Urth), it could make out the gem clearly, and it did not fear it. Its slow advance became a rapid and purposeful flowing forward. It reached the doorway—there was a burst of smoke, a crash, and it was gone. Light from below flashed through the hole it had burned in the flimsy floor that began where the stone of the outcrop ended; at first it was the colorless light of the creature, then a rapid alternation of chatoyant pastels—peacock blue, lilac, and rose. Then only the faint, reddish light of leaping flames.

X

Lead

THERE WAS A moment when I thought I would fall into the gaping hole in the center of the little room before I could regain *Terminus Est* and carry the mistress of the Duck's Nest to safety, and another when I was certain everything was going to fall—the trembling structure of the room itself and us together.

Yet in the end we escaped. When we reached the street, it was clear of dimarchi and townsfolk alike, the soldiers no doubt having been drawn to the fire below, and the people frightened indoors. I propped the woman with my arm, and though she was still too terrified to answer my questions intelligibly, I let her choose our way; as I had supposed she would, she led us unerringly to her inn.

Dorcas was asleep. I did not wake her, but sat down in the dark on a stool near the bed where there was now also a little table sufficient to hold the glass and bottle I had taken from the common room below. Whatever the wine was, it seemed strong in my mouth and yet no more than water after I had swallowed it; by the time Dorcas woke, I had drunk half the bottle and felt no more effect from it than I would have if I had swallowed so much sherbet.

She started up, then let her head fall upon the pillow again. "Severian. I should have known it was you."

"I'm sorry if I frightened you," I said. "I came to see how you were."

"That's very kind. It always seems, though, that when I wake up you're bending over me." For a moment she closed her eyes again. "You walk so very quietly in those thick-soled boots of yours, do you know that? It's one reason people are afraid of you."

"You said I reminded you of a vampire once, because I had been eating a pomegranate and my lips were stained with red. We laughed about it. Do you remember?" (It had been in a field within the Wall of Nessus, when we had slept beside Dr. Talos's theater and awakened to feast on fruit dropped the night before by our fleeing audience.)

"Yes," Dorcas said. "You want me to laugh again, don't you? But I'm afraid I can't ever laugh anymore."

"Would you like some wine? It was free, and it's not as bad as I expected."

"To cheer me? No. One ought to drink, I think, when one is cheerful already. Otherwise nothing but more sorrow is poured into the cup."

"At least have a swallow. The hostess here says you've been ill and haven't eaten all day."

I saw Dorcas's golden head move on the pillow then as she turned it to look at me; and since she seemed fully awake, I ventured to light the candle.

She said, "You're wearing your habit. You must have frightened her out of her wits."

"No, she wasn't afraid of me. She's pouring into her cup whatever she finds in the bottle."

"She's been good to me—she's very kind. Don't be hard on her if she chooses to drink so late at night."

"I wasn't being hard on her. But won't you have something? There must be food in the kitchen here, and I'll bring you up whatever you want."

My choice of phrase made Dorcas smile faintly. "I've been bringing up my own food all day. That was what she meant when she told you I'd been ill. Or did she tell you? Spewing. I should think you could smell it yet, though the poor woman did what she could to clean up after me."

Dorcas paused and sniffed. "What is it I do smell? Scorched cloth? It must be the candle, but I don't suppose you can trim the wick with that great blade of yours."

I said, "It's my cloak, I think. I've been standing too near a fire."

"I'd ask you to open the window, but I see it's open already. I'm afraid it's bothering you. It does blow the candle about. Do the flickering shadows make you dizzy?"

"No," I said. "It's all right as long as I don't actually look at the flame."

"From your expression, you feel the way I always do around water."

"This afternoon I found you sitting at the very edge of the river."

"I know," Dorcas said, and fell silent. It was a silence that lasted so long that I was afraid she was not going to speak again at all, that the pathological silence (as I now was sure it had been) that had seized her then had returned.

At last I said, "I was surprised to see you there—I remember that I looked several times before I was sure it was you, although I had been searching for you."

"I spewed, Severian. I told you that, didn't I?"

"Yes, you told me."

"Do you know what I brought up?"

She was staring at the low ceiling, and I had the feeling that there was another Severian there, the kind and even noble Severian who existed only in Dorcas's mind. All of us, I suppose, when we think we are talking most intimately to someone else, are actually addressing an image we have of the person to whom we believe we speak. But this seemed more than that; I felt that Dorcas would go on talking if I left the room. "No," I answered. "Water, perhaps?"

"Sling-stones."

I thought she was speaking metaphorically, and only ventured, "That must have been very unpleasant."

Her head rolled on the pillow again, and now I could see her blue eyes with their wide pupils. In their emptiness they might have been two little ghosts. "Sling-stones, Severian my darling. Heavy little slugs of metal, each about as big around as a nut and not quite so long as my thumb and stamped with the word *strike*. They came rattling out of my throat into the bucket, and I reached down—put my hand down into the filth that came up with them and pulled them up to see. The woman who owns this inn came and took the bucket away, but I had wiped them off and saved them. There are two, and they're in the drawer of that table now. She brought it to put my dinner on. Do you want to see them? Open it."

I could not imagine what she was talking about, and asked if she thought someone was trying to poison her.

"No, not at all. Aren't you going to open the drawer? You're so brave. Don't you want to look?"

"I trust you. If you say there are sling-stones in the table, I'm sure they're there."

"But you don't believe I coughed them up. I don't blame you. Isn't there a story about a hunter's daughter who was blessed by a pardal, so that beads of jet fell from her mouth when she spoke? And then her brother's wife stole the blessing, and when she spoke toads hopped from her lips? I remember hearing it, but I never believed it."

"How could anyone cough up lead?"

Dorcas laughed, but there was no mirth in it. "Easily. So very easily. Do you know what I saw today? Do you know why

I couldn't talk to you when you found me? And I couldn't, Severian, I swear it. I know you thought I was just angry and being stubborn. But I wasn't—I had become like a stone, wordless, because nothing seemed to matter, and I'm still not sure anything does. I'm sorry, though, for what I said about your not being brave. You are brave, I know that. It's only that it seems not brave when you're doing things to the poor prisoners here. You were so brave when you fought Agilus, and later when you would have fought with Baldanders because we thought he was going to kill Jolenta . . ."

She fell silent again, then sighed. "Oh, Severian, I'm so tired."

"I wanted to talk to you about that," I said. "About the prisoners. I want you to understand, even if you can't forgive me. It was my profession, the thing I was trained to do from boyhood." I leaned forward and took her hand; it seemed as frail as a songbird.

"You've said something like this before. Truly, I understand."

"And I could do it well. Dorcas, that's what you *don't* understand. Excruciation and execution are arts, and I have the feel, the gift, the blessing. This sword—all the tools we use live when they're in my hands. If I had remained at the Citadel, I might have been a master. Dorcas, are you listening? Does this mean anything at all to you?"

"Yes," she said. "A bit, yes. I'm thirsty, though. If you're through drinking, pour me a little of that wine now, please."

I did as she asked, filling the glass no more than a quarter full because I was afraid she might spill it on her bedclothes.

She sat up to drink, something I had not been certain until then that she was capable of, and when she had swallowed the last scarlet drop hurled the glass out the window. I heard it shatter on the street below.

"I don't want you to drink after me," she told me. "And I knew that if I didn't do that you would."

"You think whatever is wrong with you is contagious, then?"

She laughed again. "Yes, but you have it already. You caught it from your mother. Death. Severian, you never asked me what it was I saw today."

XI

The Hand of the Past

AS SOON AS Dorcas said, "You never asked me what I saw today," I realized that I had been trying to steer the conversation away from it. I had a premonition that it would be something quite meaningless to me, to which Dorcas would attach great meaning, as madmen do who believe the tracks of worms beneath the bark of fallen trees to be a supernatural script. I said, "I thought it might be better to keep your mind off it, whatever it was."

"No doubt it would, if only we could do it. It was a chair."

"A chair?"

"An old chair. And a table, and several other things. It seems that there is a shop in the Turners' Street that sells old furniture to the eclectics, and to those among the autochthons who have absorbed enough of our culture to want it. There is no source here to supply the demand, and so two or three times a year the owner and his sons go to Nessus—to the abandoned quarters of the south—and fill their boat. I talked to him, you see; I know all about it. There are tens of thousands of empty houses there. Some have fallen in long ago, but some are still standing as their owners left them. Most have been looted, yet they still find silver and bits of jewelry now and then. And though most have lost most of their furniture, the owners who moved almost always left some things behind."

I felt that she was about to weep, and I leaned forward to stroke her forehead. She showed me by a glance that she did not wish me to, and laid herself on the bed again as she had been before.

"In some of those houses, all the furnishings are still there. Those are the best, he said. He thinks that a few families, or perhaps only a few people living alone, remained behind when the quarter died. They were too old to move, or too stubborn. I've thought about it, and I'm sure some of them must have had something there they could not bear to leave. A grave, perhaps. They boarded their windows against the marauders, and they kept dogs, and worse things, to protect them. Eventually they left—or they came to the end of life, and their animals devoured their bodies and broke free; but by that time there was no one there, not even looters or scavengers, not until this man and his sons."

"There must be a great many old chairs," I said.

"Not like that one. I knew everything about it—the carving on the legs and even the pattern in the grain of the arms. So much came back then. And then here, when I vomited those pieces of lead, things like hard, heavy seeds, then I knew. Do you remember, Severian, how it was when we left the Botanic Garden? You, Agia, and I came out of that great, glass vivarium, and you hired a boat to take us from the island to the shore, and the river was full of nenuphars with blue flowers and shining green leaves. Their seeds are like that, hard and heavy and dark, and I have heard that they sink to the bottom of Gyoll and remain there for whole ages of the world. But when chance brings them near the surface they sprout no matter how old they may be, so that the flowers of a chiliad past are seen to bloom again."

"I have heard that too," I said. "But it means nothing to you or me."

Dorcas lay still, but her voice trembled. "What is the power that calls them back? Can you explain it?"

"The sunshine, I suppose—but no, I cannot explain it."

"And is there no source of sunlight except the sun?"

I knew then what it was she meant, though something in me could not accept it.

"When that man—Hildegrin, the man we met a second time on top of the tomb in the ruined stone town—was ferrying us across the Lake of Birds, he talked of millions of dead people, people whose bodies had been sunk in that water. How were they made to sink, Severian? Bodies float. How do they weight them? I don't know. Do you?"

I did. "They force lead shot down the throats."

"I thought so." Her voice was so weak now that I could scarcely hear her, even in that silent little room. "No, I knew so. I knew it when I saw them."

"You think that the Claw brought you back."

Dorcas nodded.

"It has acted, sometimes, I'll admit that. But only when I took it out, and not always then. When you pulled me out of the water in the Garden of Endless Sleep, it was in my sabretache and I didn't even know I had it."

"Severian, you allowed me to hold it once before. Could I see it again now?"

I pulled it from its soft pouch and held it up. The blue fires seemed sleepy, but I could see the cruel-looking hook at the center of the gem that had given it its name. Dorcas extended her hand, but I shook my head, remembering the wineglass.

"You think I will do it some harm, don't you? I won't. It would be a sacrilege."

"If you believe what you say, and I think you do, then you must hate it for drawing you back . . ."

"From death." She was watching the ceiling again, now

smiling as if she shared some deep and ludicrous secret with it. "Go ahead and say it. It won't hurt you."

"From sleep," I said. "Since if one can be recalled from it, it is not death—not death as we have always understood it, the death that is in our minds when we say *death*. Although I have to confess it is still almost impossible for me to believe that the Conciliator, dead now for so many thousands of years, should act through this stone to raise others."

Dorcas made no reply. I could not even be sure she was listening.

"You mentioned Hildegrin," I said, "and the time he rowed us across the lake in his boat, to pick the avern. Do you remember what he said of death? It was that she was a good friend to the birds. Perhaps we ought to have known then that such a death could not be death as we imagine it."

"If I say I believe all that, will you let me hold the Claw?"

I shook my head again.

Dorcas was not looking at me, but she must have seen the motion of my shadow; or perhaps it was only that her mental Severian on the ceiling shook his head as well. "You are right, then—I was going to destroy it if I could. Shall I tell you what I really believe? I believe I have been dead—not sleeping, but dead. That all my life took place a long, long time ago when I lived with my husband above a little shop, and took care of our child. That this Conciliator of yours who came so long ago was an adventurer from one of the ancient races who outlived the universal death." Her hands clutched the blanket. "I ask you, Severian, when he comes again, isn't he to be called the New Sun? Doesn't that sound like it? And I believe that when he came he brought with him something that had the same power over time that Father Inire's mirrors are said to have over distance. It is that gem of yours."

She stopped and turned her head to look at me defiantly; when I said nothing, she continued. "Severian, when you brought the uhlan back to life it was because the Claw twisted time for him to the point at which he still lived. When you half healed your friend's wounds, it was because it bent the moment to one when they would be nearly healed. And when you fell into the fen in the Garden of Endless Sleep, it must have touched me or nearly touched me, and for me it became the time in which I had lived, so that I lived again. But I have been dead. For a long, long time I was dead, a shrunken corpse preserved in the brown water. And there is something in me that is dead still."

"There is something in all of us that has always been dead," I said. "If only because we know that eventually we will die. All of us except the smallest children."

"I'm going to go back, Severian. I know that now, and that's what I've been trying to tell you. I have to go back and find out who I was and where I lived and what happened to me. I know you can't go with me . . ."

I nodded.

"And I'm not asking you to. I don't even want you to. I love you, but you are another death, a death that has stayed with me and befriended me as the old death in the lake did, but death all the same. I don't want to take death with me when I go to look for my life."

"I understand," I said.

"My child may still be alive—an old man, perhaps, but still alive. I have to know."

"Yes," I said. But I could not help adding, "There was a time when you told me I was not death. That I must not let others persuade me to think of myself in that way. It was behind the orchard on the grounds of the House Absolute. Do you remember?"

"You have been death to me," she said. "I have succumbed to the trap I warned you of, if you like. Perhaps you are not death, but you will remain what you are, a torturer and a carnifex, and your hands will run with blood. Since you remember that time at the House Absolute so well, perhaps you

. . . I can't say it. The Conciliator, or the Claw, or the Increate, has done this to me. Not you."

"What is it?" I asked.

"Dr. Talos gave us both money afterward, in the clearing. The money he had got from some court official for our play. When we were traveling, I gave everything to you. May I have it back? I'll need it. If not all of it, at least some of it."

I emptied the money in my sabretache onto the table. It was as much as I had received from her, or a trifle more.

"Thank you," she said. "You won't need it?"

"Not as badly as you will. Besides, it is yours."

"I'm going to leave tomorrow, if I feel strong enough. The day after tomorrow whether I feel strong or not. I don't suppose you know how often the boats put out, going downriver?"

"As often as you want them to. You push them in, and the river does the rest."

"That's not like you, Severian, or at least not much. More the sort of thing your friend Jonas would have said, from what you've told me. Which reminds me that you're not the first visitor I've had today. Our friend—your friend, at least—Hethor was here. That's not funny to you, is it? I'm sorry, I just wanted to change the subject."

"He enjoys it. Enjoys watching me."

"Thousands of people do when you perform in public, and you enjoy doing it yourself."

"They come to be horrified, so they can congratulate themselves later on being alive. And because they like the excitement, and the suspense of not knowing whether the condemned will break down, or if some macabre accident will occur. I enjoy exercising my skill, the only real skill I have—enjoy making things go perfectly. Hethor wants something else."

"The pain?"

"Yes, the pain, but something more too."

Dorcas said, "He worships you, you know. He talked with me for some time, and I think he would walk into a fire if you told him to." I must have winced at that, because she continued, "All this about Hethor is making you ill, isn't it? One sick person is enough. Let's speak of something else."

"Not ill as you are, no. But I can't think of Hethor except as I saw him once from the scaffold, with his mouth open and his eyes . . ."

She stirred uncomfortably. "Yes, those eyes—I saw them tonight. Dead eyes, though I suppose I shouldn't be the one to say that. A corpse's eyes. You have the feeling that if you touched them they would be as dry as stones, and never move under your finger."

"That isn't it at all. When I was on the scaffold in Saltus and looked down and saw him, his eyes danced. You said, though, that the dull eyes he has at most times reminded you of a corpse's. Haven't you ever looked into the glass? Your own eyes are not the eyes of a dead woman."

"Perhaps not." Dorcas paused. "You used to say they were beautiful."

"Aren't you glad to live? Even if your husband is dead, and your child is dead, and the house you once lived in is a ruin— if all those things are true—aren't you full of joy because you are here again? You're not a ghost, not a revenant like those we saw in the ruined town. Look in the glass as I told you. Or if you won't, look into my face or any man's and see what you are."

Dorcas sat up even more slowly and painfully than she had risen to drink the wine, but this time she swung her legs over the edge of the bed, and I saw that she was naked under the thin blanket. Before her illness Jolenta's skin had been perfect, with the smoothness and softness of confectionery. Dorcas's was flecked with little golden freckles, and she was so slender that I was always aware of her bones; yet she was more desirable in her imperfection than Jolenta had ever been in the lushness of her flesh. Conscious of how culpable it would be to force myself on her or even to persuade her to open to me now, when she was ill and I was on the point of leaving her, I still felt desire for her stir in me. However much I love a woman—or however little—I find I want her most when I can no longer have her. But what I felt for Dorcas was stronger than that, and more complex. She had been, though only for so brief a time, the closest friend I had known, and our possession of each other, from the frantic desire in our converted storeroom in Nessus to the long and lazy playing in the bed-chamber of the Vincula, was the characteristic act of our friendship as well as our love.

"You're crying," I said. "Do you want me to leave?"

She shook her head, and then, as though she could no longer contain the words that seemed to force themselves out, she whispered, "Oh, won't you go too, Severian? I didn't mean it. Won't you come? Won't you come with me?"

"I can't."

She sank back into the narrow bed, smaller now and more childlike. "I know. You have your duty to your guild. You can't betray it again and face yourself, and I won't ask you. It's only that I never quite gave up hoping you might."

I shook my head as I had before. "I have to flee the city—"

"Severian!"

"And to the north. You'll be going south, and if I were with you, we would have courier boats full of soldiers after us."

"Severian, what happened?" Dorcas's face was very calm, but her eyes were wide.

"I freed a woman. I was supposed to strangle her and throw her body into the Acis, and I could have done it—I didn't feel anything for her, not really, and it should have been easy. But when I was alone with her, I thought of Thecla. We were in a little summerhouse screened with shrubbery, that stood at the edge of the water. I had my hands around her neck, and I thought of Thecla and how I had wanted to free her. I couldn't find a way to do it. Have I ever told you?"

Almost imperceptibly, Dorcas shook her head.

"There were brothers everywhere, five to pass by the shortest route, and all of them knew me and knew of her." (Thecla was shrieking now in some corner of my mind.) "All I really would have had to do would have been to tell them Master Gurloes had ordered me to bring her to him. But I would have had to go with her then, and I was still trying to devise some way by which I could stay in the guild. I did not love her enough."

"It's past now," Dorcas said. "And, Severian, death is not the terrible thing you think it." We had reversed our roles, like lost children who comfort each other alternately.

I shrugged. The ghost I had eaten at Vodalus's banquet was nearly calm again; I could feel her long, cool fingers on my brain, and though I could not turn inside my own skull to see her, I knew her deep and violet eyes were behind my own. It required an effort not to speak with her voice. "At any rate, I was there with the woman, in the summerhouse, and we were alone. Her name was Cyriaca. I knew or at least suspected that she knew where the Pelerines were—she had been one of them for a time. There are silent means of excruciation that require no equipment, and although they are not spectacular, they are quite effective. One reaches into the body, as it were, and manipulates the client's nerves directly. I was going to use what we call Humbaba's Stick, but before I had touched her she told me. The Pelerines are near the pass of Orithyia caring for the wounded. This woman had a letter, she said, only a week ago, from someone she had known in the order . . ."

XII

Following the Flood

THE SUMMERHOUSE HAD boasted a solid roof, but the sides were mere latticework, closed more by the tall forest ferns planted against them than by their slender laths. Moonbeams leaked through. More came in at the doorway, reflected from the rushing water outside. I could see the fear in Cyriaca's face, and the knowledge that her only hope was that I retained some love for her; and I knew that she was thus without hope, for I felt nothing.

"At the Autarch's camp," she repeated. "That was what Einhildis wrote. In Orithyia, near the springs of Gyoll. But you must be careful if you go there to return the book—she said too that cacogens had landed somewhere in the north."

I stared at her, trying to determine whether she were lying.

"That's what Einhildis told me. I suppose they must have wished to avoid the mirrors at the House Absolute so they could escape the eyes of the Autarch. He's supposed to be their servitor, but sometimes he acts as if they were his."

I shook her. "Are you joking with me? The Autarch serves them?"

"Please! Oh, please . . ."

I dropped her.

"Everyone . . . Erebus! Pardon me." She sobbed, and though she lay in shadow I sensed that she was wiping her eyes and nose with the hem of her scarlet habit. "Everyone knows it except the peons, and the goodmen and the good women. All the armigers and even most of the optimates, and of course the exultants have always known. I've never seen the Autarch, but I'm told that he, the Viceroy of the New Sun, is scarcely taller than I am. Do you think our proud exultants would permit someone like that to rule if there weren't a thousand cannon behind him?"

"I've seen him," I said, "and I wondered about that." I sought among Thecla's memories for confirmation of what Cyriaca said, but I found only rumor.

"Would you tell me about him? Please, Severian, before—"

"No, not now. But why should the cacogens be a danger to me?"

"Because the Autarch will surely send scouts to locate them, and I suppose the archon here will too. Anyone found near them will be assumed to have been spying for them, or what's worse, seeking them out in the hope of enlisting them in some plot against the Phoenix Throne."

"I understand."

"Severian, don't kill me. I beg you. I'm not a good woman— I've never been a good woman, never since I left the Pelerines, and I can't face dying now."

I asked her, "What have you done, anyway? Why does Abdiesus want you killed? Do you know?" It is simplicity itself to strangle an individual whose neck muscles are not strong, and I was already flexing my hands for the task; yet at the same time I wished it had been permissible for me to use *Terminus Est* instead.

"Only loved too many men, men other than my husband."

As if moved by the memory of those embraces, she rose and came toward me. Again the moonlight fell upon her face; her eyes were bright with unshed tears.

"He was cruel to me, so cruel, after our marriage . . . and so I took a lover, to spite him, and afterwards, another . . ."

(Her voice dropped until I could hardly hear the words.)

"And at last taking a new lover becomes a habit, a way of pushing back the days and showing yourself that all your life has not run between your fingers already, showing yourself that you are still young enough for men to bring gifts, young enough that men still want to stroke your hair. That was what I had left the Pelerines for, after all." She paused and seemed to gather her strength. "Do you know how old I am? Did I tell you?"

"No," I said.

"I won't, then. But I might almost be your mother. If I had conceived within a year or two of the time it became possible for me. We were far in the south, where the great ice, all blue and white, sails on black seas. There was a little hill where I used to stand and watch, and I dreamed of putting on warm clothes and paddling out to the ice with food and a trained bird I never really had but only wanted to have, and so riding my own ice island north to an isle of palms, where I would discover the ruins of a castle built in the morning of the world. You would have been born then, perhaps, while I was alone on the ice. Why shouldn't an imaginary child be born on an imaginary trip? You would have grown up fishing and swimming in water warmer than milk."

"No woman is killed for being unfaithful, except by her husband," I said.

Cyriaca sighed, and her dream fell from her. "Among the landed armigers hereabout, he is one of the few who support the archon. The others hope that by disobeying him as much as they dare and fomenting trouble among the eclectics they can persuade the Autarch to replace him. I have made my husband a laughing stock—and by extension his friends and the archon."

Because Thecla was within me, I saw the country villa—half

manor and half fort, full of rooms that had scarcely changed in two hundred years. I heard the tittering ladies and the stamping hunters, and the sound of the horn outside the windows, and the deep barking of the boarhounds. It was the world to which Thecla had hoped to retreat; and I felt pity for this woman, who had been forced into that retreat when she had never known any wider sphere.

Just as the room of the Inquisitor in Dr. Talos's play, with its high judicial bench, lurked somewhere at the lowest level of the House Absolute, so we have each of us in the dustiest cellars of our minds a counter at which we strive to repay the debts of the past with the debased currency of the present. At that counter I tendered Cyriaca's life in payment for Thecla's.

When I led her from the summerhouse, she supposed, I know, that I intended to kill her at the edge of the water. Instead, I pointed to the river.

"This flows swiftly south until it meets the flood of Gyoll, which then runs more slowly to Nessus, and at last to the southern sea. No fugitive can be found in the maze of Nessus who does not wish it, for there are streets and courts and tenements there without number, and all the faces of all lands are seen a hundred times over. If you could go there, dressed as you are now, without friends or money, would you do so?"

She nodded, one pale hand at her throat.

"There is no barrier to boats yet at the Capulus; Abdiesus knows he need not fear any attack made against the current there until midsummer. But you will have to shoot the arches, and you may drown. Even if you reach Nessus, you will have to work for your bread—wash for others, perhaps, or cook."

"I can dress hair and sew. Severian, I have heard that sometimes, as the last and most terrible torture, you tell your prisoner she will be freed. If that is what you're doing to me now, I beg you to stop. You've gone far enough."

"A caloyer does that, or some other religious functionary.

No client would believe us. But I want to be certain there will be no foolishness of returning to your home or seeking a pardon from the archon."

"I am a fool," Cyriaca said. "But no. Not even such a fool as I am would do that, I swear."

We skirted the water's edge until we came to the stairs where the sentries stood to admit the archon's guests, and the little, brightly hued pleasure boats were moored. I told one of the soldiers we were going to try the river, and asked if we would have any difficulty hiring rowers to take us back upstream. He said we might leave the boat at the Capulus if we wished, and return in a fiacre. When he turned away to resume his conversation with his comrade, I pretended to inspect the boats, and slipped the painter of the one farthest from the torches of the guard post.

Dorcas said, "And so now you are going north as a fugitive, and I have taken your money."

"I won't need much, and I will get more." I stood up.

"Take back half at least." When I shook my head, she said, "Then take back two chrisos. I can whore, if worst comes to worst, or steal."

"If you steal, your hand will be struck off. And it is better that I strike off hands for my dinner than that you give your hands for yours."

I started to go, but she sprang out of bed and held my cloak. "Be careful, Severian. There is something—Hethor called it a salamander—loose in the city. Whatever it is, it burns its victims."

I told her I had much more to fear from the archon's soldiers than from the salamander, and left before she could say more. But as I toiled up a narrow street on the western bank that my boatmen had assured me would lead to the cliff top, I wondered if I would not have more to fear from the cold of the mountains, and their wild beasts, than from either. I wondered too about Hethor, and how he had followed me so far into the north, and why. But more than I thought on any of those things, I thought about Dorcas, and what she had been to me, and I to her. It was to be a long time before I would so much as glimpse her again, and I believe that in some way I sensed that. Just as when I had first left the Citadel I had pulled up my hood so that the passersby might not observe my smiles, so now I hid my face to conceal the tears running down my cheeks.

I had seen the reservoir that supplied the Vincula twice before by day, but never by night. It had appeared small then, a rectangular pond no larger than the foundation of a house and no deeper than a grave. Under the waning moon it seemed almost a lake, and might have been as deep as the cistern below the Bell Tower.

It lay no more than a hundred paces from the wall that defended the western margin of Thrax. There were towers on that wall—one quite near the reservoir—and no doubt the garrisons had by that time been ordered to apprehend me if I tried to escape from the city. At intervals, as I had walked along the cliff, I had glimpsed the sentries who patrolled the wall; their lances were unkindled, but their crested helms showed against the stars, and sometimes faintly caught the light.

Now I crouched, looking out over the city and relying on my fuligin cloak and hood to deceive their eyes. The barred iron portcullises of the arches of the Capulus had been lowered—I could detect the roiling of the Acis where it battered against them. That removed all doubt: Cyriaca had been stopped—or more probably, simply seen and reported. Abdiesus might or might not make strenuous efforts to capture her; it seemed most probable to me that he would allow her to vanish, and so avoid drawing attention to her. But he would surely apprehend me if he could, and execute me as the traitor to his rule that I was.

From the water I looked to water again, from the rushing

Acis to the still reservoir. I had the word for the sluice gate, and I used it. The ancient mechanism ground up as though moved by phantom slaves, and then the still waters rushed too, rushed faster than the raging Acis at the Capulus. Far below, the prisoners would hear their roar, and those nearest the entrance would see the white foam of the flood. In a moment those who stood would be up to their ankles in water, and those who had slept would be scrambling to their feet. In another moment, all would be waist deep; but they were chained in their places, and the weaker would be supported by the stronger—none, I hoped, would drown. The clavigers at the entrance would leave their posts and hurry up the steep trail to the cliff top to see who had tampered with the reservoir there.

And as the last water drained away, I heard the stones dislodged by their feet rattling down the slope. I closed the sluice gate again and lowered myself into the slimy and nearly vertical passage that the water had just traversed. Here my progress would have been far easier if I had not been carrying *Terminus Est*. To brace my back against one side of that crooked, chimneylike pipe, I had to unsling her; yet I could not spare a hand to hold her. I put her baldric around my neck, let her blade and sheath hang down, and managed her weight as well as I could. Twice I slipped, but each time I was saved by a turn of the narrowing sluice; and at last, after so long a time that I was certain the clavigers would have returned, I saw the gleam of red torchlight and drew forth the Claw.

I was never to see it flame so bright again. It was blinding, and I carrying it upraised down the long tunnel of the Vincula, could only wonder that my hand was not reduced to ashes. No prisoner, I think, saw *me*. The Claw fascinated them as a lantern by night does the deer of the forest; they stood motionless, their mouths open, their raddled, bearded faces uplifted, their shadows behind them as sharp as silhouettes cut in metal and dark as fuligin.

At the very end of the tunnel, where the water ran out into the long, sloping sewer that carried it below the Capulus, were the weakest and most diseased prisoners; and it was there that I saw most clearly the strength the Claw lent them all. Men and women who had not stood straight in the memory of the oldest claviger now seemed tall and strong. I waved in salute to them, though I am sure none of them observed it. Then I put the Claw of the Conciliator back into its little pouch, and we were plunged into a night beside which the night of the surface of Urth would be day.

The rush of water had swept the sewer clean, and it was easier to descend than the sluice had been, for though it was narrower, it was less steep, and I could crawl rapidly down headforemost. There was a grill at the bottom; but as I had noted on one of my inspection tours, it was nearly rusted through.

XIII

Into the Mountains

SPRING HAD ENDED and summer begun when I crept away from the Capulus in the gray light, but even so it was never warm in the high lands except when the sun was near the zenith. Yet I did not dare to go into the valleys where the villages huddled, and all day I walked up, into the mountains, with my cloak furled across one shoulder to make it look as nearly as possible like the garment of an eclectic. I also dismounted the blade of *Terminus Est* and reassembled it without the guard, so that the sheathed sword seen from a distance would have the appearance of a staff.

By noon the ground was all of stone, and so uneven that I did as much climbing as walking. Twice I saw the glint of armor far below me, and looking down beheld little parties of dimarchi cantering down trails most men could scarcely have persuaded themselves to walk, their scarlet military capes billowing behind them. I found no edible plants and sighted no game other than high soaring birds of prey. Had I seen any, I would have had no chance of taking it with my sword, and I possessed no other weapon.

All that sounds desperate enough, but the truth was that I

was thrilled by the mountain views, the vast panorama of the empire of air. As children we have no appreciation of scenery because, having not yet stored similar scenes in our imagination, with their attendant emotions and circumstances, we perceive it without psychic depth. I now looked at the cloud-crowned summits with my view of Nessus from the nose cone of our Matachin Tower and my view of Thrax from the battlements of Acies Castle before me as well, and miserable though I was, I was ready to faint with pleasure.

That night I spent huddled in the lee of a naked rock. I had not eaten since I had changed clothes in the Vincula, which now seemed weeks, if not years, before. In actuality, it had been only months since I had smuggled a worn kitchen knife to poor Thecla, and seen her blood seeping, a groping worm of crimson, from beneath her cell door.

I had chosen my stone well, at least. It blocked the wind, so that as long as I remained behind it I might almost have rested in the quiet, frigid air of some ice cave. A step or two to either side brought me into the full blast, so that I was chilled to the bone in a single frosty moment.

I slept for about a watch, I think, without any dreams that outlived my sleep, then woke with the impression—which was not a dream, but the sort of foundationless knowledge or pseudoknowledge that comes to us at times when we are weary and fearful—that Hethor was leaning over me. I seemed to feel his breath, stinking and icy cold, upon my face; his eyes, no longer dull, blazed into mine. When I was fully awake, I saw that the points of light I had taken for their pupils were in fact two stars, large and very bright in the thin, clean air.

I tried to sleep again, closing my eyes and forcing myself to remember the warmest and most comfortable places I had known: the journeyman's quarters I had been given in our tower, which had then seemed so palatial with their privacy and soft blankets after the apprentices' dormitory; the bed I had once shared with Baldanders, into which his broad back had projected heat like a stove's; Thecla's apartments in the House Absolute; the snug room in Saltus where I had lodged with Jonas.

Nothing helped. I could not sleep again, and yet I dared not to try to walk farther for fear that I would fall over some precipice in the dark. I spent the remainder of the night staring at the stars; it was the first time I had ever really experienced the majesty of the constellations, of which Master Malrubius had taught us when I was the smallest of the apprentices. How strange it is that the sky, which by day is a stationary ground on which the clouds are seen to move, by night becomes the backdrop for Urth's own motion, so that we feel her rolling beneath us as a sailor feels the running of the tide. That night the sense of this slow turning was so strong that I was almost giddy with its long, continued sweep.

Strong too was the feeling that the sky was a bottomless pit into which the universe might drop forever. I had heard people say that when they looked at the stars too long they grew terrified by the sensation of being drawn away. My own fear—and I felt fear—was not centered on the remote suns, but rather on the yawning void; and at times I grew so frightened that I gripped the rock with my freezing fingers, for it seemed to me that I must fall off Urth. No doubt everyone feels some touch of this, since it is said that there exists no climate so mild that people will consent to sleep in unroofed houses.

I have already described how I woke thinking that Hethor's face (I suppose because Hethor had been much in my mind since I talked to Dorcas) was staring into mine, yet discovered when I opened my eyes that the face retained no detail except the two bright stars that had been its own. So it was with me at first when I tried to pick out the constellations, whose names I had often read, though I had only the most imperfect idea of the part of the sky in which each might be found. At first all the stars seemed a featureless mass of lights, however beautiful, like the sparks that fly upward from a fire. Soon, of course, I began to see that some were brighter than others, and that their colors were by no means uniform. Then, quite unexpectedly, when I had been staring at them for a long time, the shape of a peryton seemed to spring out as distinctly as if the bird's whole body had been powdered with the dust ground from diamonds. In a moment it was gone again, but it soon returned, and with it other shapes, some corresponding to constellations of which I had heard, others that were, I am afraid, entirely of my own imagining. An amphisbaena, or snake with a head at either end, was particularly distinct.

When these celestial animals burst into view, I was awed by their beauty. But when they became so strongly evident (as they quickly did) that I could no longer dismiss them by an act of will, I began to feel as frightened of them as I was of falling into that midnight abyss over which they writhed; yet this was not a simple physical and instinctive fear like the other, but rather a sort of philosophical horror at the thought of a cosmos in which rude pictures of beasts and monsters had been painted with flaming suns.

After I covered my head with my cloak, which I was forced to do lest I go mad, I fell to thinking of the worlds that circled those suns. All of us know they exist, many being mere endless plains of rock, others spheres of ice or of cindery hills where lava rivers flow, as is alleged of Abaddon; but many others being worlds more or less fair, and inhabited by creatures either descended from the human stock or at least not wholly different from ourselves. At first I thought of green skies, blue grass, and all the rest of the childish exotica apt to inflict the mind that conceives of other than Urthly worlds. But in time I tired of those puerile ideas, and began in their place to think of societies and ways of thought wholly different from our own, worlds in which all the people, knowing themselves descended from a single pair of colonists, treated one another as brothers and sisters, worlds where there was no currency but honor, so that everyone worked in order that he might be entitled to associate himself with some man or woman who had saved the community, worlds in which the long war between mankind and the beasts was pursued no more. With these thoughts came a hundred or more new ones—how justice might be meted out when all loved all, for example; how a beggar who retained nothing but his humanity might beg for honor, and the ways in which people who would kill no sentient animal might be shod and fed.

When I had first come to realize, as a boy, that the green circle of the moon was in fact a sort of island hung in the sky, whose color derived from forests, now immemorially old, planted in the earliest days of the race of Man, I had formed an intention of going there, and had added to it all the other worlds of the universe as I came in time to realize their existence. I had abandoned that wish as a part (I thought) of growing up, when I learned that only people whose positions in society appeared to me unattainably high ever succeeded in leaving Urth.

Now that old longing was rekindled again, and though it seemed to have grown more absurd still with the passage of the years (for surely the little apprentice I had been had more chance of flashing between the stars at last than the hunted outcast I had become) it was immensely firmer and stronger because I had learned in the intervening time the folly of limiting desire to the possible. I would go, I was resolved. For the remainder of my life I would be sleeplessly alert for any opportunity, however slight. Already I had found myself once alone with the mirrors of Father Inire; then Jonas, wiser by far than I, had without hesitation cast himself on the tide of photons. Who could say that I would never find myself before those mirrors again?

With that thought, I snatched my cloak away from my head, resolved to look upon the stars once more, and found that the sunlight had come lancing over the crowns of the mountains to dim them almost to insignificance. The titan faces that loomed above me now were only those of the long-dead rulers of Urth, haggard by time, their cheeks fallen away in avalanches.

I stood and stretched. It was clear that I could not spend the day without food, as I had spent the day before; and clearer still that I could not spend the next night as I had spent this, with no shelter but my cloak. Thus, though I did not dare yet go down into the peopled valleys, I shaped my path to take me to the high forest I could see marching over the slopes below me.

It took most of the morning to reach it. When at last I scrambled down to stand among the scrub birches that were its outriders, I saw that although it was more steeply pitched than I had supposed, it contained, toward its center where the ground was somewhat more level and the sparse soil thus a trifle richer, trees of very considerable height, so closely spaced that the apertures between their trunks were hardly wider than the trunks themselves. They were not, of course, the glossy-leaved hardwoods of the tropical forest we had left behind on the south bank of the Cephissus. These were shaggy-barked conifers for the most part, tall, straight trees that leaned, even in their height and strength, away from the shadow of the mountain, and showed plainly in at least a quarter of their number the wounds of their wars with wind and lightning.

I had come hoping to find woodcutters or hunters from whom I might claim the hospitality that everyone (as city people fondly believe) offers to strangers in the wilds. For a long time, however, I was disappointed in that hope. Again and again I paused to listen for the ringing of an ax or the baying of hounds. There was only silence, and indeed, though the trees would have provided a great quantity of lumber, I saw no signs that any had ever been cut.

At last I came across a little brook of ice-cold water that wandered among the trees, fringed with dwarfed and tender bracken and grass as fine as hair. I drank my fill, and for perhaps half a watch followed the water down the slope through a succession of miniature falls and tarns, wondering, as no doubt others have for countless chiliads, to observe it grown slowly larger, though it had recruited no others of its kind that I could see.

Eventually it was swollen until the trees themselves were no longer safe from it, and I saw ahead the trunk of one, four cubits thick at least, that had fallen across it, its roots undermined. I approached it with no great care, for there was no sound to warn me, and bracing myself on a projecting stub vaulted to the top.

Almost I tumbled into an ocean of air. The battlement of Acies Castle, from which I had seen Dorcas in her dejection, was a balustrade compared to that height. Surely the Wall of Nessus is the only work of hands that could rival it. The brook fell silently upon a gulf that blew it to spray, so that it vanished into a rainbow. The trees below might have been toys made for a boy by an indulgent father, and at the edge of them, with a little field beyond, I saw a house no bigger than a pebble, with a wisp of white smoke, the ghost of the ribbon of water that had fallen and died, curling up to disappear like it into nothingness.

To descend the cliff appeared at first only too easy, for the momentum of my vault had nearly carried me over the fallen trunk, which itself hung half over the edge. When I had regained my balance, however, it seemed close to impossible. The rock face was sheer over large areas, so far as I could see, and though perhaps if I had carried a rope I could have let myself down and so reached the house well before night, I of course had none, and in any case would have been very slow to trust a rope of such immense length as would have been required.

I spent some time exploring the top of the cliff, however, and eventually discovered a path that, though very precipitous and very narrow, showed unmistakable signs of use. I will not recount the details of the climb down, which really have little to do with my story, although they were as may be imagined deeply absorbing at the time. I soon learned to watch only the path and the face of the cliff, to my right or left as the path wound back and forth. For most of its length it was a steep descent about a cubit wide or a little less. Occasionally it became a series of descending steps cut into the living rock, and at one point there were only hand and foot holes, which I descended like a ladder. These were far easier—viewed objectively—than the crevices to which I had clung by night at the mouth of the mine of the man-apes, and at least I was spared the shock of crossbow quarrels exploding about my ears; but the height was a hundred times greater, and dizzying.

Perhaps because I was forced to labor so hard to ignore the drop on the opposite side, I became acutely conscious of the vast, sectioned sample of the world's crust down which I crawled. In ancient times—so I read once in one of the texts Master Palaemon set me—the heart of Urth herself was alive, and the shifting motions of that living core made plains erupt like fountains, and sometimes opened seas in a night between islands that had been one continent when last seen by the sun. Now it is said she is dead, and cooling and shrinking within her stony mantle like the corpse of an old woman in one of those abandoned houses Dorcas had described, mummifying in the still, dry air until her clothing falls in upon itself. So it is, it is said, with Urth; and here half a mountain had dropped away from its mating half, falling a league at least.

XIV

The Widow's House

IN SALTUS, WHERE Jonas and I stayed for a few days and where I performed the second and third public decollations of my career, the miners rape the soil of metals, building stones, and even artifacts laid down by civilizations forgotten for chiliads before the Wall of Nessus ever rose. This they do by narrow shafts bored into the hillsides until they strike some rich layer of ruins, or even (if the tunnelers are particularly fortunate) a building that has preserved some part of its structure so that it serves them as a gallery already made.

What was done with so much labor there might have been accomplished on the cliff I descended with almost none. The past stood at my shoulder, naked and defenseless as all dead things, as though it were time itself that had been laid open by the fall of the mountain. Fossil bones protruded from the surface in places, the bones of mighty animals and of men. The forest had set its own dead there as well, stumps and limbs that time had turned to stone, so that I wondered as I descended, if it might not be that Urth is not, as we assume, older than her daughters the trees, and imagined them growing in the emptiness before the face of the sun, tree clinging to tree with tangled roots and interlacing twigs until at last their accumulation became our Urth, and they only the nap of her garment.

Deeper than these lay the buildings and mechanisms of humanity. (And it may be that those of other races lay there as well, for several of the stories in the brown book I carried seemed to imply that colonies once existed here of those beings whom we call the cacogens, though they are in fact of myriad races, each as distinct as our own.) I saw metals there that were green and blue in the same sense that copper is said to be red or silver white, colored metals so curiously wrought that I could not be certain whether their shapes had been intended as works of art or as parts for strange machines, and it may be indeed that among some of those unfathomable peoples there is no distinction.

At one point, only slightly less than halfway down, the line of the fault had coincided with the tiled wall of some great building, so that the windy path I trod slashed across it. What the design was those tiles traced, I never knew; as I descended the cliff I was too near to see it, and when I reached the base at last it was too high for me to discern, lost in the shifting mists of the falling river. Yet as I walked, I saw it as an insect may be said to see the face in a portrait over whose surface it creeps. The tiles were of many shapes, though they fit together so closely, and at first I thought them representations of birds, lizards, fish and suchlike creatures, all interlocked in the grip of life. Now I feel that this was not so, that they were instead the shapes of a geometry I failed to comprehend, diagrams so complex that the living forms seemed to appear in them as the forms of actual animals appear from the intricate geometries of complex molecules.

However that might be, these forms seemed to have little connection with the picture or design. Lines of color crossed them, and though they must have been fired into the substance of the tiles in eons past, they were so willful and bright that they might have been laid on only a moment before by some titanic artist's brush. The shades most used were beryl and white, but though I stopped several times and strove to understand what might be depicted there (whether it was writing, or a face, or perhaps a mere decorative design of lines and angles, or a pattern of intertwined verdure) I could not; and perhaps it was each of those, or none, depending on the position from which it was seen and the predisposition the viewer brought to it.

Once this enigmatic wall was passed, the way down grew easier. It was never necessary again for me to climb down a sheer drop, and though there were several more flights of steps, they were not so steep or so narrow as before. I reached the bottom before I expected it, and looked up at the path down which I had traveled with as much wonder as if I had never set foot on it—indeed, I could see several points at which it appeared to have been broken by the spalling away of sections of the cliff, so that it seemed impassable.

The house I had beheld so clearly from above was invisible now, hidden among trees; but the smoke of its chimney still showed against the sky. I made my way through a forest less precipitous than the one through which I had followed the brook. The dark trees seemed, if anything, older. The great ferns of the south were absent there, and in fact I never saw them north of the House Absolute, except for those under cultivation in the gardens of Abdiesus; but there were wild violets with glossy leaves and flowers the exact color of poor Thecla's eyes growing between the roots of the trees, and moss like the thickest green velvet, so that the ground seemed carpeted, and the trees themselves all draped in costly fabric.

Some time before I could see the house or any other sign of human presence, I heard the barking of a dog. At the sound, the silence and wonder of the trees fell back, present still but infinitely more distant. I felt that some mysterious life, old and strange, yet kindly too, had come to the very moment of revealing itself to me, then drawn away like some immensely eminent person, a master of the musicians, perhaps, whom I had struggled for years to attract to my door but who in the act of knocking had heard the voice of another guest who was unpleasing to him and had put down his hand and turned away, never to come again.

Yet how comforting it was. For almost two long days I had been utterly alone, first upon the broken fields of stone, then among the icy beauty of the stars, and then in the hushed breath of the ancient trees. Now that harsh, familiar sound made me think once more of human comfort—not only think of it, but imagine it so vividly that I seemed to feel it already. I knew that when I saw the dog himself he would be like Triskele; and so he was, with four legs instead of three, somewhat longer and narrower in the skull, and more brown than lion-colored, but with the same dancing eyes and wagging tail and lolling tongue. He began with a declaration of war, which he rescinded as soon as I spoke to him, and before I had gone twenty strides he was presenting his ears to be scratched. I came into the little clearing where the house stood with the dog romping about me.

The walls were of stone, hardly higher than my head. The thatched roof was as steep as I have ever seen, and dotted with flat stones to hold down the thatch in high winds. It was, in short, the home of one of those pioneering peasants who are the glory and despair of our Commonwealth, who in one year produce a surplus of food to support the population of Nessus, but who must themselves be fed in the next lest they starve.

When there is no paved path before a door, one can judge how often feet go out and in by the degree to which the grass encroaches on the trodden ground. Here there was only a little circle of dust the size of a kerchief before the stone step. When I saw it, I supposed that I might frighten the person who lived in that cabin (for I supposed there could only be one) if I were to appear at the door unannounced, and so since the dog had long ago ceased to bark, I paused at the edge of the clearing and shouted a greeting.

The trees and the sky swallowed it, and left only silence.

I shouted again and advanced toward the door with the dog at my heels, and had almost reached it when a woman appeared there. She had a delicate face that might easily have been beautiful had it not been for her haunted eyes, but she wore a ragged dress that differed from a beggar's only by being clean. After a moment, a round-faced little boy, larger-eyed even than his mother, peeped past her skirt.

I said, "I am sorry if I startled you, but I have been lost in these mountains."

The woman nodded, hesitated, then drew back from the door, and I stepped inside. Her house was even smaller within its thick walls than I had supposed, and it reeked with the smell of some strong vegetable boiling in a kettle suspended on a hook over the fire. The windows were few and small, and because of the depth of the walls seemed rather boxes of shadow than apertures of light. An old man sat upon a panther skin with his back to the fire; his eyes were so lacking in focus and intelligence that at first I thought him blind. There was a table at the center of the room, with five chairs about it, of which three seemed to have been made for adults. I remembered what Dorcas had told me about furniture from the abandoned houses of Nessus being brought north for eclectics who had adopted more cultivated fashions, but all the pieces showed signs of having been made on the spot.

The woman saw the direction of my glance and said, "My husband will be here soon. Before supper."

I told her, "You don't have to worry—I mean you no harm. If you'll let me share your meal and sleep here tonight out of the cold, and give me directions in the morning, I'll be glad to help with whatever work there is to be done."

The woman nodded, and quite unexpectedly the little boy

piped, "Have you seen Severa?" His mother turned on him so quickly that I was reminded of Master Gurloes demonstrating the grips used to control prisoners. I heard the blow, though I hardly saw it, and the little boy shrieked. His mother moved to block the door, and he hid himself behind a chest in the corner farthest from her. I understood then, or thought I understood, that Severa was a girl or woman whom she considered more vulnerable than herself, and whom she had ordered to hide (probably in the loft, under the thatch) before letting me in. But I reasoned that any further protestation of my good intentions would be wasted on the woman, who however ignorant was clearly no fool, and that the best way to gain her confidence was to deserve it. I began by asking her for some water so that I could wash, and said that I would gladly carry it from whatever source they had if she would permit me to heat it at her fire. She gave me a pot, and told me where the spring was.

At one time or another I have been in most of the places that are conventionally considered romantic—atop high towers, deep in the bowels of the world, in palatial buildings, in jungles, and aboard a ship—yet none of these have affected me in the same way as that poor cabin of stones. It seemed to me the archetype of those caves into which, as scholars teach, humanity has crept again at the lowest point of each cycle of civilization. Whenever I have read or heard a description of an idyllic rustic retreat (and it was an idea of which Thecla was very fond) it has dwelt on cleanliness and order. There is a bed of mint beneath the window, wood stacked by the coldest wall, a gleaming flagstone floor, and so on. There was nothing of that here, no ideality; and yet the house was more perfect for all its imperfection, showing that human beings might live and love in such a remote spot without the ability to shape their habitat into a poem.

"Do you always shave with your sword?" the woman asked. It was the first time she had spoken to me unguardedly.

"It is a custom, a tradition. If the sword were not sharp enough for me to shave with, I would be ashamed to bear it. And if it is sharp enough, what need do I have of a razor?"

"Still it must be awkward, holding such a heavy blade up like that, and you must have to take great care not to cut yourself."

"The exercise strengthens my arms. Besides, it's good for me to handle my sword every chance I get, so that it becomes as familiar as my limbs."

"You're a soldier, then. I thought so."

"I am a butcher of men."

She seemed taken aback at that, and said, "I didn't mean to insult you."

"I'm not insulted. Everyone kills certain things—you killed those roots in your kettle when you put them into the boiling water. When I kill a man, I save the lives of all the living things he would have destroyed if he had continued to live himself, including, perhaps, many other men, and women and children. What does your husband do?"

The woman smiled a little at that. It was the first time I had seen her smile, and it made her look much younger. "Everything. A man has to do everything up here."

"You weren't born here then."

"No," she said. "Only Severian . . ." The smile was gone.

"Did you say *Severian?*"

"That's my son's name. You saw him when you came in, and he's spying on us now. He is a thoughtless boy sometimes."

"That is my own name. I am Master Severian."

She called to the boy, "Did you hear that? The goodman's name is the same as yours!" Then to me again, "Do you think it's a good name? Do you like it?"

"I'm afraid I've never thought much about it, but yes, I suppose I do. It seems to suit me." I had finished shaving, and seated myself in one of the chairs to tend the blade.

"I was born in Thrax," the woman said. "Have you ever been there?"

"I just came from there," I told her. If the dimarchi were to question her after I left, her description of my habit would give me away in any case.

"You didn't meet a woman called Herais? She's my mother."

I shook my head.

"Well, it's a big town, I suppose. You weren't there long?"

"No, not long at all. While you have been in these mountains, have you heard of the Pelerines? They're an order of priestesses who wear red."

"I'm afraid not. We don't get much news here."

"I'm trying to locate them, or if I can't, to join the army the Autarch is leading against the Ascians."

"My husband could give you better directions than I can. You shouldn't have come up here so high, though. Becan— that's my husband—says the patrols never bother soldiers moving north, not even when they use the old roads."

While she spoke of soldiers moving north, someone else, much nearer, was moving as well. It was a movement so stealthy as to be scarcely audible above the crackling of the fire and the harsh breathing of the old man, but it was unmistakable nonetheless. Bare feet, unable to endure any longer the utter motionlessness that silence commands, had shifted almost imperceptibly, and the planks beneath them had chirped with the new distribution of weight.

XV

He Is Ahead of You!

THE HUSBAND WHO was supposed to have come before supper did not come, and the four of us—the woman, the old man, the boy, and I—ate the evening meal without him. I had at first thought his wife's prediction a lie intended to deter me from whatever criminality I might otherwise have committed; but as the sullen afternoon wore on in that silence that presages a storm, it became apparent that she had believed what she had said, and was now sincerely worried.

Our supper was as simple, almost, as such a meal can be; but my hunger was so great that it was one of the most gratifying I recall. We had boiled vegetables without salt or butter, coarse bread, and a little meat. No wine, no fruit, nothing fresh and nothing sweet; yet I think I must have eaten more than the other three together.

When our meal was over, the woman (whose name, I had learned, was Casdoe) took a long, iron-shod staff out of a corner and set off to look for her husband, first assuring me that she required no escort and telling the old man, who seemed not to hear her, that she would not go far and would soon return. Seeing him remain as abstracted as ever before his fire, I coaxed the boy to me, and after I had won his confidence by showing him *Terminus Est* and permitting him to hold her hilt and attempt to lift her blade, I asked him whether Severa should not come down and take care of him now that his mother was away.

"She came back last night," he told me.

I thought he was referring to his mother and said, "I'm sure she'll come back tonight too, but don't you think Severa ought to take care of you now, while she's gone?"

As children who are not sufficiently confident of language to argue sometimes do, the boy shrugged and tried to turn away.

I caught him by the shoulders. "I want you to go upstairs now, little Severian, and tell her to come down. I promise I won't hurt her."

He nodded and went to the ladder, though slowly and reluctantly. "Bad woman," he said.

Then, for the first time since I had been in the house, the old man spoke. "Becan, come over here! I want to tell you about Fechin." It was a moment before I understood that he was addressing me under the impression that I was his son-in-law.

"He was the worst of us all, that Fechin. A tall, wild boy with red hair on his hands, on his arms. Like a monkey's arms, so that if you saw them reaching around the corner to take something, you'd think, except for the size, that it was a monkey taking it. He took our copper pan once, the one Mother used to make sausage in, and I saw his arm and didn't tell who had done it, because he was my friend. I never found it again, never saw it again, though I was with him a thousand times. I used to think he had made a boat of it and sailed it on the river, because that was what I had always wanted to do with it myself. I walked down the river trying to find it, and the night came before I ever knew it, before I had even turned around to go home. Maybe he polished the bottom to look in—sometimes he drew his own likeness. Maybe he filled it with water to see his reflection."

I had gone across the room to listen to him, partly because he spoke indistinctly and partly out of respect, for his aged face reminded me a little of Master Palaemon's, though he had his natural eyes. "I once met a man of your age who had posed for Fechin," I said.

The old man looked up at me; as quickly as the shadow of a bird might cross some gray rag thrown out of the house upon the grass, I saw the realization that I was not Becan come and go. He did not stop speaking, however, or in any other way acknowledge the fact. It was as if what he was saying were so urgent that it had to be told to someone, poured into any ears before it was lost forever.

"His face wasn't a monkey's face at all. Fechin was handsome—the handsomest around. He could always get food or money from a woman. He could get anything from women. I remember once when we were walking down the trail that led to where the old mill stood then. I had a piece of paper the schoolmaster had given me. Real paper, not quite white, but with a touch of brown to it, and little speckles here and there, so it looked like a trout in milk. The schoolmaster gave it to me so I could write a letter for Mother—at the school we always wrote on boards, then washed them clean with a sponge when we had to write again, and when nobody was looking we'd hit the sponge with the board and send it flying against the wall, or somebody's head. But Fechin loved to draw, and while we walked I thought about that, and how his face would look if he had paper to make a picture he could keep.

"They were the only things he kept. Everything else he lost, or gave away, or threw away, and I knew what Mother wanted to tell pretty much, and I decided if I wrote small I could get it on half the paper. Fechin didn't know I had it, but I took it out and showed it to him, then folded it and tore it in two."

Over our heads, I could hear the fluting voice of the little boy, though I could not understand what he was saying.

"That was the brightest day I've ever seen. The sun had new life to him, the way a man will when he was sick yesterday and will be sick tomorrow, but today he walks around and laughs so that if a stranger was to come he'd think there was nothing wrong, no sickness at all, that the medicines and the bed were for somebody else. They always say in prayers that the New Sun will be too bright to look at, and I always up until that day had taken it to be just the proper way of talking, the way you say a baby's beautiful, or praise whatever a good man has made for himself, that even if there were two suns in the sky you could look at both. But that day I learned it was all true, and the light of it on Fechin's face was more than I could stand. It made my eyes water. He said thank you, and we went farther along and came to a house where a girl lived. I can't remember what her name was, but she was truly beautiful, the way the quietest are sometimes. I never knew up till then that Fechin knew her, but he asked me to wait, and I sat down on the first step in front of the gate."

Someone heavier than the boy was walking overhead, toward the ladder.

"He wasn't inside long, but when he came out, with the girl looking out the window, I knew what they had done. I looked at him, and he spread those long, thin, monkey arms. How could he share what he'd had? In the end, he made the girl give me half a loaf of bread and some fruit. He drew my picture on one side of the paper and the girl's on the other, but he kept the pictures."

The ladder creaked, and I turned to look. As I had expected, a woman was descending it. She was not tall, but fullfigured and narrow-waisted; her gown was nearly as ragged as the boy's mother's, and much dirtier. Rich brown hair spilled down her back. I think I recognized her even before she turned and I saw the high cheekbones and her long, brown eyes—it was Agia. "So you knew I was here all along," she said.

"I might make the same remark to you. You seem to have been here before me."

"I only guessed that you would be coming this way. As it happened, I arrived a little before you, and I told the mistress of this house what you would do to me if she did not hide me," she said. (I supposed she wished me to know she had an ally here, if only a feeble one.)

"You've been trying to kill me ever since I glimpsed you in the crowd at Saltus."

"Is that an accusation? Yes."

"You're lying."

It was one of the few times I have ever seen Agia caught off balance. "What do you mean?"

"Only that you were trying to kill me before Saltus."

"With the avern. Yes, of course."

"And afterward. Agia, I know who Hethor is."

I waited for her to reply, but she said nothing.

"On the day we met, you told me there was an old sailor who wanted you to live with him. Old and ugly and poor, you called him, and I could not understand why you, a lovely young woman, should even consider his offer when you were not actually starving. You had your twin to protect you, and a little money coming in from the shop."

It was my turn to be surprised. She said, "I should have gone to him and mastered him. I have mastered him now."

"I thought you had only promised yourself to him, if he would kill me."

"I have promised him that and many other things, and so mastered him. He is ahead of you, Severian, waiting word from me."

"With more of his beasts? Thank you for the warning. That was it, wasn't it? He had threatened you and Agilus with the pets he had brought from other spheres."

She nodded. "He came to sell his clothes, and they were

the kind worn on the old ships that sailed beyond the world's rim long ago, and they weren't costumes or forgeries or even tomb-tender old garments that had lain for centuries in the dark, but clothes not far from new. He said his ships—all those ships—became lost in the blackness between the suns, where the years do not turn. Lost so that even Time cannot find them."

"I know," I said. "Jonas told me."

"After I learned that you would kill Agilus, I went to him. He is iron-strong in some ways, weak in many others. If I had withheld my body I could have done nothing with him, but I did all the queer things he wished me to, and made him believe I love him. Now he will do anything I ask. He followed you for me after you killed Agilus; with his silver I hired the men you killed at the old mine, and the creatures he commands will kill you for me yet, if I don't do it here myself."

"You meant to wait until I slept, and then come down and murder me, I suppose."

"I would have waked you first, when I had my knife at your throat. But the child told me you knew I was here, and I thought this might be more pleasant. Tell me though—how did you guess about Hethor?"

A breath of wind stirred through the narrow windows. It made the fire smoke, and I heard the old man, who sat there in silence once more, cough, and spit onto the coals. The little boy, who had climbed down from the loft while Agia and I talked, watched us with large, uncomprehending eyes.

"I should have known it long before," I said. "My friend Jonas had been just such a sailor. You will remember him, I think—you glimpsed him at the mine mouth, and you must have known of him."

"We did."

"Perhaps they were from the same ship. Or perhaps it was only that each would have known the other by some sign, or that Hethor at least feared they would. However that may be, he seldom came near me when I was traveling with Jonas, though he had been so eager to be in my company before. I saw him in the crowd when I executed a woman and a man at Saltus, but he did not try to join me there. On the way to the House Absolute, Jonas and I saw him behind us, but he did not come running up until Jonas had ridden off, though he must have been desperate to get back his notule. When he was thrown into the antechamber of the House Absolute, he made no attempt to sit with us, even though Jonas was nearly dead; but something that left a trail of slime was searching the place when we left it."

Agia said nothing, and in her silence she might have been the young woman I had seen on the morning of the day after I left our tower unfastening the gratings that had guarded the windows of a dusty shop.

"You two must have lost my trail on the way to Thrax," I continued, "or been delayed by some accident. Even after you discovered we were in the city, you must not have known that I had charge of the Vincula, because Hethor sent his creature of fire prowling the streets to find me. Then, somehow, you found Dorcas at the Duck's Nest—"

"We were lodging there ourselves," Agia said. "We had only arrived a few days before, and we were out looking for you when you came. Afterward when I realized that the woman in the little garret room was the mad girl you had found in the Botanic Gardens, we still didn't guess it was you who had put her there, because that hag at the inn said the man had worn common clothes. But we thought she might know where you were, and that she would be more apt to talk to Hethor. His name isn't really Hethor, by the way. He says it's a much older one, that hardly anyone has heard of now."

"He told Dorcas about the fire creature," I said, "and she told me. I had heard of the thing before, but Hethor had a name for it—he called it a salamander. I didn't think anything of it when Dorcas mentioned it, but later I remembered that

Jonas had a name for the black thing that flew after us outside the House Absolute. He called it a notule, and said the people on the ships had named them that because they betrayed themselves with a gust of warmth. If Hethor had a name for the fire creature, it seemed likely that it was a sailor's name too, and that he had something to do with the creature itself."

Agia smiled thinly. "So now you know all, and you have me where you want me—provided you can swing that big blade of yours in here."

"I have you without it. I had you beneath my foot at the mine mouth, for that matter."

"But I still have my knife."

At that moment the boy's mother came through the doorway, and both of us paused. She looked in astonishment from Agia to me; then, as though no surprise could pierce her sorrow or alter what she had to do, she closed the door and lifted the heavy bar into place.

Agia said, "He heard me upstairs, Casdoe, and made me come down. He intends to kill me."

"And how am I to prevent that?" the woman answered wearily. She turned to me. "I hid her because she said you meant her harm. Will you kill me too?"

"No. Nor will I kill her, as she knows."

Agia's face distorted with rage, as the face of another lovely woman, molded by Fechin himself perhaps in colored wax, might have been transformed with a gout of flame, so that it simultaneously melted and burned. "You killed Agilus, and you gloried in it! Aren't I as fit to die as he was? We were the same flesh!" I had not fully believed her when she said she was armed with a knife, but without my having seen her draw it, it was out now—one of the crooked daggers of Thrax.

For some time the air had been heavy with an impending storm. Now the thunder rolled, booming among the peaks above us. When its echoings and reechoings had almost died away, something answered them. I cannot describe that voice; it was not quite a human shout, nor was it the mere bellow of a beast.

All her weariness left the woman Casdoe, replaced by the most desperate haste. Heavy wooden shutters stood against the wall beneath each of the narrow windows; she seized the nearest, and lifting it as if it weighed no more than a pie pan sent it crashing into place. Outside, the dog barked frantically then fell silent, leaving no sound but the pattering of the first rain.

"So soon," Casdoe cried. "So soon!" To her son: "Severian, get out of the way."

Through one of the still open windows, I heard a child's voice call, *"Father, can't you help me?"*

XVI

The Alzabo

I TRIED TO assist Casdoe, and in the process turned my back on Agia and her dagger. It was an error that almost cost me my life, for she was upon me as soon as I was encumbered with a shutter. Women and tailors hold the blade beneath the hand, according to the proverb, but Agia stabbed up to open the tripes and catch the heart from below, like an accomplished assassin. I turned only just in time to block her blade with the shutter, and the point drove through the wood to show a glint of steel.

The very strength of her blow betrayed her. I wrenched the shutter to one side and threw it across the room, and her knife with it. She and Casdoe both leaped for it. I caught Agia by an arm and jerked her back, and Casdoe slammed the shutter into place with the knife out, toward the gathering storm.

"You fool," Agia said. "Don't you realize you're giving a weapon to whomever it is you're afraid of?" Her voice was calm with defeat.

"It has no need of knives," Casdoe told her.

The house was dark now except for the ruddy light of the fire. I looked around for candles or lanterns, but there were none in sight; later I learned that the few the family owned had been carried to the loft. Lightning flashed outside, outlining the edges of the shutters and making a broken line of stark light at the bottom of the door—it was a moment before I realized that it had been a broken line, when it should have been a continuous one. "There's someone outside," I said. "Standing on the step."

Casdoe nodded. "I closed the window just in time. It has never come so early before. It may be that the storm wakened it."

"You don't think it might be your husband?"

Before she could answer me, a voice higher than the little boy's called, "*Let me in, Mother.*"

Even I, who did not know what it was that spoke, sensed a fearful wrongness in the simple words. It was a child's voice, perhaps, but not a human child's.

"*Mother,*" the voice called again. "*It is beginning to rain.*"

"We had better go up," Casdoe said. "If we pull the ladder after us, it cannot reach us even if it should get inside."

I had gone to the door. Without lightning, the feet of whatever it was that stood on the doorstep were invisible; but I could hear a hoarse, slow breathing above the beating of the rain, and once a scraping sound, as though the thing that waited there in the dark had shifted its footing.

"Is this your doing?" I asked Agia. "Some creature of Hethor's?"

She shook her head; the narrow, brown eyes were dancing. "They roam wild in these mountains, as you should know much better than I."

"*Mother?*"

There was a shuffle of feet—with that fretful question, the thing outside had turned from the door. One of the shutters was cracked, and I tried to look through the slit; I could see nothing in the blackness outside, but I heard a soft, heavy tread, precisely the sound that sometimes came through the barred ports of the Tower of the Bear at home.

"It took Severa three days ago," Casdoe said. She was trying to get the old man to rise; he did so slowly, reluctant to leave the warmth of the fire. "I never let her or Severian go among the trees, but it came into the clearing here, a watch before twilight. Since then it has returned every night. The dog wouldn't track it, but Becan went to hunt it today."

I had guessed the beast's identity by that time, though I had never beheld one of its kind. I said, "It is an alzabo, then? The creature from whose glands the analept is made?"

"It is an alzabo, yes," Casdoe answered. "I know nothing of any analept."

Agia laughed. "But Severian does. He has tasted the creature's wisdom, and carries his beloved about within himself. I understand one hears them whispering together by night, in the very heat and sweat of love."

I struck at her; but she dodged nimbly, then put the table between herself and me. "Aren't you delighted, Severian, that when the animals came to Urth to replace all those our ancestors slew, the alzabo was among them? Without the alzabo, you would have lost your dearest Thecla forever. Tell Casdoe here how happy the alzabo has made you."

To Casdoe I said, "I am truly sorry to hear of your daughter's death. I will defend this house from the animal outside, if it must be done."

My sword was standing against the wall, and to show that my will was as good as my words, I reached for it. It was fortunate I did so, for just at that instant a man's voice at the door called, "*Open, darling!*"

Agia and I sprang to stop Casdoe, but neither of us was swift enough. Before we could reach her, she had lifted the bar. The door swung back.

The beast that waited there stood upon four legs; even so, its hulking shoulders were as high as my head. Its own head was carried low, with the tips of its ears below the crest of fur that topped its back. In the firelight, its teeth gleamed white and its eyes glowed red. I have seen the eyes of many of these creatures that are supposed to have come from beyond the margin of the world—drawn, as certain philonoists allege, by the death of those whose genesis was here, even as tribes of enchors come slouching with their stone knives and fires into a countryside depopulated by war or disease; but their eyes are the eyes of beasts only. The red orbs of the alzabo were something more, holding neither the intelligence of humankind nor the innocence of the brutes. So a fiend might look, I thought, when it had at last struggled up from the pit of some dark star; then I recalled the man-apes, who were indeed called fiends, yet had the eyes of men.

For a moment it seemed the door might be shut again. I saw Casdoe, who had recoiled in horror, try to swing it to. The alzabo appeared to advance slowly and even lazily, yet it was too swift for her, and the edge of the door struck its ribs as it might have struck a stone.

"Let it stay open," I called. "We'll need whatever light there is." I had unsheathed *Terminus Est*, so that her blade caught the firelight and seemed itself a bitter fire. An arbalest like the ones Agia's henchmen had carried, whose quarrels are ignited by the friction of the atmosphere and burst when they strike like stones cast into a furnace, would have been a better weapon; but it would not have seemed an extension of my arm as *Terminus Est* did, and perhaps after all an arbalest would have permitted the alzabo to spring on me while I sought to recock it, if the first quarrel missed.

The long blade of my sword did not wholly obviate that danger. Her square, unpointed tip could not impale the beast, should it spring. I would have to slash at it in air, and though I had no doubt that I could strike the head from that thick neck while it flew toward me, I knew that to miss would be death. Furthermore, I needed space enough to make the stroke, for which that narrow room was scarcely adequate; and though the fire was dying, I needed light.

The old man, the boy Severian, and Casdoe were all gone—

I was not certain if they had climbed the ladder to the loft while my attention had been fixed on the eyes of the beast, or if some of them, at least, had not fled through the doorway behind it. Only Agia remained, pressed into a corner with Casdoe's iron-tipped climbing stick to use as a weapon, as a sailor might, in desperation, try to fend off a galleass with a boat hook. I knew that to speak to her would be to call attention to her; yet it might be that if the beast so much as turned its head toward her, I would be able to sever its spine.

I said, "Agia, I must have light. It will kill me in the dark. You once told your men you would front me, if only they would kill me from behind. I will front this for you now, if you will only bring a candle."

She nodded to show she understood, and as she did the beast moved toward me. It did not spring as I had expected, however, but sidled lazily yet adroitly to the right, coming nearer while contriving to keep just beyond blade reach. After a moment of incomprehension I realized that by its position near the wall it cramped further any attack I might make, and that if it could circle me (as it nearly did) to gain a position between the fire and my own, much of the benefit I had from the firelight would be lost.

So we began a careful game, in which the alzabo sought to make what use it could of the chairs, the table, and the walls, and I tried to get as much space as I could for my sword.

Then I leaped forward. The alzabo avoided my cut, as it seemed to me, by no more than the width of a finger, lunged at me, and drew back just in time to escape my return stroke. Its jaws, large enough to bite a man's head as a man bites an apple, had snapped before my face, drenching me in the reek of its putrid breath.

The thunder boomed again, so near that after its roar I could hear the crashing fall of the great tree whose death it had proclaimed; the lightning flash, illuminating every detail in its paralyzing glare, left me dazzled and blinded. I swung

Terminus Est in the rush of darkness that followed, felt her bite bone, sprang to one side, and as the thunder rumbled out slashed again, this time only sending some stick of furniture flying into ruin.

Then I could see once more. While the alzabo and I had shifted ground and feinted, Agia had been moving too, and she must have made a dash for the ladder when the lightning struck. She was halfway up, and I saw Casdoe reach down to help her. The alzabo stood before me, as whole, so it seemed, as ever; but dark blood dribbled into a pool at its forefeet. Its fur looked red and ragged in the firelight, and the nails of its feet, larger and coarser than a bear's, were darkly red as well, and seemed translucent. More hideous than the speaking of a corpse could ever be, I heard the voice that had called, *"Open darling,"* at the door. It said: *"Yes, I am injured. But the pain is nothing much, and I can stand and move as before. You cannot bar me from my family forever."* From the mouth of a beast, it was the voice of a stern, stamping honest man.

I took out the Claw and laid it on the table, but it was no more than a spark of blue. "Light!" I shouted to Agia. No light came, and I heard the rattle of the ladder on the loft's floor as the women drew it up.

"Your escape is cut off, you see," the beast said, still in the man's voice.

"So is your advance. Can you jump so high, with a wounded leg?"

Abruptly the voice became the plaintive treble of the little girl. *"I can climb. Do you think I won't think to move the table over there under the hole? I, who can talk?"*

"You know yourself a beast, then."

The man's voice came again. *"We know we are within the beast, just as once we were within the cases of flesh the beast has devoured."*

"And you would consent to its devouring your wife and your son, Becan?"

"*I would direct it. I do direct it. I want Casdoe and Severian to join us here, just as I joined Severa today. When the fire dies, you die too—joining us—and so shall they.*"

I laughed. "Have you forgotten that you got your wound when I couldn't see?" Holding *Terminus Est* at the ready, I crossed the room to the ruin of the chair, snatched up what had been its back, and threw it into the fire, making a cloud of sparks. "That was well-seasoned wood, I think, and it has been rubbed with bees' wax by some careful hand. It should burn brightly."

"*Just the same, the dark will come.*" The beast—Becan—sounded infinitely patient. "*The dark will come, and you will join us.*"

"No. When all the chair has burned and the light is failing, I will advance on you and kill you. I only wait now to let you bleed."

There was silence, the more eerie because nothing in the beast's expression hinted of thought. I knew that even as the wreck of Thecla's neural chemistry had been fixed in the nuclei of certain of my own frontal cells by a secretion distilled from the organs of just such a creature, so the man and his daughter haunted the dim thicket of the beast's brain and believed they lived; but what that ghost of life might be, what dreams and desires might enter it, I could not guess.

At last the man's voice said, "*In a watch or two, then, I will kill you or you will kill me. Or we will destroy each other. If I turn now and go out into the night and the rain, will you hunt me down when Urth turns toward the light once more? Or remain here to keep me from the woman and child that are mine?*"

"No," I said.

"*On such honor as you have? Will you swear on that sword, though you cannot point it to the sun?*"

I took a step backward and reversed *Terminus Est*, holding her by the blade in such a way that her tip was directed toward my own heart. "I swear by this sword, the badge of my Art, that if you do not return this night I will not hunt you tomorrow. Nor will I remain in this house."

As swiftly as a gliding snake it turned. For an instant I might, perhaps, have cut at its thick back. Then it was gone, and no trace of its presence remained save for the open door, the shattered chair, and the pool of blood (darker, I think, than the blood of the animals of this world) that soaked into the scrubbed planks of the floor.

I went to the door and barred it, returned the Claw to the little sack suspended from my neck, and then, as the beast had suggested, shifted the table until I could climb upon it and easily pull myself into the loft. Casdoe and the old man waited at the farther end with the boy called Severian, in whose eyes I saw the memories this night might hold for him twenty years hence. They were bathed in the vacillating radiance of a lamp suspended from one of the rafters.

"I have survived," I told them, "as you see. Could you hear what we said below?"

Casdoe nodded without speaking.

"If you had brought me the light I asked for, I would not have done what I did. As it was, I felt I owed you nothing. If I were you, I would leave this house as soon as it is day, and go to the lowlands. But that is up to you."

"We were afraid," Casdoe muttered.

"So was I. Where is Agia?"

To my surprise, the old man pointed, and looking at the place he indicated, I saw that the thick thatch had been parted to make an opening large enough for Agia's slender body.

That night I slept before the fire, after warning Casdoe that I would kill anyone who came down from the loft. In the morning, I walked around the house; as I had expected, Agia's knife had been pulled from the shutter.

XVII

The Sword of the Lictor

"WE ARE LEAVING," Casdoe told me. "But I will make breakfast for us before we go. You will not have to eat it with us if you do not wish to do so."

I nodded and waited outside until she brought out a wooden bowl of plain porridge and a wooden spoon; then I took them to the spring and ate. It was screened by rushes, and I did not come out; it was, I supppose, a violation of the oath I had given the alzabo, but I waited there, watching the house.

After a time Casdoe, her father, and little Severian emerged. She carried a pack and her husband's staff, and the old man and the boy had each their little sack. The dog, which must have crawled beneath the floor when the alzabo came (I cannot say I blame him, but Triskele would not have done that) was frisking about their heels. I saw Casdoe look around for me. When she failed to find me, she put down a bundle on the doorstep.

I watched them walk along the edge of their little field, which had been plowed and sown only a month or so before, and now would be reaped by birds. Neither Casdoe nor her father glanced behind them; but the boy, Severian, stopped and turned before going over the first ridge, to see once more the only home he had ever known. Its stone walls stood as stoutly as ever, and the smoke of the breakfast fire still curled from its chimney. His mother must have called to him then, because he hurried after her and so disappeared from view.

I left the shelter of the rushes and went to the door. The bundle on the step held two blankets of soft guanaco and dried meat wrapped in a clean rug. I put the meat into my sabretache and refolded the blankets so I could wear them across my shoulder.

The rain had left the air fresh and clean, and it was good to know that I would soon leave the stone cabin and its smells of smoke and food behind me. I looked around inside, seeing the black stain of the alzabo's blood and the broken chair. Casdoe had moved the table back to its old place, and the Claw, that had gleamed so feebly there, had left no mark upon its surface. There was nothing left that seemed worth the carrying; I went out and shut the door.

Then I set off after Casdoe and her party. I did not forgive her for having failed to give me light when I fought the al-zabo—she might easily have done so by lowering her lamp from the loft. Yet I could not greatly blame her for having sided with Agia, a woman alone among the staring faces and icy crowns of the mountains; and the child and the old man, neither of whom could be said to have much guilt in the matter, were at least as vulnerable as she.

The path was soft, so much so that I could track them in the most literal sense, seeing Casdoe's small footprints, the boy's even smaller ones beside them taking two strides to her one, and the old man's, with the toes turned out. I walked slowly in order not to overtake them, and though I knew my own danger increased with each step I took, I dared to hope that the archon's patrols, in questioning them, would warn me. Casdoe could not betray me, since whatever honest infor- mation she might tender the dimarchi would lead them astray; and if the alzabo were about, I hoped to hear or smell it before it attacked—I had not sworn, after all, to leave its prey undefended, but only not to hunt it, or to remain in the house.

The path must have been no more than a game trail enlarged by Becan; it soon vanished. The scenery here was less stark than it had been above the timberline. South-facing slopes were often covered with small ferns and mosses, and conifers grew from the cliffs. Falling water was seldom out of earshot. In me Thecla recalled coming to a place much like this to paint, accompanied by her teacher and two gruff bodyguards. I began to feel that I would soon come across the easel, palette, and untidy brush case, abandoned beside some cascade when the sun no longer lingered in the spray.

Of course I did not, and for several watches there was no sign of humanity at all. Mingled with the footprints of Casdoe's party were the tracks of deer, and twice the pug marks of one of the tawny cats that prey on them. These had been made, surely, just at dawn, when the rain had stopped.

Then I saw a line of impressions left by a naked foot larger than the old man's. Each was as large, in fact, as my own booted print, and its maker's stride had been, if anything, longer. The tracks crossed at right angles to those I followed, but one imprint fell over one of the boy's, showing that their maker had passed between us.

I hurried forward.

I assumed that the footprints were those of an autochthon, though even then I wondered at his long stride—those savages of the mountains are normally rather small. If it was indeed an autochthon, he was unlikely to do Casdoe and the others any real harm, though he might pillage the goods she carried. From all I had heard of them, the autochthons were clever hunters, but not warlike.

The impressions of bare feet resumed. Two or three more individuals, at least, had joined the first.

Deserters from the army would be another matter; about a

quarter of our prisoners in the Vincula had been such men and their women, and many of them had committed the most atrocious crimes. Deserters would be well armed, but I would have expected them to be well shod too, certainly not bare-foot.

A steep climb rose ahead of me. I could see the gouges made by Casdoe's staff, and the branches broken where she and the old man had used them to pull themselves up—some broken, possibly, by their pursuers as well. I reflected that the old man must be exhausted by now, that it was surprising that his daughter could still urge him on; perhaps he, perhaps all of them, knew by now that they were pursued. As I neared the crest I heard the dog bark, and then (at the same time it seemed almost an echo of the night before) a wild, wordless yell.

Yet it was not the horrible, half-human cry of the alzabo. It was a sound I had heard often before, sometimes, faintly, even while I lay in the cot next to Roche's, and often when I had carried their meals and the clients' to the journeymen on duty in our oubliette. It was precisely the shout of one of the clients on the third level, one of those who could no longer speak coherently and for that reason were never, for practical purposes, brought again to the examination room.

They were zoanthrops, such as I had seen feigned at Ab-diesus's ridotto. When I reached the top I could see them, as well as Casdoe with her father and son. One cannot call them men; but they seemed men at that distance, nine naked men who circled the three, bounding and crouching. I hurried for-ward until I saw one strike with his club, and the old man fall.

Then I hesitated, and it was not Thecla's fear that stopped me but my own.

I had fought the man-apes of the mine bravely, perhaps, but I had to fight them. I had stood against the alzabo to stalemate, but there had been nowhere to run but the dark-ness outside, where it would surely have killed me.

Now there was a choice, and I hung back.

Living where she had, Casdoe must have known of them, though possibly she had never encountered them before. While the boy clung to her skirt she slashed with the staff as though it were a sabre. Her voice carried to me over the yells of the zoanthrops, shrill, unintelligible, and seemingly remote. I felt the horror one always feels when a woman is attacked, but beside it or perhaps beneath it lay the thought that she who would not fight beside me must now fight alone.

It could not last, of course. Such creatures are either frightened away at once or not frightened away at all. I saw one snatch the staff from her hand, and I drew *Terminus Est* and began to run down the long slope toward her. The naked figure had thrown her to the ground and was (as I supposed) preparing to rape her.

Then something huge plunged out of the trees to my left. It was so large and moved so swiftly that I at first thought it a red destrier, riderless and saddleless. Only when I saw the flash of its teeth and heard the scream of a zoanthrop did I realize it was the alzabo.

The others were upon it at once. Rising and falling, the heads of their ironwood bludgeons seemed for a moment grotesquely like the heads of feeding hens when corn has been scattered on the ground for them. Then a zoanthrop was thrown into the air, and he, who had been naked before, now appeared to be wrapped in a cloak of scarlet.

By the time I joined the fight, the alzabo was down, and for a moment I could give no attention to it. *Terminus Est* sang in orbit about my head. One naked figure fell, then another. A stone the size of a fist whizzed past my ear, so close that I could hear the sound; if it had struck, I would have died a moment afterward.

But these were not the man-apes of the mine, so numerous they could not, in the end, be overcome. I cut one from shoulder to waist, feeling each rib part in turn and rattle across my blade, slashed at another, split a skull.

Then there was only silence and the whimpering of the

boy. Seven zoanthrops lay upon the mountain grass, four killed by *Terminus Est,* I think, and three by the alzabo. Casdoe's body was in its jaws, her head and shoulders already devoured. The old man who had known Fechin lay crumpled like a doll; that famous artist would have made something wonderful of his death, showing it from a perspective no one else could have found, and embodying the dignity and futility of all human life in the misshapen head. But Fechin was not here. The dog lay beside the old man, its jaws bloodied.

I looked about for the boy. To my horror, he was huddled against the alzabo's back. No doubt the thing had called to him in his father's voice, and he had come. Now its hindquarters trembled spasmodically and its eyes were closed. As I took him by the arm, its tongue, wider and thicker than a bull's, emerged as though to lick his hand; then its shoulders shuddered so violently that I started back. The tongue was never wholly returned to its mouth, but lay flaccid on the grass.

I drew the boy away and said, "It is over now, little Severian. Are you all right?"

He nodded and began to cry, and for a long time I held him and walked up and down.

For a moment I considered using the Claw, though it had failed me in Casdoe's house as it had failed me at times before. Yet if it had succeeded, who could say what the result might have been? I had no wish to give the zoanthrops or the alzabo new life, and what life might be granted Casdoe's headless corpse? As for the old man, he had been sitting at the doors of death already; now he had died, and swiftly. Would he have thanked me for summoning him back, to die again in a year or two? The gem flashed in the sunlight, but its flashing was mere sunshine and not the light of the Conciliator, the gegenschein of the New Sun, and I put it away again. The boy watched me with wide eyes.

Terminus Est had been bloodied to her guard and beyond. I sat upon a fallen tree and cleaned her with the rotting wood while I debated what to do, then whetted and oiled her blade. I cared nothing for the zoanthrops or the alzabo, but to leave Casdoe's body, and the old man's, to be dismembered by beasts seemed a vile thing.

Prudence warned against it as well. What if another alzabo should come, and when it had glutted itself upon Casdoe's flesh set off after the boy? I considered carrying them both back to the cabin. It was a considerable distance, however; I could not carry the two together, and it seemed sure that whichever I left behind would be violated by the time I returned for it. Drawn by the sight of so much blood, the carrion-eating teratornises were already circling overhead, each borne on wings as wide as the main yard of a caravel.

For a time I probed the ground, seeking some place soft enough that I might dig it with Casdoe's staff; in the end, I carried both bodies to a stretch of rocky ground near a watercourse, and there built a cairn over them. Under it they would lie, I hoped, for nearly a year, until the melting of the snows, at about the time of the feast of Holy Katharine, should sweep the bones of daughter and father away.

Little Severian, who had only watched at first, had himself carried small stones before the cairn was complete. When we were washing ourselves of grit and sweat in the stream, he asked, "Are you my uncle?"

I told him, "I'm your father—for now, at least. When someone's father dies, he must have a new one, if he's as young as you are. I'm the man."

He nodded, lost in thought; and quite suddenly I recalled how I had dreamed, only two nights before, of a world in which all the people knew themselves bound by ties of blood, being all descended from the same pair of colonists. I, who did not know my own mother's name, or my father's, might very well be related to this child whose name was my own, or for that matter to anyone I met. The world of which I had dreamed had been, for me, the bed on which I had lain. I wish I could describe how serious we were there by the laughing stream, how solemn and clean he looked with his wet face and the droplets sparkling in the lashes of his wide eyes.

XVIII

Severian and Severian

I DRANK AS much water as I could, and told the boy that he must do so as well, that there were many dry places in the mountains, and that we might not drink again until next morning. He had asked if we would not go home now; and though I had planned until then to retrace our route back to the house that had been Casdoe's and Becan's, I said we would not, because I knew it would be too terrible for him to see that roof again, and the field and the little garden, and then to leave them for a second time. At his age he might even suppose that his father and his mother, his sister and his grandfather were somehow still inside.

Yet we could not descend much farther—we were already well below the level at which travel was dangerous for me. The arm of the archon of Thrax stretched a hundred leagues and more, and now there was every chance that Agia would put his dimarchi on my trail.

To the northeast stood the highest peak I had yet seen. Not only its head but its shoulders too bore a shroud of snow, which descended nearly to its waist. I could not say, and perhaps no one now could, what proud face it was that stared westward over so many lesser summits; but surely he had ruled in the earliest of the greatest days of humanity, and had commanded energies that could shape granite as a carver's knife does wood. Looking at his image, it seemed to me that even the hard-bitten dimarchi, who knew the wild uplands so well, might stand in awe of him. And so we made for him, or rather for the high pass that linked the folded drapery of his robe to the mountain where Becan had once established a home. For the time being, the climbs were not severe, and we spent far more effort in walking than in climbing.

The boy Severian held my hand often when there was no need of my support. I am no great judge of the ages of children, but he seemed to me to be about of that growth when, if he had been one of our apprentices, he would first have entered Master Palaemon's schoolroom—that is to say, he was old enough to walk well, and to talk sufficiently to understand and to make himself understood.

For a watch or more he said nothing beyond what I have already related. Then, as we were descending an open, grassy slope bordered by pines, a place much like that in which his mother had died, he asked, "Severian, who were those men?"

I knew whom he meant. "They were not men, although they were once men and still resemble men. They were zoanthrops, a word that indicates those beasts that are of human shape. Do you understand what I am saying?"

The little boy nodded solemnly, then asked, "Why don't they wear clothes?"

"Because they are no longer human beings, as I told you. A dog is born a dog and a bird is born a bird, but to become a human being is an achievement—you have to think about it. You have been thinking about it for the past three or four years at least, little Severian, even though you may never have thought about the thinking."

"A dog just looks for things to eat," the boy said.

"Exactly. But that raises the question of whether a person

should be forced to do such thinking, and some people decided a long time ago that he should not. We may force a dog, sometimes, to act like a man—to walk on his hind legs and wear a collar and so forth. But we shouldn't and couldn't force a man to act like a man. Did you ever want to fall asleep? When you weren't sleepy or even tired?"

He nodded.

"That was because you wanted to put down the burden of being a boy, at least for a time. Sometimes I drink too much wine, and that is because for a while I would like to stop being a man. Sometimes people take their own lives for that reason. Did you know that?"

"Or they do things that might hurt them," he said. The way he said it told me of arguments overheard; Becan had very probably been that kind of man, or he would not have taken his family to so remote and dangerous a place.

"Yes," I told him. "That can be the same thing. And sometimes certain men, and even women, come to hate the burden of thought, but without loving death. They see the animals and wish to become as they are, answering only to instinct, and not thinking. Do you know what makes you think, little Severian?"

"My head," the boy said promptly, and grasped it with his hands.

"Animals have heads too—even very stupid animals like crayfish and oxen and ticks. What makes you think is only a small part of your head, inside, just above your eyes." I touched his forehead. "Now if for some reason you wanted one of your hands taken off, there are men you can go to who are skilled in doing that. Suppose, for example, your hand had suffered some hurt from which it would never be well. They could take it away in such a fashion that there would be little chance of any harm coming to the rest of you."

The boy nodded.

"Very well. Those same men can take away that little part

of your head that makes you think. They cannot put it back, you understand. And even if they could, you couldn't ask them to do it, once that part was gone. But sometimes people pay these men to take that part away. They want to stop thinking forever, and often they say they wish to turn their backs on all that humanity has done. Then it is no longer just to treat them as human beings—they have become animals, though animals who are still of human shape. You asked why they did not wear clothes. They no longer understand clothes, and so they would not put them on, even if they were very cold, although they might lie down on them or even roll themselves up in them."

"Are you like that, a little bit?" the boy asked, and pointed to my bare chest.

The thought he was suggesting had never occurred to me before, and for a moment I was taken aback. "It's the rule of my guild," I said. "I haven't had any part of my head taken away, if that's what you're asking, and I used to wear a shirt . . . But, yes, I suppose I am a little like that, because I never thought of it, even when I was very cold."

His expression told me I had confirmed his suspicions. "Is that why you're running away?"

"No, that's not why I'm running away. If anything, I suppose you could say it is the other side of it. Perhaps that part of my head has grown too large. But you're right about the zoanthrops, that is why they are in the mountains. When a man becomes an animal, he becomes a dangerous animal, and animals like that cannot be tolerated in more settled places, where there are farms and many people. So they are driven to these mountains, or brought here by their old friends, or by someone they paid to do it before they discarded the power of human thought. They can still think a little, of course, as all animals can. Enough to find food in the wild, though many die each winter. Enough to throw stones as monkeys throw nuts, and use their clubs, and even to hunt for mates, for there are females among them as I said. Their sons and daughters seldom live long, however, and I suppose that is for the best, because they are born just as you were—and I was— with the burden of thought."

That burden lay heavily on me when we had finished speaking; so heavily indeed that for the first time I truly understood that it could be as great a curse to others as memory has sometimes been to me.

I have never been greatly sensitive to beauty, but the beauty of the sky and the mountainside were such that it seemed they colored all my musings, so that I felt I nearly grasped ungraspable things. When Master Malrubius had appeared to me after our first performance of Dr. Talos's play— something I could not then understand and still could not understand, though I grew more confident that it had occurred, and not less—he had spoken to me of the circularity of governance, though I had no concern with governance. Now it struck me that the will itself was governed, and if not by reason, then by things below or above it. Yet it was very difficult to say on what side of reason these things lay. Instinct, surely, lay below it; but might it not be above it as well? When the alzabo rushed at the zoanthrops, its instinct commanded it to preserve its prey from others; when Becan did so, his instinct, I believe, was to preserve his wife and child. Both performed the same act, and they actually performed it in the same body. Did the higher and the lower instinct join hands at the back of reason? Or is there but one instinct standing behind all reason, so that reason sees a hand to either side?

But is instinct truly that "attachment to the person of the monarch" which Master Malrubius implied was at once the highest and the lowest form of governance? For clearly, instinct itself cannot have arisen out of nothing—the hawks that soared over our heads built their nests, doubtless, by instinct; yet there must have been a time in which nests were not built, and the first hawk to build one cannot have inherited its instinct to build from its parents, since they did not possess it. Nor could such an instinct have developed slowly, a thousand generations of hawks fetching one stick before some hawk fetched two; because neither one stick nor two could be of the slightest use to the nesting hawks. Perhaps that which came before instinct was the highest as well as the lowest principle of the governance of the will. Perhaps not. The wheeling birds traced their hieroglyphics in the air, but they were not for me to read.

As we approached the saddle that joined the mountain to that other even loftier one I have described, we seemed to move across the face of all Urth, tracing a line from pole to equator; indeed the surface over which we crawled like ants might have been the globe itself turned inside out. Far behind us and far ahead of us loomed the broad, gleaming fields of snow. Below them lay stony slopes like the shore of the ice-bound southern sea. Below these were high meadows of coarse grass, now dotted with wildflowers; I remembered well those over which I had passed the day before, and beneath the blue haze that wreathed the mountain ahead I could discern their band upon the chest, like a green fourragere; beneath it the pines shone so darkly as to appear black.

The saddle to which we descended was quite different, an expanse of montane forest where glossy-leaved hardwoods lifted sickly heads three hundred cubits toward the dying sun. Among them their dead brothers remained upright, supported by the living and wrapped in winding sheets of lianas. Near the little stream where we halted for the night the vegetation had already lost most of its mountain delicacy and was acquiring something of the lushness of the lowlands; and now that we were sufficiently near the saddle for him to have a clear view of it, and his attention was no longer monopolized by the need to walk and climb, the boy pointed and asked if we were going down there.

"Tomorrow," I said. "It will be dark soon, and I would like to get through that jungle in a day."

His eyes widened at the word *jungle*. "Is it dangerous?"

"I don't really know. From what I heard in Thrax, the insects shouldn't be nearly as bad as they are in lower places, and we're not likely to be troubled by blood bats there—a friend of mine was bitten by a blood bat once, and it's not very pleasant. But that's where the big apes are, and there will be hunting cats and so on."

"And wolfs."

"And wolves, of course. Only there are wolves high up too. As high as your house was, and much higher."

The moment I mentioned his old home I regretted it, for something of the joy in living that had been returning to his face went out of it with the word. For a moment he seemed lost in thought. Then he said, "When those men—"

"Zoanthrops."

He nodded. "When the zoanthrops came and hurt Mama, did you come to help as quick as you could?"

"Yes," I said. "I came as quickly as I could make myself come." It was true, at least in some sense, but nevertheless it was painful to say.

"Good," he said. I had spread a blanket for him, and he lay down on it now. I folded it over him. "The stars got brighter, didn't they? They get brighter when the sun goes away."

I lay beside him looking up. "It doesn't go away, really. Urth just swings her face away, so that we think it does. If you don't look at me, I don't go away, even though you don't see me."

"If the sun is still there, why do the stars shine harder?"

His voice told me he was pleased with his own cleverness in argument, and I was pleased with it too; I suddenly understood why Master Palaemon had enjoyed talking with me when I was a child. I said, "A candle flame is almost invisible in bright sunshine, and the stars, which are really suns themselves, seem to fade in the same way. Pictures painted in the ancient days, when our sun was brighter, appear to show that the stars could not be seen at all until twilight. The old legends—I have a brown book in my sabretache that tells many of them—are full of magic beings who vanish slowly and reappear in the same way. No doubt those stories are based on the look of the stars then."

He pointed. "There's the hydra."

"I think you're right," I said. "Do you know any others?"

He showed me the cross and the great bull, and I pointed out my amphisbaena, and several others.

"And there's the wolf, over by the unicorn. There's a little wolf too, but I can't find him."

We discovered it together, near the horizon.

"They're like us, aren't they? The big wolf and the little wolf. We're big Severian and little Severian."

I agreed that was so, and he stared up at the stars for a long time, chewing the piece of dried meat I had given him. Then he said, "Where is the book with stories in it?"

I showed it to him.

"We had a book too, and sometimes Mama would read to Severa and me."

"She was your sister, wasn't she?"

He nodded. "We were twins. Big Severian, did you ever have a sister?"

"I don't know. My family is all dead. They've been dead since I was a baby. What kind of story would you like?"

He asked to see the book, and I gave it to him. After he had turned a few pages he returned it to me. "It's not like ours."

"I didn't think it was."

"See if you can find a story with a boy in it who has a big friend, and a twin. There should be wolfs in it."

I did the best I could, reading rapidly to outrace the fading light.

XIX

The Tale of the Boy Called Frog

Part I
Early Summer and Her Son

ON A MOUNTAINTOP beyond the shores of Urth there once lived a lovely woman named Early Summer. She was the queen of that land, but her king was a strong, unforgiving man, and because she was jealous of him he was jealous of her in turn, and killed any man he believed to be her lover.

One day Early Summer was walking in her garden when she saw a most beautiful blossom of a kind wholly new to her. It was redder than any rose and more sweetly perfumed, but its strong stalk was thornless and smooth as ivory. She plucked it and carried it to a secluded spot, and as she reclined there contemplating it, it grew to seem to her no blossom at all but such a lover as she had longed for, powerful and yet as tender as a kiss. Certain of the juices of the plant entered her and she conceived. She told the king, however, that the child was his, and since she was well guarded, he believed her.

It was a boy, and by his mother's wish he was called Spring Wind. At his birth all those who study the stars were gathered to cast his horoscope, not only those who lived upon the mountaintop, but many of the greatest of Urth's magi. Long they labored over their charts, and nine times met in solemn conclave; and at last they announced that in battle Spring Wind would be irresistible, and that no child of his would die before it had reached full growth. These prophecies pleased the king much.

As Spring Wind grew, his mother saw with secret pleasure that he delighted most in field and flower and fruit. Every green thing thrived under his hand, and it was the pruning knife he desired to hold, and not the sword. But when he was grown a young man, war came, and he took up his spear and his shield. Because he was quiet in demeanor and obedient to the king (whom he believed to be his father, and who believed himself to be the father), many supposed the prophecy would prove false. It was not so. In the heat of battle he fought coolly, his daring well judged and his caution sober; no general was more fertile of stratagems and sleights than he was, and no officer more attentive to every duty. The soldiers he led against the king's enemies were drilled until they seemed men of bronze quickened with fire, and their loyalty to him was such that they would have followed him to the World of Shadows, the realm farthest from the sun. Then men said it was the spring wind that threw down towers, and the spring wind that capsized ships, though that was not what Early Summer had intended.

Now it happened that the chances of war often brought Spring Wind to Urth, and there he came to know of two brothers who were kings. Of these, the elder had several sons, but the younger only a single daughter, a girl named Bird of the Wood. When this girl became a woman, her father was slain; and her uncle, in order that she might never breed sons who would claim their grandfather's kingdom, entered her name on the roll of the virgin priestesses. This displeased Spring Wind, because the princess was beautiful and her father had been his friend. One day it happened that he had gone alone into the world of Urth, and there he saw Bird of the Wood sleeping beside a stream, and woke her with his kisses.

Of their coupling were engendered twin sons, but though the priestesses of her order had aided Bird of the Wood in concealing their growth in her womb from the king, her uncle, they could not hide the babes. Before Bird of the Wood ever saw them, the priestesses placed them in a winnowing basket lined with blankets of featherwork and carried them to the bank of that same stream where Spring Wind had surprised her, and launching the basket in the water went away.

Part II

How Frog Found a New Mother

FAR THAT BASKET sailed, over fresh waters and salt. Other children would have died, but the sons of Spring Wind could not die, because they were not yet grown. The armored monsters of the water splashed about their basket and the apes threw sticks and nuts into it, but it drifted ever onward until at last it came to a bank whereon two poor sisters were washing clothes. These good women saw it and shouted, and when shouting availed nothing, tucked their skirts into their belts and waded into the river and brought it to shore.

Because they had been found in the water, the boys were named Fish and Frog, and when the sisters had showed them to their husbands, and it was seen that they were children of remarkable strength and handsomeness, each sister chose one. Now the sister who chose Fish was the wife of a herdsman, and the husband of the sister who chose Frog was a woodcutter.

This sister cared well for Frog and suckled him at her own breast, for it so happened that she had recently lost a child of her own. She carried him slung behind her in a shawl when her husband went into the wild lands to cut firewood, and thus it is said by the weavers of lore that she was the strongest of all women, for she carried an empire on her back.

A year passed, and at the end of it, Frog had learned to stand upright and take a few steps. One night the woodcutter and his wife were sitting beside their own little fire in a clearing in the wild lands; and while the woodcutter's wife prepared their supper, Frog walked naked to the fire and stood warming himself before the flames. Then the woodcutter, who was a gruff, kindly man, asked him, "Do you like that?" and though he had never spoken before, Frog nodded and answered, "Red flower." At that, it is said, Early Summer stirred upon her bed on the mountaintop beyond the shores of Urth.

The woodcutter and his wife were astonished, but they had no time to tell each other what had happened, or to try to persuade Frog to speak again, or even to rehearse what they would say to the herdsman and his wife when next they met them. For there came then into the clearing a dreadful sound—those who have listened say it is the most frightening on the world of Urth. So few who have heard it have lived that it has no name, but it is something like the hum of bees, and something like the sound a cat might make if a cat were larger than a cow, and something like the noise the voice-throwers learn first to make, a droning in the throat that seems to come from everywhere at once. It was the song a smilodon sings when he has crept close to his prey, the song that frightens even mastodons so much they often charge in the wrong direction and are stabbed from behind.

Surely the Pancreator knows all mysteries. He spoke the long word that is our universe, and few things happen that are not a part of that word. By his will, then, there rose a knoll not far from the fire, where there had been a great tomb in the most ancient days; and though the poor woodcutter and his wife knew nothing of it, two wolves had built their home there, a house low of roof and thick of wall, with galleries lit by green lamps descending among the ruined memorials and broken urns, a house, that is, such as wolves love. There the he-wolf sat sucking at the thighbone of a coryphodon, and the she-wolf, his wife, held her cubs to her breasts.

From near they heard the smilodon's song and cursed it in the Gray Language as wolves can curse, for no lawful beast hunts near the home of another of the hunting kind, and wolves are on good terms with the moon.

When the curse was finished, the she-wolf said, "What prey can that be, that the Butcher, that stupid killer of river-horses, has found, when you, O my husband, who wind the lizards that frisk on the rocks of the mountains that lie beyond Urth, have been content to worry a parched stick?"

"I do not devour carrion," the he-wolf answered shortly. "Nor do I pull worms from the morning grass, nor angle for frogs in the shallows."

"No more does the Butcher sing for them," said his wife.

Then the he-wolf raised his head and sniffed the air. "He hunts the son of Meschia and the daughter of Meschiane, and you know no good can come of such meat." At this the she-wolf nodded, for she knew that alone among the living creatures, the sons of Meschia kill all when one of their own is slain. That is because the Pancreator gave Urth to them, and they have rejected the gift.

His song ended, the Butcher roared so as to shake the leaves from the trees; then he screamed, for the curses of wolves are strong curses so long as the moon shines.

"How has he come to grief?" asked the she-wolf, who was licking the face of one of her daughters.

The he-wolf sniffed again. "Burnt flesh! He has leaped into their fire." He and his wife laughed as wolves do, silently, showing all their teeth; their ears stood up as tents stand in the desert, for they were listening to the Butcher as he blundered through the thickets looking for his prey.

Now the door of the wolves' house stood open, because

when either of the grown wolves were at home they did not care who entered, and fewer departed than came in. It had been full of moonlight (for the moon is always a welcome guest in the houses of wolves) but it grew dark. A child stood there, somewhat fearful, it may be, of the darkness, but smelling the strong smell of milk. The he-wolf snarled, but the she-wolf called in her most motherly voice, "Come in, little son of Meschia. Here you may drink, and be warm and clean. Here are the bright-eyed, quick-footed playmates, the best in all the world."

Hearing this, the boy entered, and the she-wolf put down her milk-gorged cubs and took him to her breast.

"What good is such a creature?" said the he-wolf.

The she-wolf laughed. "You can suck at a bone of the last moon's kill and ask that? Do you not remember when war raged hereabouts, and the armies of Prince Spring Wind scoured the land? Then no son of Meschia hunted us, for they hunted one another. After their battles we came out, you and I and all the Senate of Wolves, and even the Butcher, and He Who Laughs, and the Black Killer, and we moved among the dead and dying, choosing what we wished."

"That is true," said the he-wolf. "Prince Spring Wind did great things for us. But that cub of Meschia's is not he."

The she-wolf only smiled and said, "I smell the battle smoke in the fur of his head, and upon his skin." (It was the smoke of the Red Flower.) "You and I shall be dust when the first column marches from the gate of his wall, but that first shall breed a thousand more to feed our children and their children, and their children's children."

The he-wolf nodded to this, for he knew that the she-wolf was wiser than he, and even as he could sniff out things that lay beyond the shores of Urth, so could she see the days beyond the next year's rains.

"I shall call him Frog," said the she-wolf. "For indeed the Butcher angled for frogs, as you said, O my husband." She believed that she said this in compliment to the he-wolf, because he had so readily acquiesced to her wishes; but the truth was that the blood of the people of the mountaintop beyond Urth ran in Frog, and the names of those who bear the blood cannot be concealed for long.

Outside wild laughter pealed. It was the voice of He Who Laughs, calling, "It is there, Lord! There, there, there! Here, here, here is the spoor! It went in at the door!"

"You see," the he-wolf remarked, "what comes of mentioning evil. To name is to call. That is the law." And he got down his sword and fingered the edge.

The doorway was darkened again. It was a narrow doorway, for none but fools and temples have wide doors, and wolves are no fools; Frog had filled most of it. Now the Butcher filled it all, turning his shoulders to get in, and stooping his great head. Because the wall was so thick, the doorway was like a passage.

"What seek you?" asked the he-wolf, and he licked the flat of his blade.

"What is my own, and only that," said the Butcher. Smilodons fight with a curved knife in either hand, and he was much larger than the he-wolf, but he did not wish to have to engage him in that close place.

"It was never yours," said the she-wolf. Setting Frog on the floor, she came so near the Butcher that he might have struck at her if he dared. Her eyes flashed fire. "The hunt was unlawful, for an unlawful prey. Now he has drunk of me and is a wolf forever, sacred to the moon."

"I have seen dead wolves," said the Butcher.

"Yes, and eaten their flesh, though it were too foul for the flies, I dare say. It may be you shall eat mine, if a falling tree kill me."

"You say he is a wolf. He must be brought before the Senate." The Butcher licked his lips, but with a dry tongue. He would have faced the he-wolf in the open, perhaps; but he had no heart to face the pair together, and he knew that if he gained the doorway they would snatch up Frog and retreat to the passages below ground among the tumbled ashlars of the tomb, where the she-wolf would soon be behind him.

"And what have you to do with the Senate of Wolves?" the she-wolf asked.

"Perhaps as much as he," said the Butcher, and went to look for easier meat.

Part III
The Black Killer's Gold

THE SENATE OF WOLVES meets under each full moon. All come who can, for it is assumed that any who do not come plot treachery, offering, perhaps, to guard the cattle of the sons of Meschia in return for scraps. The wolf who is absent for two Senates must stand trial when he returns, and he is killed by the she-wolves if the Senate finds him guilty.

Cubs too must come before the Senate, so that any grown wolf who wishes may inspect them to assure himself that their father was a true wolf. (Sometimes a she-wolf lies with a dog for spite, but though the sons of dogs often look much like wolf cubs, they have always a spot of white on them somewhere, for white was the color of Meschia, who remembered the pure light of the Pancreator; and his sons leave it still for a brand on all they touch.)

Thus the she-wolf stood before the Senate of Wolves at the full moon, and her cubs played before her feet, and Frog— who looked a frog indeed when the moonlight through the windows stained his skin green—stood beside her and clung to the fur of her skirt. The President of the Pack sat in the highest seat, and if he was surprised to see a son of Meschia brought before the Senate, his ears did not show it. He sang:

> "Here are the five!
>   The sons and daughters born alive!
>   If they be false, say how-ow-ow!
>   If ye would speak, speak now-ow-ow!"

When the cubs are brought before the Senate, their parents may not defend them if they are challenged; but at any other time it is murder if any other seek to harm them.

"Speak NOW-OW-OW!" The walls echoed it back, so that in the huts in the valley the sons of Meschia barricaded their doors, and the daughters of Meschiane clutched their own children.

Then the Butcher, who had been waiting behind the last wolf, came forward. "Why do you delay?" he said. "I am not clever—I am too strong for cleverness, as you well understand. But there are four wolf cubs here, and a fifth that is not a wolf but my prey."

At this the he-wolf asked, "What right has *he* to speak here? Surely *he* is no wolf."

A dozen voices answered, "Anyone may speak, if a wolf asks his testimony. Speak, Butcher!"

Then the she-wolf loosened her sword in the scabbard and prepared for her last fight if it came to fighting. A demon she looked with her gaunt face and blazing eyes, for an angel is often only a demon who stands between us and our enemy.

"You say I am no wolf," continued the Butcher. "And you say rightly. We know how a wolf smells, and the sound and look of a wolf. That wolf has taken this son of Meschia for her cub, but we all know that having a wolf for a mother does not make a cub a wolf."

The he-wolf shouted, "Wolves are those whose mothers and fathers are wolves! I take this cub as my son!"

There was laughter at that, and when it died, one strange voice laughed on. It was He Who Laughs, come to advise the Butcher before the Senate of Wolves. He called, "Many have talked so, ho, ho! But their cubs have fed the pack."

The Butcher said, "They were killed for their white fur. The skin is under the fur. How can this live? Give it to me!"

"Two must speak," the President announced. "That is the law. Who speaks for the cub here? It is a son of Meschia, but is it also a wolf? Two who are not its parents must speak for it."

Then the Naked One, who is counted a member of the Senate for teaching the young wolves, rose. "I have never had a son of Meschia to teach," he said. "I may learn something from it. I speak for him."

"Another," said the President. "Another must also speak."

There was only silence. Then the Black Killer strode from the back of the hall. Everyone fears the Black Killer, for though his cloak is as soft as the fur of the youngest cub, his eyes burn in the night. "Two who are no wolves have spoken here already," he said. "May I not speak also? I have gold." He held up a purse.

"Speak! Speak!" called a hundred voices.

"The law says also that a cub's life may be bought," said the Black Killer, and he poured gold into his hand, and so ransomed an empire.

Part IV

The Plowing of the Fish

IF ALL THE adventures of Frog were told—how he lived among the wolves, and learned to hunt and fight, it would fill many books. But those who bear the blood of the people of the mountaintop beyond Urth always feel its call at last; and the time came when he carried fire into the Senate of Wolves and said, "Here is the Red Flower. In his name I rule." And when no one opposed him he led forth the wolves and called them the people of his kingdom, and soon men came to him as well as wolves, and though he was still only a boy, he seemed always taller than the men about him, for he bore the blood of Early Summer.

One night when the wild roses were opening, she came to him in a dream and told him of his mother, Bird of the Wood, and of her father and her uncle, and of his brother. He found his brother, who had become a herdsman, and with the wolves and the Black Killer and many men they went to the king and demanded their heritage. He was old and his sons had died without sons, and he gave it to them, and of it Fish took the city and the farmlands, and Frog the wild hills.

But the number of the men who followed him grew. They stole women from other peoples, and bred children, and when the wolves were no longer needed and returned to the wilds, Frog judged his people should have a city to dwell in, with walls to protect them when the men were at war. He went to the herds of Fish and took a white cow and a white bull therefrom and harnessed them to a plow, and with them plowed a furrow that should mark the wall. Fish came to seek the return of his cattle while the people were preparing to build. When Frog's people showed him the furrow and told him it was to be their wall, he laughed and jumped over it; and they, knowing that small things mocked can never grow large, slew him. But he was then a man grown, so the prophecy made at the birth of Spring Wind was fulfilled.

When Frog saw the dead Fish, he buried him in the furrow to assure the fertility of the land. For so he had been taught by the Naked One, who was also called the Savage, or Squanto.

XX

The Circle of the Sorcerers

BY THE FIRST light of morning we entered the mountain jungle as one enters a house. Behind us the sunlight played on grass and bushes and stones; we passed through a curtain of tangled vines so thick I had to cut it with my sword and saw before us only shadow and the towering boles of the trees. No insect buzzed within, and no bird chirped. No wind stirred. At first the bare soil we trod was almost as stony as the mountain slopes, but before we had walked a league it grew smoother, and at last we came to a short stair that had surely been carved with the spade. "Look," said the boy, and he pointed to something red and strangely shaped that lay upon the uppermost step.

I stopped to look at it. It was a cock's head; needles of some dark metal had been run through its eyes, and it held a strip of cast snakeskin in its bill.

"What is it?" The boy's eyes were wide.

"A charm, I think."

"Left here by a witch? What does it mean?"

I tried to recall what little I knew of the false art. As a child, Thecla had been in the care of a nursemaid who tied and untied knots to speed childbirth and claimed to see the face of Thecla's future husband (was it mine, I wonder?) at midnight, reflected in a platter that had held bridal cake.

"The cock," I told the boy, "is the herald of day, and in a magical sense his crow at dawn can be said to bring the sun. He has been blinded, perhaps, so that he will not know when dawn appears. A snake's casting of his skin means cleansing or rejuvenation. The blinded cock holds onto the old skin."

"But what does it mean?" the boy asked again.

I said I did not know; but in my heart I felt sure it was a charm against the coming of the New Sun, and it somehow pained me to find that renewal, for which I had hoped so fervently when I was a boy myself, but in which I hardly believed, should be opposed by anyone. At the same time, I was conscious that I bore the Claw. Enemies of the New Sun would surely destroy the Claw, should it fall into their hands.

Before we had gone another hundred paces, there were strips of red cloth suspended from the trees; some of these were plain, but others had been written over in black in a character I did not understand—or as seemed more likely, with symbols and ideographs of the sort those who pretend to more knowledge than they possess use in imitation of the writing of the astronomers.

"We had better go back," I said. "Or go around."

I had no sooner spoken than I heard a rustling behind me. For a moment I truly thought the figures that stepped onto the path were devils, huge-eyed and striped with black, white, and scarlet; then I saw that they were only naked men with painted bodies. Their hands were fitted with steel talons, which they held up to show me. I drew *Terminus Est*.

"We will not hinder you," one said. "Go. Leave us, if you wish." It seemed to me that beneath the paint he had the pale skin and fair hair of the south.

"You would be well advised not to. With this long blade I could kill you both before you touched me."

"Go, then," the blond man told me. "If you have no objection to leaving the child with us."

At that I looked around for little Severian. He had somehow vanished from my side.

"If you wish him returned to you, however, you will surrender your sword to me and come with us." Showing no sign of fear, the painted man walked up to me and extended his hands. The steel talons emerged from between his fingers, being fastened to a narrow bar of iron he held in his palm. "I will not ask again," he said.

I sheathed the blade, then took off the baldric that held the sheath and handed the whole to him.

He closed his eyes. Their lids had been painted with dark dots rimmed with white, like the markings of certain caterpillars that would have the birds think them snakes. "This has drunk much blood."

"Yes," I said.

His eyes opened again, and he regarded me with an unblinking stare. His painted face—like that of the other, who stood just behind him—was as expressionless as a mask. "A newly forged sword would have little power here, but this might do harm."

"I trust it will be returned to me when my son and I leave. What have you done with him?"

There was no reply. The two walked around me, one to either side, and went down the path in the direction the boy and I had been going. After a moment I followed them.

I might call the place to which they led me a village, but it was not a village in the ordinary sense, not such a village as Saltus, or even a place like the clusters of autochthon huts that are sometimes called villages. Here the trees were greater, and farther separated, than I had ever seen forest trees before, and the canopy of their leaves formed an impenetrable roof several hundred cubits overhead. So great indeed were these trees that they seemed to have been growing for whole ages; a stair led to a door in the trunk of one, which had been pierced for windows. There was a house of several stories built upon the branches of another, and a thing like a great oriole's nest swung from the limbs of a third. Open hatches showed that the ground at our feet was mined.

I was taken to one of these hatches and told to descend a crude ladder that led into darkness. For a moment (I do not know why) I feared that it might go very far, into such deep caverns as lay beneath the man-apes' nighted treasure house. It was not so. After descending what was surely not more than four times my height and clambering through what then seemed to be ruined matting, I found myself in a subterranean room.

The hatch had been shut over my head, leaving everything dark. Groping, I explored the place and found it to be about three paces by four. The floor and walls were of earth, and the ceiling of unpeeled logs; there were no furnishings whatsoever.

We had been taken at about mid morning. In seven watches more, it would be dark. Before that time it might be that I would find myself led into the presence of someone in authority. If so, I would do what I could to persuade him that the child and I were harmless and should be let go in peace. If not, then I would climb the ladder again and see if I could not break out of the hatch. I sat down to wait.

I am certain I did not sleep; but I used the facility I have for calling forth past time, and so, at least in spirit, left that dark place. For a time I watched the animals in the necropolis beyond the Citadel wall, as I had as a boy. I saw the geese shape arrowheads against the sky, and the comings and goings of fox and rabbit. They raced across the grass for me once more, and in time left their tracks in snow. Triskele lay dead, as it seemed, on the refuse behind the Bear Tower; I went to him, saw him shudder and lift his head to lick my hand. I sat with Thecla in her narrow cell, where we read aloud to each other and stopped to argue what we had read. "The world runs down like a clock," she said. "The Increate is dead, and who will recreate him? Who could?"

"Surely clocks are supposed to stop when their owners die."

"That's superstition." She took the book from my hands so she could hold them in her own, which were long-fingered and very cold. "When the owner is on his deathbed, no one pours in fresh water. He dies, and his nurses look at the dial to note the time. Later they find it stopped, and the time is the same."

I told her, "You're saying that it stops before the owner; so if the universe is running down now, that does not mean that the Increate is dead—only that he never existed."

"But he is ill. Look around you. See this place, and the towers above you. Do you know, Severian, that you never have?"

"He could still tell someone else to fill the mechanism again," I suggested, and then, realizing what I had said, blushed.

Thecla laughed. "I haven't seen you do that since I took off my gown for you the first time. I laid your hands on my breasts, and you went red as a berry. Do you remember? Tell somebody to fill it? Where is the young atheist now?"

I put my hand upon her thigh. "Confused, as he was then, by the presence of divinity."

"You don't believe in me then? I think you're right. I must be what you young torturers dream of—a beautiful prisoner, as yet unmutilated, who calls on you to slake her lust."

Trying to be gallant I said, "Such dreams as you lie beyond my power."

"Surely not, since I am in your power now."

Something was in the cell with us. I looked at the barred door and Thecla's lamp with its silver reflector, then into all the corners. The cell grew darker, and Thecla and even I myself vanished with the light, but the thing that had intruded upon my memory of us did not.

"Who are you," I asked, "and what do you wish with us?"

"You know well who we are, and we know who you are." The voice was cool and, I think, perhaps the most authoritative I have ever heard. The Autarch himself did not speak so.

"Who am I, then?"

"Severian of Nessus, the lictor of Thrax."

"I am Severian of Nessus," I said. "But I am no longer lictor of Thrax."

"So you would have us believe."

There was silence again, and after a time I understood that my interrogator would not question me, but rather would force me, if I desired my freedom, to explain myself to him. I wanted greatly to seize him—he could not have been more than a few cubits away—but I knew that in all likelihood he was armed with the steel talons the guards on the path had shown me. I wanted also, as I had for some time, to draw the Claw from its leathern sack, though nothing could have been more foolish. I said, "The archon of Thrax wished me to kill a certain woman. I freed her instead, and had to flee the city."

"By magic passing the posts of the soldiers."

I had always believed all self-proclaimed wonder-workers to be frauds; now something in my interrogator's voice suggested that even as they attempted to deceive others, so they might deceive themselves. There was mockery in it, but it was mockery of me, not of magic. "Perhaps," I said. "What do you know of my powers?"

"That they are insufficient to free you from this place."

"I have not attempted to free myself, and yet I have already been free."

That disturbed him. "You were not free. You merely brought the woman here in spirit!"

I let my breath out, trying to keep the sigh inaudible. In the antechamber of the House Absolute, a little girl had once mistaken me for a tall woman, when Thecla had for a time displaced my own personality. Now, it seemed, the remembered Thecla must have spoken through my mouth. I said, "Surely I am a necromancer then, who can command the spirits of the dead. For that woman is dead."

"You told us you freed her."

"Another woman, who only slightly resembled that one. What have you done to my son?"

"He does not call you his father."

"He suffers fancies," I said.

There was no reply. After a time I rose and ran my hands once more over the walls of my underground prison; they were of plain earth, as before. I had seen no light and heard no sound, but it seemed to me that it would have been possible to cover the hatch with some portable structure to exclude the day, and if the hatch were skillfully constructed, it might be lifted silently. I mounted the first rung of the ladder; it creaked beneath my weight.

I climbed a step up, and another, and it creaked at each. I tried to rise to the fourth rung, and felt my scalp and shoulders prodded as though with the points of daggers. A trickle of blood from my right ear wet my neck.

I retreated to the third rung and groped overhead. The thing that had seemed like a torn mat when I entered the underground chamber proved to be a score or more of sharp bamboo splittings, anchored somehow in the shaft with their points directed down. I had descended with ease because my body had forced them to one side; now they prevented me from ascending much as the barbs on a fish spear prevent the fish from getting away. I took hold of one and tried to break it, but though I might have done so with both hands, it was impossible with one. Given light and time I might have worked my way through them; light perhaps I might have had, but I did not dare to take the risk. I jumped to the floor again.

Another circuit of the room told me no more than I had known before, yet it seemed beyond credence that my questioner had climbed the ladder without making a sound, though he might perhaps possess some special knowledge that would permit him to pass through the bamboo. I went about the floor on my hands and knees, and learned no more than before.

I attempted to move the ladder, but it was fixed in position; so beginning at the corner nearest the shaft, I jumped and touched the wall at a point as high as I could reach, then moved half a step to one side and jumped again. When I had arrived at a place that must have been more or less opposite the spot where I had been sitting, I found it: a rectangular hole perhaps a cubit high and two across, with its lower edge slightly higher than my head. My interrogator might have climbed from it silently, perhaps with the aid of a rope, and returned the same way; but it seemed more likely that he had merely thrust his head and shoulders through, so that his voice had sounded as if he were truly in the room with me. I gripped the edge of the hole as well as I could, jumped, and pulled myself up.

XXI

The Duel of Magic

THE CHAMBER BEYOND the one in which I had been imprisoned seemed much like it, though its floor was higher. It was, of course, utterly dark; but now that I was confident I was no longer being observed, I took the Claw from its sack and looked about me by its light which was, though not bright, sufficient.

There was no ladder, but a narrow door gave access to what I assumed was a third subterranean room. Concealing the Claw again, I stepped through it, but found myself instead in a tunnel no wider than the doorway, which turned and turned again before I had taken half a dozen strides. At first I supposed it was simply a baffled passage to prevent light from betraying the opening in the wall of the room where I had been confined. But no more than three turns should have been.necessary. The walls seemed to bend and divide; yet I remained in impenetrable darkness. I took out the Claw once more.

Perhaps because of the confined space in which I stood, it seemed somewhat brighter; but there was nothing to see beyond what my hands had already told me. I was alone. I stood in a maze with earthen walls and a ceiling (now just above my head) of rough poles; its narrow turnings quickly defeated the light.

I was about to thrust the Claw away again when I detected an odor at once pungent and alien. My nose is by no means the sensitive one of the he-wolf in the tale—if anything, I have rather a poorer sense of smell than most people. I thought I recognized the scent, but it was several moments before I placed it as the one I had experienced in the antechamber on the morning of our escape, when I returned for Jonas after talking to the little girl. She had said that something, some nameless seeker, had been snuffling among the prisoners there; and I had found a viscous substance on the floor and wall where Jonas lay.

I did not put the Claw back in its sack after that; but though I crossed a fetid trail several times as I wandered in the maze, I never glimpsed the creature that left it. After what must have been a watch or more of wandering, I reached a ladder that led up a short, open shaft. The square of daylight at its top was at once blinding and delightful. For a time I basked in it without even setting foot on the ladder. If I were to climb it, it seemed almost certain I would be recaptured at once; and yet I was so hungry and thirsty by then that I could hardly keep myself from doing so, and the thought of the foul thing that sought for me—it was surely one of Hethor's pets—made me want to bolt up it at once.

At last I climbed cautiously up and thrust my head above the level of the ground. I was not (as I had supposed) in the village I had seen; the windings of the maze had carried me beyond it to some secret exit. The great, silent trees stood closer here, and the light that had appeared so brilliant to me was the filtered green shade of their leaves. I emerged and found that I had left a hole between two roots, a place so obscure that I might have walked within a pace of it and yet not seen it. If I could, I would have blocked it with some weight to prevent or at least delay the escape of the creature that hunted me; but there was no stone or other object to hand that would serve such a purpose.

By the old trick of observing the slope of the ground and in so far as possible always walking downhill, I soon discovered a small stream. There was a little open sky above it, and as nearly as I could judge, the day appeared eight or nine watches over. Guessing that the village would not lie far from the source of the good water I had found, I soon found that as well. Wrapped in my fuligin cloak and standing in the deepest shade, I observed it for some time. Once a man—not painted like the two who had stopped us on the path—crossed the clearing. Once another left the suspended hut, went to the spring and drank, then returned to the hut.

It grew darker, and the strange village woke. A dozen men left the suspended hut and began to pile wood in the center of the clearing. Three more, robed and bearing forked staffs, emerged from the house of the tree. Still others, who must have been watching the jungle paths, slipped out of the shadows soon after the fire was kindled and spread a cloth before it.

One of the robed men stood with his back to the fire while the other two crouched at his feet; there was something extraordinary about them all, but I was reminded of the bearing of exultants, rather than of the Hierodules I had seen in the gardens of the House Absolute—it was the carriage that the consciousness of leadership confers, even as it severs the leader from common humanity. Painted and unpainted men sat cross-legged on the ground, facing the three. I heard the murmur of voices and the strong speech of the standing man, but I was too far to understand what was said. After a time the crouching men rose. One opened his robe like a tent, and Becan's son, whom I had made my own, stepped forth. The other produced *Terminus Est* in the same manner and drew her, displaying her bright blade and the black opal in her hilt to the crowd. Then one of the painted men rose, came some distance toward me (so that I feared he was about to see me, though I had covered my face with my mask) and lifted a door set into the ground. Soon afterward he emerged from another nearer the fire, and moving somewhat more rapidly went to the robed men to report.

There could be little doubt of what he was saying. I squared my shoulders and walked into the firelight. "I am not there," I said. "I am here."

There was an inrush of many breaths, and though I knew I might soon die, it was good to hear.

The midmost of the robed men said, "As you see, you cannot escape us. You were free, yet we drew you back." It was the voice that had interrogated me in my underground cell.

I said, "If you have walked far in The Way, you know you have less authority over me than the ignorant may believe." (It is not difficult to ape the way such people talk, for it is itself an aping of the speech of ascetics, and such priestesses as the Pelerines.) "You stole my son, who is also son to The Beast Who Speaks, as you must know by this time if you have much questioned him. To gain his return, I surrendered my sword to your slaves, and for a time submitted myself to you. I will take it up again now."

There is a place in the shoulder that, when pressed firmly with the thumb, paralyzes the entire arm. I laid my hand on the shoulder of the robed man who held *Terminus Est*, and he dropped it at my feet. With more presence of mind than I would have credited in a child, the boy Severian picked it up and handed it to me. The midmost robed man lifted his staff and shouted, "Arms!" and his followers rose as one man. Many had the talons I have described, and many of the others drew knives.

I fastened *Terminus Est* over my shoulder in her accustomed place and said, "You surely do not suppose that I require this ancient sword as a weapon? She has higher properties, as you of all people should know."

The robed man who had produced little Severian said hur-

riedly, "So Abundantius has just told us." The other man was
still rubbing his arm.

I looked at the midmost robed man, who was clearly the
one referred to. His eyes were clever, and as hard as stones.
"Abundantius is wise," I said. I was trying to think of some
way in which I could kill him without drawing the others
down on us. "He knows too, I think, of the curse that afflicts
those who harm the person of a magus."

"You are a magus then," Abundantius said.

"I, who took the archon's prey from out of his hands and
passed invisible through the midst of his army? Yes, I have
been called so."

"Prove then that you are a magus and we will hail you as a
brother. But if you fail the test or refuse it—we are many, and
you have but one sword."

"I will fail no fair assay," I said. "Though neither you nor
your followers have authority to make one."

He was too clever to be drawn into such a debate. "The
test is known to all here except yourself, and known, too, to
be just. Everyone you see about you has succeeded in it, or
hopes to."

They took me to a hall I had not seen before, a place
substantially built of logs, and hidden among the trees. It had
no windows, and only a single entrance. When torches were
carried inside, I saw that its one chamber was unfurnished but
for a carpet of woven grass, and so long in proportion to its
width that it seemed almost a corridor.

Abundantius said, "Here you will have your combat with
Decuman." He indicated the man whose arm I had numbed,
who was, perhaps, a trifle surprised at being thus singled out.
"You bested him by the fire. Now he must best you, if he can.
You may sit here, nearest the door, so that you may be assured we cannot enter to give him aid. He will sit at the
farther end. You shall not approach one another, or touch
one another as you touched him by the fire. You must weave

your spells, and in the morning we shall come to see who has mastered."

Taking little Severian by the hand, I led him to the blind end of that dark place. "I'll sit here," I said. "I have every confidence that you will not come to Decuman's aid, but you have no way of knowing whether I have confederates in the jungle outside. You have offered to trust me, and so I shall trust you."

"It would be better," Abundantius said, "if you were to leave the child in our keeping."

I shook my head. "I must have him with me. He is mine, and when you robbed me of him on the path, you robbed me too of half my power. I will not be separated from him again."

After a moment, Abundantius nodded. "As you wish. We but desired that he might come to no harm."

"No harm will come to him," I said.

There were iron brackets on the walls, and four of the naked men thrust their torches into them before they left. Decuman seated himself cross-legged near the door, his staff upon his lap. I sat too, and drew the boy to me. "I'm scared," he said; he buried his little face in my cloak.

"You have every right to be. The past three days have been bad ones for you."

Decuman had begun a slow, rhythmic chant.

"Little Severian, I want you to tell me what happened to you on the path. I looked around and you were gone."

It took some comforting and coaxing, but at last his sobs ceased. "They came out—the three-colored men with claws, and I was afraid and ran away."

"Is that all?"

"And then more three-colored men came out and caught me, and they made me go into a hole in the ground, where it was dark. And then they woke me and lifted me up, and I was inside a man's coat, and then you came and got me."

"Didn't anyone ask you questions?"

"A man in the dark."

"I see. Little Severian, you mustn't ever run away again, the way you did on the path—do you understand? Only run if I run too. If you hadn't run away when we met the three-colored men, we wouldn't be here."

The boy nodded.

"Decuman," I called. "Decuman, can we talk?"

He ignored me, save perhaps that his murmured chant grew a trifle louder. His face was lifted so that he appeared to be staring at the roof poles, but his eyes were closed.

"What is he doing?" the boy asked.

"He is weaving an enchantment."

"Will it hurt us?"

"No," I said. "Such magic is mostly fakery—like lifting you up through a hole so it would look as if the other one had made you appear under his robe."

Yet even as I spoke, I was conscious there was something more. Decuman was concentrating his mind on me as few minds can be concentrated, and I felt I was naked in some brightly lit place where a thousand eyes watched. One of the torches flickered, guttered, and went out. As the light in the hall dimmed, the light I could not see seemed to grow brighter.

I rose. There are ways of killing that leave no mark, and I reviewed them mentally as I stepped forward.

At once, pikes sprang from the walls, an ell on either side. They were not such spears as soldiers have, energy weapons whose heads strike bolts of fire, but simple poles of wood tipped with iron, like the pilets the villagers of Saltus had used. Nevertheless, they could kill at close range, and I sat down again. The boy said, "I think they're outside watching us through the cracks between the logs."

"Yes, I know that now too."

"What can we do?" he asked. And then when I did not reply, "Who are these people, Father?"

It was the first time he had called me that. I drew him

closer, and it seemed to weaken the net Decuman was knotting about my mind. I said, "I'm only guessing, but I would say this is an academy of magicians—of those cultists who practice what they believe are secret arts. They are supposed to have followers everywhere—though I choose to doubt that—and they are very cruel. Have you heard of the New Sun, little Severian? He is the man who prophets say will come and drive back the ice and set the world right."

"He will kill Abaia," the boy answered, surprising me.

"Yes, he is supposed to do that as well, and many other things. He is said to have come once before, long ago. Did you know that?"

He shook his head.

"Then his task was to forge a peace between humanity and the Increate, and he was called the Conciliator. He left behind a famous relic, a gem called the Claw." My hand went to it as I spoke, and though I did not loosen the drawstrings of the little sack of human skin that held it, I could feel it through the soft leather. As soon as I touched it, the invisible glare Decuman had created in my mind fell almost to nothing. I cannot say now just why I had presumed for so long that it was necessary for the Claw to be taken from its place of concealment for it to be effective. I learned that night that it was not so, and I laughed.

For a moment Decuman halted his chant, and his eyes opened. Little Severian clutched me more tightly. "Aren't you afraid anymore?"

"No," I said. "Could you see that I was frightened?"

He nodded solemnly.

"What I was going to tell you was that the existence of that relic seems to have given some people the idea that the Conciliator used claws as weapons. I have sometimes doubted that he existed; but if such a person ever lived, I'm sure that he used his weapons largely against himself. Do you understand what I am saying?"

I doubt that he did, but he nodded.

"When we were on the path, we found a charm against the coming of the New Sun. The three-colored men, who I think are the ones who have passed this test, use claws of steel. I think they must want to hold back the coming of the New Sun so they can take his place and perhaps usurp his powers. If—"

Outside, someone screamed.

XXII

The Skirts of the Mountain

MY LAUGH HAD broken Decuman's concentration, if only for a moment. The scream from outside did not. His net, so much of which had fallen in ruins when I gripped the Claw, was being knotted again, more slowly but more tightly.

It is always a temptation to say that such feelings are indescribable, though they seldom are. I felt that I hung naked between two sentient suns, and I was somehow aware that these suns were the hemispheres of Decuman's brain. I was bathed in light, but it was the glare of furnaces, consuming and somehow immobilizing. In that light, nothing seemed worthwhile; and I myself infinitely small and contemptible.

Thus my concentration too, in a sense, remained unbroken. Yet I was aware, however dimly, that the scream might signal an opportunity for me. Much later than I should have, after perhaps a dozen breaths had passed my nostrils, I stumbled to my feet.

Something was coming through the doorway. My first thought, absurd as it may sound, was that it was mud—that a convulsion had rocked Urth, and the hall was about to be inundated in what had been the bottom of some fetid marsh.

It flowed around the doorposts blindly and softly, and as it did, another torch went out. Soon it was about to touch Decuman, and I shouted to warn him.

I am not sure whether it was the touch of the creature or my voice, but he recoiled. I was conscious again of the breaking of the spell, the ruin of the snare that had held me between the twin suns. They flew apart and dimmed as they vanished, and I seemed to expand, and to turn in a direction neither up nor down, left nor right, until I stood wholly in the hall of testing, with little Severian clinging to my cloak.

Decuman's hand flashed with talons then. I had not even realized he had them. Whatever that black and nearly shapeless creature was, its side cut as fat does under the lash. Its blood was black too, or perhaps darkly green. Decuman's was red; when the creature flowed over him, it seemed to melt his skin like wax.

I lifted the boy and made him cling to my neck and clasp my waist with his legs, then jumped with all my strength. But though my fingertips touched a roof pole, I could not grasp it. The creature was turning, blindly but purposefully. Perhaps it hunted by scent, yet I have always felt it was by thought—that would explain why it was so slow to find me in the antechamber, where I had dreamed myself to Thecla, and so swift in the hall of testing, when Decuman's mind was focused on mine.

I jumped again, but this time I missed the pole by a span at least. To get one of the two remaining torches, I had to run toward the creature. I did and seized the torch, but it went out as I took it from its bracket.

Holding the bracket with one hand, I jumped a third time, assisting my legs with the strength of my arm; and now I caught a smooth, narrow pole with my left hand. The pole bent beneath my weight, but I was able to draw myself up, with the boy on my shoulders, until I could get one foot on the bracket.

Below me, the dark, shapeless creature reared, fell, and lifted itself again. Still holding the pole, I drew *Terminus Est*. A slash bit deep into the oozing flesh, but the blade was no sooner clear than the wound seemed to close and knit. I turned my sword on the roof thatch then, an expedient I confess to stealing from Agia. It was thick, of jungle leaves bound with tough fibers; my first frantic strokes seemed to make little impression on it, but at the third a great swath fell. Part of it struck the remaining torch, smothering it, then sending up a gout of flame. I vaulted through the gap and into the night.

Leaping blindly as I did with that sharp blade drawn, it is a wonder that I did not kill both the boy and myself. I dropped it and him when I struck the ground, and fell to my knees. The red blaze of the thatch grew brighter with the passing of every moment. I heard the boy whimper and called to him not to run, then pulled him to his feet with one hand and snatched up *Terminus Est* with the other and ran myself.

All the rest of that night we fled blindly through the jungle. In so far as I could, I tried to direct our steps uphill—not only because our way north would mean climbing, but because I knew we were less likely to tumble over some drop. When morning came, we were in the jungle still, with no more idea than we had before of where we were. I carried the boy then, and he fell asleep in my arms.

In another watch there could be no doubt the ground was rising steeply before us, and at last we came to a curtain of vines such as I had cut through the day before. Just as I was ready to try to put down the boy without waking him, so that I could draw my sword, I saw bright daylight streaming through a rent to my left. I went to it, walking as quickly as I could, almost running; then through it, and out onto a rocky upland of coarse grass and shrubs. A few more steps brought me to a clear stream that sang over rocks—unquestionably the stream beside which the boy and I had slept two nights before. Not knowing or caring whether the shapeless creature was on our track still, I lay down beside it and slept again.

I was in a maze, like and yet unlike the dark underground maze of the magicians. The corridors were wider here, and sometimes seemed galleries as mighty as those of the House Absolute. Some, indeed, were lined with pier glasses, in which I saw myself with ragged cloak and haggard face, and Thecla, half-transparent in a lovely, trailing gown, close beside me. Planets whistled down long, oblique, curving tracks that only they could see. Blue Urth carried the green moon like an infant, but did not touch her. Red Verthandi became Decuman, his skin eaten away, turning in his own blood.

I fled and fell, jerking all my limbs. I saw true stars in the sun-drenched sky for a moment, but sleep drew me as irresistibly as gravity. Beside a wall of glass, I walked; and through it I saw the boy, running and frightened, in the old, patched, gray shirt I had worn as an apprentice, running from the fourth level, I thought, to the Atrium of Time. Dorcas and Jolenta came hand in hand, smiling at each other, and did not see me. Then autochthons, copper-skinned and bowlegged, feathered and jeweled, were dancing behind their shaman, dancing in the rain. The undine swam in air, vast as a cloud, blotting out the sun.

I woke. Soft rain pattered on my face. Beside me, little Severian slept still. I wrapped him as well as I could in my cloak and carried him again to the rent in the curtain of vines. Beyond that curtain under the wide-boughed trees, the rain hardly penetrated; and there we lay and slept once more. This time there were no dreams, and when I woke we had slept a day and a night, and the pale light of dawn lay everywhere.

The boy was already up, wandering among the boles of the trees. He showed me where the brook was in this place, and I washed, and shaved as well as I could without hot water, which I had not done since the first afternoon in the house

beneath the cliff. Then we found the familiar path and made
our way north again.

"Won't we meet the three-colored men?" he asked, and I
told him not to worry and not to run—that I would handle
the three-colored men. The truth was that I was far more
concerned about Hethor and the creature he had set upon my
track. If it had not perished in the fire, it might be moving
toward us now; for though it had seemed an animal that
would fear the sun, the dimness of the jungle was the very
stuff of twilight.

Only one painted man stepped into the path, and he did so
not to bar the way but to prostrate himself. I was tempted to
kill him and be done with it; we are taught strictly to kill and
maim only at the order of a judge, but that training had been
weakening in me as I moved farther and farther from Nessus
and toward the war and the wild mountains. Some mystics
hold that the vapors arising from battles affect the brain, even
a long way downwind; and it may be so. Nevertheless, I lifted
him up, and merely told him to stand aside.

"Great Magus," he said, "what have you done with the
creeping dark?"

"I have sent it back to the pit, from which I drew it," I told
him, for since we had not encountered the creature, I was
fairly certain Hethor had recalled it, if it was not dead.

"Five of us transmigrated," the painted man said.

"Your powers, then, are greater than I would have credited.
It has killed hundreds in a night."

I was far from sure he would not attack us when our backs
were to him, but he did not. The path down which I had
walked as a prisoner the day before seemed deserted now. No
more guards appeared to challenge us; some of the strips of
red cloth had been torn down and trampled under foot,
though I could not imagine why. I saw many footprints on
the path, which had been smooth (perhaps raked smooth)
before.

"What are you looking for?" the boy asked.

I kept my voice low, still not sure there were no listeners behind the trees. "The slime of the animal we ran away from last night."

"Do you see it?"

I shook my head.

For a time, the boy was silent. Then he said, "Big Severian, where did it come from?"

"Do you remember the story? From one of the mountaintops beyond the shores of Urth."

"Where Spring Wind lived?"

"I don't think it was the same one."

"How did he get here?"

"A bad man brought him," I said. "Now be quiet for a while, little Severian."

If I was short with the boy, it was because I had been troubled by the same thought. Hethor must have smuggled his pets aboard the ship on which he served, that seemed clear enough; and when he had followed me out of Nessus, he might easily have carried the notules in some small, sealed container on his person—terrible though they were, they were no thicker than tissue, as Jonas had known.

But what of the creature we had seen in the hall of testing? It had appeared in the antechamber of the House Absolute too, after Hethor had come, but how? And had it followed Hethor and Agia like a dog as they journeyed north to Thrax? I summoned the memory of it, as I had seen it when it killed Decuman, and tried to estimate its weight: it must have been as heavy as several men, and perhaps as heavy as a destrier. A large cart, surely, would have been required to transport and conceal it. Had Hethor driven such a cart through these mountains? I could not believe it. Had the viscid horror we had seen shared such a cart with the salamander I had seen destroyed in Thrax? I could not believe that either.

The village seemed deserted when we reached it. Some parts of the hall of testing still stood and smoldered. I looked in vain for the remains of Decuman's body there, though I found his half-burned staff. It had been hollow, and from the smoothness of its interior, I suspected that with the head removed it had formed a sabarcane for shooting poisoned darts. No doubt it would have been used if I had proved overly resistant to the spell he wove.

The boy must have been following my thoughts from my expression and the direction of my glance. He said, "That man really was magic, wasn't he? He almost magicked you."

I nodded.

"You said it wasn't real."

"In some ways, little Severian, I am not much wiser than you. I didn't think it was. I had seen so much fakery—the secret door into the underground room where they kept me, and the way they made you appear under the other man's robe. Still, there are dark things everywhere, and I suppose that those who look hard enough for them cannot help but find some. Then they become, as you said, real magicians."

"They could tell everybody what to do, if they know real magic."

I only shook my head to that, but I have thought much about it since. It seems to me there are two objections to the boy's idea, though expressed in a more mature form it must appear more convincing.

The first is that so little knowledge is passed from one generation to the next by the magicians. My own training was in what may be called the most fundamental of the applied sciences; and I know from it that the progress of science depends much less upon either theoretical considerations or systematic investigation than is commonly believed, but rather on the transmittal of reliable information, gained by chance or insight, from one set of men to their successors. The nature of those who hunt after dark knowledge is to hoard it even in death, or to transmit it so wrapped in disguise and beclouded with self-serving lies that it is of little value. At times, one hears of those who teach their lovers well, or their children; but it is the nature of such people seldom to have either, and it may be that their art is weakened when they do.

The second is that the very existence of such powers argues a counterforce. We call powers of the first kind dark, though they may use a species of deadly light as Decuman did; and we call those of the second kind bright, though I think that they may at times employ darkness, as a good man nevertheless draws the curtains of his bed to sleep. Yet there is truth to the talk of darkness and light, because it shows plainly that one implies the other. The tale I read to little Severian said that the universe was but a long word of the Increate's. We, then, are the syllables of that word. But the speaking of any word is futile unless there are other words, words that are not spoken. If a beast has but one cry, the cry tells nothing; and even the wind has a multitude of voices, so that those who sit indoors may hear it and know if the weather is tumultuous or mild. The powers we call dark seem to me to be the words the Increate did *not* speak, if the Increate exists at all; and these words must be maintained in a quasi-existence, if the other word, the word spoken, is to be distinguished. What is not said can be important—but what is said is more important. Thus my very knowledge of the existence of the Claw was almost sufficient to counter Decuman's spell.

And if the seekers after dark things find them, may not the seekers after bright find them as well? And are they not more apt to hand their wisdom on? So the Pelerines had guarded the Claw, from generation unto generation; and thinking of this, I became more determined than ever to find them and restore it to them; for if I had not known it before, the night with the alzabo had brought home to me that I was only flesh, and would die in time certainly, and perhaps would die soon.

Because the mountain we approached stood to the north and thus cast its shadow toward the saddle of jungle, no curtain of vines grew on that side. The pale green of the leaves only faded to one more pale still, and the number of dead trees increased, though all the trees were smaller. The canopy of leaves beneath which we had walked all day broke, and in another hundred strides broke again, and at last vanished altogether.

Then the mountain rose before us, too near for us to see it as the image of a man. Great folded slopes rolled down out of a bank of cloud; they were, I knew, but the sculptured drapery of his robes. How often he must have risen from sleep and put them on, perhaps without reflecting that they would be preserved here for the ages, so huge as almost to escape the sight of humankind.

XXIII

The Cursed Town

AT ABOUT NOON of the next day we found water again, the
only water the two of us were to taste upon that mountain.
Only a few strips of the dried meat Casdoe had left for me
remained. I shared them out, and we drank from the stream,
which was no more than a trickle the size of a man's thumb.
That seemed strange, because I had seen so much snow on
the head and shoulders of the mountain; I was to discover
later that the slopes below the snow, where snow might have
melted with the coming of summer, were blown clear by the
wind. Higher, the white drifts might accumulate for centuries.

Our blankets were damp with dew, and we spread them
there on stones to dry. Even without the sun, the dry gusts of
mountain air dried them in a watch or so. I knew that we
would be spending the coming night high up the slopes, much
as I had spent the first night after leaving Thrax. Somehow,
the knowledge was powerless to depress my spirits. It was not
so much that we were leaving the dangers we had found in the
saddle of jungle, as that we were leaving behind a certain
sordidness there. I felt that I had been befouled, and that the
cold atmosphere of the mountain would cleanse me. For a

time that feeling remained with me almost unexamined; then, as we began to climb in earnest, I realized that what disturbed me was the memory of the lies I had told the magicians, pretending, as they did, to command great powers and be privy to vast secrets. Those lies had been wholly justifiable—they had helped to save my life and little Severian's. Nevertheless, I felt myself somewhat less of a man because I had resorted to them. Master Gurloes, whom I had come to hate before I left the guild, had lied frequently; and now I was not sure whether I had hated him because he lied, or hated lying because he did it.

And yet Master Gurloes had possessed as good an excuse as I did, and perhaps a better one. He had lied to preserve the guild and advance its fortunes, giving various officials and officers exaggerated accounts of our work, and when necessary concealing our mistakes. In doing that, he, the de facto head of the guild, had been advancing his own position, to be sure; yet he had also been advancing mine, and that of Drotte, Roche, Eata, and all the other apprentices and journeymen who would eventually inherit it. If he had been the simple, brutal man he wished everyone to believe he was, I could have been certain now that his dishonesty had been for his benefit alone. I knew that he was not; perhaps for years he had seen himself as I now saw myself.

And yet I could not be certain I had acted to save little Severian. When he had run and I had surrendered my sword, it might have been more to his advantage if I had fought—I myself was the one whose immediate advantage had been served by my docile capitulation, since if I had fought I might have been killed. Later, when I had escaped, I had surely returned as much for *Terminus Est* as for the boy; I had returned for her in the mine of the man-apes, when he had not been with me; and without her, I would have become a mere vagabond.

A watch after I entertained these thoughts, I was scaling a

rock face with both the sword and the boy on my back, and with no more certainty concerning how much I cared for either than I had before. Fortunately I was fairly fresh, it was not a difficult climb as such things go, and at the top we struck an ancient highway.

Although I have walked in many strange places, I have walked in none that gave me so great a sensation of anomaly. To our left, no more than twenty paces off, I could see the termination of this broad road, where some rockslide had carried its lower end away. Before us it stretched as perfect as on the day it was completed, a ribbon of seamless black stone winding up toward that immense figure whose face was lost above the clouds.

The boy gripped my hand when I put him down. "My mother said we couldn't use the roads, because of the soldiers."

"Your mother was right," I told him. "But she was going to go down, where the soldiers are. No doubt there were soldiers on this road once, but they died a long time before the biggest tree in the jungle down there was a seed." He was cold, and I gave him one of the blankets and showed him how to wrap it about him and hold it closed to make a cloak. If anyone had seen us then, we would have appeared a small, gray figure followed by a disproportionate shadow.

We entered a mist, and I thought it strange to find one that high up. It was only after we had climbed above it and could look down upon its sunlit top that I realized it had been one of the clouds that had seemed so remote when I had looked up at them from the saddle.

And yet that saddle of jungle, so far below us now, was itself no doubt thousands of cubits above Nessus and the lower reaches of Gyoll. I thought then how far I must have come, that jungles could exist at such altitudes—nearly to the waist of the world, where it was always summer, and only height produced any difference in the climate. If I were to journey to the west, out of these mountains, then from what I had learned from Master Palaemon, I would find myself in a jungle so pestilential as to make the one we had left seem a paradise, a coastal jungle of steaming heat and swarming insects; and yet there too I would see the evidences of death, for though that jungle received as much of the sun's strength as any spot on Urth, still it was less than it had received in times past, and just as the ice crept forward in the south and the vegetation of the temperate zone fled from it, so the trees and other plants of the tropics died to give the newcomers space.

While I looked down at the cloud, the boy had been walking ahead. Now he looked back at me with shining eyes and called, "Who made this road?"

"No doubt the workers who carved the mountain. They must have had great energies at their command and machines more powerful than any we know about. Still, they would have had to carry the rubble away in some fashion. A thousand carts and wains must have rolled here once." And yet I wondered, because the iron wheels of such vehicles score even the hard cobbles of Thrax and Nessus, and this road was as smooth as a processional way. Surely, I thought, only the sun and wind have passed here.

"Big Severian, look! Do you see the hand?"

The boy was pointing toward a spur of the mountain high above us. I craned my neck, but for a moment I saw nothing but what I had seen before: a long promontory of inhospitable gray rock. Then the sunlight flashed on something near the end. It seemed, unmistakably, the gleam of gold; when I had seen that, I saw also that the gold was a ring, and under it I saw the thumb lying frozen in stone along the rock, a thumb perhaps a hundred paces long, with the fingers above it hills.

We had no money, and I knew how valuable money might be when we were forced, as eventually we must be, to reenter the inhabited lands. If I was still searched for, gold might persuade the searchers to look elsewhere. Gold might also buy little Severian an apprenticeship in some worthy guild, for it was clear he could not continue to travel with me. It seemed most probable that the great ring was only gold leaf over stone; even so, so vast a quantity of gold leaf, if it could be peeled away and rolled up, must amount to a considerable total. And though I made an effort not to, I found myself wondering if mere gold leaf could have endured so many centuries. Would it not have loosened and fallen away long ago? If the ring were of solid gold, it would be worth a fortune; but all the fortunes of Urth could not have bought this mighty image, and he who had ordered its construction must have possessed wealth incalculable. Even if the ring were not solid through to the finger beneath, there might be some substantial thickness of metal.

As I considered all this, I toiled upward, my long legs soon outstripping the boy's short ones. At times the road climbed so steeply I could hardly believe vehicles burdened with stone had ever traversed it. Twice we crossed fissures, one so wide that I was forced to throw the boy across it before leaping over it myself. I was hoping to find water before we halted; I found none, and when night fell we had no better shelter than a crevice of stone where we wrapped ourselves in the blankets and my cape and slept as well as we could.

In the morning we were both thirsty. Although the rainy season would not come until autumn, I told the boy I thought it might rain today, and we started forward again in good spirits. Then too, he showed me how carrying a small stone in the mouth helps to quench thirst. It is a mountain trick, one I had not known. The wind was colder now than it had been before, and I began to feel the thinness of the air. Occasionally the road twisted to some point where we received a few moments of sunshine.

In doing so, it wound farther and farther from the ring,

until at last we found ourselves in full shadow, out of sight of the ring altogether and somewhere near the knees of the seated figure. There was a last steep climb, so abrupt that I would have been grateful for steps. And then, ahead of us where they seemed to float in the clear air, a cluster of slender spires. The boy called out "Thrax!" so happily that I knew his mother must have told him tales of it, and told him too, when she and the old man took him from the house where he had been born, that she would bring him there.

"No," I said. "It is not Thrax. This looks more like my own Citadel—our Matachin Tower, and the witches' tower, and the Bear Tower and the Bell Tower."

He looked at me, wide-eyed.

"No, it isn't that either, of course. Only I have been to Thrax, and Thrax is a city of stone. Those towers are of metal, as ours were."

"They have eyes," little Severian said.

So they did. At first I thought my imagination was deceiving me, particularly since not all the towers possessed them. At last I came to realize that some faced away from us, and that the towers had not only eyes but shoulders and arms as well; that they were, in fact, the metallic figures of cataphracts, warriors armored from head to toe. "It isn't a real city," I told the boy. "What we have found are the guardsmen of the Autarch, waiting in his lap to destroy those who would harm him."

"Will they hurt us?"

"It's a frightening thought, isn't it? They could crush you and me beneath their feet like mice. I'm sure they won't, however. They're only statues, spiritual guards left here as memorials to his powers."

"There are big houses too," the boy said.

He was right. The buildings were no more than waist-high to the towering metal figures, so that we had overlooked them at first. That again reminded me of the Citadel, where structures never meant to brave the stars are mingled with the towers. Perhaps it was merely the thin air, but I had a sudden vision of these metal men rising slowly, then ever more swiftly, lifting hands toward the sky as they dove into it as we used to dive down to the dark waters of the cistern by torchlight.

Although my boots must have grated on the wind-swept rock, I find I have no memory of such a sound. Perhaps it was lost in the immensity of the mountaintop, so that we approached the standing figures as silently as if we walked over moss. Our shadows, which had spread behind us and to our left when they had first appeared, were contracted into pools about our feet; and I noticed that I could see the eyes of every figure. I told myself that I had overlooked some at first, yet they glittered in the sun.

At last we threaded a path among them, and among the buildings that surrounded them. I had expected these buildings to be ruinous, like those in the forgotten city of Apu-Punchau. They were closed, secretive, and silent; but they might have been constructed only a few years before. No roofs had fallen in; no vines had dislodged the square gray stones of their walls. They were windowless, and their architecture did not suggest temples, fortresses, tombs, or any other type of structure with which I was familiar. They were utterly without ornament and without grace; yet their workmanship was excellent, and their differing forms seemed to indicate differences in function. The shining figures stood among them as if they had been halted in their places by some sudden, freezing wind, not as monuments stand.

I selected a building and told the boy we would break into it, and that if we were fortunate we might find water there, and perhaps even preserved food. It proved a foolish boast. The doors were as solid as the walls, the roof as strong as the foundation. Even if I had possessed an ax, I do not think I could have smashed my way in, and I dared not hew with

Terminus Est. Poking and prying for some weakness, we wasted several watches. The second and third buildings we attempted proved no easier than the first.

"There's a round house over there," the boy said at last. "I'll go and look at it for you."

Because I felt sure there was nothing in this deserted place that could harm him, I told him to go ahead.

Soon he was back. "The door's open!"

XXIV

The Corpse

I HAD NEVER discovered what uses the other buildings had served. No more did I understand this one, which was circular and covered by a dome. Its walls were metal—not the darkly lustrous metal of our Citadel towers, but some bright alloy like polished silver.

This gleaming building stood atop a stepped pedestal, and I wondered to see it there when the great images of the cataphracts in their antique armor stood plainly in the streets. There were five doorways about its circumference (for we walked around it before venturing inside), and all of them stood open. By examining them and the floor before them, I tried to judge whether they had stood so for so many years; there was little dust at this elevation, and in the end I could not be certain. When we had completed our inspection, I told the boy to let me go first, and stepped inside.

Nothing happened. Even when the boy followed me, the doors did not close, no enemy rushed at us, no energy colored the air, and the floor remained firm beneath our feet. Nevertheless, I had the feeling that we had somehow entered a trap: that outside on the mountain we had been free, however hungry and thirsty we were, and that here we were free no longer. I think I would have turned and run if he had not been with me. As it was, I did not want to appear superstitious or afraid, and I felt an obligation to try to find food and water.

There were many devices in that building to which I can give no name. They were not furniture, nor boxes, nor machines as I understand the term. Most were oddly angled; I saw some that appeared to have niches in which to sit, though the sitter would have been cramped, and would have faced some part of the device instead of his companions. Others contained alcoves where someone might once, perhaps, have rested.

These devices stood beside aisles, wide aisles that ran toward the center of the structure as straight as the spokes of a wheel. Looking down the one we had entered, I could see, dimly, some red object, and upon it, much smaller, something brown. At first, I did not pay great attention to either, but when I had satisfied myself that the devices I have described were of no value and no danger to us, I led the boy toward them.

The red object was a sort of couch, a very elaborate one, with straps so that a prisoner might be confined upon it. Around it were mechanisms that seemed intended to provide for nourishment and elimination. It stood upon a small dais, and on it lay what had once been the body of a man with two heads. The thin, dry air of the mountain had desiccated that body long ago—like the mysterious buildings, it might have been a year old or a thousand. He had been a man taller than I, perhaps even an exultant, and powerfully muscled. Now I might, I thought, tear one of his arms from its socket with a gesture. He wore no loincloth, or any other garment, and though we are accustomed to sudden changes in the size of the organs of procreation, it was strange to see them so shriveled here. Some hair remained upon the heads, and it appeared to me that the hair of the right had been black; that of the head on the left was yellowish. The eyes of both were closed, and the mouths open, showing a few teeth. I noticed that the straps that might have bound this creature to the couch were not buckled.

At the time, however, I was far more concerned with the mechanism that had once fed him. I told myself that ancient machines were often astoundingly durable, and though it had long been abandoned, it had enjoyed the most favorable conditions for its preservation; and I twisted every dial I could find, and shifted each lever, in an attempt to make it produce some nutriment. The boy watched me, and when I had been moving things here and there for some time asked if we were going to starve.

"No," I told him. "We can go a great deal longer without food than you would think. Getting something to drink is a great deal more urgent, but if we can't find anything here, there is sure to be snow further up the mountain."

"How did he die?" For some reason I had never brought myself to touch the corpse; now the boy ran his plump fingers along one withered arm.

"Men die. The wonder is that such a monster lived. Such things usually perish at birth."

"Do you think the others left him here when they went away?" He asked.

"Left him here alive, you mean? I suppose they could have. There would have been no place for him, perhaps, in the lands below. Or perhaps he did not want to go. Maybe they confined him here on this couch when he misbehaved. Possibly he was subject to madness, or fits of violent rage. If any of those things are true, he must have spent his last days wandering over the mountain, returning here to eat and drink, and dying when the food and water he depended on were exhausted."

"Then there isn't any water in there," the boy said practically.

"That's true. Still, we don't know it happened like that. He may have died for some other reason before his supplies ran out. Then too, the kind of thing we've been saying would seem to assume that he was a sort of pet or mascot for the people who carved the mountain. This is a very elaborate place in which to keep a pet. Just the same, I don't think I'm ever going to be able to reactivate this machine."

"I think we ought to go down," the boy announced as we were leaving the circular building.

I turned to look behind us, thinking how foolish all my fears had been. Its doors remained open; nothing had moved, nothing had changed. If it had ever been a trap, it seemed certain it was a trap that had rusted open centuries before.

"So do I," I said. "But the day is nearly over—see how long our shadows are now. I don't want to be overtaken by the night when we're climbing down the other side, so I'm going to find out whether I can reach the ring we saw this morning. Perhaps we'll find water as well as gold. Tonight we'll sleep in that round building out of the wind, and tomorrow we'll start down the north side by the first light."

He nodded to show that he understood, and accompanied me willingly enough as I set off to look for a path to the ring. It had been on the southern arm, so that we were in some sense returning to the side we had first climbed, though we had approached the cluster of sculptured cataphracts and buildings from the southeast. I had feared that the ascent to the arm would be a difficult climb; instead, just where the vast height of the chest and upper arm rose before us, I found what I had been wishing for much earlier: a narrow stair. There were many hundreds of steps, so it was a weary climb still, and I carried the boy up much of it.

The arm itself was smooth stone, yet so wide there seemed to be little danger that the boy would fall off as long as we kept to the center. I made him hold my hand and strode along quite eagerly, my cloak snapping in the wind.

To our left lay the ascent we had begun the day before;

beyond it was the saddle between the mountains, green under its blanket of jungle. Beyond even that, hazy now with distance, rose the mountain where Becan and Casdoe had built their home. As I walked, I tried to distinguish their cabin, or at least the area in which it stood, and at last I found what seemed to me the cliff face I had descended to reach it, a tiny fleck of color on the side of that less lofty mountain, with the glint of the falling water in its center like an iridescent mote.

When I had seen it, I halted and turned to look up at the peak on whose slope we walked. I could see the face now and its mitre of ice, and below it the left shoulder, where a thousand cavalrymen might have been exercised by their chiliarch.

Ahead of me, the boy was pointing and shouting something I could not understand, pointing down toward the buildings and the standing figures of the metal guardsmen. It was a moment before I realized what he meant—their faces were turned three-quarters toward us, as they had been turned three-quarters toward us that morning. Their heads had moved. For the first time, I followed the direction of their eyes—and found that they were looking at the sun.

I nodded to the boy and called, "I see!"

We were on the wrist, with the little plain of the hand spread before us, broader and safer even than the arm. As I strode over it, the boy ran ahead of me. The ring was on the second finger, a finger larger than a log cut from the greatest tree. Little Severian ran out upon it, balancing himself without difficulty on the crest, and I saw him throw out his hands to touch the ring.

There was a flash of light—bright, yet not blindingly so in the afternoon sunshine; because it was tinted with violet, it seemed almost a darkness.

It left him blackened and consumed. For a moment, I think, he still lived; his head jerked back and his arms were flung wide. There was a puff of smoke, carried away at once by the wind. The body fell, its limbs contracting as the legs of a dead insect do, and rolled until it had tumbled out of sight in the crevice between the second and third fingers.

I, who had seen so many brandings and abacinations, and had even used the iron myself (among the billion things I recall perfectly is the flesh of Morwenna's cheeks blistering), could scarcely force myself to go and look at him.

There were bones there, in that narrow place between the fingers, but they were old bones that broke beneath my feet when I leaped down like the bones strewn upon the paths in our necropolis, and I did not trouble to examine them. I took out the Claw. When I had cursed myself for not using it when Thecla's body was brought forth at Vodalus's banquet, Jonas had told me not to be a fool, that whatever powers the Claw might possess could not possibly have restored life to that roasted flesh.

And I could not help but think that if it acted now and restored little Severian to me, for all my joy I would take him to some safe place and slash my own throat with *Terminus Est*. Because if the Claw would do that, it would have called Thecla back too, if only it had been used; and Thecla was a part of myself, now forever dead.

For a moment it seemed that there was a glimmering, a bright shadow or aura; then the boy's corpse crumbled to black ash that stirred in the unquiet air.

I stood, and put the Claw away, and began to walk back, vaguely wondering how much trouble I would have in leaving that narrow place and regaining the back of the hand. (In the end, I had to stand *Terminus Est* on the tip of her own blade and put one foot on a quillion to get up, then crawl back, head down, until I could grasp her pommel and pull her up after me.) There was no confusion of memory, but for a time a confusion of mind, in which the boy was merged in that other boy, Jader, who had lived with his dying sister in the jacal upon the cliff in Thrax. The one, who had come to mean so much to me, I could not save; the other, who had meant little, I had cured. In some way, it seemed to me they were the same boy. No doubt that was merely some protective reaction of my mind, a shelter it sought from the storm of madness; but it seemed to me somehow that so long as Jader lived, the boy his mother had named Severian could not truly perish.

I had meant to halt upon the hand and look back; I could not—the truth is that I feared I would go to the edge and throw myself over. I did not actually stop until I had nearly regained the narrow stair that led down so many hundreds of steps to the broad lap of the mountain. Then I seated myself and once more found that fleck of color that was the cliff below which Casdoe's home had stood. I remembered the barking of the brown dog as I had come through the forest toward it. He had been a coward, that dog, when the alzabo came, but he had died with his teeth in the defiled flesh of a zoanthrop, while I, a coward too, had hung back. I remembered Casdoe's tired, lovely face, the boy peeping from behind her skirt, the way the old man had sat cross-legged with his back to the fire, talking of Fechin. They were all dead now, Severa and Becan, whom I had never seen; the old man, the dog, Casdoe, now little Severian, even Fechin, all dead, all lost in the mists that obscure our days. Time itself is a thing, so it seems to me, that stands solidly like a fence of iron palings with its endless row of years; and we flow past like Gyoll, on our way to a sea from which we shall return only as rain.

I knew then, on the arm of that giant figure, the ambition to conquer time, an ambition beside which the desire of the distant suns is only the lust of some petty, feathered chieftain to subjugate some other tribe.

There I sat until the sun was nearly hidden by the rising of the mountains in the west. It should have been easier to descend the stair than it had been to climb it, but I was very thirsty now, and the jolt of each step hurt my knees. The light was nearly gone, and the wind like ice. One blanket had been burned with the boy; I unfolded the other and wrapped my chest and shoulders in it under my cloak.

When I was perhaps halfway down, I paused to rest. Only a thin crescent of reddish brown remained of the day. That narrowed, then vanished; and as it did, each of the great metal cataphracts below me raised a hand in salute. So quiet they were, and so steady, that I could almost have believed them sculptured with lifted arms, as I saw them.

For a time the wonder of it washed all my sorrow from me, and I could only marvel. I remained where I was, staring at them, not daring to move. Night rushed across the mountains; in the last, dim twilight I watched the mighty arms come down.

Still dazed, I reentered the silent cluster of buildings that stood in the figure's lap. If I had seen one miracle fail, I had witnessed another; and even a seemingly purposeless miracle is an inexhaustible source of hope, because it proves to us that since we do not understand everything, our defeats—so much more numerous than our few and empty victories—may be equally specious.

By some idiotic error, I contrived to lose my way when I tried to return to the circular building where I had told the boy we would spend the night, and I was too fatigued to search for it. Instead I found a sheltered spot well away from the nearest metal guardsman, where I rubbed my aching legs and wrapped myself against the cold as well as I could. Although I must have fallen asleep almost at once, I was soon awakened by the sound of soft footsteps.

XXV

Typhon and Piaton

WHEN I HEARD the footsteps, I had risen and drawn my sword, and I waited in a shadow for what seemed a watch at least, though it was no doubt much less. Twice more I heard them, quick and soft, yet somehow suggestive of a large man—a powerful man hurrying, almost running, light-footed and athletic.

Here the stars were in all their glory; as bright as they must be seen by the sailors whose ports they are, when they go aloft to spread the golden gauze that would wrap a continent. I could see the motionless guardsmen almost as if by day, and the buildings around me, bathed in the many-colored lights of ten thousand suns. We think with horror of the frozen plains of Dis, the outermost companion of our sun—but of how many suns are we the outermost companion? To the people of Dis (if such exist) it is all one long, starry night.

Several times, standing there under the stars, I nearly slept; and at the borders of sleep I worried about the boy, thinking that I had probably awakened him when I rose and wondering where I should find food for him when the sun could be seen again. After such thoughts, the memory of his death would come to my mind as night had come to the mountain, a wave of blackness and despair. I knew then how Dorcas had felt when Jolenta died. There had been no sexual play between the boy and me, as I believe there had at some time been between Dorcas and Jolenta; but then it had never been their fleshly love that had aroused my jealousy. The depth of my feeling for the boy had been as great as Dorcas's for Jolenta, surely (and surely greater far than Jolenta's for Dorcas). If Dorcas had known of it, she would have been as jealous as I had sometimes been, I thought, if only she had loved me as I had loved her.

At last, when I heard the footsteps no longer, I concealed myself as well as I could and lay down and slept. I half expected I would not wake from that sleep, or that I would wake with a knife at my throat, but no such thing happened. Dreaming of water, I slept well past the dawn and woke alone, cold and stiff in every limb.

I cared nothing then for the secret of the footsteps, or the guardsmen, or the ring, or for anything else in that accursed place. My only wish was to leave it, and as quickly as possible; and I was delighted—though I could not have explained why—when I found that I would not have to repass the circular building on my way to the northwestern side of the mountain.

There have been many times when I have felt I have gone mad, for I have had many great adventures, and the greatest adventures are those that act most strongly upon our minds. So it was then. A man, larger than I and far broader of shoulder, stepped from between the feet of a cataphract, and it was as though one of the monstrous constellations of the night sky had fallen to Urth and clothed itself in the flesh of humankind. For the man had two heads, like an ogre in some forgotten tale in *The Wonders of Urth and Sky*.

Instinctively, I put my hand on the sword hilt at my shoulder. One of the heads laughed; I think it was the only laughter I was ever to hear at the baring of that great blade.

"Why are you alarmed?" he called. "I see you are as well equipped as I am. What is your friend's name?"

Even in my surprise, I admired his boldness. "She is *Terminus Est*," I said, and I turned the sword so he could see the writing on the steel.

" 'This is the place of parting.' Very good. Very good indeed, and particularly good that it should be read here and now, because this time will truly be a line between old and new such as the world has not seen. My own friend's name is Piaton, which I fear means nothing much. He is an inferior servant to that you have, though perhaps a better steed."

Hearing its name, the other head opened wide its eyes, which had been half closed, and rolled them. Its mouth moved as though to speak, but no sound emerged. I thought it a species of idiot.

"But now you may put up your weapon. As you see, I am unarmed, though already be-headed, and in any case, I mean you no hurt."

He raised his hands as he spoke, and turned to one side and then the other, so that I might see that he was entirely naked, something that was already clear enough.

I asked, "Are you perhaps the son of the dead man I saw in the round building back there?"

I had sheathed *Terminus Est* as I spoke, and he took a step nearer, saying, "Not at all. I am the man himself."

Dorcas rose in my thoughts as if through the brown waters of the Lake of Birds, and I felt again her dead hand clutch mine. Before I knew that I was speaking, I blurted, "I restored you to life?"

"Say rather that your coming awakened me. You thought me dead when I was only dry. I drank, and as you see, I live again. To drink is to live, to be bathed in water is to have a new birth."

"If what you tell me is true, it is wonderful. But I am too

much in need of water myself to think much about it now. You say that you have drunk, and the way you say it implies at least that you're friendly toward me. Prove it, please. I haven't eaten or drunk for a long time."

The head that spoke smiled. "You have the most marvelous way of falling in with whatever I plan—there is an appropriateness about you, even to your clothing, that I find delightful. I was just about to suggest that we go where there is food and drink in plenty. Follow me."

At that time, I think I would have followed anyone who promised me water anywhere. Since then I have tried to convince myself that I went out of curiosity, or because I hoped to learn the secret of the great cataphracts; but when I recall those moments and search my mind as it was then, I find nothing other than despair and thirst. The waterfall above Casdoe's house wove its silver columns before my eyes, and I remembered the Vatic Fountain of the House Absolute, and the rush of water from the cliff top in Thrax when I opened the sluice gate to flood the Vincula.

The two-headed man walked before me as if he were confident I would follow him, and equally confident that I would not attack him. When we rounded a corner, I realized for the first time that I had not been, as I had thought, on one of the radiating streets that led to the circular building. It stood before us now. A door—though it was not the one through which little Severian and I had passed—was open as before, and we entered.

"Here," the head that spoke said. "Get in."

The thing toward which he gestured was like a boat, and padded everywhere within as the nenuphar boat in the Autarch's garden had been; yet it floated not on water but in air. When I touched the gunwale, the boat rocked and bobbed beneath my hand, though the motion was almost too small to be seen. I said, "This must be a flyer. I've never seen one so close before."

"If a flyer were a swallow, this would be—I don't know—a

sparrow, perhaps. Or a mole, or the toy bird that children strike with paddles to make it fly back and forth between them. Courtesy, I fear, demands that you enter first. I assure you there is no danger."

Still, I hung back. There seemed something so mysterious about that vessel that for the moment I could not bring myself to set foot in it. I said, "I come from Nessus and from the eastern bank of Gyoll, and we were taught there that the place of honor in any craft is to be the last to enter and the first to leave."

"Precisely," the head that spoke replied, and before I realized what was happening, the two-headed man seized me about the waist and tossed me into the boat as I might have tossed the boy. It dipped and rolled under the impact of my body, and a moment later yawed violently as the two-headed man sprang in beside me. "You didn't think, I hope, that you were to take precedence over me?"

He whispered something and the vessel began to move. It glided forward slowly at first, but it was picking up speed.

"True courtesy," he continued, "earns the name. It is courtesy that is truthful. When the plebeian kneels to the monarch, he is offering his neck. He offers it because he knows his ruler can take it if he wishes. Common people like that say— or rather, they used to say, in older and better times—that I have no love of truth. But the truth is that it is precisely truth that I love, an open acknowledgment of fact."

All this time we were lying at full length, with hardly the width of a hand between us. The idiotic head the other had called Piaton goggled at me and moved its lips as he spoke, making a confused mumbling.

I tried to sit up. The two-headed man caught me with an arm of iron and pulled me down again, saying, "It's dangerous. These things were built to lie in. You wouldn't want to lose your head, would you? It's nearly as bad, believe me, as getting an extra one."

The boat nosed down and plunged into the dark. For a moment I thought we were going to die, but the sensation became one of exhilarating speed, the kind of feeling I had known as a boy when we used to slide on evergreen boughs among the mausoleums in winter. When I had become somewhat accustomed to it, I asked, "Were you born as you are? Or was Piaton actually thrust upon you in some way?" Already, I think, I had begun to realize that my life would depend on finding out as much as I could about this strange being.

The head that spoke laughed. "My name is Typhon. You might as well call me by it. Have you heard of me? Once I ruled this planet, and many more."

I was certain he lied, so I said, "Rumors of your might echo still . . . Typhon."

He laughed again. "You were on the point of calling me Imperator or something of the sort, weren't you? You shall yet. No, I was not born as I am, or born at all, as you meant it. Nor was Piaton grafted to me. I was grafted to him. What do you think of that?"

The boat moved so rapidly now that the air was whistling above our heads, but the descent seemed less steep than it had been. As I spoke, it became nearly level. "Did you wish it?"

"I commanded it."

"Then I think it very strange. Why should you desire to have such a thing done?"

"That I might have life, of course." It was too dark now for me to see either face, though Typhon's was less than a cubit from my own. "All life acts to preserve its life—that is what we call the Law of Existence. Our bodies, you see, die long before we do. In fact, it would be fair to say that we only die because they do. My physicians, of whom I naturally had the best of many worlds, told me it might be possible for me to take a new body, their first thought being to enclose my brain in the skull previously occupied by another. You see the flaw in that?"

Wondering if he were serious, I said, "No, I'm afraid I do not."

"The face—the face! The face would be lost, and it is the face that men are accustomed to obey!" His hand gripped my arm in the dark. "I told them it wouldn't do. Then one came who suggested that the entire head might be substituted. It would even be easier, he said, because the complex neural connections controlling speech and vision would be left intact. I promised him a palatinate if he should succeed."

"It would appear to me—" I began.

Typhon laughed once more. "That it would be better if the original head were removed first. Yes, I always thought so myself. But the technique of making the neural connections was difficult, and he found that the best way—all this was with experimental subjects I provided for him—was to transfer only the voluntary functions by surgery. When that was done, the involuntary ones transferred themselves, eventually. Then the original head could be removed. It would leave a scar, of course, but a shirt would cover it."

"But something went wrong?" I had already moved as far from him as I could in the narrow boat.

"Mostly it was a matter of time." The terrible vigor of his voice, which had been unrelenting, now seemed to wane. "Piaton was one of my slaves—not the largest, but the strongest of all. We tested them. It never occurred to me that someone with his strength might be strong, too, in holding to the action of the heart . . ."

"I see," I said, though in truth I saw nothing.

"It was a period of great confusion as well. My astronomers had told me that this sun's activity would decay slowly. Far too slowly, in fact, for the change to be noticeable in a human lifetime. They were wrong. The heat of the world declined by nearly two parts in a thousand over a few years, then stabilized. Crops failed, and there were famines and riots. I should have left then."

"Why didn't you?" I asked.

"I felt a firm hand was needed. There can only be one firm hand, whether it is the ruler's or someone else's . . .

"Then too, a wonder-worker had arisen, as such people do. He wasn't really a troublemaker, though some of my ministers said he was. I had withdrawn here until my treatment should be complete, and since diseases and deformities seemed to flee from him, I ordered him brought to me."

"The Conciliator," I said, and a moment later could have opened my own wrist for it.

"Yes, that was one of his names. Do you know where he is now?"

"He has been dead for many chiliads."

"And yet he remains, I think?"

That remark startled me so that I looked down at the sack suspended from my neck to see if azure light were not escaping from it.

At that moment, the vessel in which we rode lifted its prow and began to ascend. The moaning of the air about us became the roaring of a whirlwind.

XXVI

The Eyes of the World

PERHAPS THE BOAT was controlled by light—when light flashed about us, it stopped at once. In the lap of the mountain I had suffered from the cold, but that was nothing to what I felt now. No wind blew, but it was colder than the bitterest winter I could recall, and I grew dizzy with the effort of sitting up.

Typhon sprang out. "It's been a long time since I was here last. Well, it's good to be home again."

We were in an empty chamber hewn from solid rock, a place as big as a ballroom. Two circular windows at the far end admitted the light; Typhon hastened toward them. They were perhaps a hundred paces apart, and each was some ten cubits wide. I followed him until I noticed that his bare feet left distinct, dark prints. Snow had drifted through the windows and spilled upon the stone floor. I fell to my knees, scooped it up, and stuffed my mouth with it.

I have never tasted anything so delicious. The heat of my tongue seemed to melt it to nectar at once; I truly felt that I could remain where I was all my life, on my knees devouring the snow. Typhon turned back, and seeing me, laughed. "I had forgotten how thirsty you were. Go ahead. We have plenty of time. What I wanted to show you can wait."

Piaton's mouth moved too as it had before, and I thought I caught an expression of sympathy on the idiot face. That brought me to myself again, possibly only because I had already gulped several mouthfuls of the melting snow. When I had swallowed again, I remained where I was, scraping a new heap together, but I said, "You told me about Piaton. Why can't he speak?"

"He can't get his breath, poor fellow," Typhon said. Now I saw that he had an erection, which he nursed with one hand. "As I told you, I control all the voluntary functions—I will control the involuntary ones too, soon. So although poor Piaton can still move his tongue and shape his lips, he is like a musician who fingers the keys of a horn he cannot blow. When you've had enough of that snow, tell me, and I'll show you where you can get something to eat."

I filled my mouth again and swallowed. "This is enough. Yes, I am very hungry."

"Good," he said, and turning away from the windows went to the wall at one side of the chamber. When I neared it, I saw that it, at least, was not (as I had thought) plain stone. Instead, it seemed a kind of crystal, or thick, smoky glass; through it I could see loaves and many strange dishes, as still and perfect as food in a painting.

"You have a talisman of power," Typhon told me. "Now you must give it to me, so that we can open this cupboard."

"I'm afraid I don't understand what you mean. Do you want my sword?"

"I want the thing you wear at your neck," he said, and stretched out a hand for it.

I stepped back. "There is no power in it."

"Then you lose nothing. Give it to me." As Typhon spoke, Piaton's head moved almost imperceptibly from side to side.

"It is only a curio," I said. "Once I thought it had great

power, but when I tried to revive a beautiful woman who was dying, it had no effect, and yesterday it could not restore the boy who traveled with me. How did you know of it?"

"I was watching you, of course. I climbed high enough to see you well. When my ring killed the child and you went to him, I saw the sacred fire. You don't have to actually put it in my hand if you don't want to—just do what I tell you."

"You could have warned us, then," I said.

"Why should I? At that time you were nothing to me. Do you want to eat or not?"

I took out the gem. After all, Dorcas and Jonas had seen it, and I had heard the Pelerines had displayed it in a monstrance on great occasions. It lay on my palm like a bit of blue glass, all fire gone.

Typhon leaned over it curiously. "Hardly impressive. Now kneel."

I knelt.

"Repeat after me: I swear by all this talisman represents that for the food I shall receive, I shall be the creature of him I know as Typhon, evermore—"

A snare was closing beside which Decuman's net was a primitive first attempt. This one was so subtle I scarcely knew it was there, and yet I sensed that every strand was of hard-drawn steel.

"—rendering to him all I have and all I shall be, what I own now and what I shall own in days to come, living or dying at his pleasure."

"I have broken oaths before," I said. "If I took it, I should break that one."

"Then take it," he said. "It is no more than a form we must follow. Take it, and I can release you as soon as you have finished eating."

I stood instead. "You said you loved truth. Now I see why— it is truth that binds men." I put the Claw away.

If I had not done so, it would have been lost forever a

moment later. Typhon seized me, pinning my arms to my sides so I could not draw *Terminus Est,* and ran with me to one of the windows. I struggled, but it was as a puppy struggles in the hands of a strong man.

As we approached it, the great size of the window made it seem not a window at all; it was as though a part of the outer world had intruded itself into the chamber, and it was a part consisting not of the fields and trees at the mountain's base, which was what I had expected, but of mere extension, a fragment of the sky. The chamber's rock wall, less than a cubit thick, floated backward at the corner of my vision like the muddled line we see, swimming with open eyes, that is the demarcation between the water and the air.

Then I was outside. Typhon's hold had shifted to my ankles, but whether because of the thickness of my boots or merely because of my panic, for a moment I felt I was not held at all. My back was to the mass of the mountain. The Claw, in its soft bag, dangled below my head, held by my chin. I remember feeling a sudden, absurd fear that *Terminus Est* would slip from her sheath.

I pulled myself up with my belly muscles, as a gymnast does when he hangs from the bar by his feet. Typhon released one of my ankles to strike my mouth with his fist, so that I fell back again. I cried out, and tried to wipe my eyes clear of the blood trickling into them from my lips.

The temptation to draw my sword, raise myself again, and strike with it was almost too great to resist. Yet I knew that I could not do so without giving Typhon ample time to see what I intended and let me fall. Even if I succeeded, I would die.

"I urge you now . . ." Typhon's voice came above me, seeming distant in that golden immensity. ". . . to require of your talisman such help as it can provide you."

He paused, and every moment seemed Eternity itself.

"Can it aid you?"

I managed to call, "No."

"Do you understand where you are?"

"I saw. On the face. The mountain autarch."

"It is my face—did you see that? I was the autarch. It is I who come again. You are at my eyes, and it is the iris of my right eye that is to your back. Do you comprehend? You are a tear, a single black tear I weep. In an instant, I may let you fall away to stain my garment. Who can save you, Talisman-bearer?"

"You. Typhon."

"Only I?"

"Only Typhon."

He pulled me back up, and I clung to him as the boy had once clung to me, until we were well inside the great chamber that was the cranial cavity of the mountain.

"Now," he said, "we will make one more attempt. You must come with me to the eye again, and this time you must go willingly. Perhaps it will be easier for you if we go to the left eye instead of the right."

He took my arm. I suppose I could be said to have gone by my own will, since I walked; but I think I have never in my life walked with less heart. It was only the memory of my recent humiliation that kept me from refusing. We did not halt until we stood upon the very rim of the eye; then with a gesture, Typhon forced me to look out. Below us lay an ocean of undulating cloud, blue with shadow where it was not rose with sunlight.

"Autarch," I said, "how are we here, when the vessel in which we rode plunged down so long a tunnel?"

He shrugged my question aside. "Why should gravity serve Urth, when it can serve Typhon? Yet Urth is fair. Look! You see the robe of the world. Is it not beautiful?"

"Very beautiful," I agreed.

"It can be your robe. I have told you that I was autarch on many worlds. I shall be autarch again, and this time on many more. This world, the most ancient of all, I made my capital.

That was an error, because I lingered too long when disaster came. By the time I would have escaped, escape was no longer open to me—those to whom I had given control of such ships as could reach the stars had fled in them, and I was besieged on this mountain. I shall not make that mistake again. My capital will be elsewhere, and I will give this world to you, to rule as my steward."

I said, "I have done nothing to deserve so exalted a position."

"Talisman-bearer, no one, not even you, can require me to justify my acts. Instead, view your empire."

Far below us, a wind was born as he spoke. The clouds seethed under its lash and gathered themselves like soldiers into serried ranks moving eastward. Beneath them I saw mountains, and the coastal plains, and beyond the plains the faint, blue line of the sea.

"Look!" Typhon pointed, and as he did so, a pinprick of light appeared in the mountains to the northeast. "Some great energy weapon has been used there," he said. "Perhaps by the ruler of this age, perhaps by his foes. Whichever it may be, its location is revealed now, and it will be destroyed. The armies of this age are weak. They will fly before our flails as chaff at the harvest."

"How can you know all this?" I asked. "You were as dead, until my son and I came upon you."

"Yes. But I have lived almost a day and have sent my thought into far places. There are powers in the seas now who would rule. They will become our slaves, and the hordes of the north are theirs."

"What of the people of Nessus?" I was chilled to the bone; my legs trembled under me.

"Nessus shall be your capital, if you wish it. From your throne in Nessus you will send me tribute of fair women and boys, of the ancient devices and books, and all the good things this world of Urth produces."

He pointed again. I saw the gardens of the House Absolute

like a shawl of green and gold cast upon a lawn, and beyond it the Wall of Nessus, and the mighty city itself, the City Imperishable, spreading for so many hundreds of leagues that even the towers of the Citadel were lost in that endless expanse of roofs and winding streets.

"No mountain is so high," I said. "If this one were the greatest in all the world, and if it stood upon the crown of the second greatest, a man could never see as far as I do now."

Typhon took me by the shoulder. "This mountain is as lofty as I wish it to be. Have you forgotten whose face it bears?"

I could only stare at him.

"Fool," he said. "You see through my eyes. Now get out your talisman. I will have your oath upon it."

I drew forth the Claw—for the last time, as I thought—from the leathern bag Dorcas had sewn for it. As I did, there was some slight stirring far below me. The sight of the world from out of the window of the chamber was still grand beyond imagining, but it was only what a man might discern from a mighty peak: the blue dish of Urth. Through the clouds below I could glimpse the lap of the mountain, with many rectangular buildings, the circular building in the center, and the cataphracts. Slowly they were turning their faces away from the sun, upward, to look at us.

"They honor me," Typhon said. Piaton's mouth moved too, but not with his. This time I heeded it.

"You were at the other eye, previously," I told Typhon, "and they did not honor you then. They salute the Claw. Autarch, what of the New Sun, if at last he comes? Will you be his enemy too, as you were the enemy of the Conciliator?"

"Swear to me, and believe me, when he comes I shall be his master, and he my most abject slave."

I struck then.

There is a way of smashing the nose with the heel of one's hand so that the splintered bone is driven into the brain. One must be very quick, however, because without the need for thought a man will lift his hands to protect his face when he sees the blow. I was not so swift as Typhon, but it was his own face his hands were thrown up to guard. I struck at Piaton, and felt the small and terrible cracking that is the sigil of death. The heart that had not served him for so many chiliads ceased to beat.

After a moment, I pushed Typhon's body over the drop with my foot.

XXVII

On High Paths

THE FLOATING BOAT would not obey me, for I had not the word for it. (I have often thought that its word may have been among the things Piaton had tried to tell me, as he had told me to take his life; and I wish I had come to heed him sooner.) In the end, I was forced to climb from the right eye— the worst climb of my life. In this overlong account of my adventures, I have said often that I forget nothing; but I have forgotten much of that, because I was so exhausted that I moved as though in sleep. When I staggered at last into the silent, sealed town that stood among the feet of the cataracts, it must have been nearly night, and I lay down beside a wall that gave me shelter from the wind.

There is a terrible beauty in the mountains, even when they bring one near to death; indeed, I think it is most evident then, and that the hunters who enter the mountains well clothed and well fed and leave them well fed and well clothed seldom see them. There all the world can seem a natural basin of clear water, still and icy cold.

I descended far that day, and found high plains that

stretched for leagues, plains filled with sweet grass and such flowers as are never seen at lower altitudes, flowers small and quick to bloom, perfect and pure as roses can never be.

These plains were bordered as often as not by cliffs. More than once I thought I could not go north anymore and would have to retrace my steps; but I always found a way in the end, up or down, and so pressed on. I saw no soldiers riding or marching below me, and though that was in some sense a relief—for I had been afraid the archon's patrol might still be tracking me—it was also unsettling, because it showed I was no longer near the routes by which the army was supplied.

The memory of the alzabo returned to haunt me; I knew that there must be many more of its kind in the mountains. Then too, I could not feel certain it was truly dead. Who could say what recuperative powers such a creature might possess? Though I could forget it by daylight, forcing it, so to speak, away from my consciousness with worries about the presence or absence of soldiers, and the thousand lovely images of peak and cataract and swooping valley that assailed my eyes on every side, it returned by night, when, huddled in my blanket and cloak and burning with fever, I believed I heard the soft padding of its feet, the scraping of its claws.

If as is often said, the world is ordered to some plan (whether one formed prior to its creation or one derived during the billion aeons of its existence by the inexorable logic of order and growth makes no difference) then in all things there must be both the miniature representation of higher glories and the enhanced depiction of smaller matters. To hold my circling attention from the recollection of its horror, I tried sometimes to fix it on that facet of the nature of the alzabo that permits it to incorporate the memories and wills of human beings into its own. The parallel to smaller matters gave me little difficulty. The alzabo might be likened to certain insects, that cover their bodies with twigs and bits of grass, so that they will not be discovered by their enemies. Seen in one way, there is no deception—the twigs, the fragments of leaves are there and are real. Yet the insect is within. So with the alzabo. When Becan, speaking through the creature's mouth, told me he wished his wife and the boy with him, he believed himself to be describing his own desires, and so he was; yet those desires would serve to feed the alzabo, who was within, whose needs and consciousness hid behind Becan's voice.

Not surprisingly, the problem of correlating the alzabo with some higher truth was more difficult; but at last I decided that it might be likened to the absorption by the material world of the thoughts and acts of human beings who, though no longer living, have so imprinted it with activities that in the wider sense we may call works of art, whether buildings, songs, battles, or explorations, that for some time after their demise it may be said to carry forward their lives. In just this fashion the child Severa suggested to the alzabo that it might shift the table in Casdoe's house to reach the loft, though the child Severa was no more.

I had Thecla, then, to advise me, and though I had little hope when I called on her, and she little advice to give, yet she had been warned often against the dangers of the mountains, and she urged me up and onward, and down, always down to lower lands and warmth, at the first light.

I hungered no longer, for hunger is a thing that passes if one does not eat. Weakness came instead, bringing with it a pristine clarity of mind. Then, in the evening of the second day after I had climbed from the pupil of the right eye, I came upon a shepherd's bothy, a sort of beehive of stone, and found in it a cooking pot and a quantity of ground corn.

A mountain spring was only a dozen steps away, but there was no fuel. I spent the evening collecting the abandoned nests of birds from a rock face a half league distant, and that night I struck fire from the tang of *Terminus Est* and boiled the coarse meal (which took a long time to cook, because of the altitude) and ate it. It was, I think, as good a dinner as I have ever tasted, and it had an elusive yet unmistakable flavor of honey, as if the nectar of the plant had been retained in the dry grains as the salt of seas that only Urth herself recalls is held within the cores of certain stones.

I was determined to pay for what I had eaten, and went through my sabretache looking for something of at least equal value that I might leave for the shepherd. Thecla's brown book I would not give up; I soothed my conscience by reminding myself that it was unlikely the shepherd could read in any case. Nor would I surrender my broken whetstone—both because it recalled the green man, and because it would be only a tawdry gift here, where stones nearly as good lay among the young grass on every side. I had no money, having left every coin I had possessed with Dorcas. At last I settled on the scarlet cape she and I had found in the mud of the stone town, long before we reached Thrax. It was stained and too thin to provide much warmth, but I hoped that the tassels and bright color would please him who had fed me.

I have never fully understood how it came to be where we found it, or even whether the strange individual who had called us to him so that he might have that brief period of renewed life had left it behind intentionally or accidentally when the rain dissolved him again to that dust he had been for so long. The ancient sisterhood of priestesses beyond question possesses powers it seldom or never uses, and it is not absurd to suppose that such raising of the dead is among them. If that is so, he may have called them to him as he called us, and the cape may have been left behind by accident.

Yet even if that is so, some higher authority may have been served. It is in such fashion most sages explain the apparent paradox that though we freely choose to do this or the other, commit some crime or by altruism steal the sacred distinction of the Empyrian, still the Increate commands the entirety and is served equally (that is, totally) by those who would obey and those who would rebel.

Not only this. Some, whose arguments I have read in the

brown book and several times discussed with Thecla, have pointed out that fluttering in the Presence there abide a multitude of beings that though appearing minute—indeed, infinitely small—by comparison are correspondingly vast in the eyes of men, to whom their master is so gigantic as to be invisible. (By this unlimited size he is rendered minute, so that we are in relation to him like those who walk upon a continent but see only forests, bogs, hills of sand, and so on, and though feeling, perhaps, some tiny stones in their shoes, never reflect that the land they have overlooked all their lives is there, walking with them.)

There are other sages too, who doubting the existence of that power these beings, who may be called the amschaspands, are said to serve, nonetheless assert the fact of their existence. Their assertions are based not on human testimony—of which there is much and to which I add my own, for I saw such a being in the mirror-paged book in the chambers of Father Inire—but rather on irrefutable theory, for they say that if the universe was not created (which they, for reasons not wholly philosophical, find it convenient to disbelieve), then it must have existed forever to this day. And if it has so existed, time itself extends behind the present day without end, and in such a limitless ocean of time, all things conceivable must of necessity have come to pass. Such beings as the amschaspands are conceivable, for they, and many others, have conceived of them. But if creatures so mighty once entered existence, how should they be destroyed? Therefore they are still extant.

Thus by the paradoxical nature of knowledge, it is seen that though the existence of the Ylem, the primordial source of all things, may be doubted, yet the existence of his servants may not be doubted.

And as such beings certainly exist, may it not be that they interfere (if it can be called interference) in our affairs by such accidents as that of the scarlet cape I left in the bothy? It does not require illimitable might to interfere with the internal economy of a nest of ants—a child can stir it with a stick. I know of no thought more terrible than this. (That of my own death, which is popularly supposed to be so awful as to be inconceivable, does not much trouble me; it is of my life that I find, perhaps because of the perfection of my memory, that I cannot think.)

Yet there is another explanation: It may be that all those who seek to serve the Theophany, and perhaps even all those who allege to serve him, though they appear to us to differ so widely and indeed to wage a species of war upon one another, are yet linked, like the marionettes of the boy and the man of wood that I once saw in a dream, and who, although they appeared to combat each other, were nevertheless under the control of an unseen individual who operated the strings of both. If this is the case, then the shaman we saw may have been the friend and ally of those priestesses who range so widely in their civilization across the same land where he, in primitive savagery, once sacrificed with liturgical rigidity of drum and crotal in the small temple of the stone town.

In the last light of the day after I slept in the shepherd's bothy, I came to the lake called Diuturna. It was that, I think, and not the sea, that I had seen on the horizon before my mind was enchained by Typhon's—if indeed my encounter with Typhon and Piaton was not a vision or a dream, from which I awoke of necessity at the spot where I began it. Yet Lake Diuturna is nearly a sea itself, for it is sufficiently vast to be incomprehensible to the mind; and it is the mind, after all, that creates the resonances summoned by that word—without the mind there is only a fraction of Urth covered with brackish water. Though this lake lies at an altitude substantially higher than that of the true sea, I spent the greater part of the afternoon descending to its shore.

The walk was a remarkable experience, and one I treasure

even now, perhaps the most beautiful I can recall, though I now hold in my mind the experiences of so many men and women, for as I descended I strode through the year. When I left the bothy, I had above me, behind me, and to my right great fields of snow and ice, through which showed dark crags colder even than they, crags too wind-swept to retain the snow, which sifted down to melt on the tender meadow grass I trod, the grass of earliest spring. As I walked, the grass grew coarser, and of a more virile green. The sounds of insects, of which I am seldom conscious unless I have not heard them in some time, resumed, with a noise that reminded me of the tuning of the strings in the Blue Hall before the first cantilena began, a noise I sometimes used to listen to when I lay on my pallet near the open port of the apprentices' dormitory.

Bushes, which for all their appearance of wiry strength had not been able to endure the heights where the tender grasses lived, appeared now; but when I examined them with care, I found that they were not bushes at all, but plants I had known as towering trees, stunted here by the shortness of the summer and the savagery of the winter, and often split by that ill use into severe straggling trunks. In one of these dwarfed trees, I found a thrush upon a nest, the first bird I had seen in some time except for the soaring raptors of the peaks. A league farther on, and I heard the whistling of cavies, who had their holes among the rocky outcrops, and who thrust up brindled heads with sharp black eyes to warn their relatives of my coming.

A league farther on, and a rabbit went skipping ahead of me in dread of the whirling astara I did not possess. I was descending rapidly at this point, and I became aware of how much strength I had lost, not only to hunger and illness, but to the thinness of the air. It was as though I had been afflicted with a second sickness, of which I had been unaware until the return of trees and real shrubs brought its cure.

At this point, the lake was no longer a line of misted blue; I could see it as a great and almost featureless expanse of steely water, dotted by a few boats I was later to learn were built for the most part of reeds, with a perfect little village at the end of a bay only slightly to the right of my present line of travel.

Just as I had not known my weakness, until I saw the boats and the rounded curves of the thatched roofs of the village I had not known how solitary I had been since the boy died. It was more than mere loneliness, I think. I have never had much need for companionship, unless it was the companionship of someone I could call a friend. Certainly I have seldom wished the conversation of strangers or the sight of strange faces. I believe rather that when I was alone I felt I had in some fashion lost my individuality; to the thrush and the rabbit I had been not Severian, but Man. The many people who like to be utterly alone, and particularly to be utterly alone in a wilderness, do so, I believe, because they enjoy playing that part. But I wanted to be a particular person again, and so I sought the mirror of other persons, which would show me that I was not as they were.

XXVIII

The Hetman's Dinner

IT WAS NEARLY evening before I reached the first houses. The sun spread a path of red gold across the lake, a path that appeared to extend the village street to the margin of the world, so that a man might have walked down it and out into the larger universe. But the village itself, small and poor though I saw it to be when I reached it, was good enough for me, who had been walking so long in high and remote places.

There was no inn, and since none of the people who peered at me over the sills of their windows seemed at all eager to admit me, I asked for the hetman's house, pushed aside the fat woman who answered the door, and made myself comfortable. By the time the hetman arrived to see who had appointed himself his guest, I had my broken stone and my oil out and was leaning over the blade of *Terminus Est* as I warmed myself before his fire. He began by bowing, but he was so curious about me that he could not resist looking up as he bowed; so that I had difficulty in refraining from laughing at him, which would have been fatal to my plans.

"The optimate is welcome," the hetman said, blowing out his wrinkled cheeks. "Most welcome. My poor house—all our poor little settlement—is at his disposal."

"I am not an optimate," I told him. "I am the Grand Master Severian, of the Order of the Seekers for Truth and Penitence, commonly called the guild of torturers. You, Hetman, will address me as *Master*. I have had a difficult journey, and if you will provide me with a good dinner and a tolerable bed, it is not likely I will have to trouble you or your people for much else before morning."

"You will have my own bed," he said quickly. "And such food as we can provide."

"You must have fresh fish here, and waterfowl. I'll have both. Wild rice, too." I remembered that once, when Master Gurloes was discussing our guild's relations with the others in the Citadel, he had told me that one of the easiest ways to dominate a man is to demand something he cannot supply. "Honey, new bread, and butter should do it, except for the vegetable and the salad, and since I'm not particular about those, I will let you surprise me. Something good, and something I haven't had before, so that I'll have a tale to carry back to the House Absolute."

The hetman's eyes had been growing rounder and rounder as I spoke, and at the mention of the House Absolute, which was doubtless no more than the most distant of rumors in his village, they seemed about to pop out of his skull. He tried to murmur something about cattle (presumably that they could not live to supply butter at these altitudes) but I waved him out, then caught him by the scruff of the neck for not closing the door behind him.

When he was gone, I risked taking off my boots. It never pays to appear relaxed around prisoners (and he and his village were mine now, I thought, though they were not confined), but I felt sure no one would dare enter the room until some sort of meal was ready. I finished cleaning and oiling *Terminus Est*, and gave her enough strokes with the whetstone to restore her edges.

That done, I withdrew my other treasure (though it was not in fact mine) from its bag and examined it in the light of the hetman's pungent fire. Since I had left Thrax it no longer pressed against my chest like a finger of iron—indeed, while I tramped in the mountains I had sometimes forgotten for half a day that I wore it, and once or twice I had clasped it in panic, thinking, when I recalled it at last, that I had lost it. In this low-ceilinged, square room of the hetman's, where the rounded stones in the walls seemed to warm their bellies like burgesses, it did not flash as it had in the one-eyed boy's jacal; but neither was it so lifeless as it had been when I showed it to Typhon. Now, rather, it seemed to glow, and I could almost have imagined that its energies played upon my face. The crescent-shaped mark in its heart had never appeared more distinct, and though it was dark, a star-point of light emanated from it.

I put away the gem at last, a little ashamed of having toyed with so entheal a thing as if it were a bauble. I took out the brown book and would have read from it if I could; but though my fever seemed to have left me, I was still very fatigued, and the flickering firelight made the cramped, old-fashioned letters dance on the page and soon defeated my eyes, so that the story I was reading appeared at some times to be no more than nonsense, and at others to deal with my own concerns—endless journeyings, the cruelty of crowds, streams running with blood. Once I thought I saw Agia's name, but when I looked a second time it had become the word *again:* "Agia she leaped, and twisting round the columns of the carapace . . ."

The page seemed luminous yet indecipherable, like the reflection of a looking glass seen in a quiet pool. I closed the book and put it back in my sabretache, not certain I had in fact seen any of the words I had thought an instant ago I had read. Agia must indeed have leaped from the thatched roof of Casdoe's house. Certainly she twisted, for she had twisted the execution of Agilus into murder. The great tortoise that in myth is said to support the world and is thus an embodiment of the galaxy, without whose swirling order we would be a lonely wanderer in space, is supposed to have revealed in ancient times the Universal Rule, since lost, by which one might always be sure of acting rightly. Its carapace represented the bowl of heaven, its plastron the plains of all the worlds. The columns of the carapace would then be the armies of the Theologoumenon, terrible and gleaming . . .

Yet I was not sure I had read any of this, and when I took out the book again and tried to find the page, I could not. Though I knew my confusion was only the result of fatigue, hunger, and the light, I felt the fear that has always come upon me on the many occasions of my life when some small incident has made me aware of an incipient insanity. As I stared into the fire, it seemed more possible than I would have liked to believe that someday, perhaps after a blow on the head, perhaps for no discernible cause, my imagination and my reason might reverse their places—just as two friends who come every day to the same seats in some public garden might at last decide for novelty's sake to exchange them. Then I would see as if in actuality all the phantoms of my mind, and only perceive in that tenuous way in which we behold our fears and ambitions the people and things of the real world. These thoughts, occurring at this point in my narrative, must seem prescient; I can only excuse them by saying that tormented as I am by my memories, I have meditated in the same way very often.

A faint knock at the door ended my morbid revery. I pulled on my boots and called, "Come in!"

A person who took care to remain out of my sight, though I am fairly sure it was the hetman, pushed back the door; and a young woman entered carrying a brass tray heaped with dishes. It was not until she set it down that I realized she was quite naked except for what I at first took to be rude jewelry, and not until she bowed, lifting her hands to her head in the northern fashion, that I saw that the dully shining bands

about her wrists, which I had taken for bracelets, were in fact
gyves of watered steel joined by a long chain.

"Your supper, Grand Master," she said, and backed toward
the door until I could see the flesh of her rounded hips flattened where they pressed against it. With one hand she attempted to lift the latch; but though I heard its faint rattle,
the door did not give. No doubt the person who had admitted her was holding it closed from the outside.

"It smells delicious," I told her. "Did you cook it yourself?"

"A few things. The fish, and the fried cakes."

I stood, and leaning *Terminus Est* against the rough ma-
sonry of the wall so as not to frighten her, went over to examine the meal: a young duck, quartered and grilled, the fish she
had mentioned, the cakes (which later proved to be of cattail
flour mixed with minced clams), potatoes baked in the em-
bers of a fire, and a salad of mushrooms and greens.

"No bread," I said. "No butter and no honey. They will
hear of this."

"We hoped, Grand Master, that the cakes would be acceptable."

"I realize it isn't your fault."

It had been a long time since I had lain with Cyriaca, and I
had been trying not to look at this slave girl, but I did so now.
Her long, black hair hung to her waist and her skin was nearly
the color of the tray she held, yet she had a slender waist, a
thing seldom found in autochthon women, and her face was
piquant and even a trifle sharp. Agia, for all her fair skin and
freckles, had broader cheeks by far.

"Thank you, Grand Master. He wants me to stay here to
serve you while you eat. If you do not want that, you must
tell him to open the door and let me out."

"I will tell him," I said, raising my voice, "to go away from
the door and cease eavesdropping on my conversation. You
are speaking of your owner, I suppose? Of the hetman of this
place?"

"Yes, of Zambdas."

"And what is your own name?"

"Pia, Grand Master."

"And how old are you, Pia?"

She told me, and I smiled to find her precisely the same age as myself.

"Now you must serve me, Pia. I'm going to sit over here at the fire, where I was before you came in, and you can bring me the food. Have you served at table before?"

"Oh, yes, Grand Master. I serve at every meal."

"Then you should know what you're doing. What do you recommend first—the fish?"

She nodded.

"Then bring that over, and the wine, and some of your cakes. Have you eaten?"

She shook her head until the black hair danced. "Oh, no, but it would not be right for me to eat with you."

"Still I notice I can count a good many ribs."

"I would be beaten for it, Grand Master."

"Not while I am here, at least. But I won't force you. Just the same, I would like to assure myself that they haven't put anything in any of this that I wouldn't give my dog, if I still had him. The wine would be the most likely place, I think. It will be rough but sweet, if it's like most country wines." I poured the stone goblet half full and handed it to her. "You drink that, and if you don't fall to the floor in fits, I'll try a drop too."

She had some difficulty in getting it down, but she did so at last and, with watering eyes, handed the goblet back to me. I poured some wine for myself and sipped it, finding it every bit as bad as I expected.

I made her sit beside me then, and fed her one of the fish she herself had fried in oil. When she had finished it, I ate a couple too. They were so much superior to the wine as her own delicate face was to the old hetman's—caught that day, I felt sure, and in water much colder and cleaner than the muddy lower reaches of Gyoll, from which the fish I had been accustomed to in the Citadel had come.

"Do they always chain slaves here?" I asked her as we divided the cakes. "Or have you been particularly unruly, Pia?"

She said, "I am of the lake people," as though that answered my question, as no doubt it would have if I had been familiar with the local situation.

"I would think these are the lake people." I gestured to indicate the hetman's house and the village in general.

"Oh, no. These are the shore people. Our people live in the lake, on the islands. But sometimes the wind blows our islands here, and Zambdas is afraid I will see my home then and swim to it. The chain is heavy—you can see how long it is—and I can't take it off. And so the weight would drown me."

"Unless you found a piece of wood to bear the weight while you paddled with your feet."

She pretended not to have heard me. "Would you like some duck, Grand Master?"

"Yes, but not until you eat some of it first, and before you have any, I want you to tell me more about those islands. Did you say the wind blew them here? I confess I have never heard of islands that were blown by the wind."

Pia was looking longingly toward the duck, which must have been a delicacy in that part of the world. "I have heard that there are islands that do not move. That must be very inconvenient, I suppose, and I have never seen any. Our islands travel from one place to another, and sometimes we put sails in their trees to make them go faster. But they will not sail across the wind very well, because they do not have wise bottoms like the bottoms of boats, but foolish bottoms like the bottoms of tubs, and sometimes they turn over."

"I want to see your islands sometime, Pia," I told her. "I also want to get you back to them, since that seems to be where you want to go. I owe something to a man with a name much like yours, and so I'll try to do that before I leave this place. Meanwhile, you had better build up your strength with some of that duck."

She took a piece, and after she had swallowed a few mouthfuls began to peel off slivers for me that she fed me with her fingers. It was very good, still hot enough to steam and imbued with a delicate flavor suggestive of parsley, which perhaps came from some water plant on which these ducks fed; but it was also rich and somewhat greasy, and when I had eaten the better part of one thigh, I took a few bites of salad to clear my palate.

I think I ate some more of the duck after that, then a movement in the fire caught my eye. A fragment of almost-consumed wood glowing with heat had fallen from one of the logs into the ashes under the grate, but instead of lying there and becoming dim and eventually black, it seemed to straighten up, and in doing so became Roche, Roche with his fiery red hair turned to real flames, Roche holding a torch as he used to when we were boys and went to swim in the cistern beneath the Bell Keep.

It seemed so extraordinary to see him there, reduced to a glowing micromorph, that I turned to Pia to point him out to her. She appeared to have seen nothing; but Drotte, no taller than my thumb, was standing on her shoulder, half concealed in her flowing black hair. When I tried to tell her he was there, I heard myself speaking in a new tongue, hissing, grunting, and clicking. I felt no fear at any of this, only a detached wonder. I could tell that what I was saying was not human speech, and observe the horrified expression on Pia's face as though I were contemplating some ancient painting in old Rudisind's gallery in the Citadel; yet I could not turn my noises into words, or even halt them. Pia screamed.

The door flew open. It had been closed for so long that I had almost forgotten it could not be locked; but it was open now, and two figures stood there. When the door opened they were men, men whose faces had been replaced by smooth pelts of fur like the backs of two otters, but men still. An instant later they had become plants, tall stalks of viridian from which protruded the razor-sharp, oddly angled leaves of the avern. Spiders, black and soft and many-legged, had been hiding there. I tried to rise from my chair, and they leaped at me trailing webs of gossamer that shone in the firelight. I had only time to see and remember Pia's face, with its wide eyes and its delicate mouth frozen in a circle of horror before a peregrine with a beak of steel stooped to tear the Claw from my neck.

XXIX

The Hetman's Boat

AFTER THAT I was locked in the dark for what I later found had been the night and the greater part of the following morning. Yet though it was dark where I lay, it was not at first dark to me, for my hallucinations needed no candle. I can recall them still, as I can recall everything; but I will not bore you, my ultimate reader, with the entire catalog of phantoms, though it would be easy enough for me to describe them here. What is not easy is the task of expressing my feelings concerning them.

It would have been a great relief for me to believe that they were all in some way contained in the drug I had swallowed (which was, as I guessed then and learned later, when I could question those who treated the wounded of the Autarch's army, nothing more than the mushrooms that had been chopped into my salad) just as Thecla's thoughts and Thecla's personality, comforting at times and troubling at others, had been contained in the fragment of her flesh I had eaten at Vodalus's banquet. Yet I knew it could not be so, and that all the things I saw, some amusing, some horrible and terrifying, some merely grotesque, were the product of my own mind. Or of Thecla's, which was now a part of my own.

Or rather, as I first began to realize there in the dark as I watched a parade of women from the court—exultants immensely tall and imbued with the stiff grace of costly porcelains, their complexions powdered with the dust of pearls or diamonds and their eyes made large as Thecla's had been by the application of minute amounts of certain poisons in childhood—products of the mind that now existed in the combination of the minds that had been hers and mine.

Severian, the apprentice I had been, the young man who had swum beneath the Bell Keep, who had once nearly drowned in Gyoll, who had idled alone on summer days in the ruined necropolis, who had handed the Chatelaine Thecla, in the nadir of his despair, the stolen knife, was gone.

Not dead. Why had he thought that every life must end in death, and never in anything else? Not dead, but vanished as a single note vanishes, never to reappear, when it becomes an indistinguishable and inseparable part of some extemporized melody. That young Severian had hated death, and by the mercy of the Increate, whose mercy indeed (as is wisely said in many places) confounds and destroys us, he did not die.

The women turned long necks to look down at me. Their oval faces were perfect, symmetrical, expressionless yet lewd; and I understood quite suddenly that they were not—or at least no longer were—the courtiers of the House Absolute, but had become the courtesans of the House Azure.

For some while, as it seemed to me, the parade of those seductive and inhuman women continued, and at each beat of my heart (of which I was conscious at that time as I have seldom been before or since, so that it seemed as if a drum throbbed in my chest) they reversed their roles without changing the least detail of their appearance. Just as I have sometimes known in dreams that a certain figure was in fact someone whom it did not in the least resemble, so I knew at one instant that these women were the ornaments of the Autarchial presence, and at the next that they were to be sold for the night for a handful of orichalks.

During all this time, and all the much longer periods that preceded and followed it, I was acutely uncomfortable. The spiders' webs, which I came gradually to perceive were common fishing nets, had not been removed; but I had been bound with ropes as well, so that one arm was tightly pinioned by my side and the other bent until the fingers of my hand, which soon grew numb, almost touched my face. At the height of the action of the drug I had become incontinent, and now my trousers were soaked with urine, cold and stinking. As my hallucinations grew less violent and the intervals between them longer, the misery of my circumstances afflicted me more, and I became fearful of what would happen to me when I was eventually taken from the windowless storeroom into which I had been cast. I supposed that the hetman had learned from some estafette that I was not what I had pretended to be, and no doubt also that I was fleeing the archon's justice; for I assumed that he would not otherwise have dared to treat me as he had. Under these circumstances, I could only wonder whether he would dispose of me himself (doubtless by noyade, in such a place), deliver me to some petty ethnarch, or return me to Thrax. I resolved to take my own life should the opportunity be afforded me, but it seemed so improbable that I should be given the chance that I was ready to kill myself in my despair.

At last the door opened. The light, though it was only that of a dim room in that thick-walled house, seemed blinding. Two men dragged me forth as they might have pulled out a sack of meal. They were heavily bearded, and so I suppose it was they who had appeared, when they burst in upon Pia and me, to have the pelts of animals for faces. They set me upon my feet, but my legs would not hold, and they were forced to untie me and to remove the nets that had taken me when the net of Typhon had failed. When I could stand again, they gave me a cup of water and a strip of salt fish.

After a time the hetman came in. Although he stood as

importantly as he was no doubt accustomed to stand when he directed the affairs of his village, he could not keep his voice from quavering. Why he should still be frightened of me I could not understand, but plainly he still was. Since I had nothing to lose and everything to gain by the attempt, I ordered him to release me.

"That I cannot do, Grand Master," he said. "I am acting under instructions."

"May I ask who has dared tell you to act in this fashion toward the representative of your Autarch?"

He cleared his throat. "Instructions from the castle. My messenger bird carried your sapphire there last night, and another bird came this morning, with a sign that means we are to bring you."

At first I supposed he meant Acies Castle, where one of the squadrons of dimarchi had its headquarters, but after a moment I realized that here, two score leagues at least from the fortifications of Thrax, it was most unlikely that he would be so specific. I said, "What castle is that? And do your instructions preclude my cleaning myself before I present myself there? And having my clothing washed?"

"I suppose that might be done," he said uncertainly; then to one of his men: "How stands the wind?"

The man addressed gave a half shrug that meant nothing to me, though it seemed to convey information to the hetman.

"All right," he told me. "We can't set you free, but we'll wash your clothes and give you something to eat, if you wish it." As he was leaving, he turned back with an expression that was almost apologetic. "The castle is near, Grand Master, the Autarch far. You understand. We have had great difficulties in the past, but now there is peace."

I would have argued with him, but he gave me no chance. The door shut behind him.

Pia, now dressed in a ragged smock, came in a short time later. I was forced to submit to the indignity of being stripped and washed by her; but I was able to take advantage of the process to whisper to her, and I asked her to see that my sword was sent wherever I was—for I was hoping to escape, if only by confessing to the master of the mysterious castle and offering to join forces with him. Just as she had ignored me when I had suggested that she might float the weight of her chain on a stick of firewood, she gave no indication of having heard me now; but a watch or so later, when, dressed once more, I was being paraded to a boat for the edification of the village, she came running after our little procession with *Terminus Est* cradled in her arms. The hetman had apparently wanted to retain such a fine weapon, and remonstrated with her; but I was able to warn him as I was being dragged on board that when I arrived at the castle I would inform whoever received me there of the existence of my sword, and in the end he surrendered.

The boat was a kind I had never seen before. In form it might have been a xebec, sharp fore and aft, wide amidships, with a long, overhanging stern and an even longer prow. Yet the shallow hull was built of bundles of buoyant reeds tied together in a sort of wickerwork. There could be no step for a conventional mast in such a frail hull, and in its place stood a triangular lash-up of poles. The narrow base of the triangle ran from gunwale to gunwale; its long isosceles sides supported a block used, just as the hetman and I clambered aboard, to hoist a slanting yard that trailed a widely striped linen sail. The hetman now held my sword, but just as the painter was cast off, Pia leaped into the boat with her chain jangling.

The hetman was furious and struck her; but it is not an easy matter to take in the sail of such a craft and turn it about with sweeps, and in the end, though he sent her weeping to the bow, he permitted her to stay. I ventured to ask him why she had wanted to come, though I thought I knew.

"My wife is hard on her when I am not at home," he told

me. "Beats her and makes her scrub all day. It's good for the child, naturally, and it makes her happy to see me when I come back. But she would rather go with me, and I don't greatly blame her."

"Nor do I," I said, trying to turn my face away from his sour breath. "Besides, she will get to see the castle, which I suppose she has never seen before."

"She's seen the walls a hundred times. She comes of the landless lake people, and they are blown about by the wind and so see everything."

If they were blown by the wind, so were we. Air as pure as spirit filled the striped sail, made even that broad hull heel over, and sent us scudding across the water until the village vanished below the rim of the horizon—though the white peaks of the mountains were still visible, rising as it seemed from the lake itself.

XXX

Natrium

SO PRIMITIVELY ARMED were these lakeshore fisherfolk—indeed, far more primitively than the actual autochthonous primitives I had seen about Thrax—that it was some time before I understood that they were armed at all. There were more on board than were needed to steer and make sail, but I assumed at first that they had come merely as rowers, or to add to the prestige of their hetman when he brought me to his master at the castle. In their belts they carried knives of the straight, narrow-bladed kind fishermen everywhere use, and there was a sheaf of barb-headed fishing spears stowed forward, but I thought nothing of that. It was not until one of the islands I had been so eager to see came into view and I noticed one of the men fingering a club edged with animal teeth that I realized they had been brought as a guard, and there was in fact something to guard against.

The little island itself appeared unexceptional until one saw that it truly moved. It was low and very green, with a diminutive hut (built like our boat of reeds and thatched with the same material) at its highest point. A few willows grew upon it, and a long narrow boat, again built of reeds, was tied at the water's edge. When we were closer, I saw that the island was of reeds too, but of living ones. Their stems gave it its characteristic verdescence; their interlaced roots must have formed its raftlike base. Upon their massed, living tangle, soil had accumulated or been stored up by the inhabitants. The trees had sprouted there to trail their roots in the waters of the lake. A little patch of vegetables flourished.

Because the hetman and all the others on board except Pia scowled at it, I regarded this tiny land with favor; and seeing it as I saw it then, a spot of green against the cold and seemingly infinite blue of the face of Diuturna and the deeper, warmer, yet truly infinite blue of the sun-crowned, star-sprinkled sky, it was easy to love it. If I had looked upon this scene as I might have upon a picture, it would have seemed more heavily symbolic—the level line of the horizon dividing the canvas into equal halves, the dot of green with its green trees and brown hut—than those pictures critics are accustomed to deride for their symbolism. Yet who could have said what it meant? It is impossible, I think, that all the symbols we see in natural landscapes are there only because we see them. No one hesitates to brand as mad the solipsists who truly believe that the world exists only because they observe it and that buildings, mountains, and even ourselves (to whom they have spoken only a moment before) all vanish when they turn their heads. Is it not equally mad to believe that the meaning of the same objects vanishes in the same way? If Thecla had symbolized love of which I felt myself unworthy, as I know now that she did, then did her symbolic force disappear when I locked the door of her cell behind me? That would be like saying that the writing in this book, over which I have labored for so many watches, will vanish into a blur of vermilion when I close it for the last time and dispatch it to the eternal library maintained by old Ultan.

The great question, then, that I pondered as I watched the floating island with longing eyes and chafed at my bonds and cursed the hetman in my heart, is that of determining what these symbols mean in and of themselves. We are like children who look at print and see a serpent in the last letter but one, and a sword in the last.

What message was intended for me in the little homey hut and its green garden suspended between two infinities I do not know. But the meaning I read into it was that of freedom and home, and I felt then a greater desire for freedom, for the liberty to rove the upper and the lower worlds at will, carrying with me such comforts as would suffice me, then I had ever felt before—even when I was a prisoner in the antechamber of the House Absolute, even when I was client of the torturers in the Old Citadel.

Then, just at the time when I desired most to be free and we were as near the island as our course would take us, two men and a boy of fifteen or so came out of the hut. For a moment they stood before their door, looking at us as though they were taking the measure of boat and crew. There were five villagers on board in addition to the hetman, and it seemed clear the islanders could do nothing against us, but they put out in their slender craft, the men paddling after us while the boy rigged a crude sail of matting.

The hetman, who turned from time to time to look back at them, was seated beside me with *Terminus Est* across his lap. It seemed to me that at every moment he was about to set her aside and go astern to speak to the man at the tiller, or go forward to talk to the other four who lounged in the bow. My hands were tied in front of me, and it would have taken only an instant to draw the blade a thumb's width clear of her sheath and cut the cords, but the opportunity did not come.

A second island hove into view, and we were joined by another boat, this bearing two men. The odds were slightly worse now, and the hetman called one of his villagers to him and went a step or two astern, carrying my sword. They opened a metal canister that had been concealed under the steersman's platform there and took out a weapon of a type I had not seen before, a bow made by binding two slender bows, each of which carried its own string, to spacers that held them half a span apart. The strings were lashed together at their centers as well, so that the lashings made a sling for some missile.

While I was looking at this curious contrivance, Pia edged closer. "They're watching me," she whispered. "I can't untie you now. But perhaps . . ." She looked significantly toward the boats that followed ours.

"Will they attack?"

"Not unless there are more to join them. They have only fish spears and pachos." Seeing my look of incomprehension she added, "Sticks with teeth—one of these men has one too."

The villager the hetman had summoned was taking what appeared to be a wadded rag from the canister. He unwrapped it on the open lid and disclosed several silver-gray, oily-looking slugs of metal.

"Bullets of power," Pia said. She sounded frightened.

"Do you think more of your people will come?"

"If we pass more islands. If one or two follow a landboat, then all do, to share in what there is to be gotten from it. But we will be in sight of the shore again soon—" Under her ragged smock, her breasts heaved as the villager wiped his hand on his coat, picked up one of the silvery slugs, and fitted it into the sling of the double bow.

"It's only like a heavy stone—" I began. He drew the strings to his ear and let fly, sending the slug whizzing through the space between the slender bows. Pia had been so frightened that I half expected it to undergo some transformation as it flew, perhaps becoming one of those spiders I still half believed I had seen when, drugged, I had been caught in these fishermen's nets.

Nothing of the sort occurred. The slug flew—a shining streak—across the water and splashed into the lake a dozen paces or so before the bow of the nearer boat.

For the space of a breath, nothing more happened. Then there was a sharp detonation, a fireball, and a geyser of steam. Something dark, apparently the missile itself, still intact and flung up by the explosion it had caused, was thrown into the air only to fall again, this time between the two pursuing boats. A new explosion followed, only slightly less intense than the first, and one of the boats was nearly swamped. The other veered away. A third explosion came, and a fourth, but the slug, whatever other powers it might possess, seemed incapable of tracking the boats the way Hethor's notules had followed Jonas and me. Each blast carried it farther off, and after the fourth it appeared spent. The two pursuing boats fell back out of range, but I admired their courage in keeping up the chase at all.

"The bullets of power bring fire from water," Pia told me.

I nodded. "So I see." I was getting my legs set under me, finding secure footing among the bundles of reeds.

It is no great trick to swim even when your hands are bound behind you—Drotte, Roche, Eata and I used to practice swimming while gripping our own thumbs at the small of the back, and with my hands tied before me, I knew I could stay afloat for a long time if necessary; but I was worried about Pia, and told her to go as far forward as she could.

"But then I will not be able to untie you."

"You'll never be able to while they're watching us," I whispered. "Go forward. If this boat breaks up, hang onto a bunch of reeds. They'll still float. Don't argue."

The men in the bow did not stop her, and she halted only when she had reached the point at which a cable of woven reeds formed the vessel's stem. I took a deep breath and leaped overboard.

If I had wished to I could have dived with hardly a ripple, but I hugged my knees to my chest instead to make as great a splash as I could, and thanks to the weight of my boots I sank far deeper than I would have if I had been stripped for swimming. It was that point that had worried me; I had seen when the hetman's archer had fired his missile that there was a distinct pause before the explosion. I knew that as well as drenching both men, I must have wet every slug lying on the oiled rag—but I could not be certain they would go off before I came to the surface.

The water was cold and grew colder as I went down. Opening my eyes, I saw a marvelous cobalt color that grew darker as it swirled about me. I felt a panicky urge to kick off my boots; but that would have brought me up quickly, and I filled my mind instead with the wonder of the color and the thought of the indestructible corpses I had seen littering the refuse heaps about the mines of Saltus—corpses sinking forever in the blue gulf of time.

Slowly I revolved without effort until I could make out the brown hull of the hetman's boat suspended overhead. For a while that spot of brown and I seemed frozen in our positions; I lay beneath it as dead men lie below a carrion bird that, filling its wings with the wind, appears to hover only just below the fixed stars.

Then with bursting lungs I began to rise.

As if it had been a signal I heard the first explosion, a dull and distant boom. I swam upward as a frog does, hearing another explosion and another, each sounding sharper than the last.

When my head broke water, I saw that the stern of the hetman's boat had opened, the reed bundles spreading like broomstraws. A secondary explosion to my left deafened me for a moment and dashed my face with spray that stung like hail. The hetman's archer was floundering not far from me, but the hetman himself (still, I was delighted to see, gripping *Terminus Est*), Pia, and the others were clinging to what remained of the bow, and thanks to the buoyancy of the reeds it yet floated, though the lower end was awash. I tore at the cords on my wrists with my teeth until two of the islanders helped me climb into their craft, and one of them cut me free.

XXXI

The People of the Lake

PIA AND I spent the night on one of the floating islands, where I, who had entered Thecla so often when she was unchained but a prisoner, now entered Pia when she was still chained but free. She lay upon my chest afterward and wept for joy—not so much the joy she had of me, I think, but the joy of her freedom, though her kinsmen the islanders, who have no metal but that they trade or loot from the people of the shore, had no smith to strike off her shackles.

I have heard it said by men who have known many women that at last they come to see resemblances in love between certain ones, and now for the first time I found this to be true in my own experience, for Pia with her hungry mouth and supple body recalled Dorcas. But it was false too in some degree; Dorcas and Pia were alike in love as the faces of sisters are sometimes alike, but I would never have confused one with the other.

I had been too exhausted when we reached the island to fully appreciate the wonder of it, and night had been nearly upon us. Even now, all I recall is dragging the little boat to shore and going into a hut where one of our rescuers kindled a tiny blaze of driftwood, and I oiled *Terminus Est*, which the islanders had taken from the captured hetman and returned to me. But when Urth turned her face to the sun again, it was a wondrous thing to stand with one hand on the willow's graceful trunk and feel the whole of the island rock beneath me!

Our hosts cooked fish for our breakfast; before we had finished them, a boat arrived bearing two more islanders with more fish and root vegetables of a kind I had never tasted before. We roasted these in the ashes and ate them hot. The flavor was more like a chestnut's than anything else I can think of. Three more boats came, then an island with four trees and bellying, square sails rigged in the branches of each, so that when I saw it from a distance I thought it a flotilla. The captain was an elderly man, the closest thing the islanders had to a chief. His name was Llibio. When Pia introduced me to him, he embraced me as fathers do their sons, something no one had ever done to me previously.

After we separated, all the others, Pia included, drew far enough away to permit us to speak privately if we kept our voices low—some men going into the hut, and the rest (there were now about ten in all) to the farther side of the island.

"I have heard that you are a great fighter, and a slayer of men," Llibio began.

I told him that I was indeed a slayer of men, but not great.

"That is so. Every man fights backward—to kill others. Yet his victory comes not in the killing of others but in the killing of certain parts of himself."

To show that I understood him, I said, "You must have killed all the worst parts of your own being. Your people love you."

"That is also not to be trusted." He paused, looking out over the water. "We are poor and few, and had the people listened to another in these years . . ." He shook his head.

"I have traveled far, and I have observed that poor people usually have more wit and more virtue than rich ones."

He smiled at that. "You are kind. But our people have so much wit and virtue now that they may die. We have never possessed great numbers, and many perished in the winter just past, when much water froze."

"I had not thought how difficult winter must be for your people, without wool or furs. But I can see, now that you have pointed it out to me, that it must be hard indeed."

The old man shook his head. "We grease ourselves, which does much, and the seals give us finer cloaks than the shore people have. But when the ice comes, our islands cannot move, and the shore people need no boats to reach them, and so can come against us with all their force. Each summer we fight them when they come to take our fish. But each winter they kill us, coming across the ice for slaves."

I thought then of the Claw, which the hetman had taken from me and sent to the castle, and I said, "The land people obey the master of the castle. Perhaps if you made peace with him, he would stop them from attacking you."

"Once, when I was a young man, these quarrels took two or three lives in a year. Then the builder of the castle came. Do you know the tale?"

I shook my head.

"He came from the south, whence, as I am told, you come as well. He had many things the shore people wanted, such as cloth, and silver, and many well-forged tools. Under his direction they built his castle. Those were the fathers and grandfathers of those who are the shore people now. They used the tools for him, and as he had promised, he permitted them to keep them when the work was done, and he gave them many other things. My mother's father went to them while they labored, and asked if they did not see that they were setting up a ruler over themselves, since the builder of the castle could do as he chose with them, then retire behind the strong walls they had built for him where no one could reach him. They laughed at my mother's father and said they were many, which was true, and the builder of the castle only one, which was also true."

I asked if he had ever seen the builder, and if so what he looked like.

"Once. He stood on a rock talking to shore people while I passed in my boat. I can tell you he was a little man, a man who would not, had you been there, have reached higher than your shoulder. Not such a man as inspires fear." Llibio paused again, his dim eyes seeing not the waters of his lake but times long past. "Still, fear came. The outer wall was complete, and the shore people returned to their hunting, their weirs and their herds. Then their greatest man came to us and said we had stolen beasts and children, and that they would destroy us if we did not return them."

Llibio stared into my face and gripped my hand with his own, which was as hard as wood. Seeing him then, I saw the vanished years as well. They must have seemed grim enough at the time, though the future they had spawned—the future in which I sat with him, my sword across my lap, hearing his story—was grimmer than he could have known at the time. Yet there was joy in those years for him; he had been a strong young man, and though he was not, perhaps, thinking of that, his eyes remembered.

"We told them we did not devour children and had no need of slaves to fish for us, nor any pasturage for beasts. Even then, they must have known it was not we, because they did not come in war against us. But when our islands neared the shore, we heard their women wailing through the night.

"In those times, each day after the full moon was a trading day, when those of us who wished came to the shore for salt and knives. When the next trading day came, we saw that the shore people knew where their children had gone, and their beasts, and whispered it among themselves. Then we asked why they did not go to the castle and carry it by storm, for they were many. But they took our children instead, and men and women of all ages, and chained them outside their doors so that their own people might not be taken—or even marched them to the gates and bound them there."

I ventured to ask how long this had gone on.

"For many years—since I was a young man, as I told you. Sometimes the shore people fought. More often, they did not. Twice warriors came from the south, sent by the proud people of the tall houses of the southern shore. While they were here, the fighting stopped, but what was said in the castle I do not know. The builder, of whom I told you, was seen by no one once his castle was complete."

He waited for me to speak. I had the feeling, which I have often had when talking with old people, that the words he said and the words I heard were quite different, that there was in his speech a hoard of hints, clues, and implications as invisible to me as his breath, as though Time were a species of white spirit who stood between us and with his trailing sleeves wiped away before I had heard it the greater part of all that was said. At last I ventured, "Perhaps he is dead."

"An evil giant dwells there now, but no one has seen him."

I could hardly repress a smile. "Still, I would think his presence must do a great deal to prevent the shore people from attacking the place."

"Five years past, and they swarmed over it by night like the fingerlings that crowd a dead man. They burned the castle, and slew those they found there."

"Do they continue to make war on you by habit, then?"

Llibio shook his head. "After the melting of the ice this year, the people of the castle returned. Their hands were full of gifts—riches, and the strange weapons you turned against the shore people. There are others who come there too, but whether as servants or masters, we of the lake do not know."

"From the north or the south?"

"From the sky," he said, and pointed up to where the faint stars hung dimmed by the majesty of the sun; but I thought he meant only that the visitors had come in fliers, and inquired no further.

All day the lake dwellers arrived. Many were in such boats as had followed the hetman's; but others chose to sail their islands to join Llibio's, until we were in the midst of a floating continent. I was never asked directly to lead them against the castle. Yet as the day wore on, I came to realize that they wished it, and they to understand that I would so lead them. In books, I think, these things are conventionally done with fiery speeches; reality is sometimes otherwise. They admired my height and my sword, and Pia told them I was the representative of the Autarch, and that I had been sent to free them. Llibio said, "Though it is we who suffer most, the shore people were able to make the castle their own. They are stronger in war than we, but not all they burned has been rebuilt, and they had no leader from the south." I questioned him and others about the lands near the castle, and told them we should not attack until night made it difficult for sentries on the walls to see our approach. Though I did not say so, I also wanted to wait for darkness to make good shooting impossible; if the master of the castle had given the bullets of power to the hetman, it seemed probable that he had kept much more effective weapons for himself.

When we sailed, I was at the head of about one hundred warriors, though most of them had only spears pointed with the shoulder bones of seals, pachos, or knives. It would swell my self-esteem now to write that I had consented to lead this little army out of a feeling of responsibility and concern for their plight, but it would not be true. Neither did I go because I feared what might be done to me if I refused, though I suspected that unless I did so diplomatically, feigning to delay or to see some benefit to the islanders in not fighting, it might have gone hard with me.

The truth was that I felt a coercion stronger than theirs.

Llibio had worn a fish carved from a tooth about his neck; and when I had asked him what it was, he had said that it was Oannes, and covered it with his hand so that my eyes could not profane it, for he knew that I did not believe in Oannes, who must surely be the fish-god of these people.

I did not, yet I felt I knew everything about Oannes that mattered. I knew that he must live in the darkest deeps of the lake, but that he was seen leaping among the waves in storms. I knew he was the shepherd of the deep, who filled the nets of the islanders, and that murderers could not go on the water without fear, lest Oannes appear alongside, with his eyes as big as moons, and overturn the boat.

I did not believe in Oannes or fear him. But I knew, I thought, whence he came—I knew that there is an all-pervasive power in the universe of which every other is the shadow. I knew that in the last analysis my conception of that power was as laughable (and as serious) as Oannes. I knew that the Claw was his, and I felt it was only of the Claw that I knew that, only of the Claw among all the altars and vestments of the world. I had held it in my hand many times, I had lifted it above my head in the Vincula, I had touched the Autarch's uhlan with it, and the sick girl in the jacal in Thrax. I had possessed infinity, and I had wielded its power; I was no longer certain I could turn it over tamely to the Pelerines, if I ever found them, but I knew with certainty that I would not lose it tamely to anyone else.

Moreover, it seemed to me that I had somehow been chosen to hold—if only for a brief time—that power. It had been lost to the Pelerines through my irresponsibility in allowing Agia to goad our driver into a race; and so it had been my duty to care for it, and use it, and perhaps return it, and surely my duty to rescue it from the hands, monstrous hands by all accounts, into which it had now fallen through my carelessness.

I had not thought, when I began this record of my life, to

reveal any of the secrets of our guild that were imparted to me by Master Palaemon and Master Gurloes just before I was elevated, at the feast of Holy Katharine, to the rank of journeyman. But I will tell one now, because what I did that night on Lake Diuturna cannot be understood without understanding it. And the secret is only that we torturers obey. In all the lofty order of the body politic, the pyramid of lives that is immensely taller than any material tower, taller than the Bell Keep, taller than the Wall of Nessus, taller than Mount Typhon, the pyramid that stretches from the Autarch on the Phoenix Throne to the most humble clerk grubbing for the most dishonorable trader—a creature lower than the lowest beggar—we are the only sound stone. No one truly obeys unless he will do the unthinkable in obedience; no one will do the unthinkable save we.

How could I refuse to the Increate what I had willingly given the Autarch when I struck off Katharine's head?

XXXII

To the Castle

THE REMAINING ISLANDS were separated now, and though the boats moved among them and sails were bent to every limb, I could not but feel that we were stationary under the streaming clouds, our motion only the last delusion of a drowning land.

Many of the floating islands I had seen earlier that day had been left behind as refuges for women and children. Half a dozen remained, and I stood upon the highest of Llibio's, the largest of the six. Besides the old man and me, it carried seven fighters. The other islands bore four or five apiece. In addition to the islands we had about thirty boats, each crewed by two or three.

I did not deceive myself into thinking that our hundred men, with their knives and fish spears, constituted a formidable force; a handful of Abdiesus's dimarchi would have scattered them like chaff. But they were my followers, and to lead men into battle is a feeling like no other.

Not a glimmer showed upon the waters of the lake, save for the green, reflected light that fell from the myriad leaves of the Forest of Lune, fifty thousand leagues away. Those waters made me think of steel, polished and oiled. The faint wind brought no white foam, though it moved them in long swells like hills of metal.

After a time a cloud obscured the moon, and I wondered briefly whether the lake people would lose their bearings in the dark. It might have been broad noon, however, from the way they handled their vessels, and though boats and islands were often close together, I never in all that voyage saw two that were in the slightest danger of fouling each other.

To be conveyed as I was, by starlight and in darkness, in the midst of my own archipelago, with no sound but the whisper of the wind and the dipping of paddles that rose and fell as regularly as the ticking of a clock, with no motion that could be felt beyond the gentle swelling of the waves, might have been calming and even soporific, for I was tired, though I had slept a little before we set out; but the chill of the night air and the thought of what we were going to do kept me awake.

Neither Llibio nor any of the other islanders had been able to give me more than the vaguest information about the interior of the castle we were to storm. There was a principal building and a wall. Whether or not the principal building was a true keep—that is, a fortified tower high enough to look down upon the wall—I had no idea. Nor did I know whether there were other buildings in addition to the principal one (a barbican, for example), or whether the wall was strengthened with towers or turrets, or how many defenders it might have. The castle had been built in the space of two or three years with native labor; so it could not be as formidable as, say, Acies Castle; but a place a quarter of its strength would be impregnable to us.

I was acutely conscious of how little fitted I was to lead such an expedition. I had never so much as seen a battle, much less taken part in one. My knowledge of military architecture came from my upbringing in the Citadel and some casual sightseeing among the fortifications of Thrax, and what

I knew—or thought I knew—of tactics had been gleaned from equally casual reading. I remembered how I had played in the necropolis as a boy, fighting mock skirmishes with wooden swords, and the thought made me almost physically ill. Not because I feared much for my own life, but because I knew that an error of mine might result in the deaths of most of these innocent and ignorant men, who looked to me for leadership.

Briefly the moon shone again, crossed by the black silhouettes of a flight of storks. I could see the shoreline as a band of denser night on the horizon. A new mass of cloud cut off the light, and a drop of water struck my face. It made me feel suddenly cheerful without knowing why—no doubt the reason was that I unconsciously recalled the rain outside on the night when I stood off the alzabo. Perhaps I was thinking too of the icy waters that spewed from the mouth of the mine of the man-apes.

Yet leaving aside all these chance associations, the rain might be a blessing indeed. We had no bows, and if it wet our opponents' bowstrings, so much the better. Certainly it would be impossible to use the bullets of power the hetman's archer had fired. Besides, rain would favor an attack by stealth, and I had long ago decided that it was only by stealth that our attack could hope to succeed.

I was deep in plans when the cloud broke again, and I saw that we were on a course parallel to the shore, which rose in cliffs to our right. Ahead, a peninsula of rock higher still jutted into the lake, and I walked to the point of the island to ask the man stationed there if the castle was situated on it. He shook his head and said, "We will go about."

So we did. The clews of all the sails were loosed, and retied on new limbs. Leeboards weighted with stones were lowered into the water on one side of the island while three men strained at the tiller bar to bring the rudder around. I was struck by the thought that Llibio must have ordered our pres-

ent landfall, wisely enough, to escape the notice of any look-
outs who might keep watch over the waters of the lake. If that
were the case, we would still be in danger of being seen when
we no longer had the peninsula between the castle and our
little fleet. It also occurred to me that since the builder of the
castle had not chosen to put it on the high spur of rock we
were skirting now, which looked very nearly invulnerable, it
was perhaps because he had found a place yet more secure.

Then we rounded the point and sighted our destination no
more than four chains down the coast—an outthrust of rock
higher still and more abrupt, with a wall at its summit and a
keep that seemed to have the impossible shape of an immense
toadstool.

I could not believe my eyes. From the great, tapering central column, which I had no doubt was a round tower of
native stone, spread a lens-shaped structure of metal ten times
its diameter and apparently as solid as the tower itself.

All about our island, the men in the boats and on the other
islands were whispering to one another and pointing. It
seemed that this incredible sight was as novel to them as to
me.

The misty light of the moon, the younger sister's kiss upon
the face of her dying elder, shone on the upper surface of that
huge disk. Beneath it, in its thick shadow, gleamed sparks of
orange light. They moved, gliding up or down, though their
movement was so slow that I had watched them for some
time before I was conscious of it. Eventually, one rose until it
appeared to be immediately under the disk and vanished, and
just before we came to shore, two more appeared in the same
spot.

A tiny beach lay in the shadow of the cliff. Llibio's island
ran aground before we reached it, however; I had to jump
into the water once more, this time holding *Terminus Est*
above my head. Fortunately there was no surf, and though
rain still threatened, it had not yet come. I helped some of

the lake men drag their boats onto the shingle while others moored islands to boulders with sinew hawsers.

After my trip through the mountains, the narrow, treacherous path would have been easy if I had not had to climb it in the dark. As it was, I would rather have made the descent past the buried city to Casdoe's house, though that had been five times farther.

When we reached the top we were still some distance from the wall, which was screened from us by a grove of straggling firs. I gathered the islanders about me and asked—a rhetorical question—if they knew from where the sky ship above the castle had come. And when they assured me they did not, I explained that I did (and so I did, Dorcas having warned me of them, though I had never seen such a thing before), and that because of its presence here it would be better if I were to reconnoiter the situation before we proceeded with the assault.

No one spoke, but I could sense their feeling of helplessness. They had believed they had found a hero to lead them, and now they were going to lose him before the battle was joined.

"I am going inside if I can," I told them. "I will come back to you if that is possible, and I will leave such doors as I may open for you."

Llibio asked, "But suppose you cannot come back. How shall we know when the moment to draw our knives has come?"

"I will make some signal," I said, and strained my wits to think what signal I might make if I were pent in that black tower. "They must have fires on such a night as this. I'll show a brand at a window, and drop it if I can so that you'll see the streak of fire. If I make no signal and cannot return to you, you may assume they have taken me prisoner—attack when the first light touches the mountains."

· · ·

A short time later I stood at the gate of the castle, banging a great iron knocker shaped (so far as I could determine with my fingers) like the head of a man against a plate of the same metal set in oak.

There was no response. After I had waited for the space of a score of breaths, I knocked again. I could hear the echoes waked inside, an empty reverberation like the throbbing of a heart, but there was no sound of voices. The hideous faces I had glimpsed in the Autarch's garden filled my mind and I waited in dread for the noise of a shot, though I knew that if the Hierodules chose to shoot me—and all energy weapons came ultimately from them—I would probably never hear it. The air was so still it seemed the atmosphere waited with me. Thunder rolled to the east.

At last there were footsteps, so quick and light I could have thought them the steps of a child. A vaguely familiar voice called, "Who's there? What do you want?"

And I answered, "Master Severian of the Order of the Seekers for Truth and Penitence—I come as the arm of the Autarch, whose justice is the bread of his subjects."

"Do you indeed!" exclaimed Dr. Talos, and threw open the gate.

For a moment I could only stare at him.

"Tell me, what does the Autarch want with us? The last time I saw you, you were on your way to the City of Crooked Knives. Did you ever get there?"

"The Autarch wanted to know why your vassals laid hold of one of his servants," I said. "That is to say, myself. This puts a slightly different light on the matter."

"It does! It does! From our point of view too, you understand. I didn't know you were the mysterious visitor at Murene. And I'm sure poor old Baldanders didn't either. Come in and we'll talk about it."

I stepped through the gateway in the wall, and the doctor pushed the heavy gate closed behind me and fitted an iron bar into place.

I said, "There really isn't much to talk about, but we might begin with a valuable gem that was taken from me by force, and as I have been informed, sent to you."

Even while I spoke, however, my attention was drawn from the words I pronounced to the vast bulk of the ship of the Hierodules, which was directly overhead now that I was past the wall. Staring up at it gave me the same feeling of dislocation I have sometimes had on looking down through the double curve of a magnifying glass; the convex underside of that ship had the look of something alien not only to the world of human beings, but to all the visible world.

"Oh, yes," Dr. Talos said. "Baldanders has your trinket, I believe. Or rather, he had it and has stuck it away somewhere. I'm sure he'll give it back to you."

From inside the round tower that appeared (though it could not possibly have done so) to support the ship, there came faintly a lonely and terrible sound that might have been the howling of a wolf. I had heard nothing like it since I had left our own Matachin Tower; but I knew what it was, and I said to Dr. Talos, "You have prisoners here."

He nodded. "Yes. I'm afraid I've been too busy to feed the poor creatures today, what with everything." He waved vaguely toward the ship overhead. "You don't object to meeting cacogens, I hope, Severian? If you want to go in and ask Baldanders for your jewel, I'm afraid you'll have to. He's in there talking to them."

I said I had no objection, though I am afraid I shuddered inwardly as I said it.

The doctor smiled, showing above his red beard the line of sharp, bright teeth I recalled so well. "That's wonderful. You were always a wonderfully unprejudiced person. If I may say so, I suppose your training has taught you to take every being as he comes."

Ossipago, Barbatus, and Famulimus

AS IS COMMON in such pele towers, there was no entrance at
ground level. A straight stair, narrow, steep, and without rail-
ings, led to an equally narrow door some ten cubits above the
pavement of the courtyard. This door stood open already,
and I was delighted to see that Dr. Talos did not close it after
us. We went through a short corridor that was, no doubt, no
more than the thickness of the tower wall and emerged into a
room that appeared (like all the rooms I saw within that
tower) to occupy the whole of the area available at its level. It
was filled with machines that seemed to be at least as ancient
as those we had in the Matachin Tower at home, but whose
uses were beyond my conjecture. At one side of this room
another narrow stair ascended to the floor above, and at the
opposite side a dark stairwell gave access to whatever place it
was in which the howling prisoner was confined, for I heard
his voice floating from its black mouth.

"He has gone mad," I said, and inclined my head toward
the sound.

Dr. Talos nodded. "Most of them are. At least, most of
those I've examined. I administer decoctions of hellebore, but
I can't say they seem to do much good."

"We had clients like that in the third level of our oubliette, because we were forced to retain them by the legalities; they had been turned over to us, you see, and no one in authority would authorize their release."

The doctor was leading me toward the ascending stair. "I sympathize with your predicament."

"In time they died," I continued doggedly. "Either by the aftereffects of their excruciations or from other causes. No real purpose was served by confining them."

"I suppose not. Watch out for that gadget with the hook. It's trying to catch hold of your cloak."

"Then why do you keep him? You aren't a legal repository in the sense we were, surely."

"For parts, I suppose. That's what Baldanders has most of this rubbish for." With one foot on the first step, Dr. Talos turned to look back at me. "You remember to be on your good behavior now. They don't like to be called cacogens, you know. Address them as whatever it is they say their names are this time, and don't refer to slime. In fact, don't talk of anything unpleasant. Poor Baldanders has worked so hard to patch things up with them after he lost his head at the House Absolute. He'll be crushed if you spoil everything just before they leave."

I promised to be as diplomatic as I could.

Because the ship was poised above the tower, I had supposed that Baldanders and its commanders would be in the uppermost room. I was wrong. I heard the murmur of voices as we ascended to the next floor, then the deep tones of the giant, sounding, as they so often had when I was traveling with him, like the collapse of some ruinous wall far off.

This room held machines too. But these, though they might have been as old as those below, gave the impression of being in working order; and moreover, of standing in some logical though impenetrable relation to one another, like the devices in Typhon's hall. Baldanders and his guests were at the farther end of the chamber, where his head, three times the size of any ordinary man's, reared above the clutter of metal and crystal like that of a tyrannosaur over the topmost leaves of a forest. As I walked toward them, I saw what remained of a young woman who might have been a sister of Pia's lying beneath a shimmering bell jar. Her abdomen had been opened with a sharp blade and certain of her viscera removed and positioned around her body. It appeared to be in the early stages of decay, though her lips moved. Her eyes opened as I passed her, then closed again.

"Company!" Dr. Talos called. "You won't guess who."

The giant's head swung slowly around, but he regarded me, I thought, with as little comprehension as he had when Dr. Talos had awakened him that first morning in Nessus.

"Baldanders you know," the doctor continued to me, "but I must introduce you to our guests."

Three men, or what appeared to be men, rose graciously. One, if he had been truly a human being, would have been short and stout. The other two were a good head taller than I, as tall as exultants. The masks all three wore gave them the faces of refined men of middle age, thoughtful and poised; but I was aware that the eyes that looked out through the slits in the masks of the two taller figures were larger than human eyes, and that the shorter figure had no eyes at all, so that only darkness was visible there. All three were robed in white.

"Your Worships! Here's a great friend of ours, Master Severian of the torturers. Master Severian, let me present the honorable Hierodules Ossipago, Barbatus, and Famulimus. It's the labor of these noble personages to inculcate wisdom in the human race—here represented by Baldanders, and now, yourself."

The being Dr. Talos had introduced as Famulimus spoke. His voice might have been wholly human save that it was more resonant and more musical than any truly human voice I have ever heard, so that I felt I might have been listening to the speech of some stringed instrument called to life. "Welcome," it sang. "There is no greater joy for us, than greeting you, Severian. You bow to us in courtesy, but we to you will bend our knees." And he did briefly kneel, as did both the others.

Nothing he could possibly have said or done could have astounded me more, and I was too much taken by surprise to offer any reply.

The other tall cacogen, Barbatus, spoke as a courtier might to fill the silence of an otherwise embarrassing gap in the conversation. His voice was deeper than Famulimus's, and seemed to have something soldierly in it. "You are welcome here—very welcome, as my dear friend has said, and all of us have tried to indicate. But your own friends must remain outside as long as we are here. You know that, of course. I mention it only as a matter of form."

The third cacogen, in a tone so deep that one felt rather than heard it, muttered, "It doesn't matter," and as though he feared I might see the empty eye slits of his mask, turned and made a show of staring out the narrow window behind him.

"Perhaps it doesn't, then," Barbatus said. "Ossipago knows best, after all."

"You have friends here then?" Dr. Talos whispered. It was a pecularity of his that he seldom spoke to a group as most people do, but either addressed a single individual in it almost as though he and the other were alone, or else orated as if to an assembly of thousands.

"Some of the islanders gave me an escort," I said, trying to put the best face I could on things. "You must know of them. They live on the floating masses of reeds in the lake."

"They are rising against you!" Dr. Talos told the giant. "I warned you this would happen." He rushed to the window through which the being called Ossipago seemed to look, shouldering him to one side, and stared out into the night. Then, turning toward the cacogen, he knelt, seized his hand, and kissed it. This hand was quite plainly a glove of some

flexible material painted to resemble flesh, with something in
it that was not a hand.

"You will help us, Worship, will you not? You have fan-
tassins aboard your ship, surely. Once line the walls with horrors, and we will be safe for a century."

In his slow voice, Baldanders said, "Severian will be the
victor. Else why did they kneel to him? Though he may die,
and we may not. You know their ways, Doctor. The looting
may disseminate knowledge."

Dr. Talos turned upon him furiously. "Did it before? I ask
you!"

"Who can say, Doctor?"

"You know it did not. They are the same ignorant, superstitious brutes they have always been!" He whirled again.
"Noble Hierodules, answer me. You must know, if anyone
does."

Famulimus gestured, and I was never more aware of the
truth behind his mask than I was at that moment, for no
human arm could have made the motion his did, and it was a
meaningless motion, conveying neither agreement nor disagreement, neither irritation nor consolation.

"I will not speak of all the things you know," he said. "That
those you fear have learned to overcome you. It may be true
that they are simple still; still, something carried home may
make them wise."

He was addressing the doctor, but I could contain myself
no longer and said, "May I ask what you're talking about,
sieur?"

"I speak of you, of all of you, Severian. It cannot harm you
now, that I should speak."

Barbatus interjected, "Only if you don't do it too freely."

"There is a mark they use upon some world, where sometimes our worn ship finds rest at last. It is a snake with heads
at either end. One hand is dead—the other gnaws at it."

Without turning from the window, Ossipago said, "That is
this world, I think."

"No doubt Camoena could reveal its home. But then, it doesn't matter if you know it. You will understand me the more clearly. The living head stands for destruction. The head that does not live, for building. The former feeds upon the latter; and feeding, nourishes its food. A boy might think that if the first should die, the dead, constructive thing would triumph, making his twin now like himself. The truth is both would soon decay."

Barbatus said, "As so often, my good friend is less than clear. Are you following him?"

"I am not!" Dr. Talos announced angrily. He turned away as if in disgust and hurried down the stair.

"That does not matter," Barbatus told me, "since his master does."

He paused as though waiting for Baldanders to contradict him, then continued, still addressing me. "Our desire, you see, is to advance your race, not to indoctrinate it."

"Advance the shore people?" I asked.

All this time, the waters of the lake were murmuring their night-grief through the window. Ossipago's voice seemed to blend with it as he said, "All of you . . ."

"It is true then! What so many sages have suspected. We are being guided. You watch over us, and in the ages of our history, which must seem no more than days to you, you have raised us from savagery." In my enthusiasm, I drew out the brown book, still somewhat damp from the wetting I had given it earlier in the day, despite its wrappings of oiled silk. "Here, let me show you what this says: 'Man, who is not wise, is yet the object of wisdom. If wisdom finds him a fit object, is it wise in him to make light of his folly?' Something like that."

"You are mistaken," Barbatus told me. "Ages are aeons to us. My friend and I have dealt with your race for less than your own lifetime."

Baldanders said, "These things live only a score of years, like dogs." His tone told me more than is written here, for each word fell like a stone dropped down some deep cistern.

I said, "That cannot be."

"You are the work for which we live," Famulimus explained. "That man you call Baldanders lives to learn. We see that he hoards up past lore—hard facts like seeds to give him power. In time he'll die by hands that do not store, but die with some slight gain for all of you. Think of a tree that splits a rock. It gathers water, the sun's life-bringing heat . . . and all the stuff of life for its own use. In time it dies and rots to dress the earth, that its own roots have made from stone. Its shadow gone, fresh seeds spring up; in time a forest flourishes where it stood."

Dr. Talos emerged again from the stairwell, clapping slowly and derisively.

I asked, "You have left them these machines, then?" I was acutely conscious, as I spoke, of the eviscerated woman mumbling beneath her glass somewhere behind me, a thing that once would not have bothered the torturer Severian in the least.

Barbatus said, "No. Those he found, or constructed for himself. Famulimus said that he wished to learn, and that we saw to it that he did, not that we taught him. We teach no one anything, and only trade such devices as are too complex for your people to duplicate."

Dr. Talos said, "These monsters, these horrors, do nothing for us. You've seen them—you know what they are. When my poor patient ran wild through them in the theater of the House Absolute, they nearly killed him with their pistols."

The giant shifted in his great chair. "You need not feign sympathy, Doctor. It suits you badly. Playing the fool while they looked on . . ." His immense shoulders rose and fell. "I shouldn't have let it overcome me. They've agreed now to forget."

Barbatus said, "We could have killed your creator easily that night, as you know. We burned him only enough to turn aside his charges."

I recalled then what the giant had told me when we parted in the forest beyond the Autarch's gardens—that he was the doctor's master. Now, before I had time to consider what I was doing, I seized the doctor's hand. Its skin seemed as warm and living as my own, though curiously dry. After a moment he jerked away.

"What are you?" I demanded, and when he did not answer, I turned to the beings who called themselves Famulimus and Barbatus. "Once, sieurs, I knew a man who was only partly human flesh . . ."

They looked toward the giant instead of replying, and though I knew their faces were only masks, I felt the force of their demand.

"A homunculus," Baldanders rumbled.

XXXIV

Masks

THE RAIN CAME as he spoke, a cold rain that struck the rude, gray stones of the castle with a million icy fists. I sat down, clamping *Terminus Est* between my knees to keep them from shaking.

"I had already concluded," I said with as much self-possession as I could summon, "that when the islanders told me of a small man who paid for the building of this place, they were speaking of the doctor. But they said that you, the giant, had come afterward."

"I was the small man. The doctor came afterward."

A cacogen showed a dripping, nightmare face at the window, then vanished. Possibly he had conveyed some message to Ossipago, though I heard nothing. Ossipago spoke without turning. "Growth has its disadvantages, though for your species it is the only method by which youth can be reinstated."

Dr. Talos sprang to his feet. "We will overcome them! He has put himself in my hands."

Baldanders said, "I was forced to. There was no one else. I created my own physician."

I was still attempting to regain my mental balance as I

268

looked from one to the other; there was no change in the
appearance or manner of either. "But he beats you," I said. "I
have seen him."

"Once I overheard you while you confided in the smaller
woman. You destroyed another woman, whom you loved. Yet
you were her slave."

Dr. Talos said, "I must get him up, you see. He must exercise, and it is a part of what I do for him. I'm told that the
Autarch—whose health is the happiness of his subjects—has an
isochronon in his sleeping chamber, a gift from another autarch from beyond the edge of the world. Perhaps it is the
master of these gentlemen here. I don't know. Anyway, he
fears a dagger at his throat and will let no one near him when
he sleeps, so this device tells the watches of his night. When
dawn comes, it rouses him. How then should he, the master of
the Commonwealth, permit his sleep to be disturbed by a
mere machine? Baldanders created me as his physician, as he
told you. Severian, you've known me some time. Would you
say I was much afflicted with the infamous vice of false
modesty?"

I managed a smile as I shook my head.

"Then I must tell you that I am not responsible for my
virtues, such as they are. Baldanders wisely made me all that
he is not, so that I might counterweight his deficiencies. I am
not fond of money, for example. That's an excellent thing for
the patient, in a personal physician. And I am loyal to my
friends, because he is the first of them."

"Still," I said, "I have always been astounded that he did
not slay you." It was so cold in the room that I drew my cloak
closer about me, though I felt sure that the present deceptive
calm could not long endure.

The giant said, "You must know why I keep my temper in
check. You have seen me lose it. To have them sitting there,
watching me, as though I were a bear on a chain—"

Dr. Talos touched his hand; there was something womanly

in the gesture. "It's his glands, Severian. The endocrine system and the thyroid. Everything must be managed so carefully, otherwise he would grow too fast. And then I must see that his weight doesn't break his bones, and a thousand other things."

"The brain," the giant rumbled. "The brain is the worst of all, and the best."

I said, "Did the Claw help you? If not, perhaps it will, in my hands. It has performed more for me in a short time than it did for the Pelerines in many years."

When Baldanders's face showed no sign of comprehension, Dr. Talos said, "He means the gem the fishermen sent. It is supposed to perform miraculous cures."

At that Ossipago turned to face us at last. "How interesting. You have it here? May we see it?"

The doctor looked anxiously from the cacogen's expressionless mask to Baldanders's face and back again as he said, "Please, Your Worships, it is nothing. A fragment of corundum."

In all the time since I had entered this level of the tower, none of the cacogens had shifted his place by more than a cubit; now Ossipago crossed to my chair with short, waddling steps. I must have recoiled from him, for he said, "You need not fear me, though we do your kind much hurt. I want to hear about this Claw, which the homunculus tells us is only a mineral specimen."

When I heard him say that, I was afraid that he and his companions would take the Claw from Baldanders and carry it to their own home beyond the void, but I reasoned that they could not do so unless they forced him to produce it, and that if they did that, it might be possible for me to gain possession of it, which I might fail to do otherwise. So I told Ossipago all the things the Claw had accomplished while it had been in my keeping—about the uhlan on the highway, and the man-apes, and all the other instances of its power that

I have already recorded here. As I spoke, the giant's face grew harder, and the doctor's, I thought, more anxious.

When I had finished, Ossipago said, "And now we must see the wonder itself. Bring it out, please," and Baldanders rose and stalked across the wide room, making all his machines appear mere toys by his size, and at last pulled out the drawer of a little, white-topped table and took out the gem. It was more dull in his hand than I had ever seen it; it might have been a bit of blue glass.

The cacogen took it from him and held it up in his painted glove, though he did not turn up his face to look at it as a man would. There it seemed to catch the light from the yellow lamps that sprouted downward from above, and in that light it flashed a clear azure. "Very beautiful," he said. "And most interesting, though it cannot have performed the feats ascribed to it."

"Obviously," Famulimus sang, and made another of those gestures that so recalled to me the statues in the gardens of the Autarch.

"It is mine," I told them. "The shore people took it from me by force. May I have it back?"

"If it is yours," Barbatus said, "where did you get it?"

I began the task of describing my meeting with Agia and the destruction of the altar of the Pelerines, but he cut me short.

"All this is speculation. You did not see this jewel upon the altar, nor did you feel the woman's hand when she gave it to you, if in fact she did. *Where did you get it?*"

"I found it in a compartment of my sabretache." It seemed that there was nothing else to say.

Barbatus turned away as though disappointed. "And you . . ." He looked toward Baldanders. "Ossipago has the jewel now, and he got it from you. Where did you get it?"

Baldanders rumbled, "You saw me. From the drawer of that table."

The cacogen nodded by moving his mask with his hands. "You see then, Severian, his claim has become as good as yours."

"But the gem is mine and not his."

"It is not our task to judge between you; you must settle that when we are gone. But out of curiosity, which torments even such strange creatures as you believe us to be—Baldanders, will you keep it?"

The giant shook his head. "I would not have such a monument to superstition in my laboratory."

"Then there should be little difficulty in effecting a settlement," Barbatus declared. "Severian, would you like to watch our craft rise? Baldanders always comes to see us off, and though he is not the type to rhapsodize over views artificial or natural, I should think myself that it must be worth seeing." He turned away, adjusting his white robes.

"Worshipful Hierodules," I said, "I would very much like to, but I want to ask you something before you go. When I arrived, you said you had no greater joy than seeing me, and you knelt. Did you mean what you said, or anything like it? Were you confusing me with someone else?"

Baldanders and Dr. Talos had risen to their feet when the cacogen first mentioned his departure. Now, though Famulimus remained to listen to my questions, the others had already begun to move away; Barbatus was mounting the stair that led to the level above, with Ossipago, still carrying the Claw, not far behind him.

I began to walk too, because I feared to be separated from it, and Famulimus walked with me. "Though you did not now pass our test, I meant no less than what I said to you." His voice was like the music of some wonderful bird, bridging the abyss from a wood unattainable. "How often we have taken counsel, Liege. How often we have done each other's will. You know the water women, I believe. Are Ossipago, brave Barbatus, I, to be so much less sapient than they?"

I drew a deep breath. "I don't know what you mean. But somehow I feel that though you and your kind are hideous, you are good. And that the undines are not, though they are so lovely, as well as so monstrous, that I can scarcely look at them."

"Is all the world a war of good and bad? Have you not thought it might be something more?"

I had not, and could only stare.

"And you will kindly tolerate my looks. Without offense may I remove this mask? We both know it for one and it is hot. Baldanders is ahead and will not see."

"If you wish, Worship," I said. "But won't you tell—"

With a quick flick of one hand, as though with relief, Famulimus stripped away the disguise. The face revealed was no face, only eyes in a sheet of putrescence. Then the hand moved again as before, and that too fell away. Beneath it was the strange, calm beauty I had seen carved in the faces of the moving statues in the gardens of the House Absolute, but differing from that as the face of a living woman differs from her own life mask.

"Did you not ever think, Severian," she said, "that he who wore a mask might wear another? But I who wore the two do not wear three. No more untruths divide us now, I swear. Touch, Liege—your fingers on my face."

I was afraid, but she took my hand and lifted it to her cheek. It felt cool and yet living, the very opposite of the dry heat of the doctor's skin.

"All of the monstrous masks you've seen us wear are but your fellow citizens of Urth. An insect, lamprey, now a dying leper. All are your brothers, though you may recoil."

We were already close to the uppermost level of the tower, treading charred wood at times—the ruin left by the conflagration that had driven forth Baldanders and his physician. When I took my hand away, Famulimus put on her mask again. "Why do you do this?" I asked.

"So that your folk will hate and fear us all. How long, Severian, if we did not, would common men abide a reign not ours? We would not rob your race of your own rule; by sheltering your kind from us, does not your Autarch keep the Phoenix Throne?"

I felt as I sometimes had in the mountains on waking from a dream, when I sat up wondering, looked about and saw the green moon pinned to the sky with a pine, and the frowning, solemn faces of the mountains beneath their broken diadems instead of the dreamed-of walls of Master Palaemon's study, or our refectory, or the corridor of cells where I sat at the guard table outside Thecla's door. I managed to say, "Then why did you show me?"

And she answered, "Though you see us, we will not see you more. Our friendship here begins and ends, I fear. Call it a gift of welcome from departing friends."

Then the doctor, ahead of us, threw open a door, and the drumming of the rain became a roaring, and I felt the cold, deathlike air of the tower invaded by icy but living air from outside. Baldanders had to stoop and turn his shoulders to pass the doorway, and I was struck by the realization that in time he would be unable to do so, whatever care he received from Dr. Talos—the door would have to be widened, and the stairs too, perhaps, for if he fell he would surely perish. Then I understood what had puzzled me before: the reason for the huge rooms and high ceilings of this, his tower. And I wondered what the vaults in the rock were like, where he confined his starving prisoners.

XXXV

The Signal

THE SHIP, WHICH from below had appeared to rest upon the structure of the tower itself, did not. Rather it seemed to float half a chain or more above us—too high to provide much shelter from the lashing rain that made the smooth curve of its hull gleam like black nacre. As I stared up at it, I could not help but speculate on the sails such a vessel might spread to catch the winds that blow between the worlds; and then, just as I was wondering if the crew did not ever peer down to see us, the mermen, the strange, uncouth beings who for a time walked the bottom below their hull, one of them indeed came down, head foremost like a squirrel, wreathed in orange light and clinging to the hull with hands and feet, though it was wet as any stone in a river and polished like the blade of *Terminus Est*. He wore such a mask as I have often described, but I now knew it to be one. When he saw Ossipago, Barbatus, and Famulimus below, he descended no farther, and in a moment a slender line, glowing orange too so that it seemed a thread of light, was cast down from somewhere above.

"Now we must go," Ossipago told Baldanders, and he handed him the Claw. "Think well on all the things we have not told you, and remember what you have not been shown."

"I will," Baldanders said, his voice as grim as I was ever to hear it.

Then Ossipago caught the line and slid up it until it bent around the curve of the hull and he disappeared from sight. But it somehow seemed that he did not in fact slide up, but down, as if that ship were a world itself and drew everything belonging to it to itself with a blind hunger, as Urth does; or perhaps it was only that he was become lighter than our air, like a sailor who dives from his ship into the sea, and rose as I had risen after I leaped from the hetman's boat.

However that may be, Barbatus and Famulimus followed him. Famulimus waved just as the swell of the hull blocked her from view; no doubt the doctor and Baldanders thought she bade them farewell; but I knew she had waved to me. A sheet of rain struck my face, blinding my eyes despite my hood.

Slowly at first, then faster and faster, the ship lifted and receded, vanishing not upwards or to the north or the south or the east or west, but dwindling into a direction to which I could no longer point when it was gone.

Baldanders turned to me. "You heard them."

I did not understand, and said, "I spoke with them, yes. Dr. Talos invited me to when he opened the door in the wall for me."

"They told me nothing. They have shown me nothing."

"To have seen their ship," I said, "and to have spoken to them—surely those things are not nothing."

"They are driving me forward. Always forward. They drive me as an ox to slaughter."

He went to the battlement and stared out over the vast expanse of the lake, whose rain-churned waters made it seem a sea of milk. The merlons were several spans higher than my head, but he put his hands on them as upon a railing, and I saw the blue gleam of the Claw in one closed fist. Dr. Talos pulled at my cloak, murmuring that it would be better if we were to go inside out of the storm, but I would not leave.

"It began long before you were born. At first they helped me, though it was only by suggesting thoughts, asking questions. Now they only hint. Now they only let slip enough to tell me a certain thing may be done. Tonight there was not even that."

Wanting to urge that he no longer take the islanders for his experiments, but without knowing how to do so, I said that I had seen his explosive bullets, which were surely very wonderful, a very great achievement.

"Natrium," he said, and turned to face me, his huge head lifted to the dark sky. "You know nothing. Natrium is a mere elemental substance spawned by the sea in endless profusion. Do you think I'd have given it to the fishermen if it were more than a toy? No, I am my own great work. And I am my only great work!"

Dr. Talos whispered, "Look about you—don't you recognize this? It is just as he says!"

"What do you mean?" I whispered in return.

"The castle? The monster? The man of learning? I only just thought of it. Surely you know that just as the momentous events of the past cast their shadows down the ages, so now, when the sun is drawing toward the dark, our own shadows race into the past to trouble mankind's dreams."

"You're mad," I said. "Or joking."

"Mad?" Baldanders rumbled. "*You* are mad. You with your fantasies of theurgy. How they must be laughing at us. They think all of us barbarians . . . I, who have labored three lifetimes."

He extended his arm and opened his hand. The Claw blazed for him now. I reached for it, and with a sudden motion he threw it. How it flashed in the rain-swept dark! It was as if bright Skuld herself had fallen from the night sky.

I heard the yell, then, of the lake people who waited outside the wall. I had given them no signal; yet the signal had been given by the only act, save perhaps for an attack on my person, that could have induced me to give it. *Terminus Est* left her sheath while the wind still carried their battle cry. I lifted her to strike, but before I could close with the giant, Dr. Talos sprang between us. I thought the weapon he raised to parry was only his cane; if my heart had not been torn by the loss of the Claw, I would have laughed as I hewed it. My blade rang on steel, and though it drove his own back upon himself he was able to contain the blow. Baldanders rushed past me before I could recover and dashed me against the parapet.

I could not dodge the doctor's thrust, but he was deceived, I think, by my fuligin cloak, and though his point grazed my ribs, it rattled on stone. I clubbed him with the hilt and sent him reeling.

Baldanders was nowhere to be seen. After a moment I realized that his headlong charge must have been for the door behind me, and the blow he had given me no more than an afterthought, as a man intent on other things may snuff a candle before he leaves the room.

The doctor sprawled on the stone pavement that was the roof of the tower—stones that were, perhaps, merely gray in sunlight, but now appeared a rain-drowned black. His red hair and beard were visible still, permitting me to see that he lay belly down, his head twisted to one side. It had not seemed to me that I had struck him so hard, though it may be I am stronger than I know, as others have sometimes said. Still I felt that beneath all his cocksure strutting Dr. Talos had been weaker than any of us except Baldanders would have guessed. I could have slain him easily then, swinging *Terminus Est* so the corner of her blade would bury itself in his skull.

Instead I picked up his weapon, the faint line of silver that had fallen from his hand. It was a single-edged blade about as wide as my forefinger, very sharp—as befitted a surgeon's sword. After a moment I realized that the grip was only the handle of his walking stick, which I had seen so often; it was a sword cane, like the sword Vodalus had drawn in our necropolis once, and I smiled there in the rain to think of the doctor carrying his sword thus for so many leagues, unknown to me, who had labored along with my own slung over my back. The tip had shattered on the stones when he thrust at me; I flung the broken blade over the parapet, as Baldanders had flung the Claw, and went down into his tower to kill him.

When we had climbed the stair, I had been too deep in conversation with Famulimus to pay much heed to the rooms through which we passed. The uppermost I recalled only as a place where it seemed that everything was draped in scarlet cloth. Now I saw red globes, lamps that burned without a flame like the silver flowers that sprouted from the ceiling of the wide room where I had met the three beings I could no longer call cacogens. These globes stood on ivory pedestals that seemed as light and slender as the bones of birds, rising from a floor that was no floor but only a sea of fabrics, all red, but of varying shades and textures. Over this room stretched a canopy supported by atlantes. It was scarlet, but sewn with a thousand plates of silver, so well polished that they were mirrors nearly as perfect as the armor of the Autarch's praetorians.

I had nearly descended the height of the stair before I understood that what I saw was no more than the giant's bedchamber, the bed itself, five times the expanse of a normal one, being sunk level with the floor, and its cerise and carmine coverings scattered about upon the crimson carpet. Just then, I saw a face among these twisted bedclothes. I lifted my sword and the face vanished, but I left the stair to drag away one of the downy cloths. The catamite beneath (if catamite he was) rose and faced me with the boldness small children sometimes show. Indeed he was a small child, though he stood nearly as tall as I, a naked boy so fat his distended paunch obscured his tiny generative organs. His arms were like pink pillows bound with cords of gold, and his ears had been pierced for golden hoops strung with tiny bells. His hair was golden too, and curled; beneath it he looked at me with the wide, blue eyes of an infant.

Large though he was, I have never been able to believe that Baldanders practiced pederasty as that term is usually understood, though it may well be that he had hoped to do so when the boy grew larger still. Certainly it must have been that just as he held his own growth in check, permitting only as much as needed to save his mountainous body from the ravages of the years, so he had accelerated the growth of this poor boy in so far as was possible to his anthroposophic knowledge. I say that because it seemed certain that he had not had him under his control until some time after he and Dr. Talos had parted from Dorcas and me.

(I left this boy where I had found him, and to this day I have no notion of what may have become of him. It is likely enough that he perished; but it is possible also that the lake men may have preserved and nourished him, or that the hetman and his people finding him at a somewhat later time, did so.)

I had no sooner descended to the floor below than what I saw there wiped all thought of the boy from my mind. This room was as wreathed in mist (which I am certain had not been present when I had passed through before) as the other had been in red cloth; it was a living vapor that seethed as I might have imagined the logos to writhe as it left the mouth of the Pancreator. While I watched it, a man of fog, white as a grave worm, rose before me brandishing a barbed spear. Before I realized he was a mere phantom, the blade of my sword went through his wrist as it might have penetrated a column of smoke. At once he began to shrink, the fog seeming to fall in upon itself, until he stood hardly higher than my waist.

I went forward, down more steps, until I stood in the cold, roiling whiteness. Then there came bounding across its surface a hideous creature formed, like the man, of the fog itself. In dwarfs I have seen, the head and torso are of normal size or larger, but the limbs, however muscled, remain childlike; this was the reverse of such a dwarf, with arms and legs larger than my own issuing from a twisted, stunted body.

The anti-dwarf brandished an estoc, and opening its mouth in a soundless cry, it thrust its weapon into the man's neck, utterly heedless of his spear, which was plunged into its own chest.

I heard a laugh then, and though I had seldom heard him merry, I knew whose laugh it was.

"Baldanders!" I called.

His head rose from the mist, just as I have seen the mountaintops lifted above it at dawn.

XXXVI

The Fight in the Bailey

"HERE IS A real enemy," I said. "With a real weapon." I walked down into the mist, groping ahead of me with my sword blade.

"You see in my cloud chamber real enemies too," Baldanders rumbled, his voice quite calm. "Save that they are outside, in the bailey. The first was one of your friends, the second one of my foes."

As he spoke, the mist dispersed, and I saw him near the center of the room, sitting in a massive chair. When I turned toward him, he rose from it and seizing it by the back sent it hurtling toward me as easily as he might have thrown a basket. It missed me by no more than a span.

"Now you will attempt to kill me," he said. "And all for a foolish charm. I ought to have killed you, that night when you slept in my bed."

I could have said the same thing, but I did not bother to reply. It was clear that by feigning helplessness he was hoping to lure me into a careless attack, and though he appeared to be without a weapon, he was still twice my height and, as I had reason to believe, of four times or more my strength.

Then too I was conscious, as I drew nearer him, that we were reenacting here the performance of the marionettes I had seen in a dream on the night of which he had reminded me, and in that dream, the wooden giant had been armed with a bludgeon. He retreated from me step by step as I advanced; yet he seemed always ready to come to grips.

Quite suddenly, when we were perhaps three quarters across the room from the stair, he turned and ran. It was astonishing, like seeing a tree run.

It was also very quick. Ungainly though he was, he covered two paces with every step, and he reached the wall—where there was just such a slit of window as Ossipago had stared from—long before me.

For an instant I could not think what he meant to do. The window was far too narrow for him to climb through. He thrust both his great hands into it, and I heard the grinding of stone upon stone.

Just in time I guessed, and managed a few steps back. A moment later he held a block of stone wrenched from the wall itself. He lifted it above his head and hurled it at me.

As I leaped aside, he tore free another, and then another. At the third I had to roll desperately, still clutching my sword, to avoid the fourth, the stones coming quicker and quicker as the lack of those already torn away weakened the structure of the wall. By the purest chance, that roll brought me close to a casket, a thing no bigger than a modest housewife might have for her rings, lying on the floor.

It was ornamented with little knobs, and something in their form recalled to me those Master Gurloes had adjusted at Thecla's excruciation. Before Baldanders could pry out another stone, I scooped the casket up and twisted one of its knobs. At once the vanished mist came boiling out of the floor again, quickly reaching the level of my head, so that I was blinded in its sea of white.

"You have found it," Baldanders said in his deep, slow

tones. "I should have turned it off. Now I cannot see you, but you cannot see me."

I kept silent because I knew he was standing with a block of stone poised to throw, waiting for the sound of my voice. After I had drawn perhaps two dozen breaths, I began to edge toward him as silently as I could. I was certain that despite all his cunning he could not walk without my hearing him. When I had taken four steps, the stone crashed on the floor behind me, and there was the noise of another being torn from the wall.

It was one stone too many; there came a deafening roar, and I knew a whole section of the wall above the window must have gone crashing down. Briefly I dared to hope it had killed him; but the mist began to thin at once, pouring through the rent in the wall and out into the night and the rain outside, and I saw him still standing beside the gaping hole.

He must have dropped the stone he had wrenched loose when the wall fell; he was empty-handed. I dashed toward him hoping to attack him before he realized I was upon him. Once again he was too quick. I saw him grasp the wall that remained and swing himself out, and by the time I had reached the opening he was some distance below. What he had done seemed impossible; but when I looked more carefully at that part of the tower illuminated by the lights of the room in which I stood, I saw that the stones were roughly cut and laid without mortar, so there were often sizable crevices between them, and that the wall sloped inward as it rose.

I was tempted to sheathe *Terminus Est* and follow him, but I would have been utterly vulnerable if I had done so, since Baldanders would be certain to reach the ground before me. I flung the casket at him and soon lost sight of him in the rain. With no other choice left to me, I groped my way back to the stair and descended to the level I had seen when I first entered the castle.

• • •

It had been silent then, uninhabited save by its ancient mechanisms. Now it was pandemonium. Over and under and through the machines swarmed scores of hideous beings akin to the ghostly thing whose phantom I had seen in the room Baldanders called his chamber of clouds. Like Typhon, some wore two heads; some had four arms; many were cursed with disproportionate limbs—legs twice the length of their bodies, arms thicker than their thighs. All had weapons, and so far as I could judge, were mad, for they struck at one another as freely as at the islanders who fought with them. I remembered then what Baldanders had told me: that the courtyard below was filled with my friends and his foes. He had surely been correct; these creatures would have attacked him on sight, just as they attacked each other.

I cut down three before I reached the door, and I was able to rally the lake men who had entered the tower to me as I went, telling them that the enemy we sought was outside. When I saw how much they dreaded the lunatic monsters who leaped still from the dark stairwell (and whom they failed to recognize for what they undoubtedly were—the ruins of their brothers and their children) I was surprised they had dared to enter the castle at all. It was wonderful, however, to see how my presence stiffened them; they let me take the lead, but by the look of their eyes I knew that wherever I led they would follow. That was the first time, I think, that I truly understood the pleasure his position must have given Master Gurloes, which until then I had supposed must have consisted merely in a celebration of his ability to impose his will on others. I understood too why so many of the young men at court forsook their fiancées, my friends in the life I had as Thecla, to accept commissions in obscure regiments.

The rain had slackened, though it still fell in silver sheets. Dead men, and many more of the giant's creatures, lay on the steps—I was compelled to kick several over the side for fear I would fall if I tried to walk over them. Below in the bailey there was still much fighting, but none of the creatures there came up to attack us, and the lake men held the stair against those we had left behind in the tower. I saw no sign of Baldanders.

Fighting, I have found, though it is exciting in the sense that it takes one out of oneself, is difficult to describe. And when it is over, what one best remembers—for the mind is too full at the time of struggle to do much recording—is not the cuts and parries but the hiatuses between engagements. In the bailey of Baldanders's castle I traded frantic blows with four of the monsters he had forged, but I cannot now say when I fought well and when badly.

The darkness and the rain favored the style of wild combat forced on me by the design of *Terminus Est*. Not only formal fencing but any sword or spear play that resembles it requires a good light, since each antagonist must see the other's weapon. Here there was hardly light at all. Furthermore, Baldanders's creatures possessed a suicidal courage that served them badly. They tried to leap over or duck under the cuts I made at them, and for the most part they were caught by the backhand that followed. In each of these piecemeal fights, the warriors of the islands took some part, and in one case actually dispatched my opponent for me. In the others, they distracted him, or had wounded him before I engaged him. None of these encounters was satisfactory in the sense that a well-performed execution is.

After the fourth there were no more, though their dead and dying lay everywhere. I gathered the islanders about me. We were all in that euphoric state that rides with victory, and they were willing enough to attack any giant, no matter how huge; but even those who had been in the bailey when the stones fell swore they had seen none. Just as I was beginning to think they were blind, and they were no doubt ready to believe I was mad, we were saved by the moon.

How strange it is. Everyone looks for knowledge in the sky, whether in studying the influence of the constellations upon events, or like Baldanders in seeking to wrest it from those the ignorant call cacogens, or only, in the case of farmers, fishermen, and the like, in searching for weather signs; yet no one looks for immediate help there, though we often receive it, as I did that night.

It was no more than a break in the clouds. The rain, which had already grown fitful, did not truly cease; but for a very short time the light of the waning moon (high overhead and, though hardly more than half full, very bright) fell upon the giant's courtyard just as the light from one of the largest luminaries in the odeum in the oneiric level of the House Absolute used to fall upon the stage. Beneath it the smooth, wet stones of the pavement shone like pools of still, dark water; and in them I saw reflected a sight so fantastic that I wonder now that I was able to do more than stare at it until I perished—which would not have been long.

For Baldanders was falling upon us; but he was falling slowly.

XXXVII

Terminus Est

THERE ARE PICTURES in the brown book of angels swooping down upon Urth in just that posture, the head thrown back, the body inclined so that the face and the upper part of the chest are at the same level. I can imagine the wonder and horror of beholding that great being I glimpsed in the book in the Second House descending in that way; yet I do not think it could be more frightful. When I recall Baldanders now, it is thus that I think of him first. His face was set, and he held upraised a mace tipped with a phosphorescent sphere.

We scattered as the sparrows do when an owl drops among them at twilight. I felt the wind of his blow at my back and turned in time to see him alight, catching himself with his free hand and bounding from it upright as I have watched street acrobats do; he wore a belt I had not noticed before, a thick affair of linked metal prisms. I never found out, however, how he had contrived to reenter his tower to get the mace and the belt while I thought him descending the wall; perhaps there was a window somewhere larger than those I saw, or even a door that had provided access to some structure that the burning of the castle by the shore people had destroyed. It is even possible that he only reached through some window with one arm.

But, oh, the silence as he came floating down, the grace as he, who was large as the huts of so many poor folk, caught himself on that hand and turned upright. The best way to describe silence is to say nothing—but what grace!

I whirled then with my cloak wind-whipped behind me and my sword, as I had so often held it, lifted for the stroke; and I knew then what I had never troubled to think upon before— why my destiny had sent me wandering half across the continent, facing dangers from fire and the depths of Urth, from water and now from air, armed with this weapon, so huge, so heavy that fighting any ordinary man with it was like cutting lilies with an ax. Baldanders saw me and raised his mace, its head shining yellow-white; I think it was a kind of salute.

Five or six of the lake men hedged him about with spears and toothed clubs, but they did not close with him. It was as though he were the center of some hermetic circle. As we came together, we two, I discovered the reason: a terror I could neither understand nor control gripped me. It was not that I was afraid of him or of death, but simply that I was *afraid.* I felt the hair of my head moving as if beneath the hand of a ghost, a thing I had heard of but always dismissed as an exaggeration, a figure of speech grown into a lie. My knees were weak and trembled—so much so that I was glad of the dark because they could not be seen. But we closed.

I knew very well from the size of that mace and the size of the arm behind it that I would never survive a blow from it; I could only dodge and jump back. Baldanders, equally, could not endure a stroke from *Terminus Est,* for though he was large and strong enough to wear armor as thick as a destrier's bardings, he had none, and so heavy a blade, with so fine an edge, easily capable of cleaving an ordinary man to the waist, could deal him his death wound with a single cut.

This he knew, and so we fenced much as players do upon a

stage, with sweeping blows but without actually coming to grips. All that time the terror held me, so that it seemed that if I did not run my heart would burst. There was a singing in my ears, and as I watched the mace-head, whose pale nimbus made it, indeed, too easy to watch, I became aware that it was from there that the singing came. The weapon itself hummed with that high, unchanging note, like a wineglass struck with a knife and immobilized in crystalline time.

No doubt the discovery distracted me, even though it was only for a moment. Instead of a quartering stroke, the mace drove downward like a mallet hammering a tent peg. I moved to one side just in time, and the singing, shimmering head flashed past my face and crashed into the stone at my feet, which cracked and flew to pieces like a clay pot. One of its shards laid open a corner of my forehead, and I felt my blood streaming down.

Baldanders saw it, and his dull eyes lit with triumph. From that time forward he struck a stone at every stroke, and at every stroke stone shattered. I had to back away, and back away again, and soon I found myself with the curtain wall at my back. As I retreated along it, the giant used his weapon to greater advantage than ever, swinging it horizontally and striking the wall again and again. Often the stone shards, as sharp as flints, missed me; but often too they did not, and soon blood was running into my eyes, and my chest and arms were crimson.

As I leaped away from the mace for perhaps the hundredth time, something struck my heel and I nearly fell. It was the lowest step of a flight that climbed the wall. I went up, gaining a bit of advantage from the height but not enough to let me halt my retreat. There was a narrow walkway along the top of the wall. I was driven backward along it step by step. Now indeed I would have turned to run if I had dared, but I recalled how quickly the giant had moved when I surprised him in the chamber of clouds, and I knew that he would be upon me in a leap, just as I had, as a boy, overtaken the rats in the oubliette below our tower, breaking their spines with a stick.

But not every circumstance favored Baldanders. Something white flashed between us, then there was a bone-tipped spear thrust into one huge arm, like an ylespil's quill in the neck of a bull. The lake men were now far enough from the singing mace that the terror it waked no longer prevented them from throwing their weapons. Baldanders hesitated for a moment, stepping back to pull the spear out. Another struck him, grazing his face.

Then I knew hope and leaped forward, and in leaping lost my footing on a broken, rain-slick stone. I nearly went over the edge, but at the last instant caught hold of the parapet—in time to see the luminous head of the giant's mace descending. Instinctively I raised *Terminus Est* to ward off the blow.

There was such a scream as might have been made if all the specters of all the men and women she had slain were gathered on the wall—then a deafening explosion.

I lay stunned for a moment. But Baldanders was stunned as well, and the lake men, with the spell of the mace broken, were swarming along the walkway toward him from either side. Perhaps the steel of her blade, which had its own natural frequency and, as I had often observed, chimed with miraculous sweetness if tapped with a finger, was too much for whatever mechanism lent its strange powers to the giant's mace. Perhaps it was only that her edge, sharper than a surgeon's knife and as hard as obsidian, had penetrated the mace-head. Whatever had occurred, the mace was gone, and I held in my hands only the sword's hilt, from which protruded less than a cubit of shattered metal. The hydrargyrum that had labored so long in the darkness there ran from it now in silver tears.

Before I could rise, the lake men were springing over me. A spear plunged into the giant's chest, and a thrown club struck him in the face. At a sweep of his arm, two of the lake warriors tumbled screaming from the wall. Others were upon him at once, but he shook them off. I struggled to my feet, still only half comprehending what had taken place.

For an instant, Baldanders stood poised upon the parapet; then he leaped. No doubt he received great aid from the belt he wore, but the strength of his legs must have been enormous. Slowly, heavily, he arched out and out, down and down. Three who had clung to him too long fell to their deaths on the rocks of the promontory.

At last he fell too, hugely, as if he were—alone and in himself—some species of flying ship out of control. White as milk, the lake erupted, then closed over him. Something that writhed like a serpent and sometimes caught the light rose from the water and into the sky, until at last it vanished among the sullen clouds; no doubt it was the belt. But though the islanders stood with spears poised, his head never showed above the waves.

XXXVIII

The Claw

THAT NIGHT THE lake men ransacked the castle; I did not join them, nor did I sleep inside its walls. In the center of the grove of pines where we had held our council, I found a spot so sheltered by the boughs that its carpet of fallen needles was still dry. There, when my wounds had been washed and bandaged, I lay down. The hilt of the sword that had been mine, and Master Palaemon's before me, lay beside me, so that I felt I slept with a dead thing; but it brought me no dreams.

I woke with the fragrance of the pines in my nostrils. Urth had turned almost her full face to the sun. My body was sore, and the cuts I had received from the flying shards of stone smarted and burned, but it was the warmest day I had experienced since I had left Thrax and mounted into the high lands. I walked out of the grove and saw Lake Diuturna sparkling in the sun and fresh grass growing between the stones.

I sat down on a projecting rock, with the wall of Baldander's castle rising behind me and the blue lake spread at my feet, and for the last time removed the tang of the ruined blade that had been *Terminus Est* from the lovely hilt of silver and onyx. It is the blade that is the sword, and *Termi-*

nus Est is no more; but I carried that hilt with me for the rest of my journey, though I burned the manskin sheath. The hilt will hold another blade someday, even if it cannot be as perfect and will not be mine.

What remained of my blade I kissed and cast into the water.

Then I began my search among the rocks. I had only a vague idea of the direction in which Baldanders had hurled the Claw, but I knew his throw had been toward the lake, and though I had seen the gem clear the top of the wall, I felt that even such an arm as his might have failed to send so small an object far from shore.

I soon found, however, that if it had gone into the lake at all, it was lost utterly, for the water was many ells deep everywhere. Yet it still seemed possible that it had not reached the lake and was lodged in a crevice where its radiance was invisible.

And so I searched, afraid to ask the lake men to assist me, and afraid also to give up the search to rest or eat for fear someone else would take it up. Night came, and the cry of the loon at the dying of the light, and the lake men offered to take me to their islands, but I refused. They feared that shore people would come, or that they were already organizing an attack that would revenge Baldanders (I did not dare to tell them that I suspected he was not dead, but remained alive beneath the waters of the lake), and so at last, at my urging they left me alone, still crawling among the sharp-cornered rocks of the promontory.

Eventually I grew too weary to hunt more in the dark and settled myself upon a shelving slab to wait for day. From time to time it seemed that I saw azure gleaming from some crack near where I lay or from the waters below; but always when I stretched out my hand to grasp it or tried to stand to walk to the edge of the slab to look down at it, I woke with a start and found I had been dreaming.

A hundred times I wondered if someone else had not found the gem while I slept under the pine, which I cursed myself for doing. A hundred times, also, I reminded myself how much better it would be for it to be found by anyone than for it to be lost forever.

Just as summer-killed meat draws flies, so the court draws spurious sages, philosophists, and acosmists who remain there as long as their purses and their wits will maintain them, in the hope (at first) of an appointment from the Autarch and (later) of obtaining a tutorial position in some exalted family. At sixteen or so, Thecla was attracted, as I think young women often are, to their lectures on theogony, thodicy, and the like, and I recall one particularly in which a phoebad put forward as an ultimate truth the ancient sophistry of the existence of three Adonai, that of the city (or of the people), that of the poets, and that of the philosophers. Her reasoning was that since the beginning of human consciousness (if such a beginning ever was) there have been vast numbers of persons in the three categories who have endeavored to pierce the secret of the divine. If it does not exist, they should have discovered that long before; if it does, it is not possible that Truth itself should mislead them. Yet the beliefs of the populace, the insights of the rhapsodists, and the theories of the metaphysicians have so far diverged that few of them can so much as comprehend what the others say, and someone who knew nothing of any of their ideas might well believe there was no connection at all between them.

May it not be, she asked (and even now I am not certain I can answer), that instead of traveling, as has always been supposed, down three roads to the same destination, they are actually traveling toward three quite different ones? After all, when in common life we behold three roads issuing from the same crossing, we do not assume they all proceed toward the same goal.

I found (and find) this suggestion as rational as it is repellent, and it represents for me all that monomaniacal fabric of argument, so tightly woven that not even the tiniest objection or spark of light can escape its net, in which human minds become enmeshed whenever the subject is one in which no appeal to fact is possible.

As a fact the Claw was thus an incommensurable. No quantity of money, no piling up of archipelagoes or empires could approach it in value any more than the indefinite multiplication of horizontal distance could be made to equal vertical distance. If it was, as I believed, a thing from outside the universe, then its light, which I had seen shine faintly so often, and a few times brightly, was in some sense the only light we had. If it were destroyed, we were left fumbling in the dark.

I thought I had valued it highly in all the days in which I had carried it, but as I sat there upon that shelving stone overlooking the benighted waters of Lake Diuturna, I realized what a fool I had been to carry it at all, through all my wild scrapes and insane adventures, until I lost it at last. Just before sunrise I vowed to take my own life if I did not find it before the dark came again.

Whether or not I could have kept that vow I cannot say. I have loved life so long as I can remember. (It was, I believe, that love of life that gave me whatever skill I possessed at my art, because I could not bear to see the flame I cherished extinguished other than perfectly.) Surely I loved my own life, now mingled with Thecla's, as much as others. If I had broken that vow, it would not have been the first.

There was no need to. About mid morning of one of the most pleasant days I have ever experienced, when the sunlight was a warm caress and the lapping of the water below a gentle music, I found the gem—or what remained of it.

It had shattered on the rocks; there were pieces large enough to adorn a tetrarchic ring and flecks no bigger than the bright specks we see in mica, but nothing more. Weeping, I gathered the fragments bit by bit, and when I knew them to be as lifeless as the jewels miners delve up every day, the plundered finery of the long dead, I carried them to the lake and cast them in.

I made three of those climbs down to the water's edge with a tiny heap of bluish chips held in the hollow of one hand, each time returning to the place where I had found the broken gem to search for more; and after the third I found, wedged deep between two stones so that I had, in the end, to return to the pine grove to break twigs with which to free it and fish it up, something that was neither azure nor a gem, but that shone with an intense white light, like a star.

It was with curiosity rather than reverence that I drew it out. It was so unlike the treasure I had sought—or at least, unlike the broken bits of it I had been finding—that it hardly occurred to me until I held it that the two might be related. I cannot say how it is possible for an object in itself black to give light, but this did. It might have been carved in jet, so dark it was and so highly polished; yet it shone, a claw as long as the last joint of my smallest finger, cruelly hooked and needle-pointed, the reality of that dark core at the heart of the gem, which must have been no more than a container for it, a lipsanotheca or pyx.

For a long time I knelt with my back to the castle, looking from this strange, gleaming treasure to the waves and back again while I tried to grasp its significance. Seeing it thus without its case of sapphire, I felt profoundly an effect I had never noticed at all during the days before it had been taken from me in the hetman's house. Whenever I looked at it, it seemed to erase thought. Not as wine and certain drugs do, by rendering the mind unfit for it, but by replacing it with a higher state for which I know no name. Again and again I felt myself enter this state, rising always higher until I feared I should never return to the mode of consciousness I call normality; and again and again I tore myself from it. Each time I emerged, I felt I had gained some inexpressible insight into immense realities.

At last, after a long series of these bold advances and fearful retreats, I came to understand that I should never reach any real knowledge of the tiny thing I held, and with that thought (for it was a thought) came a third state, one of happy obedience to I knew not what, an obedience without reflection because there was no longer anything to reflect upon, and without the least tincture of rebellion. This state endured all that day and a large part of the next, by which time I was already deep into the hills.

Here I pause, having carried you, reader, from fortress to fortress—from the walled city of Thrax, dominating the upper Acis, to the castle of the giant, dominating the northern shore of remote Lake Diuturna. Thrax was for me the gateway to the wild mountains. So too, this lonely tower was to prove a gateway—the very threshold of the war, of which a single far-flung skirmish had taken place here. From that time to this, that war has engaged my attention almost without cease.

Here I pause. If you have no desire to plunge into the struggle beside me, reader, I do not condemn you. It is no easy one.

Appendix

A Note on Provincial Administration

SEVERIAN'S BRIEF RECORD of his career in Thrax is the best (though not the only) evidence we have concerning the business of government in the age of the Commonwealth, as it is carried out beyond the shining corridors of the House Absolute and the teeming streets of Nessus. Clearly, our own distinctions between the legislative, executive, and judicial branches do not apply—no doubt administrators like Abdiesus would laugh at our notion that laws should be made by one set of people, put into effect by a second, and judged by a third. They would consider such a system unworkable, as indeed it is proving to be.

At the period of the manuscripts, archons and tetrarchs are appointed by the Autarch, who as the representative of the people has all power in his hands. (See, however, Famulimus's remark on this topic to Severian.) These officials are expected to enforce the commands of the Autarch and to administer justice in accordance with the received usages of the populations they govern. They are also empowered to make local laws—valid only over the area governed by the lawmaker and only during his term of office—and to enforce them with the threat of death. In Thrax, as well as in the House Absolute and the Citadel, imprisonment for a fixed term—our own most common punishment—seems unknown. Prisoners in the Vincula are held awaiting torture or execution, or as hostages for the good behavior of their friends and relatives.

As the manuscript clearly shows, the supervision of the Vincula ("the house of chains") is only one of the duties of the lictor ("he who binds"). This officer is the chief subordinate of the archon involved with the administration of criminal justice. On certain ceremonial occasions he walks before his master bearing a naked sword, a potent reminder of the archon's authority. During sessions of the archon's court (as Severian complains) he is required to stand at the left of the bench. Executions and other major acts of judicial punishment are personally performed by him, and he supervises the activities of the clavigers ("those with keys").

These clavigers are not only the guards of the Vincula; they act also as a detective police, a function made easier by their opportunities for extorting information from their prisoners. The keys they bear seem sufficiently large to be used as bludgeons, and are thus their weapons as well as their tools and their emblems of authority.

The dimarchi ("those who fight in two ways") are the archon's uniformed police as well as his troops. However, their title does not appear to refer to this dual function, but to equipment and training that permits them to act as cavalry or infantry as the need arises. Their ranks appear to be filled by professional soldiers, veterans of the campaigns in the north and nonnatives of the area.

Thrax itself is clearly a fortress city. Such a place could scarcely be expected to stand for more than a day at most against the Ascian enemy—rather, it seems designed to fend off raids by brigands and rebellions by the local exultants and armigers. (Cyriaca's husband, who would have been a person almost beneath notice in the House Absolute, is clearly of some importance, and even some danger, in the neighborhood of Thrax.) Although the exultants and armigers seem to be forbidden private armies, there appears little doubt that many of their followers, though called huntsmen, stewards, and the like, are fundamentally fighting men. They are presumably essential to protect the villas from marauders and to collect rents, but in the event of civil unrest they would be a potent source of danger to such as Abdiesus. The fortified city straddling the headwaters of the river would give him an almost irresistible advantage in any such conflict.

The route chosen by Severian for his escape indicates how closely egress from the city could be controlled. The archon's own fortress, Acies Castle ("the armed camp of the point"), guards the northern end of the valley. It appears to be entirely separate from his palace in the city proper. The southern end is closed by the Capulus ("the sword haft"), apparently an elaborate fortified wall, a scaled-down imitation of the Wall of Nessus. Even the cliff tops are protected by forts linked by walls. Possessing, as it does, an inexhaustible supply of fresh water, the city appears capable of withstanding a protracted siege by any force not provided with heavy armament.

G.W.

THE CITADEL OF
THE AUTARCH

At two o'clock in the morning, if you open your window and listen,
You will hear the feet of the Wind that is going to call the sun.
And the trees in the shadow rustle and the trees in the moonlight glisten,
And though it is deep, dark dnight, you feel that the night is done.

Rudyard Kipling

The Dead Soldier

I HAD NEVER seen war, or even talked of it at length with someone who had, but I was young and knew something of violence, and so believed that war would be no more than a new experience for me, as other things—the possession of authority in Thrax, say, or my escape from the House Absolute—had been new experiences.

War is not a new experience; it is a new world. Its inhabitants are more different from human beings than Famulimus and her friends. Its laws are new, and even its geography is new, because it is a geography in which insignificant hills and hollows are lifted to the importance of cities. Just as our familiar Urth holds such monstrosities as Erebus, Abaia, and Arioch, so the world of war is stalked by the monsters called battles, whose cells are individuals but who have a life and intelligence of their own, and whom one approaches through an ever-thickening array of portents.

One night I woke long before dawn. Everything seemed still, and I was afraid some enemy had come near, so that my mind had stirred at his malignancy. I rose and looked about. The hills were lost in the darkness. I was in a nest of long grass, a nest I had trampled flat for myself. Crickets sang.

Something caught my eye far to the north: a flash, I thought, of violet just on the horizon. I stared at the point from which it seemed to have come. Just as I had convinced myself that what I believed I had seen was no more than a fault of vision, perhaps some lingering effect of the drug I had been given in the hetman's house, there was a flare of magenta a trifle to the left of the point I had been staring at.

I continued to stand there for a watch or more, rewarded from time to time with these mysteries of light. At last, having satisfied myself that they were a great way off and came no nearer, and that they did not appear to change in frequency, coming on the average with each five hundredth beat of my heart, I lay down again. And because I was then thoroughly awake, I became aware that the ground was shaking, very slightly, beneath me.

When I woke again in the morning it had stopped. I watched the horizon diligently for some time as I walked along, but saw nothing disturbing.

It had been two days since I had eaten, and I was no longer hungry, though I was aware that I did not have my normal strength. Twice that day I came upon little houses falling to ruin, and I entered each to look for food. If anything had been left, it had been taken long before; even the rats were gone. The second house had a well, but some dead thing had been thrown down it long ago, and in any case there was no way to reach the stinking water. I went on, wishing for something to drink and also for a better staff than the succession of rotten sticks I had been using. I had learned when I had used *Terminus Est* as a staff in the mountains how much easier it is to walk with one.

About noon I came upon a path and followed it, and a short time afterward heard the sound of hoofs. I hid where I could look down the road; a moment later a rider crested the next hill and flashed past me. From the glimpse I had of him, he wore armor somewhat in the fashion of the commanders of Abdiesus's dimarchi, but his wind-stiffened cape was green instead of red and his helmet seemed to have a visor like the bill of a cap. Whoever he was, he was magnificently mounted: His destrier's mouth was bearded with foam and its sides drenched, yet it flew by as though the racing signal had dropped only an instant before.

Having encountered one rider on the path, I expected others. There were none. For a long while I walked in tranquillity, hearing the calls of birds and seeing many signs of game. Then (to my inexpressible delight) the path forded a young stream. I walked up a dozen strides to a spot where deeper, quieter water flowed over a bed of white gravel. Minnows skittered away from my boots—always a sign of good water—and it was still cold from the mountain peaks and sweet with the memory of snow. I drank and drank again, and then again, until I could hold no more, then took off my clothes and washed myself, cold though it was. When I had finished my bath and dressed and returned to the place where the path crossed the stream, I saw two pug marks on the other side, daintily close together, where the animal had crouched to drink. They overlay the hoofprints of the officer's mount, and each was as big as a dinner plate, with no claws showing beyond the soft pads of the toes. Old Midan, who had been my uncle's huntsman when I was the girl-child Thecla, had told me once that smilodons drink only after they have gorged themselves, and that when they have gorged and drunk they are not dangerous unless molested. I went on.

The path wound through a wooded valley, then up into a saddle between hills. When I was near the highest point, I noticed a tree two spans in diameter that had been torn in half (as it appeared) at about the height of my eyes. The ends of both the standing stump and the felled trunk were ragged, not at all like the smooth chipping of an ax. In the next two or three leagues I walked, there were several score like it. Judging from the lack of leaves, and in some cases of bark, on-the fallen parts, and the new shoots the stumps had put forth, the damage had been done at least a year ago, and perhaps longer.

At last the path joined a true road, something I had heard of often, but never trodden except in decay. It was much like the old road the uhlans had been blocking when I had become separated from Dr. Talos, Baldanders, Jolenta, and Dorcas when we left Nessus, but I was unprepared for the cloud of dust that hung about it. No grass grew upon it, though it was wider than most city streets.

I had no choice except to follow it; the trees about it were thick set, and the spaces between them choked with brush. At first I was afraid, remembering the burning lances of the uhlans; still, it seemed probable that the law that prohibited the use of roads no longer had force here, or this one would not have seen as much traffic as it clearly had; and when, a short time later, I heard voices and the sound of many marching feet behind me, I only moved a pace or two into the trees and watched openly while the column passed.

An officer came first, riding a fine, champing blue whose fangs had been left long and set with turquoise to match his bardings and the hilt of his owner's estoc. The men who followed him on foot were antepilani of the heavy infantry, big shouldered and narrow waisted, with sun-bronzed, expressionless faces. They carried three-pointed korsekes, demilunes, and heavy-headed voulges. This mixture of armaments, as well as certain discrepancies among their badges and accouterments, led me to believe that their mora was made up of the remains of earlier formations. If that were so, the fighting they must have seen had left them phlegmatic. They swung along, four thousand or so in all, without excitement, reluctance, or any sign of fatigue, careless in their bearing but not slovenly, and seemed to keep step without thought or effort.

Wagons drawn by grunting, trumpeting trilophodons followed. I edged nearer the road as they came, for much of the baggage they carried was clearly food; but there were mounted men among the wagons, and one called to me, asking what unit I belonged to, then ordering me to him. I fled instead, and though I was fairly sure he could not ride among the trees and would not abandon his destrier to pursue me on foot, I ran until I was winded.

When I stopped at last, it was in a silent glade where greenish sunlight filtered through the leaves of spindly trees. Moss covered the ground so thickly that I felt as if I walked upon the dense carpet of the hidden picture-room where I had encountered the Master of the House Absolute. For a while I rested my back against one of the thin trunks, listening. There came no sound but the gasping of my own breath and the tidal roar of my blood in my ears.

In time I became aware of a third note: the faint buzzing of a fly. I wiped my streaming face with the edge of my guild cloak. That cloak was sadly worn and faded now, and I was suddenly conscious that it was the same one Master Gurloes had draped about my shoulders when I became a journeyman, and that I was likely to die in it. The sweat it had absorbed felt cold as dew, and the air was heavy with the odor of damp earth.

The buzzing of the fly ceased, then resumed—perhaps a trifle more insistently, perhaps merely seeming so because I had my breath again. Absently, I looked for it and saw it dart through a shaft of sunlight a few paces off, then settle on a brown object projecting from behind one of the thronging trees.

A boot.

I had no weapon whatsoever. Ordinarily I would not have been much afraid of confronting a single man with my hands alone, especially in such a place, where it would have been impossible to swing a sword; but I knew much of my strength was gone, and I was discovering that fasting destroys a part of one's courage as well—or perhaps it is only that it consumes a part of it, leaving less for other exigencies.

However that might be, I walked warily, sidelong and silently, until I saw him. He layed sprawled, with one leg crumpled under him and the other extended. A falchion had fallen near his right hand, its leather lanyard still about his wrist. His simple barbute had dropped from his head and rolled a step away. The fly crawled up his boot until it reached the bare flesh just below the knee, then flew again, with the noise of a tiny saw.

I knew, of course, that he was dead, and even as I felt relief my sense of isolation came rushing back, though I had not realized that it had departed. Taking him by the shoulder, I turned him over. His body had not yet swelled, but the smell of death had come, however faint. His face had softened like a mask of wax set before a fire; there was no telling now with what expression he had died. He had been young and blond—one of those handsome, square faces. I looked for a wound but found none.

The straps of his pack had been drawn so tight that I could neither pull it off nor even loosen the fastenings. In the end I took the coutel from his belt and cut them, then drove the point into a tree. A blanket, a scrap of paper, a fire-blackened pan with a socket handle, two pairs of rough stockings (very welcome), and, best of all, an onion and a half loaf of dark bread wrapped in a clean rag, and five strips of dried meat and a lump of cheese wrapped in another.

I ate the bread and cheese first, forcing myself, when I found I could not eat slowly, to rise after every third bite and walk up and down. The bread helped by requiring a great deal of chewing; it tasted precisely like the hard bread we used to feed our clients in the Matachin Tower, bread I had stolen, more from mischief than from hunger, once or twice. The cheese was dry and smelly and salty, but excellent all the same; I thought that I had never tasted such cheese before, and I know I have never tasted any since. I might have been eating life. It made me thirsty, and I learned how well an onion quenches thirst by stimulating the salivary glands.

By the time I reached the meat, which was heavily salted too, I was satiated enough to begin debating whether I should reserve it against the night, and I decided to eat one piece and save the other four.

The air had been still since early that morning, but now a faint breeze blew, cooling my cheeks, stirring the leaves, and catching the paper I had pulled from the dead soldier's pack and sending it rattling across the moss to lodge against a tree. Still chewing and swallowing, I pursued it and picked it up. It was a letter—I assume one he had not had the opportunity to send, or perhaps to complete. His hand had been angular, and smaller than I would have anticipated, though it may be that its smallness only resulted from his wish to crowd many words onto the small sheet, which appeared to have been the last he possessed.

O my beloved, we are a hundred leagues north of the place from which I last wrote you, having come by hard marches. We have enough to eat and are warm by day, though sometimes cold at night. Makar, of whom I told you, has fallen sick and was permitted to remain behind. A great many others claimed then to be ill and were made to march before us without weapons and carrying double packs and under guard. In all this time we have seen no sign of the Ascians, and we are told by the lochage that they are still several days' march off. The seditionists killed sentries for three nights, until we put three men on each post and kept patrols moving outside our perimeter. I was assigned to one of these patrols on the first night and found it very discomforting, since I feared one of my comrades would cut me down in the dark. My time was spent tripping over roots and listening to the singing at the fire—

> "Tomorrow night's sleep
> Will be on stained ground,
> So tonight all drink deep,
> Let the friend-cup go round.
> Friend, I hope when they shoot,

> *Every shot will fly wide,*
> *And I wish you good loot,*
> *And myself at your side.*
> *Let the friend-cup go round,*
> *For we'll sleep on stained ground."*

Naturally, we saw no one. The seditionists call themselves the Vodalarii after their leader and are said to be picked fighters. And well paid, receiving support from the Ascians. . . .

I I

The Living Soldier

I PUT ASIDE the half-read letter and stared at the man who had written it. Death's shot had not flown wide for him; now he stared at the sun with lusterless blue eyes, one nearly winking, the other fully open.

Long before that moment I should have recalled the Claw, but I had not. Or perhaps I had only suppressed the thought in my eagerness to steal the rations in the dead man's pack, never reasoning that I might have trusted him to share his food with the rescuer who had recalled him from death. Now, at the mention of Vodalus and his followers (who I felt would surely assist me if only I were able to find them), I remembered it at once and took it out. It seemed to sparkle in the summer sunlight, brighter indeed than I had ever seen it without its sapphire case. I touched him with it, then, urged by I cannot say what impulse, put it into his mouth.

When this, too, effected nothing, I took it between my thumb and first finger and pushed its point into the soft skin of his forehead. He did not move or breathe, but a drop of blood, fresh and sticky as that of a living man, welled forth and stained my fingers.

I withdrew them, wiped my hand with some leaves, and

would have gone back to his letter if I had not thought I heard a stick snap some distance away. For a moment I could not choose among hiding, fleeing, and fighting; but there was little chance of successfully doing the first, and I had already had enough of the second. I picked up the dead man's falchion, wrapped myself in my cloak, and stood waiting.

No one came—or at least, no one visible to me. The wind made a slight sighing among the treetops. The fly seemed to have gone. Perhaps I had heard nothing more than a deer bounding through the shadows. I had traveled so far without any weapon that would permit me to hunt that I had almost forgotten the possibility. Now I examined the falchion and found myself wishing it had been a bow.

Something behind me stirred, and I turned to look.

It was the soldier. A tremor seemed to have seized him—if I had not seen his corpse, I would have thought him dying. His hands shook, and there was a rattling in his throat. I bent and touched his face; it was as cold as ever, and I had the impulsive need to kindle a fire.

There had been no fire-making gear in his pack, but I knew every soldier must carry such things. I searched his pockets and found a few aes, a hanging dial with which to tell time, and a flint and striking bar. Tinder lay in plenty under the trees—the danger was that I might set fire to all of it. I swept a space clear with my hands, piling the sweepings in the center, set them ablaze, then gathered a few rotten boughs, broke them, and laid them on the fire.

Its light was brighter than I had expected—day was almost done, and it would soon be dark. I looked at the dead man. His hands no longer shook; he was silent. The flesh of his face seemed warmer. But that was, no doubt, no more than the heat of the fire. The spot of blood on his forehead had nearly dried, yet it seemed to catch the light of the dying sun, shining as some crimson gem might, some pigeon's blood ruby spilled from a treasure hoard. Though our fire gave little smoke, what there was seemed to me fragrant as incense, and like incense it rose straight until it was lost in the gathering dark, suggesting something I could not quite recall. I shook myself and found more wood, breaking and stacking it until I had a pile I thought large enough to last the night.

Evenings were not nearly so cold here in Orithyia as they had been in the mountains, or even in the region about Lake Diuturna, so that although I recalled the blanket I had found in the dead man's pack, I felt no need of it. My task had warmed me, the food I had eaten had invigorated me, and for a time I strode up and down in the twilight, brandishing the falchion when such warlike gestures accorded with my thoughts but taking care to keep the fire between the dead man and myself.

My memories have always appeared with the intensity, almost, of hallucinations, as I have said often in this chronicle. That night I felt I might lose myself forever in them, making of my life a loop instead of a line; and for once I did not resist the temptation but reveled in it. Everything I have described to you came crowding back to me, and a thousand things more. I saw Eata's face and his freckled hand when he sought to slip between the bars of the gate of the necropolis, and the storm I had once watched impaled on the towers of the Citadel, writhing and lashing out with its lightnings; I felt its rain, colder and fresher far than the morning cup in our refectory, trickle down my face. Dorcas's voice whispered in my ears: "Sitting in a window . . . trays and a rood. What will you do, summon up some Erinys to destroy me?"

Yes. Yes, indeed, I would have if I could. If I had been Hethor, I would have drawn them from some horror behind the world, birds with the heads of hags and the tongues of vipers. At my order they would have threshed the forests like wheat and beaten cities flat with their great wings . . . and yet, if I could, I would have appeared at the final moment to save her—not walking coldly off afterward in the way we all wish to do when, as children, we imagine ourselves rescuing and humiliating the loved one who has given us some supposed slight, but raising her in my arms.

Then for the first time, I think, I knew how terrible it must have been for her, who had been hardly more than a child when death had come, and who had been dead so long, to have been called back.

And thinking of that, I remembered the dead soldier whose food I had eaten and whose sword I held, and I paused and listened to hear if he drew breath or stirred. Yet I was so lost in the worlds of memory that it seemed to me the soft forest earth under my feet had come from the grave Hildegrin the Badger had despoiled for Vodalus, and the whisper of the leaves was the soughing of the cypresses in our necropolis and the rustle of the purple-flowered roses, and that I listened, listened in vain for breath from the dead woman Vodalus had lifted with the rope beneath her arms, lifted in her white shroud.

At last, the croaking of a nightjar brought me to myself. I seemed to see the soldier's white face staring at me, and went around the fire and searched until I found the blanket, and draped his corpse with it.

Dorcas belonged, as I now realized, to that vast group of women (which may, indeed, include all women) who betray us—and to that special type who betray us not for some present rival but for their own pasts. Just as Morwenna, whom I had executed at Saltus, must have poisoned her husband and her child because she recalled a time in which she was free and, perhaps, virginal, so Dorcas had left me because I had not existed (had, as she must unconsciously have seen it, failed to exist) in that time before her doom fell upon her.

(For me, also, that is the golden time. I think I must have treasured the memory of the crude, kindly boy who fetched books and blossoms to my cell largely because I knew him to be the last love before the doom, the doom that was not, as I learned in that prison, the moment at which the tapestry was cast over me to muffle my outcry, nor my arrival at the Old Citadel in Nessus, nor the slam of the cell door behind me, nor even the moment when, bathed in such a light as never shines on Urth, I felt my body rise in rebellion against me—but that instant in which I drew the blade of the greasy paring knife he had brought, cold and mercifully sharp, across my own neck. Possibly we all come to such a time, and it is the will of the Caitanya that each damn herself for what she has done. Yet can we be hated so much? Can we be hated at all? Not when I can still remember his kisses on my breasts, given, not breathing to taste the perfume of my flesh—as Aphrodisius's were, and that young man's, the nephew of the chiliarch of the Companions—but as though he were truly hungry for my flesh. Was something watching us? He has eaten of me now. Awakened by the memory, I lift my hand and run fingers through his hair.)

I slept late, wrapped in my cloak. There is a payment made by Nature to those who undergo hardships; it is that the lesser ones, at which people whose lives have been easier would complain, seem almost comfortable. Several times before I actually rose, I woke and congratulated myself to think how easily I had spent this night compared to those I had endured in the mountains.

At last the sunlight and the singing birds brought me to myself. On the other side of our dead fire, the soldier shifted and, I think, murmured something. I sat up. He had thrown the blanket aside and lay with his face to the sky. It was a pale face with sunken cheeks; there were dark shadows beneath the eyes and deeply cut lines running from the mouth; but it was a living face. The eyes were truly closed, and breath sighed in the nostrils.

For a moment I was tempted to run before he woke. I had his falchion still—I started to replace it, then took it back for fear he would attack me with it. His coutel still protruded from the tree, making me think of Agia's crooked dagger in the shutter of Casdoe's house. I thrust it back into the sheath at his belt, mostly because I was ashamed to think that I, armed with a sword, should fear any man with a knife.

His eyelids fluttered, and I drew away, remembering a time when Dorcas had been frightened to find me bending over her when she woke. So that I should not appear a dark figure, I pushed back my cloak to show my bare arms and chest, browned now by so many days' suns. I could hear the sighing of his breath; and when it changed from sleep to waking, it seemed to me a thing almost as miraculous as the passage from death to life.

Empty-eyed as a child, he sat up and looked about him. His lips moved, but only sound without sense came forth. I spoke to him, trying to make my tone friendly. He listened but did not seem to understand, and I recalled how dazed the uhlan had been, whom I had revived on the road to the House Absolute.

I wished that I had water to offer him, but I had none. I drew out a piece of the salt meat I had taken from his pack, broke it into two, and shared that with him instead.

He chewed and seemed to feel a little better. "Stand up," I said. "We must find something to drink." He took my hand and allowed me to pull him erect, but he could hardly stand. His eyes, which had been so calm at first, grew wilder as they became more alert. I had the feeling that he feared the trees might rush upon us like a pride of lions, yet he did not draw his coutel or attempt to reclaim the falchion.

When we had taken three or four steps, he tottered and nearly fell. I let him lean upon my arm, and together we made our way through the wood to the road.

III

Through Dust

I DID NOT KNOW whether we should turn north or south. Somewhere to the north lay the Ascian army, and it was possible that if we came too near the lines we would be caught up in some swift maneuver. Yet the farther south we went, the less likely we were to find anyone who would help us, and the more probable it became that we would be arrested as deserters. In the end I turned northward; no doubt I acted largely from habit, and I am still not sure if I did well or ill.

The dew had already dried upon the road, and its dusty surface showed no footprints. To either side, for three paces or more, the vegetation was a uniform gray. We soon passed out of the forest. The road wound down a hill and over a bridge that vaulted a small river at the bottom of a rock-strewn valley.

We left it there and went down to the water to drink and bathe our faces. I had not shaved since I had turned my back on Lake Diuturna, and though I had noticed none when I took the flint and striker from the soldier's pocket, I ventured to ask him if he carried a razor.

I mention this trifling incident because it was the first

thing I said to him that he seemed to comprehend. He nodded, then reaching under his hauberk produced one of those little blades that country people use, razors their smiths grind from the halves of worn oxshoes. I touched it up on the broken whetstone I still carried and stropped it on the leg of my boot, then asked if he had soap. If he did, he failed to understand me, and after a moment he seated himself on a rock from which he could stare into the water, reminding me very much of Dorcas. I longed to question him about the fields of Death, to learn all that he remembered of that time that is, perhaps, dark only to us. Instead, I washed my face in the cold river water and scraped my cheeks and chin as well as I could. When I sheathed his razor and tried to return it to him, he did not seem to know what to do with it, so I kept it.

For most of the rest of that day we walked. Several times we were stopped and questioned; more often we stopped others and questioned them. Gradually I developed an elaborate lie: I was the lictor of a civil judge who accompanied the Autarch; we had encountered this soldier on the road, and my master had ordered me to see that he was cared for; he could not speak, and so I did not know what unit he was from. That last was true enough.

We crossed other roads and sometimes followed them. Twice we reached great camps where tens of thousands of soldiers lived in cities of tents. At each, those who tended the sick told me that though they would have bandaged my companion's wounds had he been bleeding, they could not take responsibility for him as he was. By the time I spoke to the second, I no longer asked the location of the Pelerines but only to be directed to a place where we might find shelter. It was nearly night.

"There is a lazaret three leagues from here that may take you in." My informant looked from one of us to the other, and seemed to have almost as much sympathy for me as for the soldier, who stood mute and dazed. "Go west and north until you see a road to the right that passes between two big trees. It is about half as wide as the one you will have been following. Go down that. Are you armed?"

I shook my head; I had put the soldier's falchion back in his scabbard. "I was forced to leave my sword behind with my master's servants—I couldn't have carried it and managed this man too."

"Then you must beware of beasts. It would be better if you had something that would shoot, but I can't give you anything."

I turned to go, but he stopped me with a hand on my shoulder.

"Leave him if you're attacked," he said. "And if you're forced to leave him, don't feel too badly about it. I've seen cases like his before. He's not likely to recover."

"He has already recovered," I told him.

Although this man would not allow us to stay or lend me a weapon, he did provide us with something to eat; and I departed with more cheerfulness than I had felt for some time. We were in a valley where the western hills had risen to obscure the sun a watch or more before. As I walked along beside the soldier, I discovered that it was no longer necessary for me to hold his arm. I could release it, and he continued to walk at my side like any friend. His face was not really like Jonas's, which had been long and narrow, but once when I saw it sidelong I caught something there so reminiscent of Jonas that I felt almost that I had seen a ghost.

The gray road was greenish-white in the moonlight; the trees and brush to either side looked black. As we strode along I began to talk. Partially, I admit, it was from sheer loneliness; yet I had other reasons as well. Unquestionably there are beasts, like the alzabo, who attack men as foxes do fowls, but I have been told that there are many others who will flee if they are warned in time of human presence. Then too, I thought that if I spoke to the soldier as I might have to any other man, any ill-intentioned persons who heard us would be less apt to guess how unlikely he was to resist them.

"Do you recall last night?" I began. "You slept very heavily."

There was no reply.

"Perhaps I never told you this, but I have the facility of recalling everything. I can't always lay hands on it when I want, but it is always there; some memories, you know, are like escaped clients wandering through the oubliette. One may not be able to produce them on demand, but they are always there, they cannot get away.

"Although, come to think of it, that isn't entirely true. The fourth and lowest level of our oubliette has been abandoned—there are never enough clients to fill the topmost three anyway, and perhaps eventually Master Gurloes will give up the third. We only keep it open now for the mad ones that no official ever comes to see. If they were in one of the higher levels, their noise would disturb the others. Not all of them are noisy, of course. Some are as quiet as yourself."

Again there was no reply. In the moonlight I could not tell if he was paying attention to me, but remembering the razor I persevered.

"I went that way myself once. Through the fourth level, I mean. I used to have a dog, and I kept him there, but he ran away. I went after him and found a tunnel that left our oubliette. Eventually I crawled out of a broken pedestal in a place called the Atrium of Time. It was full of sundials. I met a young woman there who was really more beautiful than anyone I've ever seen since—more lovely even than Jolenta, I think, though not in the same way."

The soldier said nothing, yet now something told me he heard me; perhaps it was no more than a slight movement of his head seen from a corner of my eye.

"Her name was Valeria, and I think she was younger than I, although she seemed older. She had dark, curling hair, like

Thecla's, but her eyes were dark too. Thecla's were violet. She had the finest skin I have ever seen, like rich milk mixed with the juice of pomegranates and strawberries.

"But I didn't set out to talk about Valeria, but about Dorcas. Dorcas is lovely too, though she is very thin, almost like a child. Her face is a peri's, and her complexion is flecked with freckles like bits of gold. Her hair was long before she cut it; she always wore flowers there."

I paused again. I had continued to talk of women because that seemed to have caught his attention. Now I could not say if he were still listening or not.

"Before I left Thrax I went to see Dorcas. It was in her room, in an inn called the Duck's Nest. She was in bed and naked, but she kept the sheet over herself, just as if we had never slept together—we who had walked and ridden so far, camping in places where no voice had been heard since the land was called up from the sea, and climbing hills where no feet had ever walked but the sun's. She was leaving me and I her, and neither of us really wished it otherwise, though at the last she was afraid and asked me to come with her after all.

"She said she thought the Claw had the same power over time that Father Inire's mirrors are said to have over distance. I didn't think much of the remark then—I'm not really a very intelligent man, I suppose, not a philosopher at all—but now I find it interesting. She told me, 'When you brought the uhlan back to life it was because the Claw twisted time for him to the point at which he still lived. When you half-healed your friend's wounds, it was because it bent the moment to one when they would be nearly healed.' Don't you think that's interesting? A little while after I pricked your forehead with the Claw, you made a strange sound. I think it may have been your death rattle."

I waited. The soldier did not speak, but quite unexpectedly I felt his hand on my shoulder. I had been talking almost flippantly; his touch brought home to me the seriousness of what I had been saying. If it were true—or even some trifling approximation to the truth—then I had toyed with powers I understood no better than Casdoe's son, whom I had tried to make my own, would have understood the giant ring that took his life.

"No wonder then that you're dazed. It must be a terrible thing to move backward in time, and still more terrible to pass backward through death. I was about to say that it would be like being born again; but it would be much worse than that, I think, because an infant lives already in his mother's womb." I hesitated. "I . . . Thecla, I mean . . . never bore a child."

Perhaps only because I had been thinking of his confusion, I found I was confused myself, so that I scarcely knew who I was. At last I said lamely, "You must excuse me. When I'm tired, and sometimes when I'm near sleep, I come near to becoming someone else." (For whatever reason, his grip on my shoulder tightened when I said that.) "It's a long story that has nothing to do with you. I wanted to say that in the Atrium of Time, the breaking of the pedestal had tilted the dials so their gnomons no longer pointed true, and I have heard that when that happens, the watches of day stop, or run backward for some part of each day. You carry a pocket dial, so you know that for it to tell time truly you must direct its gnomon toward the sun. The sun remains stationary while Urth dances about him, and it is by her dancing that we know the time, just as a deaf man might still beat out the rhythm of a tarantella by observing the swaying of the dancers. But what if the sun himself were to dance? Then, too, the march of the moments might become a retreat.

"I don't know if you believe in the New Sun—I'm not sure I ever have. But if he will exist, he will be the Conciliator come again, and thus *Conciliator* and *New Sun* are only two names for the same individual, and we may ask why that individual should be called the New Sun. What do you think? Might it not be for this power to move time?"

Now I felt indeed that time itself had stopped. Around us the trees rose dark and silent; night had freshened the air. I could think of nothing more to say, and I was ashamed to talk nonsense, because I felt somehow that the soldier had been listening attentively to all I had said. Before us I saw two pines far thicker through their trunks than the others lining the road, and a pale path of white and green that threaded its way between them. "There!" I exclaimed.

But when we reached them, I had to halt the soldier with my hands and turn him by the shoulders before he followed me. I noticed a dark splatter in the dust and bent to touch it.

It was clotted blood. "We are on the right road," I told him. "They have been bringing the wounded here."

I V

Fever

I CANNOT SAY how far we walked, or how far worn the night was before we reached our destination. I know that I began to stumble some time after we turned aside from the main road, and that it became a sort of disease to me; just as some sick men cannot stop coughing and others cannot keep their hands from shaking, so I tripped, and a few steps farther on tripped again, and then again. Unless I thought of nothing else, the toe of my left boot caught at my right heel, and I could not concentrate my mind—my thoughts ran off with every step I took.

Fireflies glimmered in the trees to either side of the path, and for a long time I supposed that the lights ahead of us were only more such insects and did not hurry my pace. Then, very suddenly as it seemed to me, we were beneath some shadowy roof where men and women with yellow lamps moved up and down between long rows of shrouded cots. A woman in clothes I supposed were black took charge of us and led us to another place where there were chairs of leather and horn, and a fire burned in a brazier. There I saw that her gown was scarlet, and she wore a scarlet hood, and for a moment I thought that she was Cyriaca.

"Your friend is very ill, isn't he?" she said. "Do you know what is the matter with him?"

And the soldier shook his head and answered, "No. I'm not even sure who he is."

I was too stunned to speak. She took my hand, then released it and took the soldier's. "He has a fever. So do you. Now that the heat of summer is come, we see more disease each day. You should have boiled your water and kept yourselves as clean of lice as you could."

She turned to me. "You have a great many shallow cuts too, and some them are infected. Rock shards?"

I managed to say, "I'm not the one who is ill. I brought my friend here."

"You are both ill, and I suspect you brought each other. I doubt that either of you would have reached us without the other. Was it rock shards? Some weapon of the enemy's?"

"Rock shards, yes. A weapon of a friend's."

"That is the worst thing, I am told—to be fired upon by your own side. But the fever is the chief concern." She hesitated, looking from the soldier to me and back. "I'd like to put you both in bed now, but you'll have to go to the bath first."

She clapped her hands to summon a burly man with a shaven head. He took our arms and began to lead us away, then stopped and picked me up, carrying me as I had once carried little Severian. In a few moments we were naked and sitting in a pool of water heated by stones. The burly man splashed more water over us, then made us get out one at a time so he could crop our hair with a pair of shears. After that we were left to soak awhile.

"You can speak now," I said to the soldier.

I saw him nod in the lamplight.

"Why didn't you, then, when we were coming here?"

He hesitated, and his shoulders moved a trifle. "I was thinking of many things, and you didn't talk yourself. You seemed so tired. Once I asked if we shouldn't stop, but you didn't answer."

I said, "It seemed to me otherwise, but perhaps we are both correct. Do you recall what happened to you before you met me?"

Again there was a pause. "I don't even remember meeting you. We were walking down a dark path, and you were beside me."

"And before that?"

"I don't know. Music, perhaps, and walking a long way. In sunshine at first but later through the dark."

"That walking was while you were with me," I said. "Don't you recall anything else?"

"Flying through the dark. Yes, I was with you, and we came to a place where the sun hung just above our heads. There was a light before us, but when I stepped into it, it became a kind of darkness."

I nodded. "You weren't wholly rational, you see. On a warm day it can seem that the sun's just overhead, and when it is down behind the mountains it seems the light becomes darkness. Do you recall your name?"

At that he thought for several moments, and at last smiled ruefully. "I lost it somewhere along the way. That's what the jaguar said, who had promised to guide the goat."

The burly man with the shaven head had come back without either of us noticing. He helped me out of the pool and gave me a towel with which to dry myself, a robe to wear, and a canvas sack containing my possessions, which now smelled strongly of the smoke of fumigation. A day earlier it would have tormented me nearly to frenzy to have the Claw out of my possession for an instant. That night I had hardly realized it was gone until it was returned to me, and I did not verify that it had indeed been returned until I lay on one of the cots under a veil of netting. The Claw shone in my hand then, softly as the moon; and it was shaped as the moon sometimes is. I smiled to think that its flooding light of pale green is the reflection of the sun.

On the first night I slept in Saltus, I had awakened thinking I was in the apprentices' dormitory in our tower. Now I had the same experience in reverse: I slept and found in sleep that the shadowy lazaret with its silent figures and moving lamps had been no more than a hallucination of the day.

I sat up and looked around. I felt well—better, in fact, than I had ever felt before; but I was warm. I seemed to glow from within. Roche was sleeping on his side, his red hair tousled and his mouth slightly open, his face relaxed and boyish without the energy of his mind behind it. Through the port I could see snow drifts in the Old Court, new-fallen snow that showed no tracks of men or their animals; but it occurred to me that in the necropolis there would be hundreds of footprints already as the small creatures who found shelter there, the pets and the playmates of the dead, came out to search for food and to disport themselves in the new landscape Nature had bestowed on them. I dressed quickly and silently, holding my finger to my own lips when one of the other apprentices stirred, and hurried down the steep stair that wound through the center of the tower.

It seemed longer than usual, and I found I had difficulty in going from step to step. We are always aware of the hindrance of gravity when we climb stairs, but we take for granted the assistance it gives us when we descend. Now that assistance had been withdrawn, or nearly so. I had to force each foot down, but do it in a way that prevented it from sending me shooting up when it struck the step, as it would have if I had stamped. In that uncanny way we know things in dreams, I understood that all the towers of the Citadel had risen at last and were on their voyage beyond the circle of Dis. I felt happy in the knowledge, but I still desired to go into the necropolis and track the coatis and foxes. I was hurrying down as fast as I could when I heard a groan. The stairway no longer descended as it should but led into a cabin, just as the stairs in Baldanders's castle had stretched down the walls of its chambers.

This was Master Malrubius's sickroom. Masters are entitled to spacious quarters; still, this was larger by far than the actual cabin had been. There were two ports just as I remembered, but they were enormous—the eyes of Mount Typhon. Master Malrubius's bed was very large, yet it seemed lost in the immensity of the room. Two figures bent over him. Though their clothing was dark, it struck me that it was not the fuligin of the guild. I went to them, and when I was so near I could hear the sick man's labored breathing, they straightened up and turned to look at me. They were the Cumaean and her acolyte Merryn, the witches we had met atop the tomb in the ruined stone town.

"Ah, sister, you have come at last," Merryn said.

As she spoke, I realized that I was not, as I had thought, the apprentice Severian. I was Thecla as she had been when she was his height, which is to say at about the age of thirteen or fourteen. I felt an intense embarrassment—not because of my girl's body or because I was wearing masculine clothes (which indeed I rather enjoyed) but because I had been unaware of it previously. I also felt that Merryn's words had been an act of magic—that both Severian and I had been present before, and that she had by some means driven him into the background. The Cumaean kissed me on the forehead, and when the kiss was over wiped blood from her lips. Although she did not speak, I knew this was a signal that I had in some sense become the soldier too.

"When we sleep," Merryn told me, "we move from temporality to eternity."

"When we wake," the Cumaean whispered, "we lose the facility to see beyond the present moment."

"She never wakes," Merryn boasted.

Master Malrubius stirred and groaned, and the Cumaean

took a carafe of water from the table by his bed and poured a little into a tumbler. When she set down the carafe again, something living stirred in it. I, for some reason, thought it the undine; I drew back, but it was Hethor, no higher than my hand, his gray, stubbled face pressed against the glass.

I heard his voice as one might hear the squeaking of mice: "Sometimes driven aground by the photon storms, by the swirling of the galaxies, clockwise and counterclockwise, ticking with light down the dark sea-corridors lined with our silver sails, our demon-haunted mirror sails, our hundred-league masts as fine as threads, as fine as silver needles sewing the threads of starlight, embroidering the stars on black velvet, wet with the winds of Time that goes racing by. The bone in her teeth! The spume, the flying spume of Time, cast up on these beaches where old sailors can no longer keep their bones from the restless, the unwearied universe. Where has she gone? My lady, the mate of my soul? Gone across the running tides of Aquarius, of Pisces, of Aries. Gone. Gone in her little boat, her nipples pressed against the black velvet lid, gone, sailing away forever from the star-washed shores, the dry shoals of the habitable worlds. She is her own ship, she is the figurehead of her own ship, and the captain. Bosun, Bosun, put out the launch! Sailmaker, make a sail! She has left us behind. We have left her behind. She is in the past we never knew and the future we will not see. Put out more sail, Captain, for the universe is leaving us behind. . . ."

There was a bell on the table beside the carafe. Merryn rang it as though to overpower Hethor's voice, and when Master Malrubius had moistened his lips with the tumbler, she took it from the Cumaean, flung what remained of its water on the floor, and inverted it over the neck of the carafe. Hethor was silenced, but the water spread over the floor, bubbling as though fed by a hidden spring. It was icy cold. I thought vaguely that my governess would be angry because my shoes were wet.

A maid was coming in answer to the ring—Thecla's maid,

whose flayed leg I had inspected the day after I had saved Vodalus. She was younger, as young as she must have been when Thecla was actually a girl, but her leg had been flayed already and ran with blood. "I am so sorry," I said. "I am so sorry, Hunna. I didn't do it—it was Master Gurloes, and some journeymen."

Master Malrubius sat up in bed, and for the first time I observed that his bed was in actuality a woman's hand, with fingers longer than my arm and nails like talons. "You're well!" he said, as though I were the one who had been dying. "Or nearly well, at least." The fingers of the hand began to close upon him, but he leaped from the bed and into water that was now knee high to stand beside me.

A dog—my old dog Triskele—had apparently been hiding beneath the bed, or perhaps only lying on the farther side of it, out of sight. Now he came to us, splashing the water with his single forepaw as he drove his broad chest through it and barking joyously. Master Malrubius took my right hand and the Cumaean my left; together they led me to one of the great eyes of the mountain.

I saw the view I had seen when Typhon had led me there: The world rolled out like a carpet and visible in its entirety. This time it was more magnificent by far. The sun was behind us; its beams seemed to have multiplied their strength. Shadows were alchemized to gold, and every green thing grew darker and stronger as I looked. I could see the grain ripening in the fields and even the myriad fish of the sea doubling and redoubling with the increase of the tiny surface plants that sustained them. Water from the room behind us poured from the eye and, catching the light, fell in a rainbow.

Then I woke.

While I slept, someone had wrapped me in sheets packed with snow. (I learned later that it was brought down from the mountaintops by sure-footed sumpters.) Shivering, I longed to return to my dream, though I was already half-aware of the immense distance that separated us. The bitter taste of medicine was in my mouth, the stretched canvas felt as hard as a floor beneath me, and scarlet-clad Pelerines with lamps moved to and fro, tending men and women who groaned in the dark.

V

The Lazaret

I DO NOT BELIEVE I really slept again that night, though I may have dozed. When dawn came, the snow had melted. Two Pelerines took the sheets away, gave me a towel with which to dry myself, and brought dry bedding. I wanted to give the Claw to them then—my possessions were in the bag under my cot—but the moment seemed inappropriate. I lay down instead, and now that it was daylight, slept.

I woke again about noon. The lazaret was as quiet as it ever became; somewhere far off two men were talking and another cried out, but their voices only emphasized the stillness. I sat up and looked around, hoping to see the soldier. On my right lay a man whose close-cropped scalp made me think at first that he was one of the slaves of the Pelerines. I called to him, but when he turned his head to look at me, I saw I had been mistaken.

His eyes were emptier than any human eyes I had ever seen, and they seemed to watch spirits invisible to me. "Glory to the Group of Seventeen," he said.

"Good morning. Do you know anything about the way this place is run?"

A shadow appeared to cross his face, and I sensed that my

question had somehow made him suspicious. He answered, "All endeavors are conducted well or ill precisely in so far as they conform to Correct Thought."

"Another man was brought in at the same time I was. I'd like to talk to him. He's a friend of mine, more or less."

"Those who do the will of the populace are friends, though we have never spoken to them. Those who do not do the will of the populace are enemies, though we learned together as children."

The man on my left called, "You won't get anything out of him. He's a prisoner."

I turned to look at him. His face, though wasted nearly to a skull, retained something of humor. His stiff, black hair looked as though it had not seen a comb for months.

"He talks like that all the time. Never any other way. *Hey, you!* We're going to beat you!"

The other answered, "For the Armies of the Populace, defeat is the springboard of victory, and victory the ladder to further victory."

"He makes a lot more sense than most of them, though," the man on my left told me.

"You say he's a prisoner. What did he do?"

"Do? Why, he didn't die."

"I'm afraid I don't understand. Was he selected for some kind of suicide mission?"

The patient beyond the man on my left sat up—a young woman with a thin but lovely face. "They all are," she said. "At least, they can't go home until the war is won, and they know, really, that it will never be won."

"External battles are already won when internal struggles are conducted with Correct Thought."

I said, "He's an Ascian, then. That's what you meant. I've never seen one before."

"Most of them die," the black-haired man told me. "That's what I said."

"I didn't know they spoke our language."

"They don't. Some officers who came here to talk to him said they thought he'd been an interpreter. Probably he questioned our soldiers when they were captured. Only he did something wrong and had to go back to the ranks."

The young woman said, "I don't think he's really mad. Most of them are. What's your name?"

"I'm sorry, I should have introduced myself. I'm Severian." I almost added that I was a lictor, but I knew neither of them would talk to me if I told them that.

"I'm Foila, and this is Melito. I was of the Blue Huzzars, he a hoplite."

"You shouldn't talk nonsense," Melito growled. "I am a hoplite. You are a huzzar."

I thought he appeared much nearer death than she.

"I'm only hoping we will be discharged when we're well enough to leave this place," Foila said.

"And what will we do then? Milk somebody else's cow and herd his pigs?" Melito turned to me. "Don't let her talk deceive you—we were volunteers, both of us. I was about to be promoted when I was wounded, and when I'm promoted I'll be able to support a wife."

Foila called, "I haven't promised to marry you!"

Several beds away, someone said loudly, "Take her so she'll shut up about it!"

At that, the patient in the bed beyond Foila's sat up. "She will marry me." He was big, fair skinned, and pale haired, and he spoke with the deliberation characteristic of the icy isles of the south. "I am Hallvard."

Surprising me, the Ascian prisoner announced, "United, men and women are stronger; but a brave woman desires children, and not husbands."

Foila said, "They fight even when they're pregnant—I've seen them dead on the battlefield."

"The roots of the tree are the populace. The leaves fall, but the tree remains."

I asked Melito and Foila if the Ascian were composing his

remarks or quoting some literary source with which I was unfamiliar.

"Just making it up, you mean?" Foila asked. "No. They never do that. Everything they say has to be taken from an approved text. Some of them don't talk at all. The rest have thousands—I suppose actually tens or hundreds of thousands—of those tags memorized."

"That's impossible," I said.

Melito shrugged. He had managed to prop himself up on one elbow. "They do it, though. At least, that's what everybody says. Foila knows more about them than I do."

Foila nodded. "In the light cavalry, we do a lot of scouting, and sometimes we're sent out specifically to take prisoners. You don't learn anything from talking to most of them, but just the same the General Staff can tell a good deal from their equipment and physical condition. On the northern continent, where they come from, only the smallest children ever talk the way we do."

I thought of Master Gurloes conducting the business of our guild. "How could they possibly say something like 'Take three apprentices and unload that wagon'?"

"They wouldn't *say* that at all—just grab people by the shoulder, point to the wagon, and give them a push. If they went to work, fine. If they didn't, then the leader would quote something about the need for labor to ensure victory, with several witnesses present. If the person he was talking to still wouldn't work after that, then he would have him killed—probably just by pointing to him and quoting something about the need to eliminate the enemies of the populace."

The Ascian said, "The cries of the children are the cries of victory. Still, victory must learn wisdom."

Foila interpreted for him. "That means that although children are needed, what they say is meaningless. Most Ascians would consider us mute even if we learned their tongue, because groups of words that are not approved texts are with-

out meaning for them. If they admitted—even to themselves—that such talk meant something, then it would be
possible for them to hear disloyal remarks, and even to make
them. That would be extremely dangerous. As long as they
only understand and quote approved texts, no one can accuse
them."

I turned my head to look at the Ascian. It was clear that he
had been listening attentively, but I could not be certain of
what his expression meant beyond that. "Those who write
the approved texts," I told him, "cannot themselves be quoting from approved texts as they write. Therefore even an
approved text may contain elements of disloyalty."

"Correct Thought is the thought of the populace. The
populace cannot betray the populace or the Group of Seventeen."

Foila called, "Don't insult the populace or the Group of
Seventeen. He might try to kill himself. Sometimes they do."

"Will he ever be normal?"

"I've heard that some of them eventually come to talk
more or less the way we do, if that's what you mean."

I could think of nothing to say to that, and for some time
we were quiet. There are long periods of silence, I found, in
such a place, where almost everyone is ill. We knew that we
had watch after watch to occupy; that if we did not say what
we wished to say that afternoon there would be another opportunity that evening and another again the next morning.
Indeed, anyone who talked as healthy people normally do—
after a meal, for example—would have been intolerable.

But what had been said had set me thinking of the north,
and I found I knew next to nothing about it. When I had
been a boy, scrubbing floors and running errands in the Citadel, the war itself had seemed almost infinitely remote. I
knew that most of the matrosses who manned the major bat-
teries had taken part in it, but I knew it just as I knew that
the sunlight that fell upon my hand had been to the sun. I

would be a torturer, and as a torturer I would have no reason to enter the army and no reason to fear that I would be impressed into it. I never expected to see the war at the gates of Nessus (in fact, those gates themselves were hardly more than legends to me), and I never expected to leave the city, or even to leave that quarter of the city that held the Citadel.

The north, Ascia, was then inconceivably remote, a place as distant as the most distant galaxy, since both were forever out of reach. Mentally, I confused it with the dying belt of tropical vegetation that lay between our own land and theirs, although I would have distinguished the two without difficulty if Master Palaemon had asked me to in the classroom.

But of Ascia itself I had no idea. I did not know if it had great cities or none. I did not know if it was mountainous like the northern and eastern parts of our Commonwealth or as level as our pampas. I did have the impression (though I could not be sure it was correct) that it was a single land mass, and not a chain of islands like our south; and most distinct of all, I had the impression of an innumerable people—our Ascian's populace—an inexhaustible swarm that almost became a creature in itself, as a colony of ants does. To think of those millions upon millions without speech, or confined to parroting proverbial phrases that must surely have long ago lost most of their meaning, was nearly more than the mind could bear. Speaking almost to myself, I said, "It must surely be a trick, or a lie, or a mistake. Such a nation could not exist."

And the Ascian, his voice no louder than my own had been, and perhaps even softer, answered, "How shall the state be most vigorous? It shall be most vigorous when it is without conflict. How shall it be without conflict? When it is without disagreement. How shall disagreement be banished? By banishing the four causes of disagreement: lies, foolish talk, boastful talk, and talk which serves only to incite quarrels. How shall the four causes be banished? By speaking only Correct Thought. Then shall the state be without disagreement. Being without disagreement it shall be without conflict. Being without conflict it shall be vigorous, strong, and secure."

I had been answered, and doubly.

Miles, Foila, Melito, and Hallvard

THAT EVENING I fell prey to a fear I had been trying to put from my mind for some time. Although I had seen nothing of the monsters Hethor had brought from beyond the stars since little Severian and I had escaped from the village of the sorcerers, I had not forgotten that he was searching for me. While I traveled in the wilderness or upon the waters of Lake Diuturna, I had not been much afraid he would overtake me. Now I was traveling no longer, and I could feel the weakness in my limbs, for despite the food I had eaten I was weaker than I had ever been while starving in the mountains.

Then too, I feared Agia almost more than Hethor's notules, his salamanders and slugs. I knew her courage, her cleverness, and her malice. Any one of the scarlet-clad priestesses of the Pelerines moving between the cots might easily be she, with a poisoned stiletto beneath her gown. I slept badly that night; but though I dreamed much, my dreams were indistinct, and I will not attempt to relate them here.

I woke feeling less than rested. My fever, of which I had hardly been conscious when I came to the lazaret, and which had seemed to subside on the day previous, returned. I felt its heat in every limb—it seemed to me that I must glow, that the very glaciers of the south would melt if I came among them. I took out the Claw and clasped it to me, and for a time even held it in my mouth. My fever sank again, but left me weak and dizzied.

That morning the soldier came to see me. He wore a white gown the Pelerines had given him in place of his armor, but he appeared wholly recovered, and told me he hoped to leave the next day. I said I would like to introduce him to the acquaintances I had made in this part of the lazaret and asked if he now recalled his name.

He shook his head. "I can remember very little. I am hoping that when I go among the units of the army I will find someone there who knows me."

I introduced him anyway, calling him Miles since I could think of nothing better. I did not know the Ascian's name either and discovered that no one did, not even Foila. When we asked him what it was, he only said, "I am Loyal to the Group of Seventeen."

For a time Foila, Melito, the soldier, and I chatted among ourselves. Melito seemed to like him very well, though perhaps only because of the similarity of the name I had given him to his own. Then the soldier helped me into a sitting posture, lowered his voice, and said, "Now I have to talk to you privately. As I said, I think I will leave here in the morning. From what I have seen of you, you won't be getting out for several days—maybe not for a couple of weeks. I may never see you again."

"Let us hope that isn't so."

"I hope not either. But if I can find my legion, I may be killed by the time you're well. And if I can't find it, I'll probably go into another to keep from being arrested as a deserter." He paused.

I smiled. "And I may die here, of the fever. You didn't want to say that. Do I look as bad as poor Melito?"

He shook his head. "Not as bad, no. I think you'll make it—"

"That's what the thrush sang while the lynx chased the hare around the bay tree."

Now it was his turn to smile. "You're right; I was about to say that."

"Is it a common expression in that part of the Commonwealth where you were brought up?"

The smile vanished. "I don't know. I can't remember where my home is, and that's part of the reason I have to talk to you now. I remember walking down a road with you at night—that's the only thing I *do* remember, before I came here. Where did you find me?"

"In a wood, I suppose about five or ten leagues south of here. Do you recall what I told you about the Claw as we walked?"

He shook his head. "I think I remember you mentioning such a thing, but not what you said."

"What do you remember? Tell me all of it, and I'll tell you what I know, and what I can guess."

"Walking with you. A lot of darkness . . . I fell, or maybe flew through it. Seeing my own face, multiplied again and again. A girl with hair like red gold and enormous eyes."

"A beautiful woman?"

He nodded. "The most beautiful in the world."

Raising my voice, I asked if anyone had a mirror he would lend us for a moment. Foila produced one from the possessions beneath her cot, and I held it up for the soldier. "Is this the face?"

He hesitated. "I think so."

"Blue eyes?"

". . . I can't be sure."

I returned the mirror to Foila. "I will tell you again what I told you on the road, and I wish we had a more private place in which to do it. Some time ago a talisman came into my hands. It came innocently, but it does not belong to me, and it is very valuable—sometimes, not always, but sometimes—it has the power to heal the sick, and even to revive the dead.

Two days ago, as I was traveling north, I came across the body of a dead soldier. It was in a forest, away from the road. He had been dead less than a day; I would say it's likely he had died sometime during the preceding night. I was very hungry then, and I cut his pack straps and ate most of the food he had been carrying with him. Then I felt guilty about doing that and got out the talisman and tried to restore him to life. It has failed often before, and this time I thought for a while it was going to fail again. It didn't, although he returned to life slowly and for a long time did not seem to know where he was or what was happening to him."

"And I was that soldier?"

I nodded, looking into his honest blue eyes.

"May I see the talisman?"

I took it out and held it in the palm of my hand. He took it from me, examined both sides carefully, and tested the point against the ball of his finger. "It doesn't look magical," he said.

"I'm not sure *magical* is the right term for it. I've met magicians, and nothing they did reminded me of this or the way it acts. Sometimes it glows with light—it's very faint now, and I doubt if you can see it."

"I can't. There doesn't seem to be any writing on it."

"You mean spells or prayers. No, I've never noticed any, and I've carried it a long way. I don't really know anything about it except that it acts at times; but I think it is probably the kind of thing spells and prayers are made with, and not the kind that is made with them."

"You said it didn't belong to you."

I nodded again. "It belongs to the priestesses here, the Pelerines."

"You just came here. Two nights ago, when I did."

"I came looking for them, to give it back. It was taken from them—not by me—some time ago, in Nessus."

"And you're going to return it?" He looked at me as though he somehow doubted it.

"Yes, eventually."

He stood up, smoothing his robe with his hands.

I said, "You don't believe me, do you? Not about any of it."

"When I came here, you introduced me to the others nearby, the ones you'd talked with while you lay here on your cot." He spoke slowly, seeming to ponder every word. "Of course I've met some people too, where they put me. There's one who isn't really wounded very badly. He's just a boy, a youngster off some small holding a long way from here, and he mostly sits on his cot and looks at the floor."

"Homesick?" I asked.

The soldier shook his head. "He had an energy weapon. A korseke—that's what somebody told me. Are you familiar with them?"

"Not very."

"They project a beam straight forward, and at the same time two quartering beams, forward left and forward right. Their range isn't great, but they say they're very good for dealing with mass attacks, and I suppose they are."

He looked about for a moment to see if anyone was listening, but it is a point of honor in the lazaret to disregard completely any conversation not intended for oneself. If it were not so, the patients would soon be at each other's throats.

"His hundred was the target of one of those attacks. Most of the others broke and ran. He didn't, and they didn't get him. Another man told me there were three walls of bodies in front of him. He had dropped them until the Ascians were climbing up to the top and jumping down at him. Then he had backed away and piled them up again."

I said, "I suppose he got a medal and a promotion." I could not be sure if it was my fever returning or merely the heat of the day, but I felt sticky and somehow suffocated.

"No, they sent him here. I told you he was only a boy from the country. He had killed more people that day than he had ever seen up to the time a few months before when he went into the army. He still hasn't gotten over it, and maybe he never will."

"Yes?"

"It seems to me you might be like that."

"I don't understand you," I said.

"You talk as if you've just come here from the south, and I suppose that if you've left your legion that's the safest way to talk. Just the same, anybody can see it isn't true—people don't get cut up the way you are except where the fighting is. You were hit by rock splinters. That's what happened to you, and the Pelerine who spoke to us the first night we were here saw that right away. So I think you've been north longer than you'll admit, and maybe longer than you think yourself. If you've killed a lot of people, it might be nice for you to believe you have a way to bring them back."

I tried to grin at him. "And where does that leave you?"

"Where I am now. I'm not trying to say I owe you nothing. I had fever, and you found me. Maybe I was delirious. I think it's more likely I was unconscious, and that let you think I was dead. If you hadn't brought me here, I probably would have died."

He started to stand up; I stopped him with a hand on his arm. "There are some things I should tell you before you go," I said. "About yourself."

"You said you didn't know who I was."

I shook my head. "I didn't say that, not really. I said I found you in a wood two days ago. In the sense you mean, I *don't* know who you are—but in another sense I think I may. I think you're two people, and that I know one of them."

"Nobody is two people."

"I am. I'm two people already. Perhaps more people are two than we know. The first thing I want to tell you is much simpler, though. Now listen." I gave him detailed directions for finding the wood again, and when I was certain he understood them, I said, "Your pack is probably still there, with the straps cut, so if you find the place you won't mistake it. There was a letter in your pack. I pulled it out and read a part of it. It didn't carry the name of the person you were writing to, but if you had finished it and were just waiting for a chance to send it off, it should have at least a part of your name at the end. I put it on the ground and it blew a little and caught against a tree. It may still be possible for you to find it."

His face had tightened. "You shouldn't have read it, and you shouldn't have thrown it away."

"I thought you were dead, remember? Anyway, a good deal was going on at the time, mostly inside my head. Perhaps I was getting feverish—I don't know. Now here's the other part. You won't believe me, but it may be important that you listen. Will you hear me out?"

He nodded.

"Good. Have you heard of the mirrors of Father Inire? Do you know how they work?"

"I've heard of Father Inire's Mirror, but I couldn't tell you where I heard about it. You're supposed to be able to step into it, like you'd step into a doorway, and step out on a star. I don't think it's real."

"The mirrors are real. I've seen them. Up until now I always thought of them in much the same way you did—as if they were a ship, but much faster. Now I'm not nearly so sure. Anyway, a certain friend of mine stepped between those mirrors and vanished. I was watching him. It was no trick and no superstition; he went wherever the mirrors take you. He went because he loved a certain woman, and he wasn't a whole man. Do you understand?"

"He'd had an accident?"

"An accident had had him, but never mind that. He told me he would come back. He said, 'I will come back for her when I have been repaired, when I am sane and whole.' I didn't quite know what to think when he said that, but now I believe he has come. It was I who revived you, and I had been wishing for his return—perhaps that had something to do with it."

There was a pause. The soldier looked down at the trampled soil on which the cots had been set, then up again at me. "Possibly whenever a man loses his friend and gets another, he feels the old friend is with him again."

"Jonas—that was his name—had a habit of speech. Whenever he had to say something unpleasant, he softened it, made a joke of it, by attributing what he said to some comic situation. The first night we were here, when I asked you your name, you said, 'I lost it somewhere along the way. That's what the jaguar said, who had promised to guide the goat.' Do you recall that?"

He shook his head. "I say a lot of foolish things."

"It struck me as strange; because it was the kind of thing Jonas said, but he wouldn't have said it in that way unless he meant more by it than you seemed to. I think he would have said, 'That was the basket's story, that had been filled with water.' Something like that."

I waited for him to speak, but he did not.

"The jaguar ate the goat, of course. Swallowed its flesh and cracked its bones, somewhere along the way."

"Haven't you ever thought that it might be just the peculiarity of some town? Your friend might have come from the same place I do."

I said, "It was a time, I think, and not a place. Long ago, someone had to disarm fear—the fear that men of flesh and blood might feel when looking into a face of steel and glass. Jonas, I know you're listening. I don't blame you. The man was dead, and you still alive. I understand that. But Jonas, Jolenta is gone—I watched her die, and I tried to bring her back with the Claw, but I failed. Perhaps she was too artificial, I don't know. You will have to find someone else."

The soldier rose. His face was no longer angry, but empty as a somnambulist's. He turned and left without another word.

• • •

For perhaps a watch I lay on my cot with my hands behind my head, thinking of many things. Hallvard, Melito, and Foila were talking among themselves, but I did not attend to what they said. When one of the Pelerines brought the noon meal, Melito got my ear by rapping his platter with a fork and announced, "Severian, we have a favor to ask of you."

I was eager to put my speculations behind me, and told him I would help them in any way I could.

Foila, who had one of those radiant smiles Nature grants to some women, smiled at me now. "It's like this. These two have been bickering over me all morning. If they were well they could fight it out, but it will be a long time before they are, and I don't think I could stand it so long. Today I was thinking of my mother and father, and how they used to sit before the fire on long winter nights. If Hallvard and I marry, or Melito and I, someday we'll be doing that too. So I have decided to marry the best storyteller. Don't look at me as if I were mad—it's the only sensible thing I've done in my life. Both of them want me, both are very handsome, neither has any property, and if we don't settle this they'll kill each other or I'll kill them both. You're an educated man—we can tell by the way you talk. You listen and judge. Hallvard first, and the stories have to be original, not out of books."

Hallvard, who could walk a little, got up from his cot and came to sit on the foot of Melito's.

VII

Hallvard's Story—The Two Sealers

"This is a true story. I know many stories. Some are made up, though perhaps the made up ones were true in times everyone has forgotten. I also know many true ones, because many strange things happen in the isles of the south that you northern people never dream of. I chose this one because I was there myself and saw and heard as much of it as anyone did.

"I come from the easternmost of the southern isles, which is called Glacies. On our isle lived a man and a woman, my grandparents, who had three sons. Their names were Anskar, Hallvard, and Gundulf. Hallvard was my father, and when I grew large enough to help him on his boat, he no longer hunted and fished with his brothers. Instead, we two went out so that all we caught could be brought home to my mother, and my sisters and younger brother.

"My uncles never married, and so they continued to share a boat. What they caught they ate themselves or gave to my grandparents, who were no longer strong. In the summer they farmed my grandfather's land. He had the best on our isle, the only valley that never felt the ice wind. You could grow things there that would not ripen anywhere else on Glacies, because the growing season in this valley was two weeks longer.

"When my beard was starting to sprout, my grandfather called all the men of our family together—that was my father, my two uncles, and myself. When we got to his house, my grandmother was dead, and the priest from the big isle was there to lay out her body. Her sons wept, as I did myself.

"That night, when we sat at my grandfather's table, with him at one end and the priest at the other, he said, 'Now it is time that I dispose of my property. Bega is gone. Her family has no more claim on it, and I shall follow her shortly. Hallvard is married and has the portion that came to him from his wife. With that he provides for his family, and though they have little to spare, they do not go hungry. You, Anskar. And you, Gundulf. Will you ever marry?'

"Both my uncles shook their heads.

" 'Then this is my will. I call upon the Omnipotent to hear, and I call upon the servants of the Omnipotent also. When I die, all that I have shall go to Anskar and Gundulf. If one die, it shall go to the other. When both are dead, it shall go to Hallvard, or if Hallvard is dead, it shall be divided among his sons. You four—if you do not agree my will is just, speak now.'

"No one spoke, and thus it was decided.

"A year passed. A ship of Erebus came raiding out of the mists, and two ships put in for hides, sea ivory, and salt fish. My grandfather died, and my sister Fausta bore her girl. When the harvest was in, my uncles fished with the other men.

"When spring comes in the south, it is still too early to plant, for there will be many freezing nights to come. But when men see that the days are lengthening fast, they seek out the rookeries where the seals breed. These are on rocks far from any shore, there is much fog, and though they are growing longer, the days are still short. Often it is the men who die and not the seals.

"And so it was with my Uncle Anskar, for my Uncle Gundulf returned in their boat without him.

"Now you must know that when our men go sealing, or fishing, or hunting any other kind of sea game, they tie themselves to their boats. The rope is of braided walrus hide, and it is long enough to let the man move about in the boat as much as is needful, but not longer. The sea water is very cold and soon kills whoever remains in it, but our men dress in sealskin tight-sewn, and often a man's boat-mate can pull him back and in that way save his life.

"This is the tale my Uncle Gundulf told. They had gone far, seeking a rookery others had not visited, when Anskar saw a bull seal swimming in the water. He cast his harpoon; and when the seal sounded, a loop of the harpoon line had caught his ankle, so that he was dragged into the sea. He, Gundulf, had tried to pull him out, for he was a very strong man. But his pulling and the pulling of the seal on the harpoon line, which was tied to the base of the mast, had capsized their boat. Gundulf had saved himself by pulling himself hand over hand back to it and cutting the harpoon line with his knife. When the boat was righted he had tried to haul in Anskar, but the life rope had broken. He showed the frayed rope end. My Uncle Anskar was dead.

"Among my people, women die on land but men at sea, and therefore we call the kind of grave you make 'a woman's boat.' When a man dies as Uncle Anskar did, a hide is stretched and painted for him and hung in the house where the men meet to talk. It is never taken down until no man living can recall the man who was honored so. A hide like that was prepared for Anskar, and the painters began their work.

"Then one bright morning when my father and I were readying the tools to break ground for the new year's crop— well I remember it!—some children who had been sent to gather birds' eggs came running into the village. A seal, they said, lay on the shingle of the south bay. As everyone knows, no seal comes to land where men are. But it sometimes happens that a seal will die at sea or be injured in some fashion. Thinking of that, my father and I and many others ran to the beach, for the seal would belong to the first whose weapon pierced it.

"I was the swiftest of all, and I provided myself with an earth-fork. Such a thing does not throw well, but several other young men were at my heels, so when I was a hundred strides away I cast it. Straight and true it flew and buried its tines in the thing's back. Then followed such a moment as I hope never to see again. The weight of the fork's long handle overbalanced it, and it rolled until the handle rested on the ground.

"I saw the face of my Uncle Anskar, preserved by the cold sea brine. His beard was tangled with the dark green kelp, and his life rope of stout walrus hide had been cut only a few spans from his body.

"My Uncle Gundulf had not seen him, for he was gone to the big isle. My father took Anskar up, and I helped him, and we carried him to Gundulf's house and put the end of the rope upon his chest where Gundulf would see it, and with some other men of Glacies sat down to wait for him.

"He shouted when he saw his brother. It was not such a cry as a woman makes, but a bellow like the bull seal gives when he warns the other bulls from his herd. He ran in the dark. We set a guard on the boats and hunted him that night across the isle. The lights that spirits make in the ultimate south flamed all night, so we knew Anskar hunted with us. Brightest they flashed before they faded, when we found him among the rocks at Radbod's End."

Hallvard fell silent. Indeed, silence lay about us everywhere. All the sick within hearing had been listening to him. At last Melito said, "Did you kill him?"

"No. In the old days it was so, and a bad thing. Now the mainland law avenges bloodguilt, which is better. We bound his arms and legs and laid him in his house, and I sat with him while the older men readied the boats. He told me he had loved a woman on the big isle. I never saw her, but he said her name was Nennoc, and she was fair, and younger than he, but no man would have her because she had borne a child by a man who had died the winter before. In the boat, he had told Anskar he would carry Nennoc home, and Anskar called him *oath-breaker*. My Uncle Gundulf was strong. He seized Anskar and threw him out of the boat, then wrapped the life rope about his hands and snapped it as a woman who sews breaks her thread.

"He had stood then, he said, with one hand on the mast, as men do, and watched his brother in the water. He had seen the flash of the knife, but he thought only that Anskar sought to threaten him with it or to throw it."

Hallvard was silent again, and when I saw he would not speak, I said, "I don't understand. What did Anskar do?"

A smile, the very smallest smile, tugged at Hallvard's lips under his blond mustache. When I saw it, I felt I had seen the ice isles of the south, blue and bitterly cold. "He cut his life rope, the rope Gundulf had already broken. In that way, men who found his body would know that he had been murdered. Do you see?"

I saw, and for a while I said nothing more.

"So," Melito grunted to Foila, "the wonderful valley land went to Hallvard's father, and by this story he has managed to tell you that though he has no property, he has prospects of inheriting some. He has also told you, of course, that he comes of a murderous family."

"Melito believes me much cleverer than I am," the blond man rumbled. "I had no such thoughts. What matters now is not land or skins or gold, but who tells the best tale. And I, who know many, have told the best I know. It is true as he says that I might share my family's property when my father dies. But my unmarried sisters will have some part too for their marriage portions, and only what remained would be divided between my brother and myself. All that matters nothing, because I would not take Foila to the south, where life is so hard. Since I have carried a lance I have seen many better places."

Foila said, "I think your Uncle Gundulf must have loved Nennoc very much."

Hallvard nodded. "He said that too while he lay bound. But all the men of the south love their women. It is for them that they face the sea in winter, the storms and the freezing fogs. It is said that as a man pushes his boat out over the shingle, the sound the bottom makes grating on the stones is *my wife, my children, my children, my wife.*"

I asked Melito if he wanted to begin his story then; but he shook his head and said that we were all full of Hallvard's, so he would wait and begin next day. Everyone then asked Hallvard questions about life in the south and compared what they had learned to the way their own people lived. Only the Ascian was silent. I was reminded of the floating islands of Lake Diuturna and told Hallvard and the others about them, though I did not describe the fight at Baldanders's castle. We talked in this way until it was time for the evening meal.

VIII

The Pelerine

By the time we had finished eating, it was beginning to get dark. We were always quieter then, not only because we lacked strength, but because we knew that those wounded who would die were more liable to do so after the sun set, and particularly in the deep of the night. It was the time when past battles called home their debts.

In other ways too, the night made us more aware of the war. Sometimes—and on that night I remember them particularly—the discharges of the great energy weapons blazed across the sky like heat lightning. One heard the sentries marching to their posts, so that the word *watch*, which we so often used with no meaning beyond that of a tenth part of the night, became an audible reality, an actuality of tramping feet and unintelligible commands.

There came a moment when no one spoke, that lengthened and lengthened, interrupted only by the murmurings of the well—the Pelerines and their male slaves—who came to ask the condition of this patient or that. One of the scarlet-clad priestesses came and sat by my cot, and my mind was so slow, so nearly sleeping, that it was some time before I realized that she must have carried a stool with her.

"You are Severian," she said, "the friend of Miles?"

"Yes."

"He has recalled his name. I thought you would like to know."

I asked her what it was.

"Why, Miles, of course. I told you."

"He will recall more than that, I think, as time goes by."

She nodded. She seemed to be a woman past middle age, with a kindly, austere face. "I am sure he will. His home and family."

"If he has them."

"Yes, some do not. Some lack even the ability to make a home."

"You're referring to me."

"No, not at all. Anyway, that lack is not something the person can do something about. But it is much better, particularly for men, if they have a home. Like the man your friend talked about, most men think they make their homes for their families, but the fact is that they make both homes and families for themselves."

"You were listening to Hallvard, then."

"Several of us were. It was a good story. A sister came and got me at the place where the patient's grandfather made his will. I heard all the rest. Do you know what the trouble was with the bad uncle? With Gundulf?"

"I suppose that he was in love."

"No, that was what was right with him. Every person, you see, is like a plant. There is a beautiful green part, often with flowers or fruit, that grows upward toward the sun, toward the Increate. There is also a dark part that grows away from it, tunneling where no light comes."

I said, "I have never studied the writings of the initiates, but even I am aware of the existence of good and evil in everyone."

"Was I speaking of good and evil? It is the roots that give the plant the strength to climb toward the sun, though they know nothing of it. Suppose that some scythe, whistling along the ground, should sever the stalk from its roots. The stalk would fall and die, but the roots might put up a new stalk."

"You are saying that evil is good."

"No. I am saying that the things we love in others and admire in ourselves spring from things we do not see and seldom think about. Gundulf, like other men, had the instinct to exercise authority. Its proper growth is the founding of a family—and women, too, have a similar instinct. In Gundulf that instinct had long been frustrated, as it is in so many of the soldiers we see here. The officers have their commands, but the soldiers who have no command suffer and do not know why they suffer. Some, of course, form bonds with others in the ranks. Sometimes several share a single woman, or a man who is like a woman. Some make pets of animals, and some befriend children left homeless by the struggle."

Remembering Casdoe's son, I said, "I can see why you object to that."

"We do not object—most certainly not to that, and not to things vastly less natural. I am only speaking of the instinct to exercise authority. In the bad uncle it made him love a woman, and specifically one who already possessed a child, so there would be a larger family for him as soon as there was a family for him at all. In that way, you see, he would have regained some part of the time he had lost."

She paused, and I nodded.

"Too much time, however, had been lost already; the instinct broke out in another way. He saw himself as the rightful master of lands he only held in trust for one brother, and the master of the life of the other. That vision was delusive, was it not?"

"I suppose so."

"Others can have visions equally deluding, though less dangerous." She smiled at me. "Do you regard yourself as possessing any special authority?"

"I am a journeyman of the Seekers for Truth and Penitence, but that position carries no authority. We of the guild only do the will of judges."

"I thought the torturers' guild abolished long ago. Has it become, then, a species of brotherhood for lictors?"

"It still exists," I told her.

"No doubt, but some centuries ago it was a true guild, like that of the silversmiths. At least so I have read in certain histories preserved by our order."

As I heard her, I felt a moment of wild elation. It was not that I supposed her to be somehow correct. I am, perhaps, mad in certain respects, but I know what those respects are, and such self-deceptions are no part of them. Nevertheless, it seemed wonderful to me—if only for that moment—to exist in a world where such a belief was possible. I realized then, really for the first time, that there were millions of people in the Commonwealth who knew nothing of the higher forms of judicial punishment and nothing of the circles within circles of intrigue that ring the Autarch; and it was wine to me, or brandy rather, and left me reeling with giddy joy.

The Pelerine, seeing nothing of all this, said, "Is there no other form of special authority that you believe yourself to possess?"

I shook my head.

"Miles told me that you believe yourself to possess the Claw of the Conciliator, and that you showed him a small black claw, such as might perhaps have come from an ocelot or a caracara, and that you told him you have raised many from the dead by means of it."

The time had come then; the time when I would have to give it up. Ever since we had reached the lazaret, I had known it must come soon, but I had hoped to delay it until I was ready to depart. Now I took out the Claw, for the last time as I thought, and pressed it into the Pelerine's hand, saying, "With this you can save many. I did not steal it, and I have sought always to return it to your order."

"And with it," she asked gently, "you have revived numbers of the dead?"

"I myself would have died months ago without it," I told her, and I began to recount the story of my duel with Agilus.

"Wait," she said. "You must keep it." And she returned the Claw to me. "I am not a young woman any longer, as you see. Next year I will celebrate my thirtieth anniversary as a full member of our order. At each of the five superior feasts of the year, until this past spring, I saw the Claw of the Conciliator when it was elevated for our adoration. It was a great sapphire, as big around as an orichalk. It must have been worth more than many villas, and no doubt it was for that reason that the thieves took it."

I tried to interrupt her, but she silenced me with a gesture.

"As for its working miraculous cures and even restoring life to the dead, do you think our order would have any sick among us if it were so? We are few—far too few for the work we have to do. But if none of us had died before last spring, we would be much more numerous. Many whom I loved, my teachers and my friends, would be among us still. Ignorant people must have their wonders, even if they must scrape the mud from some epopt's boots to swallow. If, as we hope, it still exists and has not been cut to make smaller gems, the Claw of the Conciliator is the last relic we possess of the greatest of good men, and we treasured it because we still treasure his memory. If it had been the sort of thing you believe yourself to have, it would have been precious to everyone, and the autarchs would have wrested it from us long ago."

"It *is* a claw—" I began.

"That was only a flaw at the heart of the jewel. The Conciliator was a man, Severian the Lictor, and not a cat or a bird." She stood up.

"It was dashed against the rocks when the giant threw it from the parapet—"

"I had hoped to calm you, but I see that I am only exciting

you," she said. Quite unexpectedly she smiled, leaned forward, and kissed me. "We meet many here who believe things that are not so. Not many have beliefs that do them as much credit as yours do you. You and I shall talk of this again some other time."

I watched her small, scarlet-clad figure until it was lost from sight in the darkness and silence of the rows of cots. While we talked, most of the sick had fallen asleep. A few groaned. Three slaves entered, two carrying a wounded man on a litter while the third held up a lamp so they could see their way. The light gleamed on their shaven heads, which were covered with sweat. They put the wounded man on a cot, arranged his limbs as though he were dead, and went away.

I looked at the Claw. It had been lifelessly black when the Pelerine saw it, but now muted sparks of white fire ran from its base to its point. I felt well—indeed, I found myself wondering how I had endured lying all day upon the narrow mattress; but when I tried to stand my legs would hardly hold me. Afraid at every moment that I would fall on one of the wounded, I staggered the twenty paces or so to the man I had just seen carried in.

It was Emilian, whom I had known as a gallant at the Autarch's court. I was so startled to see him here that I called him by name.

"Thecla," he murmured. "Thecla . . ."

"Yes. Thecla. You remember me, Emilian. Now be well." I touched him with the Claw.

He opened his eyes and screamed.

I fled, but fell when I was halfway to my own cot. I was so weak I don't believe I could have crawled the remaining distance then, but I managed to put away the Claw and roll beneath Hallvard's cot and so out of sight.

When the slaves came back, Emilian was sitting up and able to speak—though they could not, I think, make much sense of what he said. They gave him herbs, and one of them remained with him while he chewed them, then left silently.

I rolled from under the cot, and by holding on to the edge was able to pull myself erect. All was still again, but I knew that many of the wounded must have seen me before I had fallen. Emilian was not asleep, as I had supposed he would be, but he seemed dazed. "Thecla," he murmured. "I heard Thecla. They said she was dead. What voices are here from the lands of the dead?"

"None now," I told him. "You've been ill, but you'll be well soon."

I held the Claw overhead and tried to focus my thoughts on Melito and Foila as well as Emilian—on all the sick in the lazaret. It flickered and was dark.

Melito's Story—The Cock, the Angel, and the Eagle

"ONCE NOT VERY long ago and not very far from the place where I was born, there was a fine farm. It was especially noted for its poultry: flocks of ducks white as snow, geese nearly as large as swans and so fat they could scarcely walk, and chickens that were as colorful as parrots. The farmer who had built up this place had a great many strange ideas about farming, but he had succeeded so much better with his strange ideas than any of his neighbors with their sensible ones, that few had the courage to tell him what a fool he was.

"One of his queer notions concerned the management of his chickens. Everyone knows that when chicks are observed to be little cocks they must be caponized. Only one cock is required in the barnyard, and two will fight.

"But this farmer saved himself all that trouble. 'Let them grow up,' he said. 'Let them fight, and let me tell you something, neighbor. The best and cockiest cock will win, and he is the one who will sire many more chicks to swell my flock. What's more, his chicks will be the hardiest, and the best suited to throwing off every disease—when your chickens are wiped out, you can come to me and I'll sell you some breeding stock at my own price. As for the beaten cocks, my family and I can eat them. There's no capon so tender as a cock that has been fought to death, just as the best beef comes from a bull that has died in the bull ring and the best venison from a stag the hounds have run all day. Besides, eating capons saps a man's virility.'

"This odd farmer also believed that it was his duty to select the worst bird from his flock whenever he wanted one for dinner. 'It is impious,' he said, 'for anyone to take the best. They should be left to prosper under the eye of the Pancreator, who made cocks and hens as well as men and women.' Perhaps because he felt as he did, his flock was so good that it seemed sometimes there was no worst among it.

"From all I have said, it will be clear that the cock of this flock was a very fine one. He was young, strong, and brave. His tail was as fine as the tails of many sorts of pheasants, and no doubt his comb would have been fine too, save that it had been torn to ribbons in the many desperate combats that had won him his place. His breast was of glowing scarlet—like the Pelerines' robes here—but the geese said it had been white before it was dyed in his own blood. His wings were so strong that he was a better flier than any of the white ducks, his spurs were longer than a man's middle finger, and his bill was as sharp as my sword.

"This fine cock had a thousand wives, but the darling of his heart was a hen as fine as he, the daughter of a noble race and the acknowledged queen of all the chickens for leagues around. How proudly they walked between the corner of the barn and the water of the duck pond! You could not hope to see anything finer, no, not if you saw the Autarch himself showing off his favorite at the Well of Orchids—the more so since the Autarch is a capon, as I hear it.

"Everything was bugs for breakfast for this happy pair until one night the cock was wakened by a terrible row. A great, eared owl had broken into the barn where the chickens roosted and was making his way among them as he sought for his dinner. Of course he seized upon the hen who was the particular favorite of the cock; and with her in his claws, he spread his wide, silent wings to sail away. Owls can see marvelously well in the dark, and so he must have seen the cock flying at him like a feathered fury. Who has ever seen an amazed expression on the face of an owl? Yet surely there was one on that owl in the barn that night. The cock's spurs shuffled faster than the feet of any dancer, and his bill struck for those round and shining eyes as the bill of a woodpecker hammers the trunk of a tree. The owl dropped the hen, flew from the barn, and was never seen again.

"No doubt the cock had a right to be proud, but he became too proud. Having defeated an owl in the dark, he felt he could defeat any bird, anywhere. He began to talk of rescuing the prey of hawks and bullying the teratornis, the largest and most terrible bird that flies. If he had surrounded himself with wise counselors, particularly the llama and the pig, those whom most princes choose to help guide their affairs, I feel sure his extravagances would soon have been effectively though courteously checked. Alas, he did not do so. He listened only to the hens, who were all infatuated with him, and to the geese and ducks, who felt that as his fellow barnyard fowl they shared to some extent in whatever glory he won. At last the day came, as it always does for those who show too much pride, when he went too far.

"It was sunrise, ever the most dangerous time for those who do not do well. The cock flew up and up and up, until he seemed about to pierce the sky, and at last, at the very apogee of his flight, perched himself atop the weathervane on the loftiest gable of the barn—the highest point in the entire farmyard. There as the sun drove out the shadows with lashes of crimson and gold, he screamed again and again that he was lord of all feathered things. Seven times he crowed so, and he might have got away with it, for seven is a lucky number. But he could not be content with that. An eighth time he made the same boast, and then flew down.

"He had not yet landed among his flock when there began a most marvelous phenomenon high in the air, directly above the barn. A hundred rays of sunlight seemed to tangle themselves as a kitten snarls a ball of wool, and to roll themselves together as a woman rolls up dough in a kneading pan. This collection of glorious light then put out legs, arms, a head, and at last wings, and swooped down upon the barnyard. It was an angel with wings of red and blue and green and gold, and though it seemed no bigger than the cock, he knew as soon as he had looked into its eyes that it was far larger on the inside than he.

" 'Now,' said the angel, 'hear justice. You claim that no feathered thing can stand against you. Here am I, plainly a feathered thing. All the mighty weapons of the armies of light I have left behind, and we will wrestle, we two.'

"At that the cock spread his wings and bowed so low that his tattered comb scraped the dust. 'I shall be honored to the end of my days to have been thought worthy of such a challenge,' he said, 'which no other bird has ever received before. It is with the most profound regret that I must tell you I cannot accept, and that for three reasons, the first of which is that though you have feathers on your wings, as you say, it is not against your wings that I would fight but against your head and breast. Thus you are not a feathered creature for the purposes of combat.'

"The angel closed his eyes and touched his hands to his own body, and when he drew them away the hair of his head had become feathers brighter than the feathers of the finest canary, and the linen of his robe had become feathers whiter than the feathers of the most brilliant dove.

" 'The second of which,' continued the cock, nothing daunted, 'is that you, having, as you so clearly do, the power to transform yourself, might choose during the course of our combat to change yourself into some creature that does not possess feathers—for example, a large snake. Thus if I were to fight you, I should have no guarantee of fair play.'

"At that, the angel tore open his breast, and displaying all the qualities therein to the assembled poultry, took out his ability to alter his shape. He handed it to the fattest goose to hold for the duration of the match, and the goose at once transformed himself, becoming a gray salt goose, such as stream from pole to pole. But he did not fly off, and he kept the angel's ability safe.

" 'The third of which,' continued the cock in desperation, 'is that you are clearly an officer in the Pancreator's service, and in prosecuting the cause of justice, as you do, are doing your duty. If I were to fight you as you ask, I should be committing a grave crime against the only ruler brave chickens acknowledge.'

" 'Very well,' said the angel. 'It is a strong legal position, and I suppose you think you've won your way free. The truth is that you have argued your way to your own death. I was only going to twist your wings back a bit and pull out your tail feathers.' Then he lifted his head and gave a strange, wild cry. Immediately an eagle dove from the sky and dropped like a thunderbolt into the barnyard.

"All around the barn they fought, and beside the duck pond, and across the pasture and back, for the eagle was very strong, but the cock was quick and brave. There was an old cart with a broken wheel leaning against one wall of the barn, and under it, where the eagle could not fly at him from above and he could cool himself somewhat in the shadow, the cock sought to make his final stand. He was bleeding so much, however, that before the eagle, who was almost as bloodied as he, could come at him there, he tottered, fell, tried to rise, and fell again.

" 'Now,' said the angel, addressing all the assembled birds, 'you have seen justice done. Be not proud! Be not boastful, for surely retribution will be visited upon you. You thought your champion invincible. There he lies, the victim not of this eagle but of pride, beaten and destroyed.'

"Then the cock, whom they had all thought dead, lifted

his head. 'You are doubtless very wise, Angel,' he said. 'But you know nothing of the ways of cocks. A cock is not beaten until he turns tail and shows the white feather that lies beneath his tail feathers. My strength, which I made myself by flying and running, and in many battles, has failed me. My spirit, which I received from the hand of your master the Pancreator, has not failed me. Eagle, I ask no quarter from you. Come here and kill me now. But as you value your honor, never say that you have beaten me.'

"The eagle looked at the angel when he heard what the cock said, and the angel looked at the eagle. 'The Pancreator is infinitely far from us,' the angel said. 'And thus infinitely far from me, though I fly so much higher than you. I guess at his desires—no one can do otherwise.'

He opened his chest once more and replaced the ability he had for a time surrendered. Then he and the eagle flew away, and for a time the salt goose followed them. That is the end of the story."

Melito had lain upon his back as he spoke, looking up at the canvas stretched overhead. I had the feeling he was too weak even to raise himself on one elbow. The rest of the wounded had been as quiet for his story as for Hallvard's.

At last I said, "That is a fine tale. It will be very hard for me to judge between the two, and if it is agreeable to you and Hallvard, and to Foila, I would like to give myself time to think about them both."

Foila, who was sitting up with her knees drawn under her chin, called, "Don't judge at all. The contest isn't over yet."

Everyone looked at her.

"I'll explain tomorrow," she said. "Just don't judge, Severian. But what did you think of that story?"

Hallvard rumbled, "I will tell you what I think. I think Melito is clever the way he claimed I was. He is not so well as I am, not so strong, and in this way he has drawn a woman's sympathy to himself. It was cunningly done, little cock."

Melito's voice seemed weaker than it had while he was recounting the battle of the birds. "It is the worst story I know."

"The worst?" I asked. We were all surprised.

"Yes, the worst. It is a foolish tale we tell our little children, who know nothing but the dust and the farm animals and the sky they see above them. Surely every word of it must make that clear."

Hallvard asked, "Don't you want to win, Melito?"

"Certainly I do. You don't love Foila as I love her. I would die to possess her, but I would sooner die than disappoint her. If the story I have just told can win, then I shall never disappoint her, at least with my stories. I have a thousand that are better than that."

Hallvard got up and came to sit on my cot as he had the day before, and I swung my legs over the edge to sit beside him. To me he said, "What Melito says is very clever. Everything he says is very clever. Still, you must judge us by the tales we told, and not by the ones we say we know but did not tell. I, too, know many other stories. Our winter nights are the longest in the Commonwealth."

I answered that according to Foila, who had originally thought of the contest and who was herself the prize, I was not yet to judge at all.

The Ascian said, "All who speak Correct Thought speak well. Where then is the superiority of some students to others? It is in the speaking. Intelligent students speak Correct Thought intelligently. The hearer knows by the intonation of their voices that they understand. By this superior speaking of intelligent students, Correct Thought is passed, like fire, from one to another."

I think that none of us had realized he was listening. We were all a trifle startled to hear him speak now. After a moment, Foila said, "He means you should not judge by the content of the stories, but by how well each was told. I'm not sure I agree with that—still, there may be something in it."

"I do not agree," Hallvard grumbled. "Those who listen soon tire of storyteller tricks. The best telling is the plainest."

Others joined in the argument, and we talked about it and about the little cock for a long time.

X

Ava

WHILE I WAS ILL I had never paid much attention to the people who brought our food, though when I reflected on it I was able to recall them clearly, as I recall everything. Once our server had been a Pelerine—she who had talked to me the night before. At other times they had been the shaven-headed male slaves, or postulants in brown. This evening, the evening of the day on which Melito had told his story, our suppers were carried in by a postulant I had not seen before, a slender, gray-eyed girl. I got up and helped her to pass around the trays.

When we were finished, she thanked me and said, "You will not be here much longer."

I told her I had something to do here, and nowhere else to go.

"You have your legion. If it has been destroyed, you will be assigned to a new one."

"I am not a soldier. I came north with some thought of enlisting, but I fell sick before I got the opportunity."

"You could have waited in your native town. I'm told that recruiting parties go to all the towns, twice a year at least."

"My native town is Nessus, I'm afraid." I saw her smile.

"But I left it some time ago, and I wouldn't have wanted to sit around someplace else for half a year waiting. Anyway, I never thought of it. Are you from Nessus too?"

"You're having trouble standing up."

"No, I'm fine."

She touched my arm, a timid gesture that somehow reminded me of the tame deer in the Autarch's garden. "You're swaying. Even if your fever is gone, you're no longer used to being on your feet. You have to realize that. You've been abed for several days. I want you to lie down again now."

"If I do that, there'll be no one to talk to except the people I've been talking with all day. The man on my right is an Ascian prisoner, and the man on my left comes from some village neither you nor I ever heard of."

"All right, if you'll lie down I'll sit and talk to you for a while. I've nothing more to do until the nocturne must be played anyway. What quarter of Nessus do you come from?"

As she escorted me to my cot, I told her that I did not want to talk, but to listen; and I asked her what quarter she herself called home.

"When you're with the Pelerines, that's your home—wherever the tents are set up. The order becomes your family and your friends, just as if all your friends had suddenly become your sisters too. But before I came here, I lived in the far northwestern part of the city, within easy sight of the Wall."

"Near the Sanguinary Field?"

"Yes, very near it. Do you know the place?"

"I fought there once."

Her eyes widened. "Did you, really? We used to go there and watch. We weren't supposed to, but we did anyway. Did you win?"

I had never thought about that and had to consider it. "No," I said after a moment. "I lost."

"But you lived. It's better, surely, to lose and live than to take another man's life."

I opened my robe and showed her the scar on my chest that Agilus's avern leaf had made.

"You were very lucky. Often they bring in soldiers with chest wounds like that, but we are seldom able to save them." Hesitantly she touched my chest. There was a sweetness in her face that I have not seen in the faces of other women. For a moment she stroked my skin, then she jerked her hand away. "It could not have been very deep."

"It wasn't," I told her.

"Once I saw a combat between an officer and an exultant in masquerade. They used poisoned plants for weapons—I suppose because the officer would have had an unfair advantage with the sword. The exultant was killed and I left, but afterward there was a great hullabaloo because the officer had run amok. He came dashing by me, striking out with his plant, but someone threw a cudgel at his legs and knocked him down. I think that was the most exciting fight I ever saw."

"Did they fight bravely?"

"Not really. There was a lot of argument about legalities—you know how men do when they don't want to begin."

" 'I shall be honored to the end of my days to have been thought worthy of such a challenge, which no other bird has ever received before. It is with the most profound regret that I must tell you I cannot accept, and that for three reasons, the first of which is that though you have feathers on your wings, as you say, it is not against your wings that I would fight.' Do you know that story?"

Smiling, she shook her head.

"It's a good one. I'll tell it to you some time. If you lived so near the Sanguinary Field, your family must have been an important one. Are you an armigette?"

"Practically all of us are armigettes or exultants. It's a rather aristocratic order, I'm afraid. Occasionally an optimate's daughter like me is admitted, when the optimate has been a longtime friend of the order, but there are only three of us. I'm told some optimates think all they have to do is make a large gift and their girls will be accepted, but it really isn't so—they have to help out in various ways, not just with money, and they have to have done it for a long time. The world, you see, is not really as corrupt as people like to believe."

I asked, "Do you think it is right to limit your order in that way? You serve the Conciliator. Did he ask the people he lifted out of death if they were armigers or exultants?"

She smiled again. "That's a question that has been debated many times in the order. But there are other orders that are quite open to optimates, and to the lower classes too, and by remaining as we are we get a great deal of money to use in our work and have a great deal of influence. If we nursed and fed only certain kinds of people, I would say you were right. But we don't; we even help animals when we can. Conexa Epicharis used to say we stopped at insects, but then she found one of us—I mean a postulant—trying to mend a butterfly's wing."

"Doesn't it bother you that these soldiers have been doing their best to kill Ascians?"

Her answer was very far from what I had expected. "Ascians are not human."

"I've already told you that the patient next to me is an Ascian. You're taking care of him, and as well as you take care of us, from what I've seen."

"And I've already told you that we take in animals when we can. Don't you know that human beings can lose their humanity?"

"You mean the zoanthropes. I've met some."

"Them, of course. They give up their humanity deliberately. There are others who lose theirs without intending to, often when they think they are enhancing it, or rising to some state higher than that to which we are born. Still others, like the Ascians, have it stripped from them."

I thought of Baldanders, plunging from his castle wall into

Lake Diuturna. "Surely these . . . things deserve our sympathy."

"Animals deserve our sympathy. That is why we of the order care for them. But it isn't murder for a man to kill one."

I sat up and gripped her arm, feeling an excitement I could scarcely contain. "Do you think that if something—some arm of the Conciliator, let us say—could cure human beings, it might nevertheless fail with those who are not human?"

"You mean the Claw. Close your mouth, please—you make me want to laugh when you leave it open like that, and we're not supposed to when people outside the order are around."

"You know!"

"Your nurse told me. She said you were mad, but in a nice way, and that she didn't think you would ever hurt anyone. Then I asked her about it, and she told. You have the Claw, and sometimes you can cure the sick and even raise the dead."

"Do you believe I'm mad?"

Still smiling, she nodded.

"Why? Never mind what the Pelerine told you. Have I said anything to you tonight to make you think so?"

"Or spellbound, perhaps. It isn't anything you've said at all. Or at least, not much. But you are not just one man."

She paused after saying that. I think she was waiting for me to deny it, but I said nothing.

"It is in your face and the way you move—do you know that I don't even know your name? She didn't tell me."

"Severian."

"I'm Ava. Severian is one of those brother—sister names, isn't it? Severian and Severa. Do you have a sister?"

"I don't know. If I do, she's a witch."

Ava let that pass. "The other one. Does she have a name?"

"You know she's a woman then."

"Uh huh. When I was serving the food, I thought for a moment that one of the exultant sisters had come to help me. Then I looked around and it was you. At first it seemed that it was just when I saw you from the corner of my eye, but sometimes, while we've been sitting here, I see her even when I'm looking right at you. When you glance to one side sometimes you vanish, and there's a tall, pale woman using your face. Please don't tell me I fast overmuch. That's what they all tell me, and it isn't true, and even if it were, this isn't that."

"Her name is Thecla. Do you remember what you were just saying about losing humanity? Were you trying to tell me about her?"

Ava shook her head. "I don't think so. But I wanted to ask you something. There was another patient here like you, and they told me he came with you."

"Miles, you mean. No, my case and his are quite different. I won't tell you about him. He should do it himself, or no one should. But I will tell you about myself. Do you know of the corpse-eaters?"

"You're not one of them. A few weeks ago we had three insurgent captives. I know what they're like."

"How do we differ?"

"With them . . ." She groped for words. "With them it's out of control. They talk to themselves—of course a lot of people do—and they look at things that aren't there. There's something lonely about it, and something selfish. You aren't one of them."

"But I am," I said. And I told her, without going into much detail, of Vodalus's banquet.

"They made you," she said when I was through. "If you had shown what you felt, they would have killed you."

"That doesn't matter. I drank the alzabo. I ate her flesh. And at first it was filthy, as you say, though I had loved her. She was in me, and I shared the life that had been hers, and yet she was dead. I could feel her rotting there. I had a wonderful dream of her on the first night; when I go back among my memories it is one the things I treasure most. Afterward, there was something horrible, and sometimes I seemed to be dreaming while I was awake—that was the talking and staring you mentioned, I think. Now, and for a long time, she seems alive again, but inside me."

"I don't think the others are like that."

"I don't either," I said. "At least, not from what I've heard of them. There are a great many things I do not understand. What I have told you is one of the chief ones."

Ava was quiet for the space of two or three breaths, then her eyes opened wide. "The Claw, the thing you believe in. Did you have it then?"

"Yes, but I didn't know what it could do. It had not acted—or rather, it had acted, it had raised a woman called Dorcas, but I didn't know what had happened, where she had come from. If I had known, I might have saved Thecla, brought her back."

"But you had it? You had it with you?"

I nodded.

"Then don't you see? It *did* bring her back. You just said it could act without your even knowing it. You had it, and you had her, rotting, as you say, inside you."

"Without the body . . ."

"You're a materialist, like all ignorant people. But your materialism doesn't make materialism true. Don't you know that? In the final summing up, it is spirit and dream, thought and love and act that matter."

I was so stunned by the ideas that had come crowding in on me that I did not speak again for some time, but sat wrapped in my own speculations. When I came to myself again at last, I was surprised that Ava had not gone and tried to thank her.

"It was peaceful, sitting here with you, and if one of the sisters had come, I could have said I was waiting in case one of the sick should cry out."

"I haven't decided yet about what you said about Thecla. I'll have to think about it a long time, probably for many days. People tell me I am a rather stupid man."

She smiled, and the truth was that I had said what I had (though it was true) at least in part to make her smile. "I don't think so. A thorough man, rather."

"Anyway, I have another question. Often when I tried to sleep, or when I woke in the night, I have tried to connect my failures and my successes. I mean the times when I used the Claw and revived someone, and the times when I tried to but life did not return. It seems to me that it should be more than mere chance, though perhaps the link is something I cannot know."

"Do you think you've found it now?"

"What you said about people losing their humanity—that might be a part of it. There was a woman . . . I think she may have been like that, though she was very beautiful. And a man, my friend, who was only partly cured, only helped. If it's possible for someone to lose his humanity, surely it must be possible for something that once had none to find it. What one loses another finds, everywhere. He, I think, was like that. Then too, the effect always seems less when the deaths come by violence. . . ."

"I would expect that," Ava said softly.

"It cured the man-ape whose hand I had cut away. Perhaps that was because I had done it myself. And it helped Jonas, but I—Thecla—had used those whips."

"The powers of healing protect us from Nature. Why should the Increate protect us from ourselves? We might protect ourselves from ourselves. It may be that he will help us only when we come to regret what we have done."

Still thinking, I nodded.

"I am going to the chapel now. You're well enough to walk a short distance. Will you come with me?"

While I had been beneath that wide canvas roof, it had seemed the whole of the lazaret to me. Now I saw, though only dimly and by night, that there were many tents and pavilions. Most, like ours, had their walls gathered up for coolness, furled like the sails of a ship at anchor. We entered none of them but walked between them by winding paths that seemed long to me, until we reached one whose walls were down. It was of silk, not canvas, and shone scarlet because of the lights within.

"Once," Ava told me, "we had a great cathedral. It could hold ten thousand, yet be packed into a single wagon. Our Domnicellae had it burned just before I came to the order."

"I know," I said. "I saw it."

Inside the silken tent, we knelt before a simple altar heaped with flowers. Ava prayed. I, knowing no prayers, spoke without sound to someone who seemed at times within me and at times, as the angel had said, infinitely remote.

Loyal to the Group of Seventeen's Story—The Just Man

THE NEXT MORNING, when we had eaten and everyone was awake, I ventured to ask Foila if it was now time for me to judge between Melito and Hallvard. She shook her head, but before she could speak, the Ascian announced, "All must do their share in the service of the populace. The bullock draws the plow and the dog herds the sheep, but the cat catches mice in the granary. Thus men, women, and even children can serve the populace."

Foila flashed that dazzling smile. "Our friend wants to tell a story too."

"What!" For a moment I thought Melito was actually going to sit up. "Are you going to let him—let one of them—consider—"

She gestured, and he sputtered to silence. "Why yes." Something tugged at the corners of her lips. "Yes, I think I shall. I'll have to interpret for the rest of you, of course. Will that be all right, Severian?"

"If you wish it," I said.

Hallvard rumbled, "This was not in the original agreement. I recall each word."

"So do I," Foila said. "It isn't against it either, and in fact it's in accordance with the *spirit* of the agreement, which was that the rivals for my hand—neither very soft nor very fair now, I'm afraid, though it's becoming more so since I've been confined in this place—would compete. The Ascian would be my suitor if he thought he could; haven't you seen the way he looks at me?"

The Ascian recited, "United, men and women are stronger; but a brave woman desires children, and not husbands."

"He means that he would like to marry me, but he doesn't think his attentions would be acceptable. He's wrong." Foila looked from Melito to Hallvard, and her smile had become a grin. "Are you two really so frightened of him in a storytelling contest? You must have run like rabbits when you saw an Ascian on the battlefield."

Neither of them answered, and after a time, the Ascian began to speak: "In times past, loyalty to the cause of the populace was to be found everywhere. The will of the Group of Seventeen was the will of everyone."

Foila interpreted: *"Once upon a time . . ."*

"Let no one be idle. If one is idle, let him band together with others who are idle too, and let them look for idle land. Let everyone they meet direct them. It is better to walk a thousand leagues than to sit in the House of Starvation."

"There was a remote farm worked in partnership by people who were not related."

"One is strong, another beautiful, a third a cunning artificer. Which is best? He who serves the populace."

"On this farm lived a good man."

"Let the work be divided by a wise divider of work. Let the food be divided by a just divider of food. Let the pigs grow fat. Let rats starve."

"The others cheated him of his share."

"The people meeting in counsel may judge, but no one is to receive more than a hundred blows."

"He complained, and they beat him."

"How are the hands nourished? By the blood. How does

the blood reach the hands? By the veins. If the veins are closed, the hands will rot away."

"He left that farm and took to the roads."

"Where the Group of Seventeen sit, there final justice is done."

"He went to the capital and complained of the way he had been treated."

"Let there be clean water for those who toil. Let there be hot food for them and a clean bed."

"He came back to the farm, tired and hungry after his journey."

"No one is to receive more than a hundred blows."

"They beat him again."

"Behind everything some further thing is found, forever; thus the tree behind the bird, stone beneath soil, the sun behind Urth. Behind our efforts, let there be found our efforts."

"The just man did not give up. He left the farm again to walk to the capital."

"Can all petitioners be heard? No, for all cry together. Who, then, shall be heard—is it those who cry loudest? No, for all cry loudly. Those who cry longest shall be heard, and justice shall be done to them."

"Arriving at the capital, he camped upon the very doorstep of the Group of Seventeen and begged all who passed to listen to him. After a long time he was admitted to the palace, where those in authority heard his complaints with sympathy."

"So say the Group of Seventeen: From those who steal, take all they have, for nothing that they have is their own."

"They told him to go back to the farm and tell the bad men—in their name—that they must leave."

"As a good child to its mother, so is the citizen to the Group of Seventeen."

"He did just as they had said."

"What is foolish speech? It is wind. It has come in at the ears and goes out of the mouth. No one is to receive more than a hundred blows."

"They mocked him and beat him."

"Behind our efforts, let there be found our efforts."

"The just man did not give up. He returned to the capital once more."

"The citizen renders to the populace what is due to the populace. What is due to the populace? Everything."

"He was very tired. His clothes were in rags and his shoes worn out. He had no food and nothing to trade."

"It is better to be just than to be kind, but only good judges can be just; let those who cannot be just be kind."

"In the capital he lived by begging."

At this point I could not help but interrupt. I told Foila that I thought it was wonderful that she understood so well what each of the stock phrases the Ascian used meant in the context of his story, but that I could not understand how she did it—how she knew, for example, that the phrase about kindness and justice meant that the hero had become a beggar.

"Well, suppose that someone else—Melito, perhaps—were telling a story, and at some point in it he thrust out his hand and began to ask for alms. You'd know what that meant, wouldn't you?"

I agreed that I would.

"It's just the same here. Sometimes we find Ascian soldiers who are too hungry or too sick to keep up with the rest, and after they understand we aren't going to kill them, that business about kindness and justice is what they say. In Ascian, of course. It's what beggars say in Ascia."

"Those who cry longest shall be heard, and justice shall be done to them."

"This time he had to wait a long while before he was admitted to the palace, but at last they let him in and heard what he had to say."

"Those who will not serve the populace shall serve the populace."

"They said they would put the bad men in prison."

"Let there be clean water for those who toil. Let there be hot food for them, and a clean bed."

"He went back home."

"No one is to receive more than a hundred blows."

"He was beaten again."

"Behind our efforts, let there be found our efforts."

"But he did not give up. Once more he set off for the capital to complain."

"Those who fight for the populace fight with a thousand hearts. Those who fight against them with none."

"Now the bad men were afraid."

"Let no one oppose the decisions of the Group of Seventeen."

"They said to themselves, 'He has gone to the palace again and again, and each time he must have told the rulers there that we did not obey their earlier commands. Surely, this time they will send soldiers to kill us."

"If their wounds are in their backs, who shall stanch their blood?"

"The bad men ran away."

"Where are those who in times past have opposed the decisions of the Group of Seventeen?"

"They were never seen again."

"Let there be clean water for those who toil. Let there be hot food for them, and a clean bed. Then they will sing at their work, and their work will be light to them. Then they will sing at the harvest, and the harvest will be heavy."

"The just man returned home and lived happily ever after."

. . .

Everyone applauded this story, moved by the story itself, by the ingenuity of the Ascian prisoner, by the glimpse it had afforded us of life in Ascia, and most of all, I think, by the graciousness and wit Foila had brought to her translation.

I have no way of knowing whether you, who eventually will read this record, like stories or not. If you do not, no doubt you have turned these pages without attention. I confess that I love them. Indeed, it often seems to me that of all the good things in the world, the only ones humanity can claim for itself are stories and music; the rest, mercy, beauty, sleep, clean water and hot food (as the Ascian would have said) are all the work of the Increate. Thus, stories are small things indeed in the scheme of the universe, but it is hard not to love best what is our own—hard for me, at least.

From this story, though it was the shortest and the most simple too of all those I have recorded in this book, I feel that I learned several things of some importance. First of all, how much of our speech, which we think freshly minted in our own mouths, consists of set locutions. The Ascian seemed to speak only in sentences he had learned by rote, though until he used each for the first time we had never heard them. Foila seemed to speak as women commonly do, and if I had been asked whether she employed such tags, I would have said that she did not—but how often one might have predicted the ends of her sentences from their beginnings.

Second, I learned how difficult it is to eliminate the urge for expression. The people of Ascia were reduced to speaking only with their masters' voice; but they had made of it a new tongue, and I had no doubt, after hearing the Ascian, that by it he could express whatever thought he wished.

And third, I learned once again what a many-sided thing is the telling of any tale. None, surely, could be plainer than the Ascian's, yet what did it mean? Was it intended to praise the Group of Seventeen? The mere terror of their name had routed the evildoers. Was it intended to condemn them?

They had heard the complaints of the just man, and yet they had done nothing for him beyond giving him their verbal support. There had been no indication they would ever do more.

But I had not learned those things I had most wished to learn as I listened to the Ascian and to Foila. What had been her motive in agreeing to allow the Ascian to compete? Mere mischief? From her laughing eyes I could easily believe it. Was she perhaps in truth attracted to him? I found that more difficult to credit, but it was surely not impossible. Who has not seen women attracted to men lacking every attractive quality? She had clearly had much to do with Ascians, and he was clearly no ordinary soldier, since he had been taught our language. Did she hope to wring some secret from him?

And what of him? Melito and Hallvard had accused each other of telling tales with an ulterior purpose. Had he done so as well? If he had, it had surely been to tell Foila—and the rest of us too—that he would never give up.

XII

Winnoc

THAT EVENING I had yet another visitor: one of the shaven-headed male slaves. I had been sitting up and attempting to talk with the Ascian, and he seated himself beside me. "Do you remember me, Lictor?" he asked. "My name is Winnoc."

I shook my head.

"It was I who bathed you and cared for you on the night you arrived," he told me. "I have been waiting until you were well enough to speak. I would have come last night, but you were deep in talk already with one of our postulants."

I asked what he wished to speak to me about.

"A moment ago I called you Lictor, and you did not deny it. Are you indeed a lictor? You were dressed as one that night."

"I have been a lictor," I said. "Those are the only clothes I own."

"But you are a lictor no longer?"

I shook my head. "I came north to enter the army."

"Ah," he said. For a moment he looked away.

"Surely others do the same."

"A few, yes. Most join in the south, or are made to join. A

few come north like you, because they want some special unit where a friend or relation is already. A soldier's life . . ."

I waited for him to continue.

"It's a lot like a slave's, I think. I've never been a soldier myself, but I've talked to a lot of them."

"Is your life so miserable? I would have thought the Pelerines kind mistresses. Do they beat you?"

He smiled at that and turned until I could see his back. "You've been a lictor. What do you think of my scars?"

In the fading light I could scarcely make them out. I ran my fingers across them. "Only that they are very old and were made with the lash," I said.

"I got them before I was twenty, and I'm nearly fifty now. A man with black clothes like yours made them. Were you a lictor for long?"

"No, not long."

"Then you don't know much of the business?"

"Enough to practice it."

"And that's all? The man who whipped me told me he was from the guild of torturers. I thought maybe you might have heard of them."

"I have."

"Are they real? Some people have told me they died out a long time ago, but that isn't what the man who whipped me said."

I told him, "They still exist, so far as I'm aware. Do you happen to recall the name of the torturer who scourged you?"

"He called himself Journeyman Palaemon—ah, you know him!"

"Yes. He was my teacher for a time. He's an old man now."

"He's still alive, then? Will you ever see him again?"

"I don't think so."

"I'd like to see him myself. Maybe sometime I will. The

Increate, after all, orders all things. You young men, you live wild lives—I know I did, at your age. Do you know yet that he shapes everything we do?"

"Perhaps."

"Believe me, it's so. I've seen much more than you. Since it is so, it may be that I'll never see Journeyman Palaemon again, and you've been brought here to be my messenger."

Just at that point, when I expected him to convey to me whatever message he had, he fell silent. The patients who had listened so attentively to the Ascian's story were talking among themselves now; but somewhere in the stack of soiled dishes the old slave had collected, one shifted its position with a faint clink, and I heard it.

"What do you know of the laws of slavery?" he asked me at last. "I mean, of the ways a man or a woman can become a slave under the law?"

"Very little," I said. "A certain friend of mine" (I was thinking of the green man) "was called a slave, but he was only an unlucky foreigner who'd been seized by some unscrupulous people. I knew that wasn't legal."

He nodded agreement. "Was he dark of skin?"

"You might say that, yes."

"In the olden times, or so I've heard, slavery was by skin color. The darker a man was, the more a slave they made him. That's hard to believe, I know. But we used to have a chatelaine in the order who knew a lot about history, and she told me. She was a truthful woman."

"No doubt it originated because slaves must often toil in the sun," I observed. "Many of the usages of the past now seem merely capricious to us."

At that he became a trifle angry. "Believe me, young man, I've lived in the old days and I've lived now, and I know a lot better than you which was the best."

"So Master Palaemon used to say."

As I had hoped it would, that restored him to the principal

topic of his thought. "There's only three ways a man can be a slave," he said. "Though for a woman it's different, what with marriage and the like.

"If a man's brought—him being a slave—into the Commonwealth from foreign parts, a slave he remains, and the master that brought him here can sell him if he wants. That's one. Prisoners of war—like this Ascian here—are the slaves of the Autarch, the Master of Masters and the Slave of Slaves. The Autarch can sell them if he wants to. Often he does, and because most of these Ascians aren't much use except for tedious work, you often find them rowing on the upper rivers. That's two.

"Number three is that a man can sell himself into somebody's service, because a free man is the master of his own body—he's his own slave already, as it were."

"Slaves," I remarked, "are seldom beaten by torturers. What need of it, when they can be beaten by their own masters?"

"I wasn't a slave then. That's part of what I wanted to ask Journeyman Palaemon about. I was just a young fellow that had been caught stealing. Journeyman Palaemon came in to talk to me on the morning I was going to get my whipping. I thought it was a kindly thing for him to do, although it was then that he told me he was from the guild of torturers."

"We always prepare a client, if we can," I said.

"He told me not to try to keep from yelling—it doesn't hurt quite so bad, is what he told me, if you yell out just as the whip comes down. He promised me there wouldn't be any hitting more than the number the judge said, so I could count them if I wanted to, and that way I'd know when it was about over. And he said he wouldn't hit harder than he had to, to cut the skin, and he wouldn't break any bones."

I nodded.

"I asked him then if he'd do me a favor, and he said he would if he could. I wanted for him to come back afterward

and talk to me again, and he said he would try to when I was
a little recovered. Then a caloyer came in to read the prayer.

"They tied me to a post, with my hands over my head and
the indictment tacked up above my hands. Probably you've
done it yourself many times."

"Often enough," I told him.

"I doubt the way they did me was any different. I've got
the scars of it still, but they've faded, just like you say. I've
seen many a man with worse ones. The jailers, they dragged
me back to my cell as the custom is, but I think I could have
walked. It didn't hurt as much as losing an arm or a leg. Here
I've helped the surgeons take off a good many."

"Were you thin in those days?" I asked him.

"Very thin. I think you could have counted every rib I
had."

"That was much to your advantage, then. The lash cuts
deep in a fat man's back, and he bleeds like a pig. People say
the traders aren't punished enough for short weighing and
the like, but those who speak so don't know how they suffer
when they are."

Winnoc nodded to that. "The next day I felt almost as
strong as ever, and Journeyman Palaemon came like he'd
promised. I told him how it was with me—how I lived and
all—and asked him a bit about himself. I guess it seems queer
to you that I'd talk so to a man that had whipped me?"

"No. I've heard of similar things many times."

"He told me he'd done something against his guild. He
wouldn't tell me what it was, but because of it he was exiled
for a while. He told me how he felt about it and how lone-
some he was. He said he'd tried to feel better by thinking
how other people lived, by knowing they had no more guild
than he did. But he could only feel sorry for them, and pretty
soon he felt sorry for himself too. He told me that if I
wanted to be happy, and not go through this kind of thing
again, to find some sort of brotherhood for myself and join."

"Yes?" I asked.

"And I decided to do what he's said. When I was let out, I spoke to the masters of a lot of guilds, picking and choosing them at first, then talking to any I thought might take me, like the butchers and the candlemakers. None of them would take on an apprentice as old as I was, or somebody that didn't have the fee, or somebody with a bad character—they looked at my back, you see, and decided I was a trouble-maker.

"I thought about signing on a ship or joining the army, and since then I've often wished I'd gone ahead with one or the other, although maybe if I had I'd wish now I hadn't, or maybe not be living to wish at all. Then I got the notion of joining some religious order, I don't know why. I talked to a bunch of them, and two offered to take me, even when I told them I didn't have any money and showed them my back. But the more I heard about the way they were supposed to live in there, the less I felt like I could do it. I had been drunk a lot, and I liked the girls, and I didn't really want to change.

"Then one day when I was standing around on a corner I saw a man I took to belong to some order I hadn't talked to yet. By that time I was planning to sign aboard a certain ship, but it wasn't going to sail for almost a week, and a sailor had told me a lot of the hardest work came while they were getting ready, and I'd miss it if I waited until they were about to get up the anchor. That was all a lie, but I didn't know it then.

"Anyway, I followed this man I'd seen, and when he stopped—he'd been sent to buy vegetables, you see—I went up to him and asked him about his order. He told me he was a slave of the Pelerines and it was about the same as being in an order, but better. A man could have a drink or two and nobody'd object so long as he was sober when he came to his work. He could lie with the girls too, and there were good chances for that because the girls thought they were holy men, more or less, and they traveled all around.

"I asked if he thought they'd take me, and I said I couldn't believe the life was as good as he made it out to be. He said he was sure they would, and although he couldn't prove what he'd said about the girls right then and there, he'd prove what he'd said about drinking by splitting a bottle of red with me.

"We went to a tavern by the market and sat down, and he was as good as his word. He told me the life was a lot like a sailor's, because the best part of being a sailor was seeing various places, and they did that. It was like being a soldier too, because they carried weapons when the order journeyed in wild parts. Besides all of that, they paid you to sign. In an order, the order gets an offering from every man who takes their vow. If he decides to leave later, he gets some of it back, depending on how long he's been in. For us slaves, as he explained to me, all that went the other way. A slave got paid when he signed. If he left later he'd have to buy his way out, but if he stayed he could keep all the money.

"I had a mother, and even though I never went to see her I knew she didn't have an aes. While I was thinking about the religious orders, I'd got to be more religious myself, and I didn't see how I was going to minister to the Increate with her on my mind. I signed the paper—naturally Goslin, the slave who'd brought me in, got a reward for it—and I took the money to my mother."

I said, "That made her happy, I'm sure, and you too."

"She thought it was some kind of trick, but I left it with her anyhow. I had to go back to the order right away, naturally, and they'd sent somebody with me. Now I've been here thirty years."

"You're to be congratulated, I hope."

"I don't know. It's been a hard life, but then all lives are hard, from what I've seen of them."

"I too," I said. To tell the truth, I was becoming sleepy and wished that he would go. "Thank you for telling me your story. I found it very interesting."

"I want to ask you something," he said, "and I want you to ask Journeyman Palaemon for me if you see him again."

I nodded, waiting.

"You said you thought the Pelerines would be kind mistresses, and I suppose you're right. I've had a lot of kindness from some of them, and I've never been whipped here—nothing worse than a few slaps. But you ought to know how they do it. Slaves that don't behave themselves get sold, that's all. Maybe you don't follow me."

"I don't think I do."

"A lot of men sell themselves to the order, thinking like I did that it'll be an easy life and an adventure. So it is, mostly, and it's a good feeling to help cure the sick and the wounded. But those who don't suit the Pelerines are sold off, and they get a lot more for them than they paid them. Do you see how it is now? This way, they don't have to beat anybody. About the worst punishment you get is scrubbing out the jakes. Only if you don't please them, you can find yourself getting driven down into a mine.

"What I've wanted to ask Journeyman Palaemon all these years . . ." Winnoc paused, gnawing at his lower lip. "He was a torturer, wasn't he? He said so, and so did you."

"Yes, he was. He still is."

"Then what I want to know is whether he told me what he did to torment me. Or was he giving me the best advice he could?" He looked away so that I would not see his expression. "Will you ask him that for me? Then maybe sometime I'll see you again."

I said, "He advised you as well as he could, I'm certain. If you'd stayed as you were, you might have been executed by him or another torturer long ago. Have you ever seen a man executed? But torturers don't know everything."

Winnoc stood up. "Neither do slaves. Thank you, young man."

I touched his arm to detain him for a moment. "May I ask you something now? I myself have been a torturer. If you've feared for so many years that Master Palaemon had said what he did only to give you pain, how do you know that I haven't done the same just now?"

"Because you would have said the other," he told me. "Good night, young man."

I thought for a time about what Winnoc had said, and about what Master Palaemon had said to him so long ago. He too had been a wanderer, then, perhaps ten years before I was born. And yet he had returned to the Citadel to become a master of the guild. I recalled the way Abdiesus (whom I had betrayed) had wished to have me made a Master. Surely, whatever crime Master Palaemon had committed had been hidden later by all the brothers of the guild. Now he was a master, though as I had seen all my life, being too accustomed to it to wonder at it, it was Master Gurloes who directed the guild's affairs despite his being so much younger. Outside the warm winds of the northern summer played among the tent ropes; but it seemed to me that I climbed the steep steps of the Matachin Tower again and heard the cold winds sing among the keeps of the Citadel.

At last, hoping to turn my mind to less painful matters, I stood and stretched and strolled to Foila's cot. She was awake, and I talked with her for a time, then asked if I might judge the stories now; but she said I would have to wait one more day at least.

XIII

Foila's Story—The Armiger's Daughter

"HALLVARD AND MELITO and even the Ascian have had their chances. Don't you think I'm entitled to one too? Even a man who courts a maid thinking he has no rivals has one, and that one is herself. She may give herself to him, but she may also choose to keep herself for herself. He has to convince her that she will be happier with him than by herself, and though men convince maids of that often, it isn't often true. In this competition I will make my own entry, and win myself for myself if I can. If I marry for tales, should I marry someone who's a worse teller of them than I am myself?"

"Each of the men has told a story of his own country. I will do the same. My land is the land of the far horizons, of the wide sky. It is the land of grass and wind and galloping hoofs. In summer the wind can be as hot as the breath of an oven, and when the pampas take fire, the line of smoke stretches a hundred leagues and the lions ride our cattle to escape it, looking like devils. The men of my country are brave as bulls and the women are fierce as hawks.

"When my grandmother was young, there was a villa in my country so remote that no one ever came there. It belonged to an armiger, a feudatory of the Liege of Pascua. The lands were rich, and it was a fine house, though the roof beams had been dragged by oxen all one summer to get them to the site. The walls were of earth, as the walls of all the houses in my country are, and they were three paces thick. People who live in woodlands scoff at such walls, but they are cool and make a fine appearance whitewashed and will not burn. There was a tower and a wide banqueting hall, and a contrivance of ropes and wheels and buckets by which two merychips, walking in a circle, watered the garden on the roof.

"The armiger was a gallant man and his wife a lovely woman, but of all their children only one lived beyond the first year. She was tall, brown as leather yet smooth as oil, with hair the color of the palest wine and eyes dark as thunderheads. Still, the villa where they dwelt was so remote that no one knew and no one came to seek her. Often she rode all day alone, hunting with her peregrine or dashing after her spotted hunting cats when they had started an antelope. Often too she sat alone in her bedchamber all the day, hearing the song of her lark in its cage and turning the pages of old books her mother had carried from her own home.

"At last her father determined that she must wed, for she was near the twentieth year, after which few would want her. Then he sent his servants everywhere for three hundred leagues around, crying her beauty and promising that on his death her husband should hold all that was his. Many fine riders came, with silver-mounted saddles and coral on the pommels of their swords. He entertained them all, and his daughter, with her hair in a man's hat and a long knife in a man's sash, mingled with them, feigning to be one of them, so that she might hear who boasted of many women and see who stole when he thought himself unobserved. Each night she went to her father and told him their names, and when she had gone he called them to him and told them of the stakes where no one goes, where men bound in rawhide die in the sun; and the next morning they saddled their mounts and rode away.

"Soon there remained but three. Then the armiger's daughter could go among them no more, for with so few she feared they would surely know her. She went to her bedchamber and let down her hair and brushed it, and took off her hunting clothes and bathed in scented water. She put rings on her fingers and bracelets on her arms and wide hoops of gold in her ears, and on her head that thin circlet of fine gold that an armiger's daughter is entitled to wear. In short, she did all she knew to make herself beautiful, and because her heart was brave, perhaps there was no maid anywhere more beautiful than she.

"When she was dressed as she wished, she sent her servant to call her father and the three suitors to her. 'Now behold me,' she said. 'You see a ring of gold about my brow, and smaller rings suspended from my ears. The arms that will embrace one of you are themselves embraced by rings smaller still, and rings yet smaller are on my fingers. My chest of jewels lies open before you, and there are no more rings to be found in it; but there is another ring still in this room—a ring I do not wear. Can one of you discover it and bring it to me?'

"The three suitors looked up and down, behind the arras, and beneath the bed. At last the youngest took the lark's cage from its hook and carried it to the armiger's daughter; and there, about the lark's right leg, was a tiny ring of gold. 'Now hear me,' she said. 'My husband shall be the man who shows me this little brown bird again.'

"And with that she opened the cage and thrust in her hand, then carrying the lark upon her finger took it to the window and tossed it in the air. For a moment the three suitors saw the gold ring glint in the sun. The lark rose until it was no more than a dot against the sky.

"Then the suitors rushed down the stair and out the door, calling for their mounts, the swift-footed friends that had carried them already so many leagues across the empty pampas. Their silver-mounted saddles they threw upon their backs, and in less than a moment all three were gone from the sight of the armiger and the armiger's daughter, and from each other's as well, for one rode north toward the jungles, and one east toward the mountains, and the youngest west toward the restless sea.

"When he who went north had ridden for some days, he came to a river too swift for swimming and rode along its bank, ever harkening to the songs of the birds who dwelt there, until he reached a ford. In that ford a rider in brown sat a brown destrier. His face was masked with a brown neck-cloth, his cloak, his hat, and all his clothing were of brown, and about the ankle of his brown right boot was a ring of gold.

" 'Who are you?' " called the suitor.

The figure in brown answered not a word.

" 'There was among us at the armiger's house a certain young man who vanished on the day before the last day,' said the suitor, 'and I think that you are he. In some way you have learned of my quest, and now you seek to prevent me. Well, stand clear of my road, or die where you stand.'

"And with that he drew sword and spurred his destrier into the water. For some time they fought as the men of my country fight, with the sword in the right hand and the long knife in the left, for the suitor was strong and brave, and the rider in brown was quick and blade-crafty. But at last the latter fell, and his blood stained the water.

" 'I leave you your mount,' the suitor called, 'if your strength is sufficient to get you into the saddle again. For I am a merciful man.' And he rode away.

"When he who had ridden toward the mountains had ridden for some days also, he came to such a bridge as the mountain people build, a narrow affair of rope and bamboo, stretched across a chasm like the web of a spider. No man but a fool attempts to ride across such a contrivance, and so he dismounted and led his mount by the reins.

"When he began to cross it seemed to him that the bridge was all empty before him, but he had not come a quarter of the way when a figure appeared in the center. In form it was much like a man, but it was all of brown save for one flash of white, and it seemed to fold brown wings about itself. When the second suitor was closer still he saw that it wore a ring of gold about the ankle of one boot, and the brown wings now seemed no more than a cloak of that color.

"Then he traced a Sign in the air before him to protect him from those spirits that have forgotten their creator, and he called, 'Who are you? Name yourself!'

" 'You see me,' the figure answered him. 'Name me true, and your wish is my wish.'

" 'You are the spirit of the lark sent forth by the armiger's daughter,' said the second suitor. 'Your form you may change, but the ring marks you.'

"At that, the figure in brown drew sword and presented it hilt foremost to the second suitor. 'You have named me rightly,' it said. 'What would you have me do?'

" 'Return with me to the armiger's house,' said the suitor, 'so that I may show you to the armiger's daughter and so win her.'

" 'I will return with you gladly, if that is what you wish,' said the figure in brown. 'But I warn you now that if she sees me, she will not see in me what you see.'

" 'Nevertheless, come with me,' answered the suitor, for he did not know what else to say.

"On such a bridge as the mountain people build, a man may turn about without much difficulty, but a four-legged beast finds it nearly impossible to do so. Therefore, they were forced to continue to the farther side in order that the second suitor might face his mount toward the armiger's house once more. 'How tedious this is,' he thought as he walked the great catenary of the bridge, 'and yet, how difficult and dangerous. Cannot that be used to my benefit?' At last he called to the figure in brown, 'I must walk this bridge, and then walk it again. But must you do so as well? Why don't you fly to the other side and wait there for me?'

"At that, the figure in brown laughed, a wondrous trilling. 'Did you not see that one of my wings is bandaged? I fluttered too near one of your rivals, and he slashed at me with his sword.'

" 'Then you cannot fly far?' asked the second suitor.

" 'No indeed. As you approached this bridge I was perched on the brown walkway resting, and when I heard your tread I had scarcely strength to flutter up.'

" 'I see,' said the second suitor, and no more. But to himself he thought: 'If I were to cut this bridge, the lark would be forced to take bird-form again—yet it could not fly far, and I should surely kill it. Then I could carry it back, and the armiger's daughter would know it.' "

"When they reached the farther side, he patted the neck of his mount and turned it about, thinking that it would die, but that the best such animal was a small price to set against the ownership of great herds. 'Follow us,' he said to the figure in brown, and led his mount onto the bridge again, so that over that windy and aching chasm he went first, and the destrier behind him, and the figure in brown last of all. 'The beast will rear as the bridge falls,' he thought, 'and the spirit of the lark will not be able to dash past, so it must resume its bird shape or perish.' His plans, you see, were themselves shaped by the beliefs of my land, where those who set store in shape-changers will tell you that like thoughts they will not change once they have been made prisoner.

"Down the long curve of the bridge again walked the three, and up the side from which the second suitor had come, and as soon as he set foot on the rock, he drew his sword, sharp as his labor could make it. Two handrails of rope the bridge had, and two cables of hemp to support the roadway. He ought to have cut those first, but he wasted a moment on the handrails, and the figure in brown sprang from behind into the destrier's saddle, drove spur to its flanks, and rode him down. Thus he died under the hoofs of his own mount.

"When the youngest suitor, who had gone toward the sea, had ridden some days as well, he reached its marge. There on the beach beside the unquiet sea he met someone cloaked in brown, with a brown hat, and a brown cloth across nose and mouth, and a gold ring about the ankle of a brown boot.

" 'You see me,' the person in brown called. 'Name me true, and your wish shall be my wish.'

" 'You are an angel,' replied the youngest suitor, 'sent to guide me to the lark I seek.'

"At that the brown angel drew a sword and presented it, hilt foremost, to the youngest suitor, saying, 'You have named me rightly. What would you have me do?'

" 'Never will I attempt to thwart the will of the Liege of Angels,' answered the youngest suitor. 'Since you are sent to guide me to the lark, my only wish is that you shall do so.'

" 'And so I shall,' said the angel. 'But would you go by the shortest road? Or the best?'

"At that the youngest suitor thought to himself, 'Here surely is some trick. Ever the empyrean powers rebuke the impatience of men, which they, being immortal, can easily afford to do. Doubtless the shortest way lies through the horrors of caverns underground, or something like.' Therefore he answered the angel, 'By the best. Would not it dishonor her whom I shall wed to travel any other?'

" 'Some say one thing and some another,' replied the angel. 'Now let me mount up behind you. Not far from here there is a goodly port, and there I have just sold two destriers as good as yours or better. We shall sell yours as well, and the gold ring that circles my boot.'

"In the port they did as the angel had indicated, and with their money purchased a ship, not large but swift and sound, and hired three knowing seamen to work her.

"On the third day out from port, the youngest suitor had

such a dream by night as young men have. When he woke he touched the pillow near his head and found it warm, and when he lay down to sleep again, he winded some delicate perfume—the odor, it might have been, of the flowering grasses the women of my land dry in spring to braid in their hair.

"An isle they reached where no men come, and the youngest suitor went ashore to search for the lark. He found it not, but at the dying of the day stripped off his garments to cool himself in the surging sea. There, when the stars had brightened, another joined him. Together they swam, and together lay telling tales on the beach.

"One day while they were peering over the prow of their ship for another (for they traded at times and at times fought also) a great gust of wind came and the angel's hat was blown into the all-devouring sea, and soon the brown cloth that had covered her face went to join it.

"At last they grew weary of the unresting sea and thought of my land, where the lions ride our cattle in autumn when the grass burns, and the men are brave as bulls and the women fierce as hawks. Their ship they had called the *Lark*, and now the *Lark* flew across blue waters, each morn impaling the red sun upon her bowsprit. In the port where they had bought her they sold her and received three times the price, for she had become a famous vessel, renowned in song and story; and indeed, all who came to the port wondered at how small she was, a trim, brown craft hardly a score of paces from stem to rudderpost. Their loot they sold also, and the goods they had gained by trading. The people of my land keep the best destriers they breed for themselves, but it is to this port that they bring the best of those they sell, and there the youngest suitor and the angel bought good mounts and filled their saddlebags with gems and gold, and set out for the armiger's house that is so remote that no one ever comes there.

"Many a scrape did they have upon the way, and many a

time bloody the swords that had been washed so often in the cleansing sea and wiped on sailcloth or sand. Yet at last come they did. There the angel was welcomed by the armiger, shouting, and by his wife, weeping, and by all the servants, talking. And there she doffed her brown clothing and became the armiger's daughter of old once more.

"A great wedding was planned. In my land such things take many days, for there are roasting pits to be dug anew, and cattle to be slaughtered, and messengers who must ride for days to fetch guests who must ride for days also. On the third day, as they waited, the armiger's daughter sent her servant to the youngest suitor, saying, "My mistress will not hunt today. Rather, she invites you to her bedchamber, to talk of times past upon sea and land."

"The youngest suitor dressed himself in the finest of the clothes he had bought when they had returned to port, and soon was at the door of the armiger's daughter.

"He found her sitting on a window seat, turning the pages of one of the old books her mother had carried from her own home and listening to the singing of a lark in a cage. To that cage he went, and saw that the lark had a ring of gold about one leg. Then he looked at the armiger's daughter, wondering.

" 'Did the angel you met upon the strand not promise you should be guided to this lark?' she said. 'And by the best road? Each morning I open his cage and cast him out upon the wind to exercise his wings. Soon he returns to it again, where there is food for him, clean water, and safety.'

"Some say the wedding of the youngest suitor and the armiger's daughter was the finest ever seen in my land."

XIV

Mannea

THAT NIGHT THERE WAS much talk of Foila's story, and this time it was I who postponed making any judgment among the tales. Indeed, I had formed a sort of horror of judging, the residue, perhaps, of my education among the torturers, who teach their apprentices from boyhood to execute the instructions of the judges appointed (as they themselves are not) by the officials of our Commonwealth.

In addition, I had something more pressing on my mind. I had hoped that our evening meal would be served by Ava, but when it was not, I rose anyway, dressed myself in my own clothes, and slipped off in the gathering dark.

It was a surprise—a very pleasant one—to find that my legs were strong again. I had been free of fever for several days, yet I had grown accustomed to thinking myself ill (just as I had earlier been accustomed to thinking myself well) and had lain in my cot without complaint. No doubt many a man who walks about and does his work is dying and ignorant of it, and many who lie abed all day are healthier than those who bring their food and wash them.

I tried to recall, as I followed the winding paths between

the tents, when I had felt so well before. Not in the mountains or upon the lake—the hardships I had suffered there had gradually reduced my vitality until I fell prey to the fever. Not when I fled Thrax, for I was already worn out from my duties as lictor. Not when I had arrived at Thrax; Dorcas and I had undergone privations in the roadless country nearly as severe as I was to bear alone in the mountains. Not even when I had been at the House Absolute (a period that now seemed as remote as the reign of Ymar), because I had still been suffering the aftereffects of the alzabo and my ingestion of Thecla's dead memories.

At last it came to me: I felt now as I had on that memorable morning when Agia and I had set out for the Botanic Gardens, the first morning after I had left the Citadel. That morning, though I had not known it, I had acquired the Claw. For the first time I wondered if it had not been cursed as well as blessed. Or perhaps it was only that all the past months had been needed for me to recover fully from the leaf of the avern that had pierced me that same evening. I took out the Claw and stared at its silvery gleam, and when I raised my eyes, I saw the glowing scarlet of the Pelerines' chapel.

I could hear the chanting, and I knew it would be some time before the chapel would be empty, but I proceeded anyway, and at last slipped through the door and took a place in the back. Of the liturgy of the Pelerines, I will say nothing. Such things cannot always be well described, and even when they can, it is less than proper to do so. The guild called the Seekers for Truth and Penitence, to which I at one time belonged, has its own ceremonies, one of which I have described in some detail in another place. Certainly those ceremonies are peculiar to it, and perhaps those of the Pelerines were peculiar to them as well, though they may once have been universal.

Speaking in so far as I can as an unprejudiced observer, I

would say that they were more beautiful than ours but less theatrical, and thus in the long run perhaps less moving. The costumes of the participants were ancient, I am sure, and striking. The chants possessed a queer attraction I have not encountered in other music. Our ceremonies were intended chiefly to impress the role of the guild upon the minds of our younger members. Possibly those of the Pelerines had a similar function. If not, then they were designed to engage the particular attention of the All-Seeing, and whether they did so I cannot say. In the event, the order received no special protection.

When the ceremony was over and the scarlet-clad priestesses filed out, I bowed my head and feigned to be deep in prayer. Very readily, I found, the pretense became the thing itself. I remained conscious of my kneeling body, but only as a peripheral burden. My mind was among the starry wastes, far from Urth and indeed far from Urth's archipelago of island worlds, and it seemed to me that that to which I spoke was farther still—I had come, as it were, to the walls of the universe, and now shouted through the walls to one who waited outside.

"Shouted," I said, but perhaps that is the wrong word. Rather I whispered, as Barnoch, perhaps, walled up in his house, might have whispered through some chink to a sympathetic passerby. I spoke of what I had been when I wore a ragged shirt and watched the beasts and birds through the narrow window of the mausoleum, and what I had become. I spoke too, not of Vodalus and his struggle against the Autarch, but of the motives I had once foolishly attributed to him. I did not deceive myself with the thought that I had it in me to lead millions. I asked only that I might lead myself; and as I did so, I seemed to see, with a vision increasingly clear, through the chink in the universe to a new universe bathed in golden light, where my listener knelt to hear me. What had seemed a crevice in the world had expanded until

I could see a face and folded hands, and the opening, like a tunnel, running deep into a human head that for a time seemed larger than the head of Typhon carved upon the mountain. I was whispering into my own ear, and when I realized it I flew into it like a bee and stood up.

Everyone was gone, and a silence as profound as any I have ever heard seemed to hang in the air with the incense. The altar rose before me, humble in comparison to that Agia and I had destroyed, yet beautiful with its lights and purity of line and panels of sunstone and lapis lazuli.

Now I came forward and knelt before it. I needed no scholar to tell me the Theologoumenon was no nearer now. Yet he seemed nearer, and I was able—for the final time—to take out the Claw, something I had feared I could not do. Forming the syllables only in my mind, I said, "I have carried you over many mountains, across rivers, and across the pampas. You have given Thecla life in me. You have given me Dorcas, and you have restored Jonas to this world. Surely I have no complaint of you, though you must have many of me. One I shall not deserve. It shall not be said that I did not do what I might to undo the harm I have done."

I knew the Claw would be swept away if I were to leave it openly on the altar. Mounting the dais, I searched among its furnishings for a place of concealment that should be secure and permanent, and at last noticed that the altar-stone itself was held from below with four clamps that had surely never been loosed since the altar was constructed, and seemed likely to remain in place so long as it stood. I have strong hands, and I was able to free them, though I do not think most men could. Beneath the stone some wood had been chiseled away so that it should be supported at the edges only and would not rock—it was more than I had dared to hope for. With Jonas's razor I cut a small square of cloth from the edge of my now-tattered guild cloak. In it I wrapped the Claw, then I laid it under the stone and retightened the clamps, bloodying my fingers in my effort to make sure they would not come loose by accident.

As I stepped away from the altar I felt a profound sorrow, but I had not gone halfway to the door of the chapel before I was seized with wild joy. The burden of life and death had been lifted from me. Now I was only a man again, and I was delirious with delight. I felt as I had felt as a child when the long lessons with Master Malrubius were over and I was free to play in the Old Yard or clamber across the broken curtain wall to run among the trees and mausoleums of our necropolis. I was disgraced and outcast and homeless, without friend and without money, and I had just given up the most valuable object in the world, which was, perhaps, in the end the only valuable object in the world. And yet I knew that all would be well. I had climbed to the bottom of existence and felt it with my hands, and I knew that there *was* a bottom, and that from this point onward I could only rise. I swirled my cloak about me as I had when I was an actor, for I knew that I was an actor and no torturer, though I had been a torturer. I leaped into the air and capered as the goats do on the mountainside, for I knew that I was a child, and that no man can be a man who is not.

Outside, the cool air seemed expressly made for me, a new creation and not the ancient atmosphere of Urth. I bathed in it, first spreading my cloak then raising my arms to the stars, filled my lungs as does one who has just escaped drowning in the fluids of birth.

All this took less time than it has required to describe it, and I was about to start back to the lazaret tent from which I had come when I became aware of a motionless figure watching me from the shadows of another tent some distance off. Ever since the boy and I had escaped the blindly questing creature that had destroyed the village of the magicians, I had been afraid that some of Hethor's servants might search me out again. I was about to flee when the figure stepped into the moonlight, and I saw it was only a Pelerine.

"Wait," she called. Then, coming nearer, "I am afraid I frightened you."

Her face was a smooth oval that seemed almost sexless. She was young, I thought, though not so young as Ava and a good two heads taller—a true exultant, as tall as Thecla had been.

I said, "When one has lived long with danger . . ."

"I understand. I know nothing of war, but much of the men and women who have seen it."

"And now how may I serve you, Chatelaine?"

"First I must know if you are well. Are you?"

"Yes," I said. "I will leave this place tomorrow."

"You were in the chapel giving thanks, then, for your recovery."

I hesitated. "I had much to say, Chatelaine. That was a part of it, yes."

"May I walk with you?"

"Of course, Chatelaine."

I have heard it said that a tall woman seems taller than any man, and perhaps it is true. This woman was far less in stature than Baldanders had been, yet walking beside her made me feel almost dwarfish. I recalled too how Thecla had bent over me when we embraced, and how I had kissed her breasts.

When we had taken two score steps or so, the Pelerine said, "You walk well. Your legs are long, and I think they have covered many leagues. You are not a cavalry trooper?"

"I have ridden a bit, but not with the cavalry. I came through the mountains on foot, if that's what you mean, Chatelaine."

"That is well, for I have no mount for you. But I do not believe I have told you my name. I am Mannea, mistress of the postulants of our order. Our Domnicellae is away, and so for the moment I am in charge of our people here."

"I am Severian of Nessus, a wanderer. I wish that I could give you a thousand chrisos to help carry out your good work, but I can only thank you for the kindness I have received here."

"When I spoke of a mount, Severian of Nessus, I was neither offering to sell you one nor offering to give you one in the hope of thus earning your gratitude. If we do not have your gratitude now, we shall not get it."

"You have it," I told her, "as I've said. As I've also said, I will not linger here presuming on your kindness."

Mannea looked down at me. "I did not think you would. This morning a postulant told me how one of the sick had gone to the chapel with her two nights ago and described him. This evening, when you remained behind after the rest left, I knew you were he. I have a task, you see, and no one to perform it. In calmer days I would send a party of our slaves, but they are trained in the care of the sick, and we have need of every one of them and more. Yet it is said, 'He sends the beggar a stick and to the hunter a spear.' "

"I have no wish to insult you, Chatelaine, but I think that if you trust me because I went to your chapel you trust me for a bad reason. For all you know, I could have been stealing gems from the altar."

"You mean that thieves and liars often come to pray. By the blessing of the Conciliator they do. Believe me, Severian, wanderer from Nessus, no one else does—in the order or out of it. But you molested nothing. We have not half the power ignorant people suppose—nevertheless, those who think us without power are more ignorant still. Will you go on an errand for me? I'll give you a safe-conduct so you will not be taken up as a deserter."

"If the errand is within my powers, Chatelaine."

She put her hand on my shoulder. It was the first time she had touched me, and I felt a slight shock, as though I had been brushed unexpectedly by the wing of a bird.

"About twenty leagues from here," she said, "is the hermitage of a certain wise and holy anchorite. Until now he has been safe, but all this summer the Autarch has been driven back, and soon the fury of the war will roll over that place. Someone must go to him and persuade him to come to us—or if he cannot be persuaded, force him to come. I believe the Conciliator has indicated that you are to be the messenger. Can you do it?"

"I'm no diplomatist," I told her. "But for the other business, I can honestly say I have received long training."

The Last House

MANNEA HAD GIVEN me a rough map showing the location of the anchorite's retreat, emphasizing that if I failed to follow the course indicated on it precisely, I would almost certainly be unable to locate it.

In what direction that house lay from the lazaret I cannot say. The distances shown on the map were in proportion to their difficulty, and turnings were adjusted to suit the dimensions of the paper. I began by walking east, but soon found that the route I followed had turned north, then west through a narrow canyon threaded by a rushing stream, and at last south.

On the earliest leg of my journey, I saw a great many soldiers—once a double column lining both sides of the road while mules carried back the wounded down the center. Twice I was stopped, but each time the display of my safe-conduct permitted me to proceed. It was written on cream-colored parchment, the finest I had then seen, and bore the narthex sigil of the order stamped in gold. It read:

To Those Who Serve—
  The letter you read shall identify our servant Severian of Nessus, a young man dark of hair and eye, pale of face, thin,

and well above the middle height. As you honor the memory
we guard, and yourselves may wish in time for succor and if
need be an honorable interment, we beg you not hinder this
Severian as he prosecutes the business we have entrusted to
him, but rather provide him such aid as he may require and
you can supply.

For the Order of the Journeying Monials of the Conciliator, called *Pelerines*, I am

> The Chatelaine Mannea
> Instructress and
> Directress

Once I had entered the narrow canyon, however, all the
armies of the world seemed to vanish. I saw no more soldiers,
and the rushing water drowned the distant thundering of the
Autarch's sacars and culverins—if indeed they could have
been heard in that place at all.

The anchorite's house had been described to me and the
description augmented by a sketch on the map I carried;
moreover, I had been told that two days would be required
for me to reach it. I was considerably surprised, therefore,
when, at sunset, I looked up and saw it perched atop the cliff
looming over me.

There was no mistaking it. Mannea's sketch had captured
perfectly that high, peaked gable with its air of lightness and
strength. Already a lamp shone in one small window.

In the mountains I had climbed many cliffs; some had
been much higher than this one, and some—at least in appearance—more sheer. I had by no means been looking forward to camping among the rocks, and as soon as I saw the
anchorite's house, I decided I would sleep in it that night.

The first third of the climb was easy. I scaled the rock face
like a cat and was more than halfway up the whole of it
before the fading of the light.

I have always had good night vision; I told myself the
moon would soon be out and continued. In that I was wrong.
The old moon had died while I lay in the lazaret, and the

new would not be born for several days. The stars shed some light, though they were crossed and recrossed by bands of hurrying clouds; but it was a deceptive light that seemed worse than none, save when I did not have it. I found myself recalling then how Agia had waited with her assassins for me to emerge from the underground realm of the man-apes. The skin of my back crawled as though in anticipation of the arbalests' blazing bolts.

Soon a worse difficulty overtook me: I lost my sense of balance. I do not mean that I was entirely at the mercy of vertigo. I knew, in a general way, that *down* was in the direction of my feet and *up* in the direction of the stars; but I could be no more precise than that, and because I could not, I could judge only poorly how far I might lean out to search for each new handhold.

Just when this feeling was at its worst, the hurrying clouds closed their ranks, and I was left in total darkness. Sometimes it seemed to me that the cliff face had assumed a more gentle slope, so that I might almost have stood erect and walked up it. Sometimes I felt that it was beetling out—I must cling to the underside or fall. Often I felt certain I had not been climbing at all, but edging long distances to the left or right. Once I found myself almost head downward.

At last I reached a ledge, and there I determined to stay until the light came again. I wrapped myself in my cloak, lay down, and shifted my body to bring my back firmly against the rock. No resistance met it. I shifted once more and still felt nothing. I grew afraid that my sense of direction had deserted me even as my sense of balance had, and that I had somehow turned myself about and was edging toward the drop. After feeling the rock to either side, I rolled on my back and extended my arms.

At that moment there came a flash of sulfurous light that dyed the belly of every cloud. Not far off, some great bombard had loosed its cargo of death, and in that hectic illumination I saw that I had gained the top of the cliff, and that the house I had seen there was nowhere to be found. I lay upon an empty expanse of rock and felt the first drops of the coming rain patter against my face.

Next morning, cold and miserable, I ate some of the food I had carried from the lazaret and made my way down the farther side of the high hill of which the cliff had formed a part. The slope there was easier, and it was my intention to double about the shoulder of the hill until I again reached the narrow valley indicated on my map.

I could not do so. It was not that my way was blocked, but rather that when, after long walking, I arrived at what should have been the location I sought, I found an entirely different place, a shallower valley and a broader stream. After several watches wasted searching there, I discovered the spot from which (as it seemed to me) I had seen the anchorite's house perched upon the cliff top. Needless to say, it was not there now, nor was the cliff so high nor so steep as I recalled it.

It was there that I took out the map again, and studying it noticed that Mannea had written, in a hand so fine that I could scarcely believe it had been done with the pen I had seen her use, the words *THE LAST HOUSE* beneath the image of the anchorite's dwelling. For some reason those words and the picture of the house itself atop its rock recalled to me the house Agia and I had seen in the Jungle Garden, where husband and wife had sat listening to the naked man called Isangoma. Agia, who had been wise in the ways of all the Botanic Gardens, had told me there that if I turned on the path and attempted to go back to the hut I should not find it. Reflecting upon that incident, I discovered that I did not now believe her, but that I had believed her at the time. It might be, of course, that my loss of credulity was only a reaction to her treachery, of which I had by now had a sufficient sample. Or it might merely be that I was far more ingenuous then, when I was less than a day gone from the Citadel and the nurturing of the guild. But it was also possible—so it seemed to me now—that I had believed then because I had just seen the thing for myself, and that the sight of it, and the knowledge of those people, had carried its own conviction.

Father Inire was alleged to have built the Botanic Gardens. Might it not be that some part of the knowledge he commanded was shared by the anchorite? Father Inire, too, had built the secret room in the House Absolute that had appeared to be a painting. I had discovered it by accident but only because I had followed the instructions of the old picture cleaner, who had meant that I should. Now I was no longer following the instructions of Mannea.

I retraced my way around the shoulder of the hill and up the easy slope. The steep cliff I recalled dropped before me, and at its base rushed a narrow stream whose song filled all the strait valley. The position of the sun indicated that I had at most two watches of light remaining, but by that light the cliff was far easier to descend than it had been to climb by night. In less than a watch I was down, standing in the narrow valley I had left the evening before. I could see no lamp at any window, but the Last House stood where it had been, founded upon stone over which my boots had walked that day. I shook my head, turned away from it, and used the dying light to read the map Mannea had drawn for me.

Before I go further, I wish to make it clear that I am by no means certain there was anything preternatural in all that I have described. I saw the Last House thus twice, but on both occasions under similar lighting, the first time being by late twilight and the second by early twilight. It is surely possible that what I saw was no more than a creation of rocks and shadows, the illuminated window a star.

As to the vanishing of the narrow valley when I tried to come upon it from the other direction, there is no geographical feature more prone to disappear from sight than such a narrow declivity. The slightest unevenness in the ground conceals it. To protect themselves from marauders, some of the autochthonous peoples of the pampas go so far as to build their villages in that form, first digging a pit whose bottom can be reached by a ramp, then excavating houses and stables from the sides of it. As soon as the grass has covered the cast-out earth, which occurs very rapidly after the winter rains, one may ride to within half a chain of such a place without realizing it exists.

But though I may have been such a fool, I do not believe I was. Master Palaemon used to say that the supernatural exists in order that we may not be humiliated at being frightened by the night wind; but I prefer to believe that there was some element truly uncanny surrounding that house. I believe it now more firmly than I did then.

However it may be, I followed the map I had been given from that time forward, and before the night was more than two watches old, found myself climbing a path that led to the door of the Last House, which stood at the edge of just such a cliff as I remembered. As Mannea had said, the trip had taken just two days.

XVI

The Anchorite

THERE WAS A PORCH. It was hardly higher than the stone upon which it stood, but it ran to either side of the house and around the corners, like those long porches one sometimes sees on the better sort of country houses, where there is little to fear and the owners like to sit in the cool of the evening and watch Urth fall below Lune. I rapped at the door, and then, when no one answered, walked around this porch, first right, then left, peering in the windows.

It was too dark inside for me to see anything, but I found that the porch circled the house as far as the edge of the cliff, and there ended without a railing. I knocked again as fruitlessly as before and had laid myself on the porch to sleep (for having a roof over it, it was a better place than any I was likely to find among the rocks) when I heard faint footsteps.

Somewhere high in that high house, a man was walking. His steps were but slow at first, so that I thought he must be an old man or a sick one. As they came nearer, however, they became firmer and more swift, until as they neared the door they seemed the regular tread of a man of purpose, such a one as might, perhaps, command a maniple, or an ile of cavalry.

I had stood again by then and dusted my cloak and made myself as presentable as I could, yet I was only poorly prepared for him I saw when the door swung back. He carried a candle as thick as my wrist, and by its light I beheld a face that was like the faces of the Hierodules I had met in Baldanders's castle, save that it was a human face—indeed, I felt that as the faces of the statues in the gardens of the House Absolute had imitated the faces of such beings as Famulimus, Barbatus, and Ossipago, so their faces were only imitations, in some alien medium, of such faces as the one I saw now. I have said often in this account that I remember everything, and so I do; but when I try to sketch that face beside these words of mine I find I cannot do so. No drawing that I make resembles it in the least. I can only say that the brows were heavy and straight, the eyes deep-set and deep blue, as Thecla's were. This man's skin was fine as a woman's too, but there was nothing womanish about him, and the beard that flowed to his waist was of darkest black. His robe seemed white, but there was a rainbow shimmering where it caught the candlelight.

I bowed as I had been taught in the Matachin Tower and told him my name and who had sent me. Then I said, "And are you, sieur, the anchorite of the Last House?"

He nodded. "I am the last man here. You may call me Ash."

He stood to one side, indicating that I should enter, then led me to a room at the rear of the house, where a wide window overlooked the valley from which I had climbed the night before. There were wooden chairs there and a wooden table. Metal chests, dully gleaming in the candlelight, rested in the corners and in the angles between floor and walls.

"You must pardon the poor appearance of this place," he said. "It is here that I receive company, but I have so little company that I have begun to use it as a storeroom."

"When one lives alone in such a lonely spot, it is well to seem poor, Master Ash. This room, however, does not."

I had not thought that face capable of smiling, yet he smiled. "You wish to see my treasures? Look." He rose and opened a chest, holding the candle so that it lit the interior. There were square loaves of hard bread and packages of pressed figs. Seeing my expression he asked, "Are you hungry? There is no spell upon this food, if you are fearful of such things."

I was ashamed, because I had carried food for the journey and still had some left for the return; but I said, "I would like some of that bread, if you can spare it."

He gave me half a loaf already cut (and with a very sharp knife), cheese wrapped in silver paper, and dry yellow wine.

"Mannea is a good woman," he told me. "And you, I think, are a good man of the kind who does not know himself to be one—some say that is the only kind. Does she think I can help you?"

"Rather she believes that I can help you, Master Ash. The armies of the Commonwealth are in retreat, and soon the battle will overwhelm all this part of the country, and after the battle, the Ascians."

He smiled again. "The men without shadows. It is one of those names, of which there are many, that are in error and yet perfectly correct. What would you think if an Ascian told you he really cast no shadow?"

"I don't know," I said. "I never heard of such a thing."

"It is an old story. Do you like old stories? Ah, I see a light in your eyes, and I wish I could tell it better. You call your enemies Ascians, which of course is not what they call themselves, because your fathers believed they came from the waist of Urth, where the sun is precisely overhead at noon. The truth is that their home is much farther north. Yet Ascians they are. In a fable made in the earliest morning of our race, a man sold his shadow and found himself driven out everywhere he went. No one would believe that he was human."

Sipping wine, I thought of the Ascian prisoner whose cot

had stood beside my own. "Did this man ever regain his shadow, Master Ash?"

"No. But for a time he traveled with a man who had no reflection."

Master Ash fell silent. Then he said, "Mannea is a good woman; I wish that I could oblige you. But I cannot go, and the war will never reach me here, no matter how its columns march."

I said, "Perhaps it would be possible for you to come with me and reassure the Chatelaine."

"That I cannot do either."

I saw then that I would have to force him to accompany me, but there seemed to be no reason to resort to duress now; there would be plenty of opportunity in the morning. I shrugged my shoulders as though in resignation and asked, "May I then at least sleep here tonight? I will have to return and report your decision, but the distance is fifteen leagues or more, and I could not walk much farther now."

Again I saw his faint smile, just such a smile as a carving of ivory might make when the motion of a torch altered the shadow of its lips. "I had hoped to have some news of the world from you," he said. "But I see that you are weary. Come with me when you have finished eating. I will show you to your bed."

"I have no courtly manners, Master, but I am not so ill-bred as to sleep when my host still desires my conversation—though I'm afraid I have little enough news to give. From what I've learned from my fellow sufferers in the lazaret, the war proceeds and waxes hotter each day. We are reinforced with legions and half legions, they by whole armies sent down from the north. They have much artillery too, and therefore we must rely more upon our mounted lances, who can charge swiftly and engage the enemy closely before his heavy pieces can be pointed. They have more fliers also than they boasted last year, although we have destroyed many. The Autarch himself has come to command, bringing many of his household troops from the House Absolute. But . . ." Shrugging again, I paused to take a bite of bread and cheese.

"The study of war has always seemed to me the least interesting part of history. Even so, there are certain patterns. When one side in a long war shows sudden strength, it is usually for one of three reasons. The first is that it has formed some new alliance. Do the soldiers of these new armies differ in any way from those in the old?"

"Yes," I said. "I have heard that they are younger and on the whole less strong. And there are more women among them."

"No differences in tongue or dress?"

I shook my head.

"Then for the present at least we can dismiss an alliance. The second possibility would be the termination of another war, fought elsewhere. If that were so, the reinforcements would be veterans. You say they are not, thus only the third remains. For some reason your foes have need of an immediate victory and are straining every limb."

I had finished the bread, but I was truly curious by now. "Why should that be?"

"Without knowing more than I do, I cannot say. Perhaps their leaders fear their people, who have sickened of the war. Perhaps all the Ascians are only servants, and their masters now threaten to act for themselves."

"You extend hope at one moment and snatch it away at the next."

"Not I, but history. Have you yourself been at the front?"

I shook my head.

"That is well. In many respects, the more a man sees of war the less he knows of it. How stand the people of your Commonwealth? Are they united behind their Autarch? Or has the war so worn them that they shout for peace?"

I laughed at that, and all the old bitterness that had helped draw me to Vodalus came rushing back. "Unite? Shout? I know that you have isolated yourself, Master, to fix your mind on higher things, but I would not have thought any man could know so little of the land in which he lives. Careerists, mercenaries, and young would-be adventurers fight the war. A hundred leagues south it is less than a rumor, outside the House Absolute."

Master Ash pursed his lips. "Your Commonwealth is stronger than I would have believed, then. No wonder your foes are in despair."

"If that is strength, may the All Merciful preserve us from weakness. Master Ash, the front may collapse at any time. It would be wise for you to come with me to a safer place."

He appeared not to have heard. "If Erebus and Abaia and the rest enter the field themselves, it will be a new struggle. If and when. Interesting. But you are tired. Come with me. I will show you your bed and the high matters that, as you said a moment ago, I came here to study."

We ascended two flights and entered a room that must have been the one in which I had seen a light the evening before. It was a wide chamber of many windows, and it occupied the entire story. There were machines there, but they were smaller and fewer than those I had seen in Baldanders's castle, and there were tables too, and papers, and many books, and near the center a narrow bed.

"Here I nap," Master Ash explained, "when my work will not let me retire. It is not large for a man of your frame, but I think you will find it comfortable."

I had slept on stone the night before; it looked very appealing indeed.

After showing me where I could relieve myself and wash, he left. My last glimpse of him before he darkened the light caught the same perfect smile I had seen before.

An instant later, when my eyes had grown accustomed to the dark, I ceased to wonder about it, for outside all those many windows there shone an unbounded pearly radiance. "We are above the clouds," I said to myself (I, too, half smiling), "or rather, some low clouds have come to shroud this hilltop, unnoticed by me in the darkness but known in some fashion to him. Now I see the tops of those clouds, high matters surely, as I saw the tops of clouds from Typhon's eyes." And I laid myself down to sleep.

XVII

Ragnarok—The Final Winter

IT SEEMED STRANGE to wake without a weapon, though for some reason I cannot explain, that was the first morning on which I had felt so. After the destruction of *Terminus Est* I had slept at the sacking of Baldanders's castle without fear, and later journeyed north without fear. Only the night before, I had slept upon the bare rock of the cliff top weaponless and—perhaps only because I had been so tired—had not been afraid. I now think that during all those days, and indeed during all the days since I had left Thrax, I had been putting the guild behind me and coming to believe that I was what those who encountered me took me for—the sort of would-be adventurer I had mentioned the night before to Master Ash. As a torturer, I had not so much considered my sword a weapon as a tool and a badge of office. Now in retrospect it had become a weapon to me, and I had no weapon.

I thought about that as I lay upon my back on Master Ash's comfortable mattress, my hands behind my head. I would have to acquire another sword if I remained in the war-torn lands, and it would be wise to have one even if I turned south again. The question was whether to turn south or not. If I remained where I was, I risked being drawn into the fighting, where I might well be killed. But for me a return to the south would be even more dangerous. Abdiesus, the archon of Thrax, had no doubt posted a reward for my capture, and the guild would almost certainly procure my assassination if they learned I was anywhere near Nessus.

After vacillating over this decision for some time, as one does when only half-awake, I recalled Winnoc and what he had told me of the slaves of the Pelerines. Because it is a disgrace to us if our clients die after torment, we are taught a good deal of leech-craft in the guild; I thought I knew already at least as much as they. When I had cured the girl in the jacal, I had felt suddenly uplifted. The Chatelaine Mannea had a good opinion of me already and would have a better one when I returned with Master Ash.

A few moments before, I had been disturbed because I lacked a weapon. Now I felt I had one—resolution and a plan are better than a sword, because a man whets his own edges on them. I threw off the blankets, noticing then for the first time, I think, how soft they were. The big room was cold but filled with sunlight; it was almost as though there were suns on all four sides, as though all the walls were east walls. I walked naked to the nearest window and saw that undulating field of white I had vaguely noted the evening before.

It was not a mass of cloud but a plain of ice. The window would not open, or if it would, I could not solve the puzzle of its mechanism; but I put my face close to the glass and peered downward as well as I could. The Last House rose, as I had seen before, from a high hill of rock. Now this hilltop alone remained above the ice. I went from window to window, and the view from each was the same. Going back to the bed that had been mine, I pulled on my trousers and boots, and slung my cloak about my shoulders, hardly knowing what it was I did.

Master Ash appeared just as I finished dressing. "I hope I do not intrude," he said. "I heard you walking up here."

I shook my head.

"I did not want you to become disturbed."

Without my willing it, my hands had gone to my face. Now some foolish part of me became aware of my bristling beard. I said, "I meant to shave before putting on my cloak. That was stupid of me. I haven't shaved since I left the lazaret." It was as though my mind were trudging across the ice, leaving my tongue and lips to get along as best they might.

"There is hot water here, and soap."

"That's good," I said. And then, "If I go downstairs . . ."

That smile again. "Will it be the same? The ice? No. You are the first to have guessed. May I ask how you did it?"

"A long time ago—no, only a few months, actually, though it seems like such a long time now—I went to the Botanic Gardens in Nessus. There was a place called the Lake of Birds, where the bodies of the dead seemed to remain fresh forever. I was told it was some property of the water, but I wondered even then that there should be so much power in water. There was another place too, that they called the Jungle Garden, where the leaves were greener than I have ever known leaves to be—not a bright green but dark with greenness, as if the plants could never use all the energy the sun poured down. The people there seemed not of our time, though I could not say if they were of the past, or the future, or some third thing that is neither. They had a little house. It was much smaller than this, but this reminds me of it. I've thought often of the Botanic Gardens since I left them, and sometimes I've wondered if their secret were not that the time never changed in the Lake of Birds, and that one moved forward or backward—however it might be—when walking the path of the Jungle Garden. Am I perhaps speaking overmuch?"

Master Ash shook his head.

"Then when I was coming here, I saw your house at the top of this hill. But when I climbed to it, it was gone, and the valley below was not as I remembered it." I did not know what else to say, and fell silent.

"You are correct," Master Ash told me. "I have been put here to observe what you see about you now. The lower stories of my home, however, reach into older periods, of which yours is the oldest."

"That seems a great wonder."

He shook his head. "It is almost more wonderful that this spur of rock has been spared by the glaciers. The tops of peaks far higher are submerged. It is sheltered by a geographic pattern so subtle that it could only be achieved by accident."

"But it too will be covered at last?" I asked.

"Yes."

"And what then?"

"I shall leave. Or rather, I shall leave some time before it occurs."

I felt a surge of irrational anger, the same emotion I had sometimes known as a boy when I could not make Master Malrubius understand my questions. "I meant, what of Urth?"

He shrugged. "Nothing. What you see is the last glaciation. The surface of the sun is dull now; soon it will grow bright with heat, but the sun itself will shrink, giving less energy to its worlds. Eventually, should anyone come and stand upon the ice, he will see it only as a bright star. The ice he stands upon will not be that which you see but the atmosphere of this world. And so it will remain for a very long time. Perhaps until the close of the universal day."

I went to another window and looked out again on the expanse of ice. "Will this happen soon?"

"The scene you see is many thousands of years in your future."

"But before this, the ice must have come from the south."

Master Ash nodded. "And down from the mountaintops. Come with me."

We descended to the second level of the house, which I had scarcely noticed when I had come upstairs the night before. The windows were far fewer there, but Master Ash placed chairs before one and indicated that we would sit and look out. It was as he had said—ice, lovely in its purity, crept down the mountainsides to war with the pines. I asked if this too were far in the future, and he nodded once more. "You will not live to see it again."

"But so near that the life of a man will nearly reach it?"

He twitched his shoulders and smiled beneath his beard. "Let us say it is a thing of degree. You will not see this. Nor will your children, nor theirs. But the process has already begun. It began long before you were born."

I knew nothing of the south, but I found myself thinking of the island people of Hallvard's story, the precious little sheltered places with a growing season, the hunting of the seals. Those islands would not hold men and their families much longer. The boats would scrape over their stony beaches for the last time. *"My wife, my children, my children, my wife."*

"At this time, many of your people are already gone," Master Ash continued. "Those you call the cacogens have mercifully carried them to fairer worlds. Many more will leave before the final victory of the ice. I am myself, you see, descended from those refugees."

I asked if everyone would escape.

He shook his head. "No, not everyone. Some would not go, some could not be found. No home could be found for others."

For some time I sat looking out at the beleaguered valley and trying to order my thoughts. At last I said, "I have always found that men of religion tell comforting things that are not true, while men of science recount hideous truths. The Chatelaine Mannea said you were a holy man, but you appear to be a man of science, and you said your people had sent you to our dead Urth to study the ice."

"The distinction you mention no longer holds. Religion and science have always been matters of faith in something.

It is the same something. You are yourself what you call a man of science, so I talk of science to you. If Mannea were here with her priestesses, I would talk differently."

I have so many memories that I often become lost among them. Now as I looked at the pines, waving in a wind I could not feel, I seemed to hear the beating of a drum. "I met another man who said he was from the future once," I said. "He was green—nearly as green as those trees—and he told me that his time was a time of brighter sun."

Master Ash nodded. "No doubt he spoke truly."

"But you tell me that what I see now is but a few lifetimes away, that it is part of a process already begun, and that this will be the last glaciation. Either you are a false prophet or he was."

"I am not a prophet," answered Master Ash, "nor was he. No one can know the future. We are speaking of the past."

I was angry again. "You told me this was only a few lifetimes away."

"I did. But you, and this scene, are past events for me."

"I am not a thing of the past! I belong to the present."

"From your own viewpoint you are correct. But you forget I cannot see you from your viewpoint. This is my house. It is through my windows that you have looked. My house strikes its roots into the past. Without that I should go mad here. As it is, I read these old centuries like books. I hear the voices of the long dead, yours among them. You think that time is a single thread. It is a weaving, a tapestry that extends forever in all directions. I follow a thread backward. You will trace a color forward, what color I cannot know. White may lead you to me, green to your green man."

Not knowing what to say, I could only mutter that I had conceived of time as a river.

"Yes—you came from Nessus, did you not? And that was a city built about a river. But it was once a city by the sea, and you would do better to think of time as a sea. The waves ebb and flow, and currents run beneath them."

"I would like to go downstairs," I said. "To return to my own time."

Master Ash said, "I understand."

"I wonder if you do. Your time, if I have heard you rightly, is that of this house's highest story, and you have a bed there, and other necessary things. Yet when you are not over-whelmed by your labors you sleep here, according to what you have told me. Yet you say this is nearer my time than your own."

He stood up. "I meant that I too flee the ice. Shall we go? You will want food before you begin the long trip back to Mannea."

"We both will," I said.

He turned to look at me before he started down the stair. "I told you I could not go with you. You have discovered for yourself how well hidden this house is. For all who do not walk the path correctly, even the lowest story stands in the future."

I caught both his arms behind him in a double lock and used my free hand to search him for weapons. There were none, and though he was strong, he was not as strong as I had feared he might be.

"You plan to carry me to Mannea. Is that correct?"

"Yes, Master, and we'll have a great deal less trouble if you will go willingly. Tell me where I can find some rope—I don't want to have to use the belt of your robe."

"There is none," he told me.

I bound his hands with his cincture, as I had first planned. "When we are some distance from here," I said, "I will loose you if you will give me your word to behave well."

"I made you welcome in my house. What harm have I done you?"

"Quite a bit, but that doesn't matter. I like you, Master Ash, and I respect you. I hope that you won't hold what I am doing to you against me any more than I hold what you have done to me against you. But the Pelerines sent me to fetch you, and I find I am a certain sort of man, if you understand what I mean. Now don't go down the steps too fast. If you fall, you won't be able to catch yourself."

I led him to the room to which he had first taken me and got some of the hard bread and a package of dried fruit. "I don't think of myself as one anymore," I continued, "but I was brought up as—" It was at my lips to say *torturer*, but I realized (then, I think, for the first time) that it was not quite the correct term for what the guild did and used the official one instead. "—as a Seeker for Truth and Penitence. We do what we have said we will do."

"I have duties to perform. In the upper level, where you slept."

"I am afraid they must go unperformed."

He was silent as we went out the door and onto the rocky hilltop. Then he said, "I will go with you, if I can. I have often wished to walk out of this door and never halt."

I told him that if he would swear upon his honor, I would untie him at once.

He shook his head. "You might think that I betrayed you."

I did not know what he meant.

"Perhaps somewhere there is the woman I have called Vine. But your world is your world. I can exist there only if the probability of my existence is high."

I said, "I existed in your house, didn't I?"

"Yes, but that was because your probability was complete. You are a part of the past from which my house and I have come. The question is whether I am the future to which you go."

I remembered the green man in Saltus, who had been solid enough. "Will you vanish like a soap bubble then?" I asked. "Or blow away like smoke?"

"I do not know," he said. "I do not know what will happen to me. Or where I will go when it does. I may cease to exist in any time. That was why I never left of my own will."

I took him by one arm, I suppose because I thought I could keep him with me in that way, and we walked on. I followed the route Mannea had drawn for me, and the Last House rose behind us as solidly as any other. My mind was busy with all the things he had told me and showed me, so that for a while, the space of twenty or thirty paces, perhaps, I did not look around at him. At last his remark about the tapestry suggested Valeria to me. The room where we had eaten cakes had been hung with them, and what he had said about tracing threads suggested the maze of tunnels through which I had run before encountering her. I started to tell him of it, but he was gone. My hand grasped empty air. For a moment I seemed to see the Last House afloat like a ship upon its ocean of ice. Then it merged into the dark hilltop on which it had stood; the ice was no more than what I had once taken it to be—a bank of cloud.

XVIII

Foila's Request

FOR ANOTHER HUNDRED paces or more, Master Ash was not entirely gone. I felt his presence, and sometimes even caught sight of him, walking beside me and half a step behind, when I did not try to look directly at him. How I saw him, how he could in some sense be present while in another absent, I do not know. Our eyes receive a rain of photons without mass or charge from swarming particles like a billion, billion suns—so Master Palaemon, who was nearly blind, had taught me. From the pattering of those photons we believe we see a man. Sometimes the man we believe we see may be as illusory as Master Ash, or more so.

His wisdom I felt with me too. It had been a melancholy wisdom, but a real one. I found myself wishing he had been able to accompany me, though I realized it would have meant the coming of the ice was certain. "I'm lonely, Master Ash," I said, not daring to look back. "How lonely I didn't realize until now. You were lonely also, I think. Who was the woman you called Vine?"

Perhaps I only imagined his voice. "*The first woman.*"

"Meschiane? Yes, I know her, and she is very lovely. My Meschiane was Dorcas, and I am lonely for her, but for all

the others too. When Thecla became a part of me, I thought
I would never be lonely again. But now she is so much a part
that we're only one person, and I can be lonely for others.
For Dorcas, for Pia the island girl, for little Severian and
Drotte and Roche. If Eata were here, I could hug him.

"Most of all, I'd like to see Valeria. Jolenta was the most
beautiful woman I've ever seen, but there was something in
Valeria's face that tore my heart out. I was only a boy, I
suppose, though I didn't think so then. I crawled up out of
the dark and found myself in a place they called the Atrium
of Time. Towers—the towers of Valeria's family—rose on all
sides of it. In the center was an obelisk covered with sundials,
and though I remember its shadow on the snow, it couldn't
have had sunlight there for more than two or three watches
of each day; the towers must shade it most of the time. Your
understanding is deeper than mine, Master Ash—can you tell
me why they might have built it so?"

A wind that played among the rocks seized my cloak so
that it billowed from my shoulders. I secured it again and
pulled up my hood. "I was following a dog. I called him
Triskele, and I said, even to myself, that he was mine, though
I had no right to keep a dog. It was a winter day when I
found him. We'd been doing laundry—washing the clients'
bedclothes—and the drain plugged with rags and lint. I'd
been shirking my work, and Drotte told me to go outside and
ram a clothes prop up it. The wind was terribly cold. That
was your ice coming, I suppose, though I didn't know it at
the time—the winters getting a little worse each year. And of
course when I got the drain open, a gush of filthy water
would come out and wet my hands.

"I was angry because I was the oldest, except for Drotte
and Roche, and I thought the younger apprentices ought to
have to do the work. I was poking at the clog with my stick
when I saw him across the Old Yard. The keepers in the Bear
Tower had held a private fight, I suppose, the night before,
and the dead beasts were lying outside their door waiting for

the nacker. There was an arsinoither and a smilodon, and several dire wolves. The dog was lying on top. I suppose he had been the last to die, and from his wounds one of the dire wolves had killed him. Of course, he wasn't really dead, but he looked dead.

"I went over to see him—it was an excuse to stop what I was doing for a moment and blow on my fingers. He was as stiff and cold as . . . well, as anything I've ever seen. I killed a bull once with my sword, and when it was lying dead in its own blood it still looked quite a bit more living than Triskele did then. Anyway, I reached out and stroked his head. It was as big as a bear's, and they had cut off his ears, so that only two little points were left. When I touched him he opened his eyes. I dashed back across the Yard and rammed the stick up so hard it broke through at once, because I was afraid Drotte would send Roche down to see what I was doing.

"When I think back on it, it was as if I had the Claw already, more than a year before I got it. I can't describe how he looked when he rolled his eye up to see me. He touched my heart. I never revived an animal when I had the Claw, but then I never tried. When I was among them, I was usually wishing I could kill one, because I wanted something to eat. Now I'm no longer sure that killing animals to eat is something we are meant to do. I noticed that you had no meat in your supplies—only bread and cheese, and wine and dried fruit. Do your people, on whatever world it is where people live in your time, feel so too?"

I paused, hoping for an answer, but none came. All the mountaintops had dropped below the sun now; I was no longer certain whether some thin presence of Master Ash followed me or only my shadow.

I said, "When I had the Claw I found that it would not revive those dead by human acts, though it seemed to heal the man-ape whose hand I had struck off. Dorcas thought it was because I had done it myself. I can't say—I never thought the Claw knew who held it, but perhaps it did."

A voice—not Master Ash's but a voice I had never heard before—called out, "A fine new year to you!"

I looked up and and saw, perhaps forty paces off, just such an uhlan as Hethor's notules had killed on the green road to the House Absolute. Not knowing what else to do, I waved and shouted, "Is it New Year's Day, then?"

He touched spurs to his destrier and came galloping up. "Mid summer today, the beginning of the new year. A glorious one for our Autarch."

I tried to recall some of the phrases Jolenta had been so fond of. "Whose heart is the shrine of his subjects."

"Well said! I'm Ibar, of the Seventy-eighth Xenagie, patrolling the road until evening, worse luck."

"Surely it's lawful to use the road here."

"Entirely. Provided, of course, that you are prepared to identify yourself."

"Yes," I said. "Of course." I had almost forgotten the safe-conduct Mannea had written for me. Now I took it out and handed it to him.

When I had been stopped on my way to the Last House, I had by no means been sure that the soldiers who had questioned me could read. Each had stared wisely at the parchment, but it might well have been that they took in no more than the sigil of the order and Mannea's regular and vigorous, though slightly eccentric, penmanship. The uhlan unquestionably could. I could see his eyes traveling the lines of script, and even guess, I think, when they paused momentarily at "honorable interment."

He refolded the parchment carefully but retained it. "So you are a servant of the Pelerines."

"I have that honor, yes."

"You were praying, then. I thought you were talking to yourself when I saw you. I don't hold with any religious nonsense. We have the standard of the xenagie near at hand and the Autarch at a distance, and that's all I need of reverence and mystery; but I have heard that they were good women."

I nodded. "I believe—perhaps somewhat more than you. But they are indeed."

"And you were sent on a task for them. How many days ago?"

"Three."

"Are you returning to the lazaret at Media Pars now?"

I nodded again. "I hope to reach it before nightfall."

He shook his head. "You won't. Take it easy, that's my advice to you." He held out the parchment.

I took it and returned it to my sabretache. "I was traveling with a companion, but we were separated. I wonder if you've seen him." I described Master Ash.

The uhlan shook his head. "I'll keep an eye out for him and tell him which way you went if I see him. Now—will you answer a question for me? It's not official, so you can tell me it's none of my affair if you want."

"I will if I can."

"What will you do when you leave the Pelerines?"

I was somewhat taken aback. "Why, I hadn't planned to leave at all. Someday, perhaps."

"Well, keep the light cavalry in mind. You look like a man of your hands, and we can always use one. You'll live half as long as you would in the infantry, and have twice as much fun."

He urged his mount forward, and I was left to ponder what he had said. I did not doubt that he had been serious in telling me to sleep on the road; but that very seriousness made me hurry forward all the faster. I have been blessed with long legs, so that when I need to I can walk as fast as most men can trot. I used them then, dropping all thoughts of Master Ash and my own troubled past. Perhaps some thin presence of Master Ash still accompanied me; perhaps it does so yet. But if it did, I was and remain unaware of it.

Urth had not yet turned her face from the sun when I came to that narrow road the dead soldier and I had taken only a little over a week before. There was blood in its dust still, much more than I had seen there previously. I had feared from what the uhlan had said that the Pelerines had been accused of some misdeed; now I felt sure that it was only that a great influx of wounded had been brought to the lazaret, and he had decided I deserved a night's rest before being set to work on them. That thought was a vast relief to me. A superabundance of the injured would give me an opportunity to show my skills and render it that much more likely that Mannea would accept me when I offered to sell myself to the order, if only I could contrive some tale to account for my failure at the Last House.

When I turned the final bend in the road, however, what I saw was entirely different.

Where the lazaret had stood, the ground seemed to have been plowed by a host of madmen, plowed and dug—its bottom already a small lake of shallow water. Shattered trees rimmed the circle.

Until darkness came, I walked back and forth across it. I was looking for some sign of my friends, and also for some trace of the altar that had held the Claw. I found a human hand, a man's hand, blown off at the wrist. It might have been Melito's, or Hallvard's, or the Ascian's, or Winnoc's. I could not tell.

I slept beside the road that night. When morning came I began my inquiries, and before evening I had located the survivors, some half dozen leagues from the original site. I went from cot to cot, but many were unconscious and so bandaged about the head that I could not have known them. It is possible that Ava, Mannea, and the Pelerine who had carried a stool to my bedside were among them, though I did not discover them there.

The only woman I recognized was Foila, and that only because she recognized me, calling "Severian!" as I walked among the wounded and dying. I went to her and tried to question her, but she was very weak and could tell me little. The attack had come without warning and shattered the

lazaret like a thunderbolt; her memories were all of the after-
math, of hearing the screams that for a long time had
brought no rescuers, and at last being dragged forth by soldiers who knew little of medicine. I kissed her as well as I
could, and promised to come and see her again—a promise, I
think, that both of us knew I would not be able to keep. She
said, "Do you recall the time when all of us told stories? I
thought of that."

I said I knew she had.

"I mean while they were carrying us here. Melito and Hallvard and the rest are dead, I think. You will be the only one
who remembers, Severian."

I told her I would remember always.

"I want you to tell other people. On winter days, or a night
when there is nothing else to do. Do you remember the
stories?"

"'My land is the land of far horizons, of the wide sky.'"

"Yes," she said, and seemed to sleep.

My second promise I have kept, first copying all the stories
onto the blank pages at the close of the brown book, then
giving them here, just as I heard them in the long, warm
noons.

Guasacht

THE NEXT TWO DAYS I spent in wandering. I will not say much
of them here, for there is little to say. I might, I suppose,
have enlisted in several units, but I was far from sure I
wanted to enlist. I would have liked to return to the Last
House, but I was too proud to cast myself on Master Ash's
charity, assuming that Master Ash was again to be found
there. I told myself I would gladly have returned to the post
of Lictor of Thrax, yet if that had been possible, I am not
certain I would have done so. I slept like an animal in
wooded places and took what food I could, which was little.

On the third day I discovered a rusty falchion, dropped, as
it appeared, in some campaign of the year before. I got out
my little flask of oil and my broken whetstone (both of which
I had retained, together with her hilt, when I had cast the
wreck of *Terminus Est* into the water) and spent a happy
watch in cleaning and sharpening it. When that was done, I
trudged on, and soon struck a road.

With the protection of Mannea's safe-conduct effectively
removed, I was more chary of showing myself than I had
been on my way from Master Ash's. But it seemed probable
that the dead soldier the Claw had raised, who now called

himself Miles though I knew some part of him to be Jonas, had by now joined some unit. If so, he would be on a road or in camp near one, if he was not actually in battle; and I wished to speak to him. Like Dorcas, he had paused a time in the country of the dead. She had dwelt there longer, but I hoped that if I could question him before too much time had erased his memories of it, I might learn something that would—if not permit me to regain her—at least help reconcile me to her loss.

For I found I loved her now as I never had when we tramped cross-country to Thrax. Then my thoughts had been too much of Thecla; I had always been reaching inside myself to find her. Now it seemed, if only because she had been a part of me so long, that I had grasped her indeed, in an embrace more final than any coupling—or rather, that as the male's seed penetrates the female body to produce (if it be the will of Apeiron) a new human being, so she, entering my mouth, by my will had combined with the Severian that was to establish a new man: I who still call myself Severian but am conscious, as it were, of my double root.

Whether I could have learned what I sought from Miles-Jonas, I do not know. I have never found him, though I have persevered in the search from that day to this. By midafternoon I had entered a realm of broken trees, and from time to time I passed corpses in more or less advanced stages of decay. At first I tried to pillage them as I had the body of Miles-Jonas, but others had been there before me, and indeed the fennecs had come in the night with their sharp little teeth to loot the flesh.

Somewhat later, as my energies were beginning to flag, I paused at the smoldering remains of an empty supply wagon. The draft animals, which had not, it appeared, been dead long, lay in the road, with their driver pitched on his face between them; and it occurred to me that I might do worse than to cut as much meat as I wanted from their flanks and carry it to some isolated spot where I could kindle a fire. I had fleshed the point of the falchion in the haunch of one of these animals when I heard the drumming of hoofs, and supposing them to belong to the destrier of an estafette, moved to the edge of the road to let him pass.

It was instead a short, thick-bodied, energetic-looking man on a tall, ill-used mount. He reined up at the sight of me, but something in his expression told me there was no need for fight or flight. (If there had been, it would have been *fight*. His destrier would have done him little good among the stumps and fallen logs, and despite his haubergeon and brass-ringed buff cap, I thought I could best him.)

"Who are you?" he called. And when I told him, "Severian of Nessus, eh? You're civilized then, or half-civilized, but you don't look like you've been eating too well."

"On the contrary," I said. "Better than I've been accustomed to, recently." I did not want him to think me weak.

"But you could use some more—that's not Ascian blood on your sword. You're a schiavoni? An irregular?"

"My life has been pretty irregular of late, certainly."

"But you're attached to no formation?" With startling dexterity he vaulted from his saddle, threw the reins to the ground, and came striding over. He was slightly bowlegged and had one of those faces that appear to have been molded in clay and flattened from the top and bottom before firing, so that the forehead and chin are shallow but broad, the eyes slits, the mouth wide. Still I liked him at once for his verve, and because he took so little trouble to hide his dishonesty.

I said, "I'm attached to nothing and no one—memories excepted."

"Ahh!" He sighed, and for an instant rolled his eyes upward. "I know—I know. We have all had our difficulties, every one of us. What was it, a woman or the law?"

I had not previously viewed my troubles in that light, but after thinking for a moment I admitted it had been a bit of both.

"Well, you've come to the right place and you've met the

right man. How'd you like a good meal tonight, a whole crowd of new friends, and a handful of orichalks tomorrow? Sound good? Good!"

He returned to his mount, and his hand darted out as quickly as a fencer's blade to grasp her bridle before she could shy away. When he had the reins again, he leaped into the saddle as readily as he had left it. "Now you get up behind me," he called. "It's not far, and she'll carry two easily enough."

I did as he told me, though with considerably more difficulty since I had no stirrup to assist me. The instant I was seated, the destrier struck like a bushmaster at my leg; but her master, who had clearly been anticipating the maneuver, clubbed her so hard with the brass pommel of his poniard that she stumbled and nearly fell.

"Pay no mind," he said. The shortness of his neck did not permit him to look over his shoulder, so he spoke out of the left side of his mouth to make it clear he was addressing me. "She's a fine animal and a plucky fighter, and she just wants to make sure you understand her value. A sort of initiation, you know. You know what an initiation is?"

I told him I thought myself familiar with the term.

"Anything that's worth belonging to has one, you'll find— I've found that out myself. I've never seen one that a plucky lad couldn't handle and laugh about afterwards."

With that cryptic encouragement he set his enormous spurs to the sides of his fine animal as if he meant to eviscerate her on the spot, and we went flying down the road, trailed by a cloud of dust.

Since the time I had ridden Vodalus's charger out of Saltus, I had supposed in my innocence that all mounts might be divided into two sorts: the highbred and swift, and the cold-blooded and slow. The better, I thought, ran with the graceful ease, almost, of a coursing cat; the worse moved so tardily that it hardly mattered how they did it. It used to be a maxim of one of Thecla's tutors that all two-valued systems are false, and I discovered on that ride a new respect for him. My benefactor's mount belonged to that third class (which I have since discovered is fairly extensive) comprising those animals that outrace the birds but seem to run with legs of iron upon a road of stone. Men have numberless advantages over women and for that reason are rightly charged to protect them, yet there is one great one women may boast over men: No woman has ever had her organs of generation crushed between her own pelvis and the bony spine of one of these galloping brutes. That happened to me twenty or thirty times before we reined up, and when I slid over the crupper at last and leaped aside to dodge a kick, I was in no very good mood.

We had halted in one of those little, lost fields one sometimes finds among the hills, an area more or less level and a hundred strides or so across. A tent the size of a cottage had been erected in the center, with a faded flag of black and green flapping before it. Several score hobbled mounts grazed at will over the field, and an equal number of ragged men, with a sprinkling of unkempt women, lounged about cleaning armor, sleeping, and gambling.

"Look here!" my benefactor shouted, dismounting to stand beside me. "Here's a new recruit!" To me he announced, "Severian of Nessus, you're standing in the presence of the Eighteenth Bacele of the Irregular Contarii, every one of us a fighter of dauntless courage whenever there's a speck of money to be made."

The ragged men and women were standing and drifting toward us, many of them frankly grinning. A tall and very thin man led the way.

"Comrades, I give you Severian of Nessus!

"Severian," my benefactor continued, "I'm your condottiere. Call me Guasacht. This fishing pole here, taller even than you are, is my second, Erblon. The rest will introduce themselves, I'm sure.

"Erblon, I want to talk to you. There'll be patrols tomor-

row." He took the tall man by the arm and led him into the
tent, leaving me with the crowd of troopers who had by now
surrounded me.

One of the largest, an ursine man almost my height and at
least twice my weight, gestured toward the falchion. "Don't
you have a scabbard for that? Let's see it."

I surrendered it without argument; whatever might happen next, I felt certain it would not be an occasion for killing.

"So, you're a rider, are you?"

"No," I said. "I've ridden a bit, but I don't consider myself
an expert."

"But you know how to manage them?"

"I know men and women better."

Everyone laughed at that, and the big man said, "Well,
that's just fine, because you probably won't do much riding,
but a good understanding of women—and destriers—will be a
help to you."

As he spoke, I heard the sound of hoofs. Two men were
leading up a piebald, muscular and wild-eyed. His reins had
been divided and lengthened, permitting the men to stand at
either side of his head, about three paces away. A trollop
with fox-colored hair and a laughing face sat the saddle with
ease, and in lieu of the reins held a riding whip in each hand.
The troopers and their women cheered and clapped, and at
the sound the piebald reared like a whirlwind and pawed the
air, showing the three horny growths on each forefoot that
we call hoofs for what they were—talons adapted almost as
well to combat as to gripping turf. Their feints outsped my
eyes.

The big man slapped me on the back. "He's not the best I
ever had, but he's good enough, and I trained him myself.
Mesrop and Lactan there are going to pass you those reins,
and all you have to do is get up on him. If you can do it
without knocking Daria off, you can have her until we run
you down." He raised his voice: "*All right, let him go!*"

I had expected the two men to give me the reins. Instead

they threw them at my face, and in snatching for them I missed them both. Someone goaded the piebald from behind, and the big man gave a peculiar, piercing whistle. The piebald had been taught to fight, like the destriers in the Bear Tower, and though his long teeth had not been augmented with metal, they had been left as nature made them and stood out from his mouth like knives.

I dodged a flashing forefoot and tried to grasp his halter; a blow from one of the whips caught me full across the face, and the piebald's rush knocked me sprawling.

The troopers must have held him back or I would have been trampled. Perhaps they also helped me to my feet—I cannot be sure. My throat was full of dust, and blood from my forehead trickled into my eyes.

I went for him again, circling to the right to keep clear of his hoofs, but he turned more quickly than I, and the girl called Daria snapped both lashes before my face to throw me off. More from anger than any plan I seized one. The thong of the whipstock was around her wrist; when I jerked the lash she came with it, falling into my arms. She bit my ear, but I got her by the back of the neck, spun her around, dug fingers into one firm buttock and lifted her. Kicking the air, her legs seemed to startle the piebald. I backed him through the crowd until one of his tormentors goaded him toward me, then stepped on his reins.

After that, it was easy. I dropped the girl, caught his halter, twisted his head, and kicked his forefeet from under him as we were taught to do with unruly clients. With a high-pitched, animal scream he came crashing down. I was in the saddle before he could get his legs beneath him, and from there I lashed his flanks with the long reins and sent him bolting through the crowd, then turned him and charged them again.

All my life I had heard of the excitement of this kind of fighting, though I had never experienced it. Now I found everything more than true. The troopers and their women were yelling and running, and a few flourished swords. They might have threatened a thunderstorm with more effect—I rode over half a dozen at a sweep. The girl's red hair flew like a banner as she fled, but no human legs could have outdistanced that steed. We flashed past her, and I caught her by that flaming banner and threw her over the arcione before me.

A twisting trail led to a dark ravine, and that ravine to another. Deer scattered ahead of us; in three bounds we overtook a buck in velvet and shouldered him out of the way. While I had been Lictor of Thrax, I had heard that the eclectics often raced game and leaped from their mounts to stab it. I believed those stories now—I could have cut the buck's throat with a butcher knife.

We left him behind, crested a new hill and dashed down into a silent, wooded valley. When the piebald had run himself out, I let him find his own path among the trees, which were the largest I had seen since leaving Saltus; and when he stopped to crop the sparse, tender grass that grew between their roots, I halted and threw the reins on the ground as I had seen Guasacht do, then dismounted and helped the redhaired girl off.

"Thanks," she said. And then, "You did it. I didn't think you could."

"Or you wouldn't have agreed to this? I had supposed they made you."

"I wouldn't have given you that cut with the whip. You'll want to repay me now, won't you? With the reins, I suppose."

"What makes you think that?" I was tired and sat down. Yellow flowers, each blossom no bigger than a drop of water, grew in the grass; I picked a few and found they smelled of calambac.

"You look the type. Besides, you carried me bottom up, and men who do that always want to hit it."

"I never knew that. It's an interesting thought."

"I have a lot of them—that kind." Quickly and gracefully she seated herself beside me and put a hand on my knee. "Listen, it was the initiation, that's all. We take turns, and it was my turn and I was supposed to hit you. Now it's over."

"I understand."

"Then you won't hurt me? That's wonderful. We can have a good time here, really. Whatever you want and as much as you want, and we won't go back until it's time to eat."

"I didn't say I wouldn't hurt you."

Her face, which had been wreathed with forced smiles, fell, and she looked at the ground. I suggested that she might run away.

"That would only make it more fun for you, and you'd hurt me more before we were through." Her hand crept up my thigh as she spoke. "You're nice looking, you know. And so tall." She made a sitting bow, pressing her face into my lap to give me a tingling kiss, then straightening up at once. "It could be nice. Really it could."

"Or you could kill yourself. Have you a knife?"

For an instant, her mouth formed a perfect little circle. "You're crazy, aren't you? I should have known." She leaped to her feet.

I caught her by one ankle and sent her sprawling to the soft forest floor. Her shift was rotten with wear—a pull and it fell away. "You said you wouldn't run."

She looked over her shoulder at me with large eyes.

I said, "You have no power over me, neither you nor they. I am not afraid of pain, or of death. There is only one living woman I desire, and no man but myself."

X X

Patrol

WE HELD A PERIMETER no more than a couple of hundred paces across. For the most part, our enemies had only knives and axes—the axes and their ragged clothes recalled the volunteers I had helped Vodalus against in our necropolis—but there were hundreds of them already, and more coming.

The bacele had saddled up and left camp before dawn. The shadows were still long, somewhere along the shifting front, when a scout showed Guasacht the deep ruts of a coach traveling north. For three watches we tracked it.

The Ascian raiders who had captured it fought well, turning south to surprise us, then west, then north again like a writhing serpent; but always leaving a trail of dead, caught between our fire and that of the guards inside, who shot them through the loopholes. It was only toward the end, when the Ascians could no longer flee, that we grew aware of other hunters.

By noon, the little valley was surrounded. The gleaming steel coach with its dead and dying prisoners stood mired to the axles. Our Ascian prisoners squatted in front of it, guarded by our wounded. The Ascian officer spoke our tongue, and a watch earlier Guasacht had ordered him to free the coach and shot several Ascians when he had failed; thirty or more remained, nearly naked, listless and empty-eyed. Their weapons were piled some distance off, near our tethered mounts.

Now Guasacht was making the rounds, and I saw him pause at the stump that sheltered the trooper next to me. One of the enemy put her head from behind a clump of brush some way up the slope. My contus struck her with a bolt of flame; she leaped by reflex, then curled up as spiders do when someone tosses them among the coals of a campfire. She had been white-faced beneath her red bandana, and I suddenly understood that she had been made to look—that there were those behind that brush who had disliked her, or at least not valued her, and who had forced her to look out. I fired again, slashing the green growth with the bolt and bringing a puff of acrid smoke that drifted toward me like her ghost.

"Don't waste those charges," Guasacht said at my elbow. More from habit, I think, than from fear, he had thrown himself flat beside me.

I asked if the charges would be exhausted before night if I fired six times a watch.

He shrugged, then shook his head.

"That's how fast I've been shooting this thing, as well as I can judge by the sun. And when night comes . . ."

I looked at him, and he could only shrug again.

"When night comes," I continued, "we won't be able to see them until they're only a few steps away. We'll fire more or less at random and kill a few score, then draw swords and stand back to back, and they'll kill us."

He said, "Help will arrive before then," and when he saw I did not believe him, he spat. "I wish I'd never looked at the damned thing's track. I wish I'd never heard of it."

It was my turn to shrug. "Give it back to the Ascians, and we'll break out."

"It's coin, I tell you! Gold to pay our troops. It's too heavy to be anything else."

"The armor must weigh a good deal."

"Not that much. I've seen these coaches before, and it's gold from Nessus or the House Absolute. But those things inside—who's ever seen such creatures?"

"I have."

Guasacht stared at me.

"When I went out through the Piteous Gate in the Wall of Nessus. They are man-beasts, contrived by the same lost arts that made our destriers faster than the road engines of old." I tried to recall what else Jonas had told me of them, and finished rather weakly by saying, "The Autarch employs them in duties too laborious for men, or for which men cannot be trusted."

"I suppose that might be right enough. They can't very well steal the money. Where would they go? Listen, I've had my eye on you."

"I know," I said. "I've felt it."

"I've had my eye on you, I say. Particularly since you made that piebald of yours go for the man that trained him. Up here in Orithyia we see a lot of strong men and a lot of brave ones—mostly when we step over their bodies. We see a lot of smart ones too, and nineteen out of twenty are too smart to be of use to anybody, including themselves. What's valuable are men, and sometimes women, who've got a kind of power, the power that makes other people want to do what they say. I don't mean to brag, but I've got it. You've got it too."

"It hasn't been overwhelmingly apparent in my life before this."

"Sometimes it takes the war to bring it out. That's one of the benefits of the war, and since it hasn't got many we ought to appreciate the ones it does. Severian, I want you to go down to the coach and treat with these man-animals. You say you know something about them. Get them to come out and help us fight. We're both on the same side, after all."

I nodded. "And if I can get them to open the doors, we can divide the money among us. Some of us, at least, may escape."

Guasacht shook his head in disgust. "What did I tell you just a moment ago about being too smart? If you were really smart, you wouldn't have ignored it. No, you tell them that even if there's only three or four of them, every fighter counts. Besides, there's at least a chance the sight of them will frighten these damn freebooters away. Let me have your contus, and I'll hold your position for you until you come back."

I handed over the long weapon. "Who are these people, anyway?"

"These? Camp followers. Sutlers and whores—men as well as women. Deserters. Every so often the Autarch or one of his generals has them rounded up and put to work, but they slip away before long. Slipping away's their specialty. They ought to be wiped out."

"I have your authority to treat with our prisoners in the coach? You'll back me up?"

"They're not prisoners—well, yes, I suppose they are. You tell them what I said and make the best deal you can. I'll back you."

I looked at him for a moment, trying to decide whether he meant it. Like so many middle-aged men, he carried the old man he would become in his face, soured and obscene, already muttering the objections and complaints that would be his in the final skirmish.

"You've got my word. Go on."

"All right." I rose. The armored coach resembled the carriages that had been used to bring important clients to our tower in the Citadel. Its windows were narrow and barred, its rear wheels as high as a man. The smooth steel sides suggested those lost arts I had mentioned to Guasacht, and I knew the man-beasts inside had better weapons than ours. I extended my hands to show I was unarmed and walked as steadily as I could toward them until a face showed at one window grill.

When one hears of such creatures, one imagines something stable, midway between beast and human; but when one actually sees them—as I now saw this man-beast, and as I had seen the man-apes in the mine near Saltus—they are not like that at all. The best comparison I can make is to the flickering of a silver birch tossed by the wind. At one moment it seems a common tree, at the next, when the undersides of the leaves appear, a supernatural creation. So it is with the man-beasts. At first I thought a mastiff peered at me through the bars; then it seemed rather a man, nobly ugly, tawny-faced and amber-eyed. I raised my hands to the grill to give him my scent, thinking of Triskele.

"What do you want?" His voice was harsh but not unpleasant.

"I want to save your lives," I said. It was the wrong thing to say, and I knew it as soon as the words had left my mouth.

"We want to save our honor."

I nodded. "Honor is the higher life."

"If you can tell us how to save our honor, speak. We will listen. But we will never surrender our trust."

"You have already surrendered it," I said.

The wind died, and the mastiff was back in an instant, flashing teeth and blazing eyes.

"It was not to safeguard gold from the Ascians that you were put into this coach, but to safeguard it from those of our own Commonwealth who would steal it if they could. The Ascians are beaten—look at them. We are the Autarch's loyal humans. Those you were set to guard against will overwhelm us soon."

"They must kill me and my fellows before they can get the gold."

It *was* gold, then. I said, "They will do so. Come out and help us fight, while there is still a chance of victory."

He hesitated, and I was no longer sure that I had been

entirely wrong to speak first of saving his life. "No," he said. "We cannot. What you say may be reason, I do not know. Our law is not the law of reason. Our law is honor and obedience. We stay."

"But you know that we are not your enemies?"

"Anyone seeking what we guard is our enemy."

"We're guarding it too. If these camp followers and deserters came within range of your weapons, would you fire on them?"

"Yes, of course."

I walked over to the spiritless cluster of Ascians and asked to speak with their commander. The man who stood was only slightly taller than the rest; the intelligence in his face was the kind one sometimes sees in cunning madmen. I told him Guasacht had sent me to treat in his stead because I had often spoken with Ascian prisoners and knew their ways. This was, as I intended, overheard by his three wounded guards, who could see Guasacht manning my position on the perimeter.

"Greetings in the name of the Group of Seventeen," the Ascian said.

"In the name of the Group of Seventeen."

The Ascian looked startled but nodded.

"We are surrounded by the disloyal subjects of our Autarch, who are thus the enemies of both the Autarch and the Group of Seventeen. Our own commander, Guasacht, has devised a plan that will leave us all alive and free."

"The servants of the Group of Seventeen must not be expended without purpose."

"Precisely. Here is the plan. We will harness some of our destriers to the steel coach—as many as necessary to pull it free. You and your people must work to free it too. When it's free, we'll return your weapons and help you fight your way out of this cordon. Your soldiers and ours will go north, and you can keep the coach and the money inside to take to your superiors, just as you hoped when you captured it."

"The light of Correct Thought penetrates every darkness."

"No, we haven't gone over to the Group of Seventeen. You have to help us in return. In the first place, help get the coach out of the mud. In the second, help us fight our way out. In the third, provide us with an escort that will get us through your army and back to our own lines."

The Ascian officer glanced toward the gleaming coach. "No failure is permanent failure. But inevitable success may require new plans and greater strength."

"Then you approve of my new plan?" I had not been aware that I was perspiring, but now the sweat ran stinging into my eyes. I wiped my forehead with the edge of my cloak, just as Master Gurloes used to.

The Ascian officer nodded. "Study of Correct Thought eventually reveals the path of success."

"Yes," I said. "All right, I've studied it. Behind our efforts, let there be found our efforts."

When I returned to the coach, the same man-beast I had seen before came to the window again, not quite so hostile this time. I said, "The Ascians have agreed to try to push this thing out once more. We're going to have to unload it."

"That is impossible."

"If we don't, the gold will be lost with the sun. I'm not asking you to give it up—just take it out and mount guard over it. You'll have your weapons, and if any human bearing arms comes close to you, you can kill him. I'll be with you, unarmed. You can kill me too."

It took a great deal more talking, but eventually they did it. I got the wounded who had been watching the Ascians to lay down their conti and harness eight of our destriers to the coach, and got the Ascians positioned to pull on the harness and heave at the wheels. Then the door in the side of the steel coach swung open and the man-beasts carried out small metal chests, two working while the one I had spoken to stood guard. They were taller than I had expected and had fusils, with pistols in their belts to supplement them—the first pistols I had seen since I had watched the Hierodules use them to turn Baldanders's charges in the gardens of the House Absolute.

When all the chests were out and the three man-beasts were standing around them with their weapons at the ready, I shouted. The wounded troopers lashed every destrier in the new team, the Ascians heaved until their eyes started from their straining faces . . . and just when we all thought it would not, the steel coach lifted itself from the mud and lumbered half a chain before the wounded could bring it to a halt. Guasacht nearly got us both killed by running down from the perimeter waving my contus, but the man-beasts had just sense enough to see that he was merely excited and not dangerous.

He got a great deal more excited when he saw the man-beasts carry their gold inside again, and when he heard what I had promised the Ascians. I reminded him that he had given me leave to act in his name.

"When I act," he sputtered, "it's with the idea of winning."

I confessed I lacked his military experience, but told him I had found that in some situations winning consisted of disentangling oneself.

"Just the same, I had hoped you would work out something better."

Rising inexorably while we remained unaware of their motion, the mountain peaks to the west were already clawing for the lower edge of the sun; I pointed to it.

Suddenly, Guasacht smiled. "After all, these are the same Ascians we took it from before."

He called the Ascian officer over and told him our mounted troopers would lead the attack, and that his soldiers could follow the steel coach on foot. The Ascian agreed, but when his soldiers had rearmed themselves, he insisted on placing half a dozen on top of the coach and leading the attack himself with the rest. Guasacht agreed with an apparent bad grace that seemed to me entirely assumed. We put an armed trooper astride each of the eight destriers of the new team, and I saw Guasacht conversing earnestly with their cornet.

I had promised the Ascian we would break through the cordon of deserters to the north, but the ground in that direction proved to be unsuited to the steel coach, and in the end a route north by northwest was agreed upon. The Ascian infantry advanced at a pace not much short of a full run, firing as they came. The coach followed. The narrow, enduring bolts of the troopers' conti stabbed at the ragged mob who tried to close about it, and the Ascian arquebuses on its roof sent gouts of violet energy crashing among them. The man-beasts fired their fusils from the barred windows, slaughtering half a dozen with a single blast.

The remainder of our troops (I among them) followed the coach, having maintained our perimeter until it was gone. To save precious charges, many put their conti through the saddle rings, drew their swords, and rode down the straggling remnant the Ascians and the coach had left behind.

Then the enemy was past, and the ground clearer. At once the troopers whose mounts pulled the coach clapped spurs to them, and Guasacht, Erblon, and several others who were riding just behind it swept the Ascians from its top in a cloud of crimson flame and reeking smoke. Those on foot scattered, then turned to fire.

It was a fight I did not feel I could take part in. I reined up, and so saw—I believe, before any of the others—the first of the anpiels who dropped, like the angel in Melito's fable, from the sun-dyed clouds. They were fair to look upon, naked and having the slender bodies of young women; but their rainbow wings spread wider than any teratornis's, and each anpiel held a pistol in either hand.

* * *

Late that night, when we were back in camp and the wounded had been cared for, I asked Guasacht if he would do as he had again.

He thought for a moment. "I hadn't any way of knowing those flying girls would come. Looking at it from this end, it's natural enough—there must have been enough in that coach to pay half the army, and they wouldn't hesitate to send elite troops looking for it. But before it happened, would you have guessed it?"

I shook my head.

"Listen, Severian, I shouldn't be talking to you like this. But you did what you could, and you're the best leech I ever saw. Anyway, it came out all right in the end, didn't it? You saw how friendly their seraph was. What did she see, after all? Plucky lads trying to save the coach from the Ascians. We'll get a commendation, I should think. Maybe a reward."

I said, "You could have killed the man-beasts, and the Ascians too, when the gold was out of the coach. You didn't because I would have died with them. I think you deserve a commendation. From me, at least."

He rubbed his drawn face with both hands. "Well, I'm just as happy. It would have been the end of the Eighteenth; in another watch we'd have been killing each other for the money."

XXI

Deployment

BEFORE THE BATTLE there were other patrols and days of idleness. Often enough we saw no Ascians, or saw only their dead. We were supposed to arrest deserters and drive from our area such peddlers and vagabonds as fatten on an army; but if they seemed to us such people as had surrounded the steel coach, we killed them, not executing them in any formal style but cutting them down from the saddle.

The moon waxed again nearly to the full, hanging like a green apple in the sky. Experienced troopers told me the worst fights always came at or near the full of the moon, which is said to breed madness. I suppose this is actually because its refulgence permits generals to bring up reinforcements by night.

On the day of the battle, the graisle's bray summoned us from our blankets at dawn. We formed a ragged double column in the mist, with Guasacht at our head and Erblon following him with our flag. I had supposed that the women would stay behind—as most had when we had gone on patrol—but more than half drew conti and came with us. Those who had helmets, I noticed, thrust their hair up into the bowl, and many wore corslets that flattened and concealed their breasts. I mentioned it to Mesrop, who rode opposite me.

"There might be trouble about the pay," he said. "Somebody with sharp eyes will be counting us, and the contracts usually call for men."

"Guasacht said there'd be more money today," I reminded him.

He cleared his throat and spat, the white phlegm vanishing into the clammy air as though Urth herself had swallowed it. "They won't pay until it's over. They never do."

Guasacht shouted and waved an arm; Erblon gestured with our flag, and we were off, the hoofbeats sounding like the thudding of a hundred muffled drums. I said, "I suppose that way they don't have to pay for those who are killed."

"They pay triple—once because he fought, once for blood money, and once for discharge money."

"Or she fought, I suppose."

Mesrop spat again.

We rode for some time, then halted at a spot that seemed no different from any other. As the column fell silent, I heard a humming or murmuring in the hills all around us. A scattered army, dispersed no doubt for sanitary reasons and to deprive the Ascian enemy of a concentrated target, was assembling now just as particles of dust in the stone town had come together in the bodies of its resuscitated dancers.

Not unnoticed. Even as birds of prey had once followed us before we reached that town, now five-armed shapes that spun like wheels pursued us above the scattered clouds that dimmed and melted in the level red light of dawn. At first, when they were highest, they seemed merely gray; but as we watched they dropped toward us, and I saw they were of a hue for which I can find no name but that stands to achroma as gold to yellow, or silver to white. The air groaned with their turning.

Another that we had not seen came leaping across our path, hardly higher than the treetops. Each spoke was the length of a tower, pierced with casements and ports. Though it lay flat upon the air, it seemed to stride along. Its wind whistled down upon us as if to blow away the trees. My piebald screamed and bolted, and so did many other destriers, often falling in that strange wind.

In the space of a heartbeat it was over. The leaves that had swirled about us like snow fell to earth. Guasacht shouted and Erblon sounded the graisle and brandished our flag. I got the piebald under control and cantered from one destrier to another, taking them by the nostrils until their riders could manage them again.

I rescued Daria, who I had not known was in the column, in this way. She looked very pretty and boyish dressed as a trooper, with a contus, and a slender sabre at either side of her saddle horn. I could not help thinking when I saw her of how other women I had known would appear in the same situation: Thea a theatrical warrior maid, beautiful and dramatic but essentially the figure of a figurehead; Thecla—now part of myself—a vengeful mimalone brandishing poisoned weapons; Agia astride a slender-legged sorrel, wearing a cuirass molded to her figure, while her hair, plaited with bowstrings, flew wild in the wind; Jolenta a floriate queen in armor spikey with thorns, her big breasts and fleshy thighs absurd at any gait faster than a walk, smiling dreamily at each halt and attempting to recline in the saddle; Dorcas a naiad riding, lifted momentarily like a fountain flashing with sunshine; Valeria, perhaps, an aristocratic Daria.

I had supposed, when I saw our people scatter, that it would be impossible to reassemble the column; but within a few moments of the time the pentadactyl air-strider had passed over us, we were together again. We galloped for a league or more—mostly, I suspect, to dissipate some of the nervous energy of our destriers—then halted by a brook and gave them just as much water as would wet their mouths without making them sluggish. When I had fought the piebald back from the bank, I rode to a clearing from which I could watch the sky. Soon Guasacht trotted over and asked me jocularly, "You looking for another one?"

I nodded and told him I had never seen such craft before.

"You wouldn't have, unless you've been close to the front. They'd never come back if they tried to go down south."

"Soldiers like us wouldn't stop them."

He grew suddenly serious, his tiny eyes mere slits in the sun-browned flesh. "No. But plucky lads can stop their raiding parties. The guns and air-galleys can't do that."

The piebald stirred and stamped with impatience. I said, "I come from a part of the city you've probably never heard of, the Citadel. There are guns there that look out over the whole quarter, but I've never known them to be fired except ceremonially." Still staring at the sky, I thought of the wheeling pentadactyls over Nessus, and a thousand blasts, issuing not just from the Barbican and the Great Keep, but from all the towers; and I wondered with what weapons the pentadactyls would reply.

"Come along," Guasacht said. "I know it's a temptation to keep a lookout for them, but it doesn't do any good."

I followed him back to the brook, where Erblon was lining up the column. "They didn't even fire at us. They must surely have guns in those fliers."

"We're pretty small fish." I could see that Guasacht wanted me to rejoin the column, though he hesitated to order me to do so directly.

For my part, I could feel fear grip me like a specter, strongest about my legs, but lifting cold tentacles into my bowels, touching my heart. I wanted to be silent, but I could not stop talking. "When we go onto the field of battle—" (I think I imagined this field like the shaven lawn of the Sanguinary Field, where I had fought Agilus.)

Guasacht laughed. "When we go into the fight, our gunners would be delighted to see them out after us." Before I understood what he was about to do, he struck the piebald with the flat of his blade and sent me cantering off.

Fear is like those diseases that disfigure the face with running sores. One becomes almost more afraid of their being seen than of their source, and comes to feel not only disgraced but defiled. When the piebald began to slow, I dug my heels into him and fell into line at the very end of the column.

Only a short time before I had been on the point of replacing Erblon; now I was demoted, not by Guasacht but by myself, to the lowest position. And yet when I had helped reassemble the scattered troopers, the thing I feared had already passed; so that the entire drama of my elevation had been played out after it had ended in debasement. It was as though one were to see a young man idling in a public garden stabbed—then watch him, all unknowing, strike up an acquaintance with the voluptuous wife of his murderer, and at last, having ascertained, as he thought, that her husband was in another part of the city, clasp her to him until she cried out from the pain of the dagger's hilt protruding from his chest.

When the column lurched forward, Daria detached herself from it and waited until she could fall in beside me. "You're afraid," she said. It was not a question but a statement, and not a reproach but almost a password, like the ridiculous phrases I had learned at Vodalus's banquet.

"Yes. You're about to remind me of the boast I made to you in the forest. I can only say that I did not know it to be an empty one when I made it. A certain wise man once tried to teach me that even after a client has mastered one excruciation, so that he can put it from his mind even while he screams and writhes, another quite different excruciation may be as effectual in breaking his will as in breaking a child's. I learned to explain all this when he asked me but never until now to apply it, as I should, to my own life. But if I am the client here, who is the torturer?"

"We're all more or less afraid," she said. "That was why—yes, I saw it—Guasacht sent you away. It was to keep you from making his own feeling worse. If it were worse, he wouldn't be able to lead. When the time comes, you'll do what you have to, and that's all any of them do."

"Hadn't we better go?" I asked. The end of the column was moving off in that surging way the tail of a long line always does.

"If we go now, a lot of them will know we're at the rear because we're afraid. If we wait just a little while longer, many of those who saw you talking with Guasacht will think he sent you back here to speed up stragglers, and that I came back to be with you."

"All right," I said.

Her hand, damp with sweat and as thin as Dorcas's, came sliding into mine.

Until that moment, I had been certain she had fought before. Now I asked her, "Is this your first time too?"

"I can fight better than most of them," she declared, "and I'm sick of being called a whore."

Together, we trotted after the column.

XXII

Battle

I SAW THEM first as a scattering of colored dots on the farther side of the wide valley, skirmishers who seemed to move and mix, as bubbles do that dance upon the surface of a mug of cider. We were trotting through a grove of shattered trees whose white and naked wood was like the living bone of a compound fracture. Our column was much larger now, perhaps the whole of the irregular contarii. It had been under fire, in a more or less dilatory way, for about half a watch. Some troopers had been wounded (one, near me, quite badly) and several killed. The wounded cared for themselves and tried to help each other—if there were medical attendants for us they were too far behind us for me to be conscious of them.

From time to time we passed corpses among the trees; usually these were in little clusters of two or three, sometimes they were merely solitary individuals. I saw one who had contrived in dying to hook the collar of his brigandine jacket to a splinter protruding from one of the broken trunks, and I was struck by the horror of his situation, his being dead and yet unable to rest, and then by the thought that such was the plight of all those thousands of trees, trees that had been killed but could not fall.

At about the same time I became aware of the enemy, I realized that there were troops of our own army to either side. To our right a mixture, as it were, of mounted men and infantry, the riders helmetless and naked to the waist, with red and blue blanket rolls slung across their bronzed chests. They were better mounted, I thought, than most of us. They carried lancegays not much longer than the height of a man, many of them holding them aslant their saddle-bows. Each had a small copper shield bound to the upper part of his left arm. I had no idea from what part of the Commonwealth these men might come; but for some reason, perhaps only because of their long hair and bare chests, I felt sure they were savages.

If they were, the infantry that moved among them was something lower still, brown and stooped and shaggy-haired. I had only glimpses through the broken trees, but I thought they dropped to all fours at times. Occasionally one seemed to grasp the stirrup of some rider, as I had sometimes taken Jonas's when he rode his merychip; whenever that occurred, the rider struck at his companion's hand with the butt of his weapon.

A road ran through lower ground to our left; and down it, and to either side of it, there moved a force far more numerous than our column and the savage riders and their companions all combined: battalions of peltasts with blazing spears and big, transparent shields; hobilers on prancing mounts, with bows and arrow cases crossed over their backs; lightly armed cherkajis whose formations were seas of plumes and flags.

I could know nothing of the courage of all these strange soldiers who had suddenly become my comrades, but I unconsciously assumed it to be no greater than my own, and they seemed a slender defense indeed against the moving dots on the farther side. The fire to which we were subjected grew more intense, and so far as I could see, our enemies were under none at all.

Only a few weeks before (though it felt like at least a year now) I would have been terrified at the thought of being shot at with such a weapon as Vodalus had used on the foggy night in our necropolis with which I have begun this account. The bolts that struck all around us made that simple beam appear as childish as the shining slugs thrown from the hetman's archer's pellet bow.

I had no idea what sort of device was used to project these bolts, or even whether they were in fact pure energy or some type of missile; but as they landed among us, their nature was that of an explosion lengthened into something like a rod. And though they could not be seen until they struck, they whistled as they came, and by that whistled note, which endured no longer than the blink of an eye, I soon learned to tell how near they would hit and how powerful the extended detonation would be. If there was no change in the tone, so that it resembled the note a coryphaeus sounds on his pitch pipe, the strike would be some distance off. But if it rose quickly, as though a note first sounded for men had become one for women, its impact would be nearby; and though only the loudest of the monotonal bolts were dangerous, each that rose to a scream claimed at least one of us and often several.

It seemed madness to trot forward as we did. We should have scattered, or dismounted to take refuge among the trees; and if one of us had done it, I think all the rest would have followed him. With every bolt that fell, I was almost that one. But again and again, as if my mind were chained in some narrow circle, the memory of the fear I had shown earlier held me in my place. Let the rest run and I would run with them; but I would not run first.

Inevitably, a bolt struck parallel to our column. Six troopers flew apart as though they themselves had contained small bombs, the head of the first bursting in a gout of scarlet, the neck and shoulders of the second, the chest of the third, the bellies of the fourth and fifth, and the groin (or perhaps on the saddle and the back of his destrier) of the sixth, before the bolt struck the ground and sent up a geyser of dust and stones. The men and animals opposite those who were destroyed in this way were killed too, wracked by the force of the explosions and bombarded with the limbs and armor of the others.

Holding the piebald to a trot, and often to a walk, was the worst of it; if I could not run, I wanted to press forward, to get the fighting begun, to die if I was in fact to die. This hit gave me some opportunity to relieve my feelings. Waving to Daria to follow, I let the piebald lope past the little group of survivors who had been riding between us and the last trooper to die, and moved into the space in the column that had been the casualties'. Mesrop was there already, and he grinned at me. "Good thinking. Chances are there won't be another one here for quite a while." I forbore to disabuse him.

For a time it seemed he was correct anyway. Having hit us, the enemy gunners diverted their fire to the savages on our right. Their shambling infantry shrieked and gibbered as the bolts fell among them, but the riders reacted, so it appeared, by calling on magic to protect them. Often their chants sounded so clearly that I could make out the words, though they were in no language I had ever heard. Once one actually stood on his saddle like a performer in a riding exhibition, lifting a hand to the sun and extending the other toward the Ascians. Each rider seemed to have a personal spell; and it was easy to see, as I watched their numbers shrink under the bombardment, how such primitive minds come to believe in their charms, for the survivors could not but feel their thaumaturgy had saved them, and the rest could not complain of the failure of theirs.

Though we were advancing, for the most part, at the trot, we were not the first to engage the enemy. On the lower ground, the cherkajis had streaked across the valley, crashing against a square of foot soldiers like a wave of fire.

I had vaguely supposed that the enemy would be provided with weapons far superior to anything we had in the contarii—perhaps pistols and fusils, such as the man-beasts had carried—and that a hundred fighters so armed would easily destroy any quantity of cavalry. Nothing of the kind happened. Several rows of the square gave way, and I was close enough now to hear the riders' war cries, distant yet distinct, and see individual foot soldiers in flight. Some were casting aside immense shields, shields even larger than the glassy ones of the peltasts, though they shone with the luster of metal. Their offensive arms seemed to be splay-headed spears no more than three cubits long, weapons that could produce sheets of cleaving flame, but short in range.

A second infantry square emerged behind the first, then another and another, farther down the valley.

Just as I was sure we were about to ride to the assistance of the cherkajis, we received the order to halt. Looking to the right, I saw that the savages had already done so, stopping some distance behind us, and were now driving the hairy creatures that had accompanied them toward the side of their position farthest from us.

Guasacht called, "We're blocking! Sit easy, lads!"

I looked at Daria, who returned a look equally bewildered. Mesrop waved an arm toward the eastern end of the valley. "We're watching the flank. If nobody comes, we ought to have a good enough time of it today."

I said, "Except for the ones who've already died." The bombardment, which had been diminishing, now seemed to have stopped altogether. The silence of its absence lay all about us, almost more frightening than its screaming bolts had been.

"I suppose so." His shrug announced eloquently that we had lost a few dozen from a force of hundreds.

The cherkajis had recoiled, retreating behind a screen of hobilers who directed a shower of arrows at the leading edge of the Ascians' checkerboard battle line. Most seemed to glance off the shields, but a few must have buried their heads in the metal, which took fire from them and burned with a flame as bright as theirs and billowing white smoke.

When the arrows slackened, the squares of the checkerboard advanced again with a mechanical jerkiness. The cherkajis had continued to fall back and were now in the rear of a line of peltasts, very little in advance of us. I could see their dark faces clearly. They were all men and bearded, and numbered about two thousand; but they had among them a dozen or so bejeweled young women borne in gilded howdahs on the backs of caparisoned arsinoithers.

These women were dark-eyed and dark complexioned like the men, yet in their lush figures and languishing looks they reminded me of Jolenta. I pointed them out to Daria and asked if she knew how they were armed, since I could see no weapons.

"You'd like one, would you? Or two. I'll bet they look good to you even from here."

Mesrop winked and said, "I wouldn't mind a couple myself."

Daria laughed. "They'd fight like alraunes if either of you tried to have anything to do with them. They're sacred and forbidden, the Daughters of War. Have you ever been around those animals they're riding?"

I shook my head.

"They charge easy and nothing stops them, but they always go the same way—straight at whatever it is that bothers them and past it for a chain or two. Then they stop and go back."

I watched. Arsinoithers have two big horns—not spreading horns like the horns of bulls, but horns that diverge about as much as a man's first and second fingers can. As I soon saw, they charge head down, with those horns level with the ground, and these did just as Daria had said. The cherkajis rallied and attacked again with their slender lances and forked swords. Trailing far behind that lightning dash, the arsinoithers lumbered forward, gray-black heads down and tails up, with the deep-bosomed, dark-faced maidens standing erect under their canopies and gripping the gilded poles. One could see from the way these women held themselves that their thighs were as full as the udders of milch cows and round as the trunks of trees.

The charge carried them through the swirling fight and deep—but not too deep—into the checkerboard. The Ascian foot soldiers blasted the sides of their beasts, which must have been like burning horn or *cuir boli*; they tried to mount their heads and were tossed into the air; they struggled to climb the gray flanks. The cherkajis came crashing to the rescue, and the checkerboard flowed and ebbed and lost a square.

Watching it from such a distance, I recalled my own thoughts of battle as a game of chess, and I felt that somewhere someone else had entertained the same thoughts and unconsciously allowed them to shape his plan.

"They're lovely," Daria continued, teasing me. "Chosen at twelve and fed on honey and pure oils. I've heard their flesh is so tender they can't lie on the ground without being bruised. Bags of feathers are carried about for them to sleep on. If those are lost, the girls have to lie in mud that shapes itself to support their bodies. The eunuchs who care for them mix it with wine warmed over a fire, so they will sleep and not be cold."

"We should dismount," Mesrop said. "It'll spare the animals."

But I wanted to watch the battle and would not get down, though soon only Guasacht and I remained in the saddle out of our entire bacele.

The cherkajis had been driven back once again, and now came under a withering bombardment from unseen artillery.

The peltasts dropped to the ground, covering themselves with their shields. New squares of Ascian infantry emerged from the forest on the north side of the valley. There seemed to be no end to them; I felt we had been committed against an inexhaustible enemy.

The feeling grew stronger when the cherkajis charged a third time. A bolt struck an arsinoither, blowing it and the lovely woman it had carried to bloody ruin. The infantry was firing at those women now; one crumpled, and howdah and canopy vanished in a puff of flame. The infantry squares advanced over brightly clad corpses and dead destriers.

By each step in war the winner loses. The ground the checkerboard had won exposed the side of its leading square to us, and to my astonishment we were ordered to mount, spread into line, and wheeled against it, first trotting, then cantering, and at last, with the brass throats of all the graisles shouting, in a desperate rush that nearly blew the skin from our faces.

If the cherkajis were lightly armed, we were armed more lightly still. Yet there was a magic in the charge more powerful than the chants of our savage allies. The wildfire of our weapons played along the distant ranks as scythes attack a wheat field. I lashed the piebald with his reins to keep from being outdistanced by the roaring hoofs I heard behind me. Yet I was, and glimpsed Daria as she shot past, the flame of her hair flying free, her contus in one hand and a sabre in the other, her cheeks whiter than the foaming flanks of her destrier. I knew then how the custom of the cherkajis had begun, and I tried to charge faster still so that she should not die, though Thecla laughed through my lips at the thought.

Destriers do not run like common beasts—they skim the ground as arrows do air. For an instant, the fire of the Ascian infantry half a league away rose before us like a wall. A moment later we were among them, the legs of every mount bloody to the knee. The square that had seemed as solid as a building stone had become only a crowd of frantic soldiers

with big shields and cropped heads, soldiers who often slew
one another in their eagerness to slay us.

Fighting is a stupid business at best; but there are things to
be learned about it, of which the first is that numbers tell
only in time. The immediate struggle is always that of an
individual against one or two others. In this our destriers gave
us the upper hand—not only because of their height and
weight, but because they bit and struck out with their forefeet, and the blows of their hoofs were more powerful than
any man save Baldanders could have delivered with a mace.

Fire cut through my contus. I dropped it but continued to
kill, slashing left, then right, then left again with the falchion
and hardly noticing that the blast had laid open my leg.

I think I must have cut down half a dozen Ascians before I
saw that they all looked the same—not that they all had the
same face (as the men in some units of our own army do, who
are indeed closer than brothers), but that the differences
among them seemed accidental and trivial. I had observed
this among our prisoners when we had retrieved the steel
coach, but it had not really impressed itself upon my mind.
In the madness of battle it did so, for it seemed a part of that
madness. The frenzied figures were male and female: the
women had small but pendulous breasts and were half a head
shorter, but there was no other distinction. All had large,
brilliant, wild eyes, hair clipped nearly to the skull, starved
faces, screaming mouths, and prominent teeth.

We fought free as the cherkajis had; the square had been
dented but not destroyed. While we let our mounts catch
breath it reformed, the light, polished shields to the front. A
spearman broke ranks and came running toward us waving his
weapon. At first I thought it mere bluster; then, as he came
nearer (for a normal man runs much less swiftly than a destrier), that he wished to surrender. At last, when he had almost reached our line, he fired, and a trooper shot him down.
In his convulsions he threw his blazing spear into the air; I
remember how it twisted against the dark blue sky.

Guasacht came trotting over. "You're bleeding bad. Can you ride when we charge them again?"

I felt as strong as I ever had in my life and told him so.

"Still, you'd better get a bandage on that leg."

The seared flesh had cracked; blood was oozing out. Daria, who had not been hurt at all, bound it up.

The charge for which I had been prepared never took place. Quite unexpectedly (at least as far as I was concerned) the order came to turn about, and we went trotting off to the northeast over open, rolling country whisperous with coarse grass.

The savages seemed to have vanished. A new force appeared in their place, on the flank that had now become our front. At first I thought they were cavalry on centaurs, creatures whose pictures I had encountered in the brown book. I could see the heads and shoulders of the riders above the human heads of their mounts, and both appeared to bear arms. When they drew nearer, I saw they were nothing so romantic: merely small men—dwarfs, in fact—upon the shoulders of very tall ones.

Our directions of advance were nearly parallel but slowly converged. The dwarfs watched us with what seemed a sullen attention. The tall men did not look at us at all. At last, when our column was no more than a couple of chains from theirs, we halted and turned to face them. With a horror I had not felt before, I realized that these strange riders and strange steeds were Ascians; our maneuver had been intended to prevent them from taking the peltasts in the flank, and had now succeeded in that they would now have to make their attack, if they could, through us. There seemed to be about five thousand of them, however, and there were certainly many more than we had fit to fight.

Yet no attack came. We had halted and formed a tight line, stirrup to stirrup. Despite their numbers, they surged nervously up and down before it as though attracted first by the thought of passing it on the right, then on the left, then on the right again. It was clear, however, that they could not pass at all unless a part of their force engaged our front to prevent our striking the rest from behind. As if hoping to postpone the fight, we did not fire.

Now we saw repetitions of the behavior of the lone spearman who had left his square to attack us. One of the tall men dashed forward. In one hand he held a slender staff, hardly more than a switch; in the other, a sword of the kind called a *shotel*, which has a very long, double-edged blade whose forward half is curved into a semicircle. As he drew nearer he slowed, and I saw that his eyes were unfocused; that he was in fact blind. The dwarf on his shoulders had an arrow nocked to the string of a short, recurved bow.

When these two were within half a chain of us, Erblon detailed two men to drive them off. Before they could close with the blind man, he broke into a run as swift as any destrier's but eerily silent, and came flying toward us. Eight or ten troopers fired, but I saw then how difficult it is to hit a target moving at such speed. The arrow struck and burst in a blaze of orange light. A trooper tried to parry the blind man's wand—the shotel flashed down, and its hooked blade laid open the trooper's skull.

Then a group of three of the blind men with three riders detached itself from the mass of the enemy. Before they reached us, there were clusters of five or six coming. Far down the line, our hipparch raised his arm; Guasacht waved us forward and Erblon blew the charge, echoed to right and left—a bellowing note that seemed to have deep-mouthed bells in it.

Though I did not know it at the time, it is axiomatic that encounters purely between cavalry rapidly degenerate into mere skirmishes. So it was with ours. We rode at them, and though we lost twenty or thirty in doing so, we rode through them. At once we turned to engage them again, both to prevent their flanking the peltasts and to regain contact with our own army. They, of course, turned to face us; and in a short time neither we nor they had anything that could be called a front, or any tactics beyond those each fighter forged for himself.

My own were to veer away from any dwarf who looked ready to shoot and try to catch others from behind or from the side. They worked well enough when I could apply them, but I quickly found that though the dwarfs appeared almost helpless when the blind men they rode were killed under them, their tall steeds ran amok without their riders, attacking anything that stood in their path with frantic energy, so that they were more dangerous than ever.

Very soon the dwarfs' arrows and our conti had kindled scores of fires in the grass. The choking smoke rendered the confusion worse than ever. I had lost sight of Daria and Guasacht—of everyone I knew—sometime before. Through the acrid gray haze I could just make out a figure on a plunging destrier fighting off four Ascians. I went to him, and though one dwarf turned his blind steed and sent an arrow whizzing by my ear, I rode over them and heard the blind man's bones snap under the piebald's hoofs. A hairy figure rose from the smoldering grass behind the other pair and cut them down as a peon hews a tree—three or four strokes of his ax to the same spot until the blind man fell.

The mounted soldier I had come to rescue was not one of our troopers, but one of the savages who had been on our right earlier. He had been wounded, and when I saw the blood I recalled that I had been wounded too. My leg was stiff, my strength nearly gone. I would have ridden back toward the south crest of the valley and our own lines if I had known which way to go. As it was, I gave the piebald his head and a good slap from the reins, having heard that these animals will often return to the place where they last had water and rest. He broke into a canter that soon became a gallop. Once he jumped, nearly throwing me from the saddle, and I looked down to glimpse a dead destrier with Erblon dead beside him, and the brass graisle and the black and green flag lying on the burning turf. I would have turned the piebald and gone back for them, but by the time I pulled him up, I no longer knew the spot. To my right, a mounted line showed through the smoke, dark and almost formless, but serrated. Far behind it loomed a machine that flashed fire, a machine that was like a tower walking.

At one moment they were nearly invisible; at the next they were upon me like a torrent. I cannot say who the riders were or on what beasts they rode; not because I have forgotten (for I forget nothing) but because I saw nothing clearly. There was no question of fighting, only of seeking in some way to live. I parried a blow from a twisted weapon that was neither sword nor ax; the piebald reared, and I saw an arrow protruding from his chest like a horn of fire. A rider crashed against us, and we fell into the dark.

XXIII

The Pelagic Argosy Sights Land

WHEN I REGAINED consciousness, it was the pain in my leg that I felt first. It was pinned beneath the body of the piebald, and I struggled to free it almost before I knew who I was or how I found myself where I did. My hands and face, the very ground on which I lay, were crusted with blood.

And it was quiet—so quiet. I listened for the thudding of hoofs, the drum roll that makes Urth herself its drum. It was not there. The shouts of the cherkajis were no more, nor the shrill, mad cries that had come from the checkerboard of Ascian infantry. I tried to turn to push against the saddle, but I could not do so.

Somewhere far off, no doubt on one of the ridges that rimmed the valley, a dire wolf raised its maw to Lune. That inhuman howling, which Thecla had heard once or twice before when the court went to hunt near Silva, made me realize that the dimness of my sight was not due to the smoke of the grass fires that had burned earlier that day, or, as I had half feared, to some head injury. The land was twilit, though whether by dusk or dawn I could not say.

I rested and perhaps I slept, then roused again at the sound of footsteps. It was darker than I remembered. The footsteps were slow, soft, and heavy. Not the sound of cavalry on the move, nor yet the measured tread of marching infantry—a walk heavier than Baldanders's and more slow. I opened my mouth to cry for help, then closed it again, thinking I might call upon myself something more terrible than that I had once waked in the mine of the man-apes. I lunged away from the dead piebald until it seemed I would wrench my leg from its socket. Another dire wolf, as frightful as the first and much closer, howled to the green isle overhead.

As a boy, I was often told I lacked imagination. If it were ever true, Thecla must have brought it to our nexus, for I could see the dire wolves in my mind, black and silent shapes, each as large as an onyger, pouring down into the valley; and I could hear them cracking the ribs of the dead. I called, and called again, before I knew what it was I did.

It seemed to me that the heavy footsteps paused. Certainly they moved toward me, whether they had been coming toward me before or not. I heard a rustling in the grass, and a little phenocod, striped like a melon, bounded out, terrified by something I still could not see. It shied at the sight of me and in a moment was gone.

I have said that Erblon's graisle was silenced. Another blew now, a deeper, longer, wilder note than I had ever heard. The outline of a bent orphicleide showed against the dusky sky. When its music was ended it fell, and in a moment more I saw the head of the player blotting out the brightening moon at three times the height of a mounted trooper's helmet—a domed head shaggy with hair.

The orphicleide sounded once more, deep as a waterfall, and this time I saw it rise, and the white, curling tusks that guarded it on each side, and I knew I lay in the path of the very symbol of dominion, the beast called Mammoth.

Guasacht had said I held some mastery over animals, even without the Claw. I strove to use it now, whispering I know not what, concentrating my thought until it seemed my temples would burst. The mammoth's trunk came questing toward me, its tip nearly a cubit across. Lightly as a child's hand it touched my face, flooding me with moist, hot breath sweet with hay. The corpse of the piebald was lifted away; I tried to stand but somehow fell. The mammoth caught me up, winding its trunk about my waist, and lifted me higher than its own head.

The first thing I saw was the muzzle of a trilhoen with a dark, bulging lens the size of a dinner plate. It was fitted with a seat for the operator, but no one sat there. The gunner had come down and stood upon the mammoth's neck as a sailor might upon the deck of a ship, with one hand on the barrel for balance. For a moment a light shone in my face, blinding me.

"It's you. Miracles converge on us." The voice was not truly either a man's or a woman's; it might almost have been a boy's. I was laid at the speaker's feet, and he said, "You're hurt. Can you stand on that leg?"

I managed to say I did not think I could.

"This is a poor place to lie, but a good one to fall from. There's a gondola farther back, but I'm afraid Mamillian can't reach it with his trunk. You'll have to sit up here, with your back against the swivel."

I felt his hands, small, soft, and moist, beneath my arms. Perhaps it was their touch that told me who he was: The androgyne I had met in the snow-covered House Azure, and later in that artfully foreshortened room that posed as a painting hanging in a corridor of the House Absolute.

The Autarch.

In Thecla's memories I saw him robed in jewels. Although he had said he recognized me, I could not believe in my dazed state that it was so, and I gave him the code phrase he had once given me, saying, "The pelagic argosy sights land."

"It does. It does indeed. Yet if you fall overboard now, I'm afraid Mamillian's not quite quick enough to catch you . . . despite his undoubted wisdom. Give him as much help as you can. I'm not as strong as I look."

I got some part of the trilhoen's mount in one hand and was able to pull myself around on the musty-smelling mat that was the mammoth's hide. "To speak the truth," I said, "you've never looked strong to me."

"You have the professional eye and ought to know, but I'm not even as strong as that. You, on the other hand, have always seemed to me a construction of horn and boiled leather. And you must be, or you'd be dead by now. What happened to your leg?"

"Burned, I think."

"We'll have to get you something for it." He raised his voice slightly. "*Home! Back home, Mamillian!*"

"May I ask what you're doing here?"

"Having a look at the field of battle. You fought here today, I take it."

I nodded, though I felt my head would tumble from my shoulders.

"I didn't . . . or rather, I did, but not personally. I ordered certain bodies of light auxiliaries into action, with a legion of peltasts in support. I suppose you must have been one of the auxiliaries. Were any of your friends killed?"

"I only had one. She was all right the last time I saw her."

His teeth flashed in the moonlight. "You maintain your interest in women. Was it the Dorcas you told me of?"

"No. It doesn't matter." I did not quite know how to phrase what I was about to say. (It is the worst of bad manners to state openly that one has penetrated an incognito.) At last I managed, "I can see you hold high rank in our Commonwealth. If it won't get me pushed from the back of this animal, can you tell me what someone who commands legions was doing conducting that place in the Algedonic Quarter?"

While I spoke, the night had grown rapidly darker, the stars winking out one after another like the tapers in a hall when the ball is over and footmen walk among them with snuffers like mitres of gold dangling from spidery rods. At a great distance I heard the androgyne say, "You know who we are. We are the thing itself, the self-ruler, the Autarch. We know more. We know who you are."

Master Malrubius was, as I realize now, a very sick man before he died. At the time I did not know it, because the thought of sickness was foreign to me. At least half our apprentices, and perhaps more than half, died before they were raised to journeyman; but it never occurred to me that our tower might be an unhealthy place, or that the lower reaches of Gyoll, where we so often swam, were little purer than a cesspool. Apprentices had always died, and when we living apprentices dug their graves we turned up small pelvises and skulls, which we, the succeeding generation, reburied again and again until they were so much injured by the spade that their chalky particles were lost in the tarlike soil. I, however, never suffered more than a sore throat and a running nose, forms of sickness that serve only to deceive healthy people into the belief that they know in what disease consists. Master Malrubius suffered real illness, which is to see death in shadows.

As he stood at his little table, one felt that he was conscious of someone standing behind him. He looked straight to the front, never turning his head and hardly moving a shoulder, and he spoke as much for that unknown listener as for us.

"I have done my best to teach you boys the rudiments of learning. They are the seeds of trees that should grow and blossom in your minds. Severian, look to your Q. It should be round and full like the face of a happy boy, but one of its cheeks is as fallen-in as your own. You have all, all you boys, seen how the spinal cord, lifting itself toward its culmination, expands and at last blossoms in the myriad pathways of the brain. And this one, one cheek round, the other seared and shriveled."

His trembling hand reached for the slate pencil, but it

escaped his fingers and rolled over the edge of the table to clatter on the floor. He did not stoop to pick it up, fearful, I think, that in stooping he might glimpse the invisible presence.

"I have spent much of my life, boys, in trying to implant those seeds in the apprentices of our guild. I have had a few successes, but not many. There was a boy, but he—"

He went to the port and spat, and because I was sitting near it I saw the twisted shapes formed by the seeping blood and knew that the reason I could not see the dark figure (for death is of the color that is darker than fuligin) that accompanied him was that it stood within him.

Just as I had discovered that death in a new form, in the shape of war, could frighten me when it could no longer do so in its old ones, so I learned now that the weakness of my body could afflict me with the terror and despair my old teacher must have felt. Consciousness came and went.

Consciousness went and came like the errant winds of spring, and I, who so often have had difficulty in falling asleep among the besieging shades of memory, now fought to stay awake as a child struggles to lift a faltering kite by the string. At times I was oblivious to everything except my injured body. The wound in my leg, which I had hardly felt when I received it, and whose pain I had so effortlessly locked away when Daria had bandaged it, throbbed with an intensity that formed the background to all my thoughts, like the rumbling of the Drum Tower at the solstice. I turned from side to side, thinking always that I lay upon that leg.

I had hearing without sight and occasionally sight without hearing. I rolled my cheek from the matted hair of Mamillian and laid it on a pillow woven of the minute, downy feathers of hummingbirds.

Once I saw torches with dancing flames of scarlet and radiant gold held by solemn apes. A man with the horns and muzzled face of a bull bent over me, a constellation sprung to life. I spoke to him and found myself telling him that I was unsure of the precise date of my birth, that if his benign spirit of meadow and unfeigning force had governed my life I thanked him for it; then remembered that I knew the date, that my father had given a ball for me each year until his death, that it fell under the Swan. He listened intently, turning his head to watch me from one brown eye.

XXIV

The Flier

SUNLIGHT IN MY FACE.

I tried to sit up, and in fact succeeded in getting one elbow beneath me. All about me shimmered an orb of color—purple and cyan, ruby and azure, with the orpiment of the sun piercing these enchanted tints like a sword to fall upon my eyes. Then it was blotted out, and its extinction revealed what its splendor had obscured: I lay in a domed pavilion of variegated silk, with an open door.

The rider of the mammoth was walking toward me. He was robed in saffron, as I had always seen him, and carried an ebony rod too light to be a weapon. "You have recovered," he said.

"I'd try and say yes, but I'm afraid the effort of speaking might kill me."

He smiled at that, though the smile was no more than a twitching of the mouth. "As you should know better than almost anyone, the sufferings we endure in this life make possible all the happy crimes and pleasant abominations we shall commit in the next . . . aren't you eager to collect?"

I shook my head and laid it on the pillow again. The softness smelled faintly of musk.

"That is just as well, because it will be some time before you do."

"Is that what your physician says?"

"I am my own, and I've been treating you myself. Shock was the principal problem. . . . It sounds like a disorder for old women, as you are no doubt thinking at this moment. But it kills a great many men with wounds. If all of mine who die of it would only live, I would readily consent to the death of those who take a thrust in the heart."

"While you were being your own physician—and mine— were you telling the truth?"

He smiled more broadly at that. "I always do. In my position, I have to talk too much to keep a skein of lies in order; of course, you must realize that the truth . . . the little, ordinary truths that farm wives talk of, not the ultimate and universal Truth, which I'm no more capable of uttering than you . . . that truth is more deceptive."

"Before I lost consciousness, I heard you say you are the Autarch."

He threw himself down beside me like a child, his body making a distinct sound as it struck the piled carpets. "I did. I am. Are you impressed?"

"I would be more impressed," I said, "if I did not recall you so vividly from our meeting in the House Azure."

(That porch, covered with snow, heaped with snow that deadened our footsteps, stood in the silken pavilion like a specter. When the Autarch's blue eyes met mine, I felt that Roche stood beside me in the snow, both of us dressed in unfamiliar and none-too-well-fitting clothes. Inside, a woman who was not Thecla was transforming herself into Thecla as I was later to make myself Meschia, the first man. Who can say to what degree an actor assumes the spirit of the person he portrays? When I played the Familiar, it was nothing, because it was so close to what I was—or had at least believed myself to be—in life; but as Meschia I had sometimes had thoughts that could never have occurred to me otherwise, thoughts alien equally to Severian and to Thecla, thoughts of the beginnings of things and the morning of the world.)

"I never told you, you will recall, that I was *only* the Autarch."

"When I met you in the House Absolute, you appeared to be a minor official of the court. I admit you never told me that, and in fact I knew then who you were. But it was you, wasn't it, who gave the money to Dr. Talos?"

"I would have told you that without a blush. It is completely true. In fact, I am several of the minor officials of my court. . . . Why shouldn't I be? I have the authority to appoint such officials, and I can just as well appoint myself. An order from the Autarch is often too heavy an instrument, you see. You would never have tried to slit a nose with that big headsman's sword you carried. There is a time for a decree from the Autarch, and a time for a letter from the third bursar, and I am both and more besides."

"And in that house in the Algedonic Quarter—"

"I am also a criminal . . . just as you are."

There is no limit to stupidity. Space itself is said to be bounded by its own curvature, but stupidity continues beyond infinity. I, who had always thought myself, though not truly intelligent, at least prudent and quick to learn simple things, who had always counted myself the practical and foreseeing one when I had traveled with Jonas or Dorcas, had never until that instant connected the Autarch's position at the very apex of the structure of legality with his certain knowledge that I had penetrated the House Absolute as an emissary of Vodalus. At that moment, I would have leaped up and fled from the pavilion if I could, but my legs were like water.

"All of us are—all of us must be who must enforce the law. Do you think your guild brothers would have been so severe with you—and my agent reports that many of them wished to kill you—if they had themselves been guilty of something of the same kind? You were a danger to them unless you were terribly punished because they might otherwise someday be tempted. A judge or a jailer who has no crime of his own is a monster, alternately purloining the forgiveness that belongs to the Increate alone and practicing a deathly rigor that belongs to no one and nothing.

"So I became a criminal. The violent crimes offended my love of humanity, and I lack the quickness of hand and thought required of a thief. After blundering about for some time . . . that would be in about the year you were born, I suppose . . . I found my true profession. It takes care of certain emotional needs I cannot now satisfy otherwise . . . and I have, I really do have, a knowledge of human nature. I know just when to offer a bribe and how much to give, and, the most important thing, when not to. I know how to keep the girls who work for me happy enough with their careers to continue, and discontented enough with their fates. . . . They're khaibits, of course, grown from the body cells of exultant women so an exchange of blood will prolong the exultants' youth. I know how to make my clients feel that the encounters I arrange are unique experiences instead of something midway between dewy-eyed romance and solitary vice. You felt that you had a unique experience, didn't you?"

"That's what we call them too," I said. "*Clients.*" I had been listening as much to the tone of his voice as to his words. He was happy, as I thought he had not been on either of the other occasions on which I had encountered him, and to hear him was like hearing a thrush speak. He almost seemed to know it himself, lifting his face and extending his throat, the Rs in *arrange* and *romance* trilled into the sunlight.

"It is useful too. It keeps me in touch with the underside of the population, so I know whether or not taxes are really being collected and whether they're thought fair, which elements are rising in society and which are going down."

I sensed that he was referring to me, though I had no idea what he meant. "Those women from the court," I said.

"Why didn't you get the real ones to help you? One of them was pretending to be Thecla when Thecla was locked under our tower."

He looked at me as though I had said something particularly stupid, as no doubt I had. "Because I can't trust them, of course. A thing like that has to remain a secret. . . . Think of the opportunities for assassination. Do you believe that because all those gilded personages from ancient families bow so low in my presence, and smile, and whisper discreet jokes and lewd little invitations, they feel some loyalty to me? You will learn differently, you may be sure. There are few at my court I can trust, and none among the exultants."

"You say I'll learn differently. Does that mean you don't intend to have me executed?" I could feel the pulse in my neck and see the scarlet gout of blood.

"Because you know my secret now? No. We have other uses for you, as I told you when we talked in the room behind the picture."

"Because I was sworn to Vodalus."

At that his amusement mastered him. He threw back his head and laughed, a plump and happy child who had just discovered the secret of some clever toy. When the laughter subsided at last into a merry gulping, he clapped his hands. Soft though they looked, the sound was remarkably loud.

Two creatures with the bodies of women and the heads of cats entered. Their eyes were a span apart and as large as plums; they strode on their toes as dancers sometimes do, but more gracefully than any dancers I have ever seen, with something in their motions that told me it was their normal gait. I have said they had the bodies of women, but that was not quite true, for I saw the tips of claws sheathed in the short, soft fingers that dressed me. In wonder, I took the hand of one and pressed it as I have sometimes pressed the paw of a friendly cat, and saw the claws barred. My eyes brimmed with tears at the sight of them, because they were shaped like that claw that is the Claw, that once lay concealed in the gem that I, in my ignorance, called the Claw of the Conciliator. The Autarch saw I was weeping, and told the woman-cats they were hurting me and must put me down. I felt like an infant who has just learned he will never see his mother again.

"We do not harm him, Legion," one protested in such a voice as I had never heard before.

"Put him down, I said!"

"They have not so much as grazed my skin, Sieur," I told him.

With the woman-cats' support I was able to walk. It was morning, when all shadows flee the first sight of the sun; the light that had wakened me had been the earliest of the new day. Its freshness filled my lungs now, and the coarse grass over which we walked darkened my scuffed old boots with its dew; a breeze faint as the dim stars stirred my hair.

The Autarch's pavilion stood on the summit of a hill. All around lay the main bivouac of his army—tents of black and gray, and others like dead leaves; huts of turf and pits that led to shelters underground, from which streams of soldiers issued now like silver ants.

"We must be careful, you see," he said. "Though we are some distance behind the lines here, if this place were plainer it would invite attack from above."

"I used to wonder why your House Absolute lay beneath its own gardens, Sieur."

"The need has long passed now, but there was a time when they laid waste to Nessus."

Below us and all around us, the silver lips of trumpets sounded.

"Was it only the night?" I asked. "Or have I slept a whole day away?"

"No. Only the night. I gave you medicines to ease your pain and keep infection from your wound. I would not have roused you this morning, but I saw you were awake when I came in . . . and there is no more time."

I was not certain what he meant by that. Before I could ask, I caught sight of six nearly naked men hauling at a rope. My first impression was that they were bringing down some huge balloon, but it was a flier, and the sight of its black hull brought vivid memories of the Autarch's court.

"I was expecting—what was its name? Mamillian."

"No pets today. Mamillian is an excellent comrade, silent and wise and able to fight with a mind independent of my own, but when all is said and done, I ride him for pleasure. We will thieve a string from the Ascians' bow and use a mechanism today. They steal many from us."

"Is it true that it consumes their power to land? I think one of your aeronauts once told me that."

"When you were the Chatelaine Thecla, you mean. Thecla purely."

"Yes, of course. Would it be impolitic, Autarch, to ask why you had me killed? And how you know me now?"

"I know you because I see your face in the face of my young friend and hear your voice in his. Your nurses know you too. Look at them."

I did, and saw the woman-cats' faces twisted in snarls of fear and amazement.

"As to why you died, I will speak of that—to him—on board the flier . . . have we time. Now, go back. You find it easy to manifest yourself because he is weak and ill, but I must have him now, not you. If you will not go, there are means."

"Sieur—"

"Yes, Severian? Are you afraid? Have you entered such a contrivance before?"

"No," I said. "But I am not afraid."

"Do you recall your question about their power? It is true,

in a sense. Their lift is supplied by the antimaterial equivalent of iron, held in a penning trap by magnetic fields. Since
the anti-iron has a reversed magnetic structure, it is repelled
by promagnetism. The builders of this flier have surrounded
it with magnets, so that when it drifts from its position at the
center it enters a stronger field and is forced back. On an
antimaterial world, that iron would weigh as much as a boul-
der, but here on Urth it counters the weight of the promatter
used in the construction of the flier. Do you follow me?"

"I believe so, Sieur."

"The trouble is that it is beyond our technology to seal the
chamber hermetically. Some atmosphere—a few molecules—
is always creeping in through porosities in the welds, or by
penetrating the insulation of the magnetic wires. Each such
molecule neutralizes its equivalent in anti-iron and produces
heat, and each time one does so, the flier loses an infinitesimal amount of lift. The only solution anyone has found is to
keep fliers as high as possible, where there is effectively no air
pressure."

The flier was nosing down now, near enough for me to
appreciate the beautiful sleekness of its lines. It had precisely
the shape of a cherry leaf.

"I didn't understand all of that," I said. "But I would
think the ropes would have to be immensely long to allow
the fliers to float high enough to do any good, and that if the
Ascian pentadactyls came over by night they would cut them
and let the fliers drift away."

The woman-cats smiled at that with tiny, secretive twitch-
ings of their lips.

"The rope is only for landing. Without it, our flier would
require sufficient distance for its forward speed to drive it
down. Now, knowing we're below, it drops its cable just as a
man in a pond might extend his hand to someone who would
pull him out. It has a mind of its own, you see. Not like
Mamillian's—a mind we have made for it, but enough of a

mind to permit it to stay out of difficulties and come down when it receives our signal."

The lower half of the flier was of opaque black metal, the upper half a dome so clear as to be nearly invisible—the same substance, I suppose, as the roof of the Botanic Gardens. A gun like the one the mammoth had carried thrust out from the stern, and another twice as large protruded from the bow.

The Autarch lifted one hand to his mouth and seemed to whisper into his palm. An aperture appeared in the dome (it was as if a hole had opened in a soap bubble) and a flight of silver steps, as thin and insubstantial looking as the web ladder of a spider, descended to us. The bare-chested men had left off pulling. "Do you think you can climb those?" the Autarch asked.

"If I can use my hands," I said.

He went before me, and I crawled up ignominiously after him, dragging my wounded leg. The seats, long benches that followed the curve of the hull on either side, were upholstered in fur; but even this fur felt colder than any ice. Behind me, the aperture narrowed and vanished.

"We will have surface pressure in here no matter how high we go. You don't have to worry about suffocating."

"I am afraid I am too ignorant to feel the fear, Sieur."

"Would you like to see your old bacele? They're far to the right, but I'll try to locate them for you."

The Autarch had seated himself at the controls. Almost the only machinery I had seen before had been Typhon's and Baldanders's, and that which Master Gurloes controlled in the Matachin Tower. It was of the machines, not of suffocation, that I was afraid; but I fought the fear down.

"When you rescued me last night, you indicated that you had not known I was in your army."

"I made inquiries while you slept."

"And it was you who ordered us forward?"

"In a sense . . . I issued the order that resulted in your

movement, though I had nothing to do with your bacele directly. Do you resent what I did? When you joined, did you think you would never have to fight?"

We were soaring upward. Falling, as I had once feared to do, into the sky. But I remembered the smoke and the brassy shout of the graisle, the troopers blown to red paste by the whistling bolts, and all my terror turned to rage. "I knew nothing of war. How much do you know? Have you ever really been in a battle?"

He glanced over his shoulder at me, his blue eyes flashing. "I've been in a thousand. You are two, as people are usually counted. How many do you think I am?"

It was a long while before I answered him.

XXV

The Mercy of Agia

AT FIRST I THOUGHT there could be nothing stranger than to
see the army stretch across the surface of Urth until it lay like
a garland before us, coruscant with weapons and armor,
many-hued; the winged anpiels soaring above it nearly as
high as we, circling and rising on the dawn wind.

Then I beheld something stranger still. It was the army of
the Ascians, an army of watery whites and grayish blacks,
rigid as ours was fluid, deployed toward the northern horizon.
I went forward to stare at it.

"I could show them to you more closely," the Autarch
said. "Still, you would see only human faces."

I realized he was testing me, though I did not know how.
"Let me see them," I said.

When I had ridden with the schiavoni and watched our
troops go into action, I had been struck by their look of
weakness in the mass, the cavalry all ebb and flow like a wave
that crashes with great force—then drains away as mere water,
too weak to bear the weight of a mouse, pale stuff a child
might scoop up in his hands. Even the peltasts, with their
serried ranks and crystal shields, had seemed hardly more formidable than toys on a tabletop. Now I saw how strong the

rigid formations of our enemy appeared, rectangles that held machines as big as fortresses and a hundred thousand soldiers shoulder to shoulder.

But on a screen in the center of the control panel I looked under the visors of their helmets, and all that rigidity, all that strength, melted into a kind of horror. There were old people and children in the infantry files, and some who seemed idiots. Nearly all had the mad, famished faces I had observed the day before, and I recalled the man who had broken from his square and thrown his spear into the air as he died. I turned away.

The Autarch laughed. His laughter held no joy now; it was a flat sound, like the snapping of a flag in a high wind. "Did you see one kill himself?"

"No," I said.

"You were fortunate. I often do, when I look at them. They are not permitted arms until they are ready to engage us, and so many take advantage of the opportunity. The spearmen drive the butts of their weapons into soft ground, usually, then blast off their own heads. Once I saw two swordsmen—a man and a woman—who had made a compact. They stabbed each other in the belly, and I watched them counting first, moving their left hands . . . one . . . two . . . three, and dead."

"Who are they?" I asked.

He shot me a look I could not interpret. "What did you say?"

"I asked who they are, Sieur. I know they're our enemies, that they live to the north in the hot countries, and that they're said to be enslaved by Erebus. But who are they?"

"Up until now I doubt you knew you did not know. Did you?"

My throat felt parched, though I could not have told why. I said, "I suppose not. I'd never seen one until I came into the lazaret of the Pelerines. In the south, the war seems very remote."

He nodded. "We have driven them half as far to the north as they once drove us south, we autarchs. Who they are you will discover in due time. . . . What matters is that you wish to know." He paused. "Both could be ours. Both armies, not just the one to the south. . . . Would you advise me to take both?" As he spoke, he manipulated some control and the flier canted forward, its stern pointing at the sky and its bow to the green earth, as though he meant to pour us out upon the disputed ground.

"I don't understand what you mean," I told him.

"Half what you said of them was incorrect. They do not come from the hot countries of the north, but from the continent that lies across the equator. But you were right when you called them the slaves of Erebus. They think themselves the allies of those who wait in the deep. In truth, Erebus and his allies would give them to me if I would give our south to them. Give you and all the rest."

I had to grip the back of the seat to keep from falling toward him. "Why are you telling me this?"

The flier righted itself like a child's boat in a puddle, bobbing.

"Because it will soon be necessary for you to know that others have felt what you will feel."

I could not frame a question I dared to ask. At last I ventured, "You said you'd tell me here why you killed Thecla."

"Does she not live in Severian?"

A windowless wall in my mind fell to ruins. I shouted: "I *died!*" Not realizing what I had said until the words were past my lips.

The Autarch took a pistol from beneath the control panel, letting it lie across his thighs as he turned to face me.

"You won't need that, Sieur," I said. "I'm too weak."

"You have remarkable powers of recovery. . . . I have seen them already. Yes, the Chatelaine Thecla is gone, save as she endures in you, and though the two of you are always together, you are both lonely. Do you still seek for Dorcas? You told me of her, you remember, when we met in the Secret House."

"Why did you kill Thecla?"

"I did not. Your error lies in thinking I am at the bottom of everything. No one is. . . . Not I, or Erebus, or any other. As to the Chatelaine, you are she. Were you arrested openly?"

The memory came more vividly than I would have thought possible. I walked down a corridor whose walls were lined with sad masks of silver and entered one of the abandoned rooms, high-ceilinged and musty with ancient hangings. The courier I was to meet had not yet come. Because I knew the dusty divans would soil my gown, I took a chair, a spindly thing of gilt and ivory. The tapestry spilled from the wall behind me; I recalled looking up and seeing Destiny crowned in chains and Discontent with her staff and glass, all worked in colored wool, descending upon me.

The Autarch said, "You were taken by certain officers, who had learned that you were conveying information to your half sister's lover. Taken secretly, because your family has so much influence in the north, and conveyed to an almost forgotten prison. By the time I learned what had occurred, you were dead. Should I have punished those officers for acting in my absence? They are patriots, and you were a traitor."

"I, Severian, am a traitor too," I said, and I told him, then for the first time in detail, how I had once saved Vodalus, and of the banquet I had later shared with him.

When I had concluded, he nodded to himself. "Much of the loyalty you felt for Vodalus comes, surely, from the Chatelaine. Some she imparted to you while she was yet living, more after her death. Naive though you have been, I am certain you are not so naive as to think it a coincidence that it was she whose flesh was served to you by the corpse-eaters."

I protested, "Even if he had known of my connection with her, there was no time to bring her body from Nessus."

The Autarch smiled. "Have you forgotten that you told me a moment ago that when you had saved him, he fled in such a craft as this? From that forest, hardly a dozen leagues outside the City Wall, he could have flown to the center of Nessus, unearthed a corpse preserved by the chill soil of early spring, and returned in less than a watch. Actually, he need not have known so much or moved so swiftly. While you were imprisoned by your guild, he may have learned that the Chatelaine Thecla, who had been loyal to him even to death, was no more. By serving her flesh to his followers, he would strengthen them in his cause. He would require no additional motive to take her body, and no doubt he reinterred her in hoarded snow in some cellar, or in one of the abandoned mines with which that region abounds. You arrived, and wishing to bind you to him, he ordered her brought out."

Something passed too swiftly to be seen—an instant later the flier rocked with the violence of its motion. Sparks maneuvered on the screen.

Before the Autarch could take the controls again, we were scudding backward. There was a detonation so loud it seemed to paralyze me, and the reverberating sky opened in a blossom of yellow fire. I have seen a sparrow, struck by a stone from Eata's sling, reel in the air just as we did, and fall, like us, fluttering to one side.

I woke to darkness, pungent smoke, and the smell of fresh earth. For a moment or a watch I forgot my rescue and believed I lay on the field where Daria and I, with Guasacht, Erblon, and the rest, had fought the Ascians.

Someone lay near me—I heard the sigh of his breath, and the creakings and scrapings that betray movement—but at first I paid no heed to them, and later I came to believe that these sounds were made by foraging animals, and grew afraid; later still, I recalled what had happened and knew they were surely made by the Autarch, who must have survived the crash with me, and I called to him.

"So you still live, then." His voice was very weak. "I feared you would die . . . though I should have known better. I could not revive you, and your pulse was but faint."

"I have forgotten! Do you remember when we flew over the armies? For a time I forgot it! I know now what it is to forget."

There was pale laughter in his voice. "Which you will now remember always."

"I hope so, but it fades even as we speak. It vanishes like mist, which must itself be a forgetting. What was that weapon that brought us down?"

"I do not know. But listen. These are the most important words of my life. Listen. You have served Vodalus, and his dream of renewed empire. You still wish, do you not, that humankind should go again to the stars?"

I recalled something Vodalus had told me in the wood and said, "Men of Urth, sailing between the stars, leaping from galaxy to galaxy, the masters of the daughters of the sun."

"They were so once . . . and brought all the old wars of Urth with them, and in the young suns kindled new ones. Even they," (I could not see him, yet I knew by his tone that he had indicated the Ascians) "understand it must not be so again. They wish the race to become a single individual . . . the same, duplicated to the end of number. We wish each to carry all the race and its longings within himself. Have you noticed the phial I wear at my neck?"

"Yes, often."

"It contains a pharmacon like alzabo, already mixed and held in suspension. I am cold already below the waist. I will die soon. Before I die . . . you must use it."

"I cannot see you," I said. "And I can scarcely move."

"Nevertheless, you will find a way. You remember everything, and so you must recall the night you came to my House Azure. That night someone else came to me. I was a servant once, in the House Absolute. . . . That is why they hate me. As they will hate you, for what you once were. Paeon, who trained me, who was honey-steward fifty years gone by. I knew what he was in truth, for I had met him before. He told me you were the one . . . the next. I did not think it would be quite so soon. . . ."

His voice fell away, and I began to grope for him, pulling myself along. My hand found his, and he whispered, "Use the knife. We are behind the Ascian line, but I have called upon Vodalus to rescue you. . . . I hear the hoofs of his destriers."

The words were so faint I could hardly hear, though my ear was within a span of his mouth. "Rest," I said. Knowing that Vodalus hated him and sought to destroy him, I thought him delirious.

"I am his spy. That is another of my offices. He draws the traitors. . . . I learn who they are and what they do, what they think. That is one of his. Now I have told him the Autarch is trapped in this flier and given him our location. He has served me . . . as my bodyguard . . . before this."

Now even I could hear the sound of feet on the ground outside. I reached up, searching for some means by which to signal; my hand touched fur, and I knew the flier had overturned, leaving us like hidden toads beneath it.

There was a snap and the scream of tearing metal. Moonlight, seeming bright as day but green as willow leaves, came flooding through a rent in the hull that gaped as I watched. I saw the Autarch, his thin white hair darkened with dried blood.

And above him silhouettes, green shades looking down upon us. Their faces were invisible; but I knew those gleaming eyes and narrow heads belonged to no followers of Vodalus. Frantically, I searched for the Autarch's pistol. My hands were seized. I was drawn up, and as I emerged I could not help thinking of the dead woman I had seen pulled from her grave in the necropolis, for the flier had fallen on soft ground and half buried itself. Where the Ascian bolt had struck it, its side was torn away, leaving a tangle of ruined wiring. The metal was twisted and burned.

I did not have much time to look at it. My captors turned me around and around as one after another took my face in his hands. My cloak was fingered as though they had never seen cloth. With their large eyes and hollow cheeks, these evzones seemed to me much like the infantry we had fought against, but though there were women among them, there were no old people and no children. They wore silvery caps and shirts in place of armor, and carried strangely shaped jezails, so long barreled that when their butt plates rested on the ground their muzzles were higher than their owners' heads. As I saw the Autarch lifted from the flier, I said, "Your message was intercepted, Sieur, I think."

"Nevertheless, it arrived." He was too weak to point, but I followed the direction of his eyes, and after a moment I saw flying shapes against the moon.

It almost seemed they slid down the beams to us, they came so quickly and so straight. Their heads were like the skulls of women, round and white, capped with miters of bone and stretched at the jaws into curved bills lined with pointed teeth. They were winged, the pinions so great they seemed to have no bodies at all. Twenty cubits at least these pinions stretched from tip to tip; when they beat they made no sound, but far below I felt the rush of air.

(Once I had imagined such creatures threshing the forests of Urth and beating flat her cities. Had my thought helped bring these?)

It seemed a long time before the Ascian evzones saw them. Then two or three fired at once, and the converging bolts caught one at their intersection and blew it to rags, then another and another. For an instant the light was blotted out, and something cold and flaccid struck my face, knocking me down.

When I could see again, half a dozen of the Ascians were

gone, and the rest were firing into the air at targets almost imperceptible to me. Something whitish fell from them. I thought it would explode and put my head down, but instead the hull of the wrecked flier rang like a cymbal. A body—a human body broken like a doll's—had struck it, but there was no blood.

One of the evzones jammed his weapon in my back and pushed me forward. Two more were supporting the Autarch much as the woman-cats had supported me. I discovered that I had lost all sense of direction. Though the moon still shone, masses of cloud veiled most of the stars. I looked in vain for the cross and for those three stars that are, for reasons no one understands, called *The Eight* and hang forever over the southern ice. Several of the evzones were still firing when there came blazing among us some arrow or spear that burst in a mass of blinding white sparks.

"That will do it," the Autarch whispered.

I was rubbing my eyes as I stumbled along, but I managed to ask what he meant.

"Can you see? No more can they. Our friends above . . . Vodalus's, I think . . . did not know our captors were so well armed. Now there will be no more good shooting, and as soon as that cloud drifts across the disc of Lune . . ."

I felt cold, as though a chill mountain wind had cut the tepid air around us. A few moments before I had been in despair to find myself among these gaunt soldiers. Now I would have given anything for some guarantee that I would remain among them.

The Autarch was to my left, hanging limp between two evzones who had slung their long-barreled jezails aslant their backs. As I watched, his head lolled to one side, and I knew he was unconscious or dead. "Legion" the woman-cats had called him, and it did not take great intellect to combine that name with what he had told me in the wrecked flier. Just as Thecla and Severian had joined in me, many personalities were surely united in him. Ever since the night I had first seen him, when Roche had brought me to the House Azure (whose odd name I was now, perhaps, beginning to grasp) I had sensed the complexity of his thought, as we sense, even in a bad light, the complexity of a mosaic, the myriad, infinitesimal chips that combine to produce the illuminated face and staring eyes of the New Sun.

He had said I was destined to succeed him, but for how long a reign? Preposterous as it was in a prisoner, and in a man so injured and so weak that a watch of rest on the coarse grass would have seemed like paradise, I was consumed with ambition. He had said I must eat his flesh and swallow the drug while he still lived; and, loving him, I would have torn my own from the grasp of my captors, if I had possessed the strength, to claim that luxury and pomp and power. I was Severian and Thecla united now, and perhaps the torturers' ragged apprentice had, without fully knowing it, longed for those things more than the young exultant held captive at court. I knew then what poor Cyriaca had felt in the gardens of the archon; yet if she had felt fully what I felt at that moment, it would have burst her heart.

An instant later I was unwilling. Some part of me treasured the privacy that not even Dorcas had entered. Deep inside the convolutions of my mind, in the embrace of the molecules, Thecla and I were twined together. For others—a dozen or a thousand, perhaps, if in absorbing the personality of the Autarch I was also to absorb those he had incorporated into himself—to come where we lay would be for the crowds of the bazaar to enter a bower. I clasped my heart's companion to me, and felt myself clasped. I felt myself clasped, and clasped my heart's companion to me.

The moon dimmed as a dark lantern does when one presses the lever that makes its plates iris closed until there remains no more than a point of light, then nothing. The Ascian evzones fired their jezails in a lattice of lilac and heliotrope, beams that diverged high in the atmosphere and at last pricked the clouds like colored pins; but without effect.

There was a wind, hot and sudden, and what I can only call a flash of black. Then the Autarch was gone, and something huge rushed toward me. I threw myself down.

Perhaps I struck the ground, but I do not remember it. In an instant, it seemed, I was swooping through the air, turning, climbing surely, the world below no more than a darker night. An emaciated hand, hard as stone and three times human size, clutched me about the waist.

We ducked, turned, lurched, slipped sidewise down a slope of air, then, catching a rising wind, climbed till the cold stung and stiffened my skin. When I craned my neck to look upward, I could see the white, inhuman jaws of the creature that bore me. It was the nightmare I had known months earlier when I had shared Baldanders's bed, though in my dream I had ridden the thing's back. Why that difference between dream and truth should be, I cannot say. I cried out (I do not know what) and above me the thing opened its scimitar beak to hiss.

From above, too, I heard a woman's voice call, "Now I have repaid you for the mine—you are still alive."

XXVI

Above the Jungle

WE LANDED BY STARLIGHT. It was like awakening; I felt that it was not the sky but the country of nightmare I was leaving behind. Like a falling leaf, the immense creature settled in narrowing circles through regions of progressively warmer air until I could smell the odor of the Jungle Garden: the mingling of green life and rotting wood with the perfume of wide, waxen, unnamed blossoms.

A ziggurat lifted its dark head above the trees—yet carried the trees with it, for they sprouted from its crumbling walls like fungi from a dead tree. We settled on it weightlessly, and at once there came torches and excited voices. I was still faint from the thin and icy air I had been breathing only moments before.

Human hands replaced the claws that had grasped me for so long. We wound down ledges and stairways of broken stone until at last I stood before a fire and saw across it the handsome, unsmiling face of Vodalus and the heart-shaped one of his consort, Thea, our half sister.

"Who is this?" Vodalus asked.

I tried to lift my arms, but they were held. "Liege," I said, "you must know me."

From behind me, the voice I had heard in the air answered, "This is the man of the price, the killer of my brother. For him, I—and Hethor, who serves me—have served you."

"Then why do you bring him to me?" Vodalus asked. "He is yours. Did you think that when I had seen him, I would repent of our agreement?"

Perhaps I was stronger than I felt myself to be. Perhaps I only caught the man on my right off-balance; however it was, I succeeded in twisting about, jerking him into the fire, where his feet sent the red brands flying.

Agia stood behind me, naked to the waist, and Hethor behind her, showing all his rotten teeth as he cupped her breasts. I fought to escape. She slapped me with an open hand—there was a pull at my cheek, tearing pain, then the warm rush of blood.

Since then, I have learned that the weapon is called a *lucivee*, and that Agia had it because Vodalus had forbidden any but his own bodyguard to carry arms in his presence. It is no more than a small bar with rings for the thumb and fourth finger, and four or five curved blades that can be concealed in the palm; but few have survived its blow.

I was one of those few, and rose after two days to find myself shut in a bare room. Perhaps in each life one room must become better known than any other: for prisoners, it is always a cell. I, who had worked outside so many, thrusting in trays of food to the disfigured and demented, now knew again a cell of my own. What the ziggurat had once been, I never guessed. Perhaps a prison indeed; perhaps a temple, or the atelier of some forgotten art. My cell was about twice the size of the one I had occupied beneath the tower of the torturers, six paces wide and ten long. A door of ancient, gleaming alloy stood against the wall, useless to Vodalus's jailers because they could not lock it; a new one, roughly made of the ironlike timbers of some jungle tree, closed the doorway. A window I believe had never been meant for one, a circular opening hardly bigger than my arm, pierced the discolored wall high up and gave light to the cell.

Three days more passed before I was strong enough to jump and, gripping its lower edge with one hand, pull myself up to look out. When that day came, I saw a rolling green country dotted with butterflies—a place so foreign to what I had expected that I felt I might be mad and lost my hold upon the window in my astonishment. It was, as I eventually realized, the country of treetops, where ten-chain hardwoods spread a lawn of leaves, seldom seen save by the birds.

An old man with a knowledgeable, evil face had bandaged my cheek and changed the dressings on my leg. Later he brought a lad of about thirteen whose bloodstream he linked with mine until the boy's lips turned the hue of lead. I asked the old leech where he came from, and he, apparently thinking me a native of these parts, said, "From the big city in the south, in the valley of the river that drains the cold lands. It is a longer river than yours, is the Gyoll, though its flood is not so fierce."

"You have great skill," I said. "I've never heard of a physician who did as much. I feel well already, and wish you would stop before this boy dies."

The old man pinched his cheek. "He'll recover quickly—in time to warm my bed tonight. At his age they always do. Nay, it's not what you think. I only sleep beside him because the night-breath of the young acts as a restorative to those of my years. Youth, you see, is a disease, and we may hope to catch a mild case. How stands your wound?"

There was nothing—not even an admission, which might have been rooted in some perverse desire to maintain an appearance of potency—that could have convinced me so completely as his denial. I told him the truth, that my right cheek was numb save for a vague burning as irritating as an itch, and wondered which of his duties the miserable boy minded most.

The old man stripped away my bandages and gave my wounds a second coating of the foul-smelling brown salve he had used previously. "I'll be back tomorrow," he told me. "Although I don't think you'll need Mamas here again. You're coming along nicely. Her exultancy" (with a jerk of the head to show this was an ironical reference to Agia's stature) "will be most pleased."

I said, in what I sought to make an offhand way, that I hoped all his patients were doing as well.

"You mean the delator who was brought in with you? He's as well as can be expected." He turned aside as he spoke, so that I would not see his frightened expression.

On the chance that I might gain influence with him that would enable me to aid the Autarch, I praised his understanding of his craft extravagantly and ended by saying that I failed to comprehend why a physician of his ability consorted with these wicked people.

He looked at me narrowly, and his face grew serious. "For knowledge. There is nowhere a man in my profession can learn as I learn here."

"You mean the eating of the dead? I have shared in that too, though they may not have told you so."

"No, no. Learned men—particularly those of my profession—practice that everywhere, and usually with better effect, since we are more selective of our subjects and confine ourselves to the most retentive tissues. The knowledge I seek cannot be learned in that way, since none of the recently dead possessed it, and perhaps no one has ever possessed it."

He was leaning against the wall now, and seemed to be speaking as much to some invisible presence as to me. "The past's sterile science led to nothing but the exhaustion of the planet and the destruction of its races. It was founded in the mere desire to exploit the gross energies and material substances of the universe, without regard to their attractions, antipathies, and eventual destinies. Look!" He thrust his hand into the beam of sunshine that was then issuing from my high, circular window. "Here is light. You will say that it is not a living entity, but you miss the point that it is more, not less. Without occupying space, it fills the universe. It nourishes everything, yet itself feeds upon destruction. We claim to control it, but does it not perhaps cultivate us as a source of food? May it not be that all wood grows so that it can be set ablaze, and that men and women are born to kindle fires? Is it not possible that our claim to master light is as absurd as wheat's claiming to master us because we prepare the soil for it and attend its intercourse with Urth?"

"All that is well said," I told him. "But nothing to the point. Why do you serve Vodalus?"

"Such knowledge is not gained without experiment." He smiled as he spoke, and touched the shoulder of the boy, and I had a vision of children in flames. I hope that I was wrong.

That had been two days before I pulled myself up to the window. The old leech did not come again; whether he had fallen from favor, or been dispatched to another place, or had merely decided no further attentions were necessary, I had no way of knowing.

Agia came once, and standing between two of Vodalus's armed women spat in my face as she described the torments she and Hethor had contrived for me when I was strong enough to endure them. When she finished, I told her quite truthfully that I had spent most of my life assisting at operations more terrible, and advised her to obtain trained assistance, at which she went away.

Thereafter for the better part of several days I was left alone. Each time I woke, I felt myself almost a different person, for in that solitude the isolation of my thoughts in the dark intervals of sleep was nearly sufficient to deprive me of my sense of personality. Yet all these Severians and Theclas sought freedom.

The retreat into memory was easy; we made it often, reliving those idyllic days when Dorcas and I had journeyed toward Thrax, the games played in the hedge-walled maze behind my father's villa and in the Old Yard, the long walk down the Adamnian Steps that Agia and I had taken before I knew her for my enemy.

But often too, I left memory and forced myself to think, sometimes limping up and down, sometimes only waiting for insects to enter the window so that I might for my amusement pluck them from the air. I planned escape, though until my circumstances altered there seemed no possibility of it; I pondered passages from the brown book and sought to match them to my own experiences in order to produce, insofar as possible, some general theory of human action that would be of benefit to me should I ever free myself.

For if the leech, who was an elderly man, could still pursue knowledge despite the certainty of imminent death, could not I whose death appeared more imminent still, take some comfort in the surety that it was less certain?

Thus I sifted the actions of the magicians, and of the man who had accosted me outside the jacal of the sick girl, and of many other men and women I had known, seeking for a key that would unlock all hearts.

I found none that could be expressed in few words: "Men and women do as they do because of thus and so. . . ." None of the ragged bits of metal fit—the desire for power, the lust of love, the need for reassurance, or the taste for seasoning life with romance. But I did find one principle, which I came to call that of Primitivity, that I believe is widely applicable, and which, if it does not initiate action, at least seems to influence the forms that action takes. I might state it this way: *Because the prehistoric cultures endured for so many chiliads, they have shaped our heritage in such a way as to cause us to behave as if their conditions obtained today.*

For example, the technology that once might have permitted Baldanders to observe all the actions of the hetman of the lakeside village has been dust now for thousands of years; but during the eons of its existence, it laid upon him a spell, as it were, by which it remained effective though no longer extant.

In the same way, we all have in us the ghosts of long-vanished things, of fallen cities and marvelous machines. The story I once read to Jonas when we were imprisoned (with how much less anxiety and how much more companionship) showed that clearly, and I read it over again in the ziggurat. The author, having need for some sea-born fiend like Erebus or Abaia, in a mythical setting, gave it a head like a ship—which was the whole of its visible body, the remainder being underwater—so that it was removed from protoplasmic reality and became the machine that the rhythms of his mind demanded.

While I amused myself with these speculations, I became increasingly aware of the impermanent nature of Vodalus's occupation of the ancient building. Though the leech came no more, as I have said, and Agia never visited me again, I frequently heard the sound of running feet in the corridor outside my door and occasionally a few shouted words.

Whenever such sounds came, I put my unbandaged ear to the planks; and in fact I often anticipated them, sitting that way for long periods in the hope of overhearing some snatch of conversation that would tell me something of Vodalus's plans. I could not help but think then, as I listened in vain, of the hundreds in our oubliette who must have listened to me when I carried their food to Drotte, and how they must have strained to overhear the fragments of conversation that drifted from Thecla's cell into the corridor, and thus into their own cells, when I visited her.

And what of the dead? I own that I thought of myself, at times, almost as dead. Are they not locked below ground in chambers smaller than mine was, in their millions of millions? There is no category of human activity in which the dead do not outnumber the living many times over. Most beautiful children are dead. Most soldiers, most cowards. The fairest women and the most learned men—all are dead.

Their bodies repose in caskets, in sarcophagi, beneath arches of rude stone, everywhere under the earth. Their spirits haunt our minds, ears pressed to the bones of our foreheads. Who can say how intently they listen as we speak, or for what word?

XXVII

Before Vodalus

ON THE MORNING of the sixth day, two women came for me. I had slept very little the night before. One of the blood bats common in those northern jungles had entered my room by the window, and though I had succeeded in driving it out and staunching the blood, it had returned again and again, attracted, I suppose, by the odor of my wounds. Even now I cannot see the vague green darkness that is diffused moonlight without imagining I see the bat crawling there like a big spider, then springing into the air.

The women were as surprised to find me awake as I was to see them; it was just dawn. They made me stand, and one bound my hands while the other held her dirk to my throat. She asked how my cheek was healing, however, and added that she had been told I was a handsome fellow when I was brought in.

"I was almost as near to death then as I am now," I said to her. The truth was that though the concussion I had suffered when the flier crashed had healed, my leg, as well as my face, was still giving me considerable pain.

The women brought me to Vodalus; not, as I had more or less expected, somewhere in the ziggurat or on the ledge where he had sat in state with Thea, but in a clearing embraced on three sides by slow green water. It was a moment or two—I had to stand waiting while some other business was conducted—before I realized that the course of this river was fundamentally to the north and east, and that I had never seen northeastward-flowing water before; all streams, in my previous experience, ran south or southwest to join south-western-flowing Gyoll.

At last Vodalus inclined his head toward me, and I was brought forward. When he saw that I could scarcely stand, he ordered my guards to seat me at his feet, then waved them back out of hearing distance. "Your entrance is somewhat less impressive than that you made in the forest beyond Nessus," he said.

I agreed. "But, Liege, I come now, as I did then, as your servant. Just as I was the first time you met me, when I saved your neck from the ax. If I appear before you in bloody rags and with bound hands, it is because you treat your servants so."

"Certainly I would agree that securing your wrists seems a trifle excessive in your condition." He smiled faintly. "Is it painful?"

"No. The feeling is gone."

"Still, the cords aren't needed." Vodalus stood and drew a slender blade, and leaning over me, flicked my bonds with the point.

I flexed my shoulders and the last strands parted. A thousand needles seemed to pierce my hands.

When he had taken his seat again, Vodalus asked if I were not going to thank him.

"You never thanked me, Liege. You gave me a coin instead. I think I have one here somewhere." I fumbled in my sabretache for the money I had been paid by Guasacht.

"You may keep your coin. I'm going to ask you for much more than that. Are you ready to tell me who you are?"

"I've always been ready to do that, Liege. I'm Severian, formerly a journeyman of the guild of torturers."

"But are you nothing else besides a former journeyman of that guild?"

"No."

Vodalus sighed and smiled, then leaned back in his chair and sighed again. "My servant Hildegrin always insisted you were important. When I asked him why, he had any number of speculations, none of which I found convincing. I thought he was trying to get silver from me for a little easy spying. Yet he was right."

"I have only been important once to you, Liege."

"Each time we meet, you remind me that you saved my life once. Did you know that Hildegrin once saved yours? It was he who shouted 'Run!' to your opponent when you dueled in the city. You had fallen, and he might have stabbed you."

"Is Agia here?" I asked. "She'll try to kill you if she hears that."

"No one can hear you but myself. You may tell her later, if you like. She will never believe you."

"You can't be sure of that."

He smiled more broadly. "Very well, I'll turn you over to her. You can then test your theory against mine."

"As you wish."

He brushed my acquiescence aside with an elegant motion of one hand. "You think you can stalemate me with your willingness to die. Actually you're offering me an easy exit from a dilemma. Your Agia came to me with a very valuable thaumaturgist in her train, and asked as the price of his service and her own only that you, Severian of the Order of the Seekers for Truth and Penitence, should be put into her hands. Now you say you are that Severian the Torturer and no one else, and it is with great embarrassment that I resist her demands."

"And whom do you wish me to be?" I asked.

"I have, or I should say I had, a most excellent servant in the House Absolute. You know him, of course, since it was to him that you gave my message." Vodalus paused and smiled again. "A week or so ago we received one from him. It was not, to be sure, openly addressed to me, but I had seen to it not long before that he was aware of our location, and we were not far from him. Do you know what he said?"

I shook my head.

"That's odd, because you must have been with him at the time. He said he was in a wrecked flier—and that the Autarch was in the flier with him. He would have been an idiot to have sent such a message in the ordinary course of things, because he gave his location—and he was behind our lines, as he must have known."

"You are a part of the Ascian army, then?"

"We serve them in certain scouting capacities, yes. I see you are troubled by the knowledge that Agia and the thaumaturgist killed a few of their soldiers to take you. You need not be. Their masters value them even less than I do, and it was not a time for negotiation."

"But they did not capture the Autarch." I am not a good liar, but I was too exhausted, I think, for Vodalus to read my face easily.

He leaned forward, and for a moment his eyes glowed as though candles burned in their depths. "He was there, then. How wonderful. You have seen him. You have ridden in the royal flier with him."

I nodded once more.

"You see, ridiculous though it sounds, I feared you were he. One never knows. An Autarch dies and another takes his place, and the new Autarch may be there for half a century or a fortnight. There were three of you then? No more?"

"No."

"What did the Autarch look like? Let me have every detail."

I did as he asked, describing Dr. Talos as he had appeared in the part.

"Did he escape both the thaumaturgist's creatures and the

Ascians? Or do the Ascians have him? Perhaps the woman and her paramour are holding him for themselves."

"I told you the Ascians did not take him."

Vodalus smiled again, but beneath his glowing eyes his twisted mouth suggested only pain. "You see," he repeated, "for a time I thought you might be the one. We have my servant, but he has suffered a head injury and is never conscious for more than a few moments. He will die very shortly, I'm afraid. But he has always told me the truth, and Agia says that you were the only one with him."

"You think that I am the Autarch? No."

"Yet you are changed from the man I met before."

"You yourself gave me the alzabo, and the life of the Chatelaine Thecla. I loved her. Did you think that to thus ingest her essence would leave me unaffected? She is with me always, so that I am two, in this single body. Yet I am not the Autarch, who in one body is a thousand."

Vodalus answered nothing, but half closed his eyes as though he were afraid I would see their fire. There was no sound but the lapping of the river water and the much-muted voices of the little knot of armed men and women, who talked among themselves a hundred paces off and glanced from time to time at us. A macaw shrieked, fluttering from one tree to another.

"I would still serve you," I told Vodalus, "if you would permit it." I was not certain it was a lie until the words had left my lips, and then I was bewildered in mind, seeking to understand how those words, which would have been true in the past for Thecla and for Severian too, were now false for me.

" 'The Autarch, who in one body is a thousand,' " Vodalus quoted me. "That is correct, but how few of us know it."

XXVIII

On the March

TODAY, THIS BEING the last before I am to leave the House
Absolute, I participated in a solemn religious ceremony. Such
rituals are divided into seven orders according to their importance, or as the heptarchs say, their "transcendence"—something I was quite ignorant of at the time of which I was
writing a moment ago. At the lowest level, that of Aspira-
tion, are the private pieties, including prayers pronounced
privately, the casting of a stone upon a cairn, and so forth.
The gatherings and public petitionings that I, as a boy,
thought constituted the whole of organized religion, are actually at the second level, which is that of Integration. What
we did today belonged to the seventh and highest, the level
of Assimilation.

In accordance with the principle of circularity, most of the
accretions gathered in the progression through the first six
were now dispensed with. There was no music, and the rich
vestments of Assurance were replaced by starched robes
whose sculptural folds gave all of us something of the air of
icons. It is no longer possible for us to carry out the ceremony, as once we did, wrapped in the shining belt of the

galaxy; but to achieve the effect as nearly as possible, Urth's attractive field was excluded from the basilica. It was a novel sensation for me, and though I was unafraid, I was reminded again of that night I spent among the mountains when I felt myself on the point of falling off the world—something I will undergo in sober earnest tomorrow. At times the ceiling seemed a floor, or (what was to me far more disturbing) a wall became the ceiling, so that one looked upward through its open windows to see a mountainside of grass that lifted itself forever into the sky. Startling as it was, this vision was no less true than that we commonly see.

Each of us became a sun; the circling, ivory skulls were our planets. I said we had dispensed with music, yet that was not entirely true, for as they swung about us there came a faint, sweet humming and whistling, caused by the flow of air through their eye sockets and teeth; those in nearly circular orbits maintained an almost steady note, varying only slightly as they rotated on their axes; the songs of those in elliptical orbits waxed and waned, rising as they approached me, sinking to a moan as they receded.

How foolish we are to see in those hollow eyes and marble calottes only death. How many friends are among them! The brown book, which I carried so far, the only one of the possessions I took from the Matachin Tower that still remains with me, was sewn and printed and composed by men and women with those bony faces; and we, engulfed by their voices, now on behalf of those who are the past, offered ourselves and the present to the fulgurant light of the New Sun.

Yet at that moment, surrounded by the most meaningful and magnificent symbolism, I could not but think how different the actuality had been when we had left the ziggurat on the day after my interview with Vodalus and had marched (I under the guard of six women, who were sometimes forced to carry me) for what must have been a week or more through pestilential jungle. I did not know—and still do not know—

whether we were fleeing the armies of the Commonwealth or the Ascians who had been Vodalus's allies. Perhaps we were merely seeking to rejoin the major part of the insurgent force. My guards complained of the moisture that dripped from the trees to eat at their weapons and armor like acid, and of suffocating heat; I felt nothing of either. I remember looking down once at my thigh and noticing with surprise that the flesh had fallen away so that the muscles there stood out like cords and I could see the sliding parts of my knee as one sees the wheels and shafts of a mill.

The old leech was with us, and now visited me two or three times each day. At first he tried to keep dry bandages on my face; when he saw the effort was futile, he removed them all and contented himself with plastering the wounds there with his salve. After that, some of my women guards refused to look at me, and if they had reason to speak to me did so with downcast eyes. Others seemed to take pride in their ability to confront my torn face, standing straddle-legged (a pose they appeared to consider warlike) and resting their left hands upon the hilts of their weapons with studied casualness.

I talked with them as often as I could. Not because I desired them—the illness that had come with my wounds had taken all such desire from me—but because in the midst of the straggling column I was lonely in a way I had never been when I was alone in the war-torn north or even when I had been locked in my ancient, mold-streaked cell in the ziggurat, and because in some absurd corner of my mind I still hoped to escape. I questioned them about every subject of which they might conceivably have knowledge, and I was endlessly amazed to find how few were the points on which our minds coincided. Not one of the six had joined Vodalus because of an appreciation of the difference between the restoration of progress he sought to represent and the stagnation of the Commonwealth. Three had merely followed some man into the ranks; two had come in the hope of gaining revenge for

some personal injustice, and one because she had been fleeing from a detested stepfather. All but the last now wished
they had not joined. None knew with any precision where we
had been or had the slightest idea where we were going.

For guides our column had three savages: a pair of young
men who might have been brothers or even twins, and a
much older one, twisted, I thought, by deformities as well as
age, who perpetually wore a grotesque mask. Though the first
two were younger and the third much older, all three of them
recalled to me the naked man I had once seen in the Jungle
Garden. They were as naked as he and had the same dark,
metallic-looking skin and straight hair. The younger two carried cerbotanas longer than their outstretched arms and dart
bags hand-knotted of wild cotton and dyed a burnt umber,
doubtless with the juice of some plant. The old man had a
staff as crooked as himself, topped with the dried head of a
monkey.

A covered palanquin whose place in the column was considerably more advanced than my own bore the Autarch,
whom my leech gave me to understand was still alive; and
one night when my guards were chattering among themselves and I sat crouched over our little fire, I saw the old
guide (his bent figure and the impression of an immense head
conferred by his mask were unmistakable) approach this palanquin and slip beneath it. Some time passed before he scut-
tled away. This old man was said to be an *uturuncu,* a
shaman capable of assuming the form of a tiger.

Within a few days of our leaving the ziggurat, without
encountering anything that might be called a road or even a
path, we struck a trail of corpses. They were Ascians, and
they had been stripped of their clothing and equipment, so
that their starved bodies seemed to have dropped from the
air to the places where they lay. To me, they appeared to be
about a week dead; but no doubt decay had been accelerated

by the dampness and heat, and the actual time was much
less. The cause of death was seldom apparent.

Until then we had seen few animals larger than the grotesque beetles that buzzed about our fires by night. Such
birds as called from the treetops remained largely invisible,
and if the blood-bats visited us, their inky wings were lost in
the smothering dark. Now we moved, as it seemed, through
an army of beasts drawn to the corpse trail as flies are to a
dead sumpter. Hardly a watch passed without our hearing
the sound of bones crushed by great jaws, and by night green
and scarlet eyes, some of them two spans apart, shone outside
our little circles of firelight. Though it was preposterous to
suppose these carrion-gorged predators would molest us, my
guards doubled their sentries; those who slept did so in their
corslets, with curtelaxes in their hands.

With each new day the bodies were fresher, until at last
not all were dead. A madwoman with cropped hair and staring eyes stumbled into the column just ahead of our party,
shouted words no one could understand, and fled among the
trees. We heard cries for help, screams, and ravings, but
Vodalus permitted no one to turn aside, and on the afternoon of that day we plunged—much in the same sense
we might earlier have been said to have plunged into the
jungle—into the Ascian horde.

Our column consisted of the women and supplies, Vodalus
himself and his household, and a few of his aides with their
retinues. In all it surely amounted to no more than a fifth of
his force; but if every insurgent he could have called to his
banner had been there, and every fighter become a hundred,
they would still have been among that multitude as a cupful
of water in Gyoll.

Those we encountered first were infantry. I recalled that
the Autarch had told me their weapons were kept from them
until the time of battle; but if it were so, their officers must
have thought that time to be at hand, or nearly. I saw thou-

sands armed with the ransieur, so that at length I came to believe that all their infantry was equipped in that way; then, as night was falling, we overtook thousands more carrying demilunes.

Because we marched faster than they, we moved more deeply into their force; but we camped sooner than they (if they camped at all) and all that night, until at last I fell asleep, I heard their hoarse cries and the shuffling of their feet. In the morning we were again among their dead and dying, and it was a watch or more before we overtook the stumbling ranks.

These Ascian soldiers had a rigidity, a will-less attachment to order, that I have never seen elsewhere, and that appeared to me to have no roots in either spirit or discipline as I understand them. They seemed to obey because they could not conceive of any other course of action. Our soldiers nearly always carry several arms—at the very least an energy weapon and a long knife (among the schiavoni I was exceptional in not possessing such a knife in addition to my falchion). But I never saw an Ascian with more than one, and most of their officers bore no weapon at all, as if they regarded actual fighting with contempt.

XXIX

Autarch of the Commonwealth

By the middle of the day, we had again passed all those whom we had passed the afternoon before and came upon the baggage train. I think all of us were amazed to discover that the enormous force we had seen was no more than the rear guard of an army inconceivably greater.

The Ascians used uintathers and platybelodons as beasts of burden. Mixed with them were machines with six legs, machines apparently built to serve that purpose. So far as I could see, the drivers made no distinction between these devices and the animals; if a beast lay down and could not be made to rise again, or a machine fell and did not right itself, its load was distributed among those nearest to hand, and it was abandoned. There appeared to be no effort to slaughter the beasts for their meat or to repair or take parts from the machines.

Late in the afternoon some great excitement passed down our column, though neither I nor my guards could discover what it was. Vodalus himself and several of his lieutenants came hurrying by, and afterward there was much coming and going between the end of the column and its head. When dark came we did not camp, but continued to tramp through the night with the Ascians. Torches were passed back to us, and since I had no weapons to carry and was somewhat stronger than I had been, I carried them, feeling almost as though I commanded the six swords who surrounded me.

About midnight, as nearly as I could judge, we halted. My guards found sticks for a fire, which we kindled from a torch. Just as we were about to lie down, I saw a messenger rouse the palanquin bearers ahead of us and send them blundering forward in the dark. They were no sooner gone than he loped back to us and held a quick, whispered conversation with the sergeant of my guards. At once my hands were bound (as they had not been since Vodalus had cut them free) and we were hurrying after the palanquin. We passed the head of the column, marked by the Chatelaine Thea's little pavilion, without pausing, and were soon wandering among the myriad Ascian soldiers of the main body.

Their headquarters was a dome of metal. I suppose it must have folded or collapsed in some way as a tent does, but it appeared as permanent and solid as any building, black externally but glowing with a sourceless, pale light within when the side opened to admit us. Vodalus was there, stiff and deferential; beside him the palanquin stood with its curtains opened to show the immobile body of the Autarch. At the center of the dome, three women sat around a low table. Neither then nor later did they look at Vodalus, or the Autarch in his palanquin, or at me when I was brought forward, save for an occasional glance. There were stacks of papers before them, but they did not look at those at all—only at one another. In appearance they were much like the other Ascians I had seen, save that their eyes were saner and they were less starved looking.

"Here he is," Vodalus said. "Now you see them both before you."

One of the Ascians spoke to the other two in their own tongue. Both nodded and the one who had spoken said, "Only he who acts against the populace need hide his face."

There was a lengthy pause, then Vodalus hissed at me, "Answer her!"

"Answer what? There has been no question."

The Ascian said, "Who is the friend of the populace? He who aids the populace. Who is the enemy of the populace?"

Speaking very rapidly, Vodalus asked, "To the best of your knowledge are you, or is this unconscious man here, the leader of the peoples of the southern half of this hemisphere?"

"No," I said. It was an easy lie, since from what I had seen, the Autarch was the leader of very few in the Commonwealth. To Vodalus I added under my breath, "What kind of foolishness is this? Do they believe I would tell them if I were the Autarch?"

"All we say is being transmitted to the north."

One of the Ascians who had not spoken previously spoke now. Once she gestured in our direction. When she was finished, all three sat deathly still. I had the impression that they heard some voice inaudible to me, and that they did not dare move while it spoke; but that may have been mere imagination on my part. Vodalus fidgeted, I shifted my position to put a little less weight on my injured leg, and the Autarch's narrow chest heaved to the unsteady rhythm of his breathing, but the three of them remained as immobile as figures in a painting.

At last the one who had spoken first said, "All persons belong to the populace." At that the others seemed to relax.

"This man is ill," Vodalus said, looking toward the Autarch, "and he has been a useful servant to me, though I suppose his usefulness is now ended. The other I have promised to one of my followers."

"The merit of sacrifice falls on him who without thought to his own convenience offers what he has toward the service of the populace." The Ascian woman's tone made it clear that no further argument was possible.

Vodalus looked toward me and shrugged, then turned on

his heel and strode out of the dome. Almost at once a file of Ascian officers entered carrying lashes.

We were imprisoned in an Ascian tent perhaps twice the size of my cell in the ziggurat. There was a fire there but no bedding, and the officers who had carried in the Autarch had merely dropped him on the ground beside it. After working my hands free, I tried to make him comfortable, turning him over on his back as he had been in the palanquin and arranging his arms at his sides.

About us the army lay quiet, or at least as quiet as an Ascian army ever is. From time to time someone far off cried out—in sleep, it seemed—but for the most part there was no sound but the slow pacing of the sentries outside. I cannot express the horror that the thought of going north to Ascia evoked in me then. To see only the Ascians' wild, starved faces and to encounter myself, no doubt for the remainder of my life, whatever it was that had driven them mad, seemed to me a more horrible fate than any the clients in the Matachin Tower were ever forced to endure. I tried to lift the skirt of the tent, thinking that the sentries could do nothing worse than take my life; but the edges were welded to the ground by some means I did not understand. All four walls were of a slick, tough substance I could not tear, and Miles's razor had been taken from me by my six female guards. I was about to rush out the door when the Autarch's well-remembered voice whispered, "Wait." I dropped to my knees beside him, suddenly afraid we would be overheard.

"I thought you were—sleeping."

"I suppose I have been in a coma most of the time. But when I was not, I feigned, so Vodalus would not question me. Are you going to escape?"

"Not without you, Sieur. Not now. I had given you up for dead."

"You were not far wrong . . . certainly not by so much as a day. Yes, I think that is best, you must escape. Father Inire is with the insurgents. He was to bring you what is necessary, then help you get away. But we are no longer there . . . are we? He may not be able to aid you. Open my robe. What you first require is thrust into my waistband."

I did as he asked; the flesh my fingers brushed was as cold as a corpse's. Near his left hip I saw a hilt of silvery metal no thicker than a woman's finger. I drew the weapon forth; the blade was not half a span in length, but thick and strong, and of that deadly sharpness I had not felt since Baldanders's mace had shattered *Terminus Est*.

"You must not go yet," the Autarch whispered.

"I will not leave you while you live," I said. "Do you doubt me?"

"We will both live, and both go. You know the abomination . . ." His hand closed on mine. "The eating of the dead, to devour their dead lives. But there is another way you do not know, and another drug. You must take it, and swallow the living cells of my forebrain."

I must have drawn away, for his hand gripped my own harder.

"When you lie with a woman, you thrust your life into hers so that perhaps there will be new life. When you do as I have commanded you, my life and the lives of all those who live in me will be continued in you. The cells will enter your own nervous system and multiply there. The drug is in the vial I wear at my neck, and that blade will split the bones of my skull like pine. I have had occasion to use it, and I promise it. Do you recall how you swore to serve me when I shut the book? Use the knife now, and go as quickly as you can."

I nodded and promised I would.

"The drug will be stronger than any you have known, and though all but mine will be faint, there will be hundreds of personalities. . . . We are many lives."

"I understand," I said.

"The Ascians march at dawn. Can there be more than a single watch remaining of the night?"

"I hope that you will live it out, Sieur, and many more. That you'll recover."

"You must kill me now, before Urth turns to face the sun. Then I will live in you . . . never die. I live by mere volition now. I am relinquishing my life as I speak."

To my utter surprise, my eyes were streaming with tears. "I've hated you since I was a boy, Sieur. I've done you no harm, but I would have harmed you if I could, and now I'm sorry."

His voice had faded until it was softer than the chirping of a cricket. "You were right to hate me, Severian. I stand . . . as you will stand . . . for so much that is wrong."

"Why?" I asked. "Why?" I was on my knees beside him.

"Because all else is worse. Until the New Sun comes, we have but a choice of evils. All have been tried, and all have failed. Goods in common, the rule of the people . . . everything. You wish for progress? The Ascians have it. They are deafened by it, crazed by the death of Nature till they are ready to accept Erebus and the rest as gods. We hold humankind stationary . . . in barbarism. The Autarch protects the people from the exultants, and the exultants . . . shelter them from the Autarch. The religious comfort them. We have closed the roads to paralyze the social order. . . ."

His eyes fell shut. I put my hand upon his chest to feel the faint stirring of his heart.

"Until the New Sun . . ."

This was what I had sought to escape, not Agia or Vodalus or the Ascians. As gently as I could, I lifted the chain from his neck, unstoppered the vial and swallowed the drug. Then with that short, stiff blade I did what had to be done.

When it was over, I covered him from head to toe with his own saffron robe and hung the empty vial about my own neck. The effect of the drug was as violent as he had warned me it would be. You that read this, who have never, perhaps, possessed more than a single consciousness, cannot know what it is to have two or three, much less hundreds. They lived in me and were joyful, each in his own way, to find they had new life. The dead Autarch, whose face I had seen in scarlet ruin a few moments before, now lived again. My eyes and hands were his, I knew the work of the hives of the bees of the House Absolute and the sacredness of them, who steer by the sun and fetch gold of Urth's fertility. I knew his course to the Phoenix Throne, and to the stars, and back. His mind was mine and filled mine with lore whose existence I had never suspected and with the knowledge other minds had brought to his. The phenomenal world seemed dim and vague as a picture sketched in sand over which an errant wind veered and moaned. I could not have concentrated on it if I had wished to, and I had no such wish.

The black fabric of our prison tent faded to a pale dove-gray, and the angles of its top whirled like the prisms of a kaleidoscope. I had fallen without being aware of it and lay near the body of my predecessor, where my attempts to rise resulted in nothing more than the beating of my hands upon the ground.

How long I lay there I do not know. I had wiped the knife—now, still, *my* knife—and concealed it as he had. I could vividly picture a self of dozens of superposed images slitting the wall and slipping out into the night. Severian, Thecla, myriad others all escaping. So real was the thought that I often believed I had done it; but always, when I ought to have been running between the trees, avoiding the exhausted sleepers of the army of the Ascians, I found myself instead in the familiar tent, with the draped body not far from my own.

Hands clasped mine. I supposed that the officers had returned with their lashes, and tried to see and to rise so I would not be struck. But a hundred random memories intruded themselves like the pictures the owner holds up to us in rapid succession in a cheap gallery: a footrace, the towering pipes of an organ, a diagram with labeled angles, a woman riding in a cart.

Someone said, "Are you all right? What's happened to you?" I felt the spittle dribbling from my lips, but no words came.

XXX

The Corridors of Time

SOMETHING STRUCK MY FACE a tingling blow.

"What's happened? He's dead. Are you drugged?"

"*Yes. Drugged.*" Someone else was speaking, and after a moment I knew who it was: Severian, the young torturer.

But who was I?

"Get up. We've got to get out."

"*Sentry.*"

"Sentries," the voice corrected us. "There were three of them. We killed them."

I was walking down a stair white as salt, down to nenuphars and stagnant water. Beside me walked a suntanned girl with long and slanting eyes. Over her shoulder peered the sculptured face of one of the eponyms. The carver had worked in jade; the effect was that of a face of grass.

"Is he dying?"

"He sees us now. See his eyes."

I knew where I was. Soon the pitchman would thrust his head through the doorway of the tent to tell me to be gone. "Above ground," I said. "You told me I would see her above ground. But that was easy. She is here."

"We must go." The green man took my left arm and Agia my right, and they led me out.

We walked a long way, just as I had envisioned myself running, stepping sometimes over sleeping Ascians.

"They keep little guard," Agia whispered. "Vodalus told me their leaders are so well obeyed they can scarcely conceive of treacherous attack. In the war, our soldiers surprise them often."

I did not understand and repeated, " 'Our soldiers . . .' " like a child.

"Hethor and I will no longer fight for them. How could we, after we have seen them? My business is with you."

I was beginning to find myself again, the minds that made up *my* mind all falling into place. I had been told once that *autarch* meant "self-ruler," and I glimpsed the reason that title had come into being. I said, "You wanted to kill me. Now you are freeing me. You could have stabbed me." I saw a crooked dagger from Thrax quivering in Casdoe's shutter.

"I could have killed you more readily than that. Hethor's mirrors have given me a worm, no longer than your hand, that glows with white fire. I have only to fling it, and it kills and crawls back to me—one by one I slew the sentries so. But this green man would not permit it, and I would not wish it. Vodalus promised me your agony spread over weeks, and I will not have less."

"You're taking me back to him?"

She shook her head, and in the faint, gray dawn light that had crept through the leaves I saw her brown curls bounce on her shoulders as they had when I had watched her raise the gratings outside the rag shop. "Vodalus is dead. With the worm at my command, do you think I would let him cheat me and live? They would have taken you away. Now I will let you go free—because I have some inkling of where you will go—and in the end you will come into my hands again, as you did when our pteriopes took you from the evzones."

"You are rescuing me because you hate me then," I said, and she nodded. Vodalus, I suppose, had hated that part of me that had been the Autarch in the same way.

Or rather, he had hated his conception of the Autarch, for he had been loyal, in so far as he was capable of it, to the real Autarch, whom he supposed his servant. When I had been a boy in the kitchens of the House Absolute, there was a cook who so despised the armigers and exultants for whom he prepared food that, in order that he should never have to bear the indignity of their reproaches, he did everything with a feverish perfection. He was eventually made chief of the cooks of that wing. I thought of him, and while I did, Agia's touch on my arm, which had become almost imperceptible as we hastened along, vanished altogether. When I looked for her, she was gone; I was alone with the green man.

"How did you come to be here?" I asked him. "You nearly lost your life in these times, and I know you cannot thrive under our sun."

He smiled. Though his lips were green, his teeth were white; they gleamed in the faint light. "We are your children, and we are not less honest than you, though we do not kill to eat. You gave me half your stone, the stone that gnawed the iron and set me free. What did you think I would do when the chain no longer bound me?"

"I supposed you would return to your own day," I said. The spell of the drug had faded sufficiently for me to fear our talk would wake the Ascian soldiers. Yet I could see none— only the dark, towering boles of the jungle hardwoods.

"We requite our benefactors. I have been running up and down the corridors of Time, seeking for a moment in which you also were imprisoned, that I might free you."

When I heard that, I did not know what to say. At last I told him, "You cannot imagine how strange I feel now, knowing that someone has been searching my future, looking for an opportunity to do me good. But now, now that we are quits, surely you understand that I did not help you because I believed you could help me."

"You did—you desired my help in finding the woman who just left us, the woman whom since that occasion you have found several times. However, you ought to know that I was not alone: There are others questing there—I shall send two of them to you. And you and I are not yet at a balance, for although I found you captive here, the woman found you also and would have freed you without my help. So I shall see you again."

As he said these words, he let go of my arm and stepped in that direction I had never seen until I watched the ship vanish into it from the top of Baldanders's castle and could only see, it seemed, when there was something there. Immediately he turned and began to run, and despite the dimness of the dawn sky I could see his running figure for a long time, illuminated by intermittent but regular flashes. At last he faded to a point of darkness; but then, just when I expected that point to disappear utterly, it began to grow, so that I had the impression of something huge rushing toward me down that strangely angled tunnel.

It was not the ship I had seen but another and much smaller one. Still, it was so large that when it moved at last entirely into our field of consciousness, its gunwales touched several of the thick trunks at once. The hull dilated, and a pont, much shorter than the steps that had descended from the Autarch's flier, slid out to touch the ground.

Down it came Master Malrubius and my dog, Triskele.

At that moment I regained a command of my personality that I had not truly possessed since I had drunk alzabo with Vodalus and eaten Thecla's flesh. It was not that Thecla was gone (and indeed I could not wish her gone, though I knew that in many respects she had been a cruel and foolish woman) or that my predecessor and the hundred minds that had been enveloped in his had vanished. The old, simple structure of my single personality was no more; but the new, complex structure no longer dazzled and bewildered me. It was a maze, but I was the owner and even the builder of that maze, with the print of my thumb on every passageway. Malrubius touched me, and then taking my wondering hand in his laid it gently against his own cool cheek.

"You are real, then," I said.

"No. We are almost what you think us—powers from above the stage. Only not quite deities. You are an actor, I believe."

I shook my head. "Don't you know me, Master? You taught me when I was a boy, and I have become a journeyman of the guild."

"Yet you are an actor too. You have as much right to think of yourself in that way as the other. You had been performing when we spoke to you in the field near the Wall, and the next time we saw you, at the House Absolute, you were acting again. It was a good play; I should have liked to see the end."

"You were in our audience?"

Master Malrubius nodded. "As an actor, Severian, you surely know the phrase I hinted at a moment ago. It refers to some supernatural force, personified and brought onto the stage in the last act in order that the play may end well. None but poor playwrights do it, they say, but those who say so forget that it is better to have a power lowered on a rope, and a play that ends well, than to have nothing, and a play that ends badly. Here is our rope—many ropes, and a stout ship too. Will you come aboard?"

I said, "Is that why you are as you are? In order that I will trust you?"

"Yes, if you like." Master Malrubius nodded, and Triskele, who had been sitting at my feet and looking up into my face, ran with his bumping, three-legged gallop halfway up the pont and turned to look back at me, his stump tail wagging and his eyes pleading as a dog's eyes do.

"I know you can't be what you seem. Perhaps Triskele is, but I saw you buried, Master. Your face is no mask, but there's a mask somewhere, and under that mask you're what the common people call a cacogen, although Dr. Talos explained to me once that you prefer to be called Hierodules."

Again Malrubius laid his hand on mine. "We would not deceive you if we could. But I hope that you will deceive yourself, to your good and all Urth's. Some drug now dulls your mind—more than you realize—just as you were under the sway of sleep when we spoke to you in that meadow near the Wall. If you were undrugged now, perhaps you would lack the courage to come with us, even if you saw us, even if your reason convinced you that you should."

I said, "So far it hasn't convinced me of that, or of anything else. Where do you want to take me, and why do you want to take me there? Are you Master Malrubius or a Hierodule?" As I spoke I became more conscious of the trees, standing as soldiers stand while the officers of the staff discuss some point of strategy. Night was upon us still, but it had become a thinner darkness, even here.

"Do you know the meaning of that word *Hierodule* you use? I am Malrubius, and no Hierodule. Rather I serve those the Hierodules serve. *Hierodule* means *holy slave*. Do you think there can be slaves without masters?"

"And you take me—"

"To Ocean, to preserve your life." As if he had read my thought, he continued, "No, we do not take you to the paramours of Abaia, those who spared and succored you because you had been a torturer and would be Autarch. In any event, you have much worse to fear. Soon the slaves of Erebus, who held you captive here, will discover you have escaped; and Erebus would hurl that army, and many others like it, into the abyss to capture you. Come." He drew me onto the pont.

XXXI

The Sand Garden

THAT SHIP WAS worked by hands I could not see. I had supposed we would float up as the flier had or vanish like the green man down some corridor in time. Instead we rose so quickly I felt sick; alongside I heard the crashing of great limbs.

"You are the Autarch now," Malrubius told me. "Do you know it?" His voice seemed to blend with the whistle of the wind in the rigging.

"Yes. My predecessor, whose mind is now one of mine, came to office as I have. I know the secrets, the words of authority, though I haven't had time yet to think about them. Are you returning me to the House Absolute?"

He shook his head. "You are not ready. You believe that all the old Autarch knew is available to you now. You are correct—but it is not yet in your grasp, and when the tests come, you will encounter many who will slay you should you falter. You were nurtured in the Citadel of Nessus—what are the words for its castellan? How are the man-apes of the treasure mine to be commanded? What phrases unlock the vaults of the Secret House? You need not tell me, because these things are the arcana of your state, and I know them in any case. But do you yourself know them, without thinking long?"

The phrases I required were present in my mind, yet I failed when I sought to pronounce them to myself. Like little fish, they slipped aside, and in the end I could only lift my shoulders.

"And there is one thing more for you to do. One adventure more, beside the waters."

"What is it?"

"If I were to tell you, it would not come to pass. Do not be alarmed. It is a simple thing, over in a breath. But I must explain a great deal, and I have not much time in which to do it. Have you faith in the coming of the New Sun?"

As I had looked within myself for the words of command, so I looked within for my belief; and I could no more find it than I had found them. "I have been taught so all my life," I said. "But by teachers—the true Malrubius was one—who I think did not themselves believe. So I cannot now say whether I believe or not."

"Who is the New Sun? A man? If a man, how can it be that every green thing is to grow darkly green again at his coming, and the granaries full?"

It was unpleasant to be drawn back to things half heard in childhood now, when I was just beginning to understand that I had inherited the Commonwealth. I said, "He will be the Conciliator come again—his avatar, bringing justice and peace. In pictures he is shown with a shining face, like the sun. I was an apprentice of the torturers, not an acolyte, and that is all I can tell you." I drew my cloak about me for shelter from the cold wind. Triskele was huddled at my feet.

"And which does humanity need more? Justice and peace? Or a New Sun?"

At that I tried to smile. "It has occurred to me that though you cannot possibly be my old teacher, you may incorporate his personality as I do the Chatelaine Thecla's. If that is so, you already know my answer. When a client is driven to the utmost extremity, it is warmth and food and ease from pain he wants. Peace and justice come afterward. Rain symbolizes mercy and sunlight charity, but rain and sunlight are better than mercy and charity. Otherwise they would degrade the things they symbolize."

"To a large extent you are correct. The Master Malrubius you knew lives in me, and your old Triskele in this Triskele. But that is not important now. If there is time, you will understand before we go." Malrubius closed his eyes and scratched the gray hair on his chest, just as I remembered him doing when I was among the youngest of the apprentices. "You were afraid to board this little ship, even when I told you it would not carry you away from Urth, or even to a continent other than your own. Suppose I were to tell you—I do *not* tell you, but suppose I did—that it would in fact take you from Urth, past the orbit of Phaleg, which you call Verthandi, past Bethor and Aratron, and at last into the outer dark, and across the dark to another place. Would you be frightened, now that you have sailed with us?"

"No man enjoys saying he is afraid. But yes, I would."

"Afraid or not, would you go if it might bring the New Sun?"

It seemed then that some icy spirit from the gulf had already wrapped its hands about my heart. I was not deceived, nor, I think, did he mean I should be. To answer yes would be to undertake the journey. I hesitated, in silence except for the roar of my own blood in my ears.

"You need not answer now if you cannot. We will ask again. But I can tell you nothing more until you answer."

For a long time I stood on that strange deck, sometimes walking up and down, blowing on my fingers in the freezing wind while all my thoughts crowded around me. The stars watched us, and it seemed to me that Master Malrubius's eyes were two more such stars.

At last I returned to him and said, "I have long wanted . . . if it would bring the New Sun, I would go."

"I can give you no assurance. If it *might* bring the New Sun, would you then? Justice and peace, yes, but a New Sun—such an outpouring of warmth and energy upon Urth as she knew before the birth of the first man?"

Now came the strangest happening I have to tell in all this already overlong tale; yet there was no sound or sight associated with it, no speaking beast or gigantic woman. It was only that as I heard him I felt a pressure against my breastbone, as I had felt it in Thrax when I knew I should be going north with the Claw. I remembered the girl in the jacal. "Yes," I said. "If it might bring the New Sun, I would go."

"What if you were to stand trial there? You knew him who was autarch before you, and in the end you loved him. He lives in you. Was he a man?"

"He was a human being—as you, I think, are not, Master."

"That was not my question, as you know as well as I. Was he a man as you are a man? Half the dyad of man and woman?"

I shook my head.

"So you will become, should you fail the trial. Will you still go?"

Triskele laid his scarred head against my knee, the ambassador of all crippled things, of the Autarch who had carried a tray in the House Absolute and lain paralyzed in the palanquin waiting to pass to me the humming voices in his skull, of Thecla writhing under the Revolutionary, and of the woman even I, who had boasted I could forget nothing, had nearly forgotten, bleeding and dying beneath our tower. Perhaps after all it was my discovery of Triskele, which I have said changed nothing, that in the end changed everything. I did not have to answer this time; Master Malrubius saw my answer in my face.

"You know of the chasms of space, which some call the Black Pits, from which no speck of matter or gleam of light ever returns. But what you have not known until now is that these chasms have their counterparts in White Fountains, from which matter and energy rejected by a higher universe flow in endless cataract into this one. If you pass—if our race is judged ready to reenter the wide seas of space—such a white fountain will be created in the heart of our sun."

"But if I fail?"

"If you fail, your manhood will be taken from you, so that you cannot bequeath the Phoenix Throne to your descendants. Your predecessor also accepted the challenge."

"And failed. That is clear from what you said."

"Yes. Still, he was braver than many who are called heroes, the first to go in many reigns. Ymar, of whom you may have heard, was the last before him."

"Yet Ymar too must have been judged unfit. Are we going now? I can see only stars beyond the rail."

Master Malrubius shook his head. "You are not looking as carefully as you think. We are already near our destination."

Swaying, I walked to the railing. Some of my unsteadiness had its origin in the motion of the ship, I think; but some, too, came from the lingering effects of the drug.

Night still covered Urth, for we had flown swiftly to the west, and the faint dawn that had come to the Ascian army in the jungle had not yet appeared here. After a moment I saw that the stars over the side seemed to slip, and slide in their heaven, with an uneasy and wavering motion. Almost it seemed that something moved among the stars as the wind moves through wheat. Then I thought, *It is the sea* . . . and at that moment Master Malrubius said, "It is that great sea called Ocean."

"I have longed to visit it."

"In a short time you will be standing at its margin. You asked when you would leave this planet. Not until your rule here is secure. When the city and the House Absolute obey you and your armies have repelled the incursions of the slaves of Erebus. Within a few years, perhaps. But perhaps not for decades. We two will come for you."

"You are the second tonight to tell me I will see you

again," I said. Just as I spoke, there was a slight shock, like the sensation one feels when a boat is brought skillfully to the dock. I walked down the pont and out upon sand, and Master Malrubius and Triskele followed me. I asked if they would not stay with me for a time to counsel me.

"For a short time only. If you have further questions, you must ask them now."

The silver tongue of the pont was already creeping back into the hull. It seemed that it had hardly come home before the ship lifted itself and scudded down the same aperture in reality into which the green man had run.

"You spoke of the peace and justice that the New Sun is to bring. Is there justice in his calling me so far? What is the test I must pass?"

"It is not he who calls you. Those who call hope to summon the New Sun to them," Master Malrubius said, but I did not understand him. Then he recounted to me in brief words the secret history of Time, which is the greatest of all secrets, and which I will set down here in the proper place. When he had finished, my mind reeled and I feared I would forget all he had said, because it seemed too great a thing for any living man to know, and because I had learned at last that the mists close for me as for other men.

"You will not forget, you above all. At Vodalus's banquet, you said you felt sure you would forget the foolish passwords he taught you in imitation of the words of authority. But you did not. You will remember everything. Remember too, not to be afraid. It may be that the epic penance of mankind is at an end. The old Autarch told you the truth—we will not go to the stars again until we go as a divinity, but that time may not be far off now. In you all the divergent tendencies of our race may have achieved synthesis."

Triskele stood on his hind legs for a moment as he used to, then spun around and galloped down the starlit beach, three paws scattering the little cat's-paw waves. When he was a hundred strides off he turned and looked back at me, as though he wished me to follow.

I took a few steps toward him, but Master Malrubius said, "You cannot go where he is going, Severian. I know you think us cacogens of a kind, and for a time I felt it would not be wise to wholly undeceive you, but I must do so now. We are aquastors, beings created and sustained by the power of the imagination and the concentration of thought."

"I have heard of such things," I told him. "But I have touched you."

"That is no test. We are as solid as most truly false things are—a dance of particles in space. Only the things no one can touch are true, as you should know by now. Once you met a woman named Cyriaca, who told you tales of the great thinking machines of the past. There is such a machine on the ship in which we sailed. It has the power to look into your mind."

I asked, "Are you that machine, then?" A feeling of loneliness and vague fear grew in me.

"I am Master Malrubius, and Triskele is Triskele. The machine looked among your memories and found us. Our lives in your mind are not so complete as those of Thecla and the old Autarch, but we are there nevertheless, and live while you live. But we are maintained in the physical world by the energies of the machine, and its range is but a few thousand years."

As he spoke these final words, his flesh was already fading into bright dust. For a moment it glinted in the cold starlight. Then it was gone. Triskele remained with me a few breaths longer, and when his yellow coat was already silvered and blowing away in the gentle breeze, I heard his bark.

Then I stood alone at the edge of the sea I had longed for so often; but though I was alone, I found it cheering, and breathed the air that is like no other, and smiled to hear the soft song of the little waves. Land—Nessus, the House Absolute, and all the rest—lay to the east; west lay the sea; I walked north because I was reluctant to leave it too soon, and because Triskele had run in that direction, along the margin of the sea. There great Abaia might wallow with his women, yet the sea was older far, and wiser than he; we human beings, like all the life of the land, had come from the sea; and because we could not conquer it, it was ours always. The old, red sun rose on my right and touched the waves with his fading beauty, and I heard the calling of the sea birds, the innumerable birds.

By the time the shadows were short, I was tired. My face and my wounded leg pained me; I had not eaten since noon of the previous day and had not slept save for my trance in the Ascian tent. I would have rested if I could, but the sun was warm, and the line of cliffs beyond the beach offered no shade. At last I followed the tracks of a two-wheeled cart and came to a clump of wild roses growing from a dune. There I halted, and seated myself in their shadow to take off my boots and pour out the sand that had entered their splitting seams.

A thorn caught my forearm and broke from its branch, remaining embedded in my skin, with a scarlet drop of blood, no bigger than a grain of millet, at its tip. I plucked it out— then fell to my knees.

It was the Claw.

The Claw perfect, shining black, just as I had placed it under the altar stone of the Pelerines. All that bush and all the other bushes growing with it were covered with white blossoms and these perfect Claws. The one in my palm flamed with transplendent light as I looked at it.

I had surrendered the Claw, but I had retained the little leather sack Dorcas had sewn for it. I took it from my sabretache and hung it about my neck in the old way, with the Claw once more inside. It was only when I had thus put it away that I recalled seeing just such a bush in the Botanic Gardens at the beginning of my journey.

• • •

No one can explain such things. Since I have come to the House Absolute, I have talked with the heptarch and with various acaryas; but they have been able to tell me very little save that the Increate has chosen before this to manifest himself in these plants.

At that time I did not think of it, being filled with wonder—but may it not be that we were guided to the unfinished Sand Garden? I carried the Claw even then, though I did not know it; Agia had already slipped it under the closure of my sabretache. Might it not be that we came to the unfinished garden so that the Claw, flying as it were against the wind of Time, might make its farewell? The idea is absurd. But then, all ideas are absurd.

What struck me on the beach—and it struck me indeed, so that I staggered as at a blow—was that if the Eternal Principle had rested in that curved thorn I had carried about my neck across so many leagues, and if it now rested in the new thorn (perhaps the same thorn) I had only now put there, then it might rest in anything, and in fact probably did rest in everything, in every thorn on every bush, in every drop of water in the sea. The thorn was a sacred Claw because all thorns were sacred Claws; the sand in my boots was sacred sand because it came from a beach of sacred sand. The cenobites treasured up the relics of the sannyasins because the sannyasins had approached the Pancreator. But everything had approached and even touched the Pancreator, because everything had dropped from his hand. Everything was a relic. All the world was a relic. I drew off my boots, that had traveled with me so far, and threw them into the waves that I might not walk shod on holy ground.

XXXII

The *Samru*

AND I WALKED ON as a mighty army, for I felt myself in the company of all those who walked in me. I was surrounded by a numerous guard; and I was the guard about the person of the monarch. There were women in my ranks, smiling and grim, and children who ran and laughed and, daring Erebus and Abaia, hurled seashells into the sea.

In half a day I came to the mouth of Gyoll, so wide that the farther shore was lost in distance. Three-sided isles lay in it, and through them vessels with billowing sails picked their way like clouds among the peaks of the mountains. I hailed one passing the point on which I stood and asked for passage to Nessus. A wild figure I must have appeared, with my scarred face and tattered cloak and every rib showing.

Her captain sent a boat for me nonetheless, a kindness I have not forgotten. I saw fear and awe in the eyes of the rowers. Perhaps it was only at the sight of my half-healed wounds; but they were men who had seen many wounds, and I recalled how I had felt when I first saw the face of the Autarch in the House Azure, though he was not a tall man, or even a man, truly.

· · ·

Twenty days and nights the *Samru* made her way up Gyoll. We sailed when we could, and rowed, a dozen sweeps to a side, when we could not. It was a hard passage for the sailors, for though the current is almost imperceptibly slow, it runs day and night, and so long and so wide are the meanders of the channel that an oarsman often sees at evening the spot from which he labored when the beating of the drum first roused the watch.

For me it was as pleasant as a yachting expedition. Although I offered to make sail and row with the rest, they would not permit it. Then I told the captain, a sly-faced man who looked as though he lived by bargaining as much as by sailing, that I would pay him well when we reached Nessus; but he would not hear of it, and insisted (pulling at his mustache, which he did whenever he wished to show the greatest sincerity) that my presence was reward enough for him and his crew. I do not believe they guessed I was their Autarch, and for fear of such as Vodalus had been I was careful to drop no hints to them; but from my eyes and manner they seemed to feel I was an adept.

The incident of the captain's sword must have strengthened their superstition. It was a craquemarte, the heaviest of the sea swords, with a blade as wide as my palm, sharply curved and graven with stars and suns and other things the captain did not understand. He wore it when we were close enough to a riverbank village or another ship to make him feel the occasion demanded dignity; but for the most part he left it lying on the little quarterdeck. I found it there, and having nothing else to do but watch sticks and fruit skins bob in the green water, I took out my half stone and sharpened it. After a time he saw me testing the edge with my thumb and began to boast of his swordsmanship. Since the craquemarte was at least two-thirds the weight of *Terminus Est*, with a short grip, it was amusing to hear him; I listened with delight for half a watch or so. As it happened there was a hempen cable about the thickness of my wrist coiled nearby, and

when he began to lose interest in his own inventions, I had
him and the mate hold up three cubits or so between them.
The craquemarte severed it like a hair; then before either of
them could recover breath, I threw it flashing toward the sun
and caught it by the hilt.

As I fear that incident shows too well, I was beginning to
feel better. There is nothing to enthrall the reader in rest,
fresh air, and plain food; but they can work wonders against
wounds and exhaustion.

The captain would have given me his cabin if I had let
him, but I slept on deck rolled in my cloak, and on our one
night of rain found shelter under the boat, which was stowed
bottom-up amidships. As I learned on board, it is the nature
of breezes to die when Urth turns her back to the sun; so I
went to sleep, on most nights, with the chant of the rowers in
my ears. In the morning I woke to the rattle of the anchor
chain.

Sometimes, though, I woke before morning, when we lay
close to shore with only a sleepy lookout on deck. And sometimes the moonlight roused me to find us gliding forward
under reefed sails, with the mate steering and the watch
asleep beside the halyards. On one such night, shortly after
we had passed through the Wall, I went aft and saw the
phosphorescence of our wake like cold fire on the dark water
and thought for a moment that the man-apes of the mine
were coming to be cured by the Claw, or to gain an old
revenge. That, of course, was not truly strange—only the
foolish error of a mind still half in dream. What happened
the next morning was not truly strange either, but it affected
me deeply.

The oarsmen were rowing a slow beat to get us around a
leagues-long bend to a point where we could catch what little
wind there was. The sound of the drum and the hissing of
the water falling from the long blades of the sweeps are hyp-
notic, I think because they are so similar to the beating of

one's own heart in sleep and the sound the blood makes as it
moves past the inner ear on its way to the brain.

I was standing by the rail looking at the shore, still marshy
here where the plains of old have been flooded by silt-choked
Gyoll; and it seemed to me that I saw forms in the hillocks
and hummocks, as though all that vast, soft wilderness had a
geometrical soul (as certain pictures do) that vanished when I
stared at it, then reappeared when I took my eyes away. The
captain came to stand beside me, and I told him I had heard
that the ruins of the city extended far downriver and asked
when we would sight them. He laughed and explained that
we had been among them for the past two days, and loaned
me his glass so I could see that what I had taken for a stump
was in actuality a broken and tilted column covered with
moss.

At once everything—walls, streets, monuments—seemed to
spring from hiding, just as the stone town had reconstructed
itself while we watched from the tomb roof with the two
witches. No change had occurred outside my own mind, but
I had been transported, far faster than Master Malrubius's
ship could have taken me, from the desolate countryside to
the midst of an ancient and immense ruin.

Even now I cannot help but wonder how much any of us
see of what is before us. For weeks my friend Jonas had
seemed to me only a man with a prosthetic hand, and when I
was with Baldanders and Dr. Talos, I had overlooked a hundred clues that should have told me Baldanders was master.
How impressed I was outside the Piteous Gate because Baldanders did not escape the doctor when he could.

As the day wore on, the ruins became plainer and plainer
still. At each loop of the river, the green walls rose higher,
from ever firmer ground. When I woke the next morning,
some of the stronger buildings retained their upper stories.

Not long afterward, I saw a little boat, newly built, tied to an ancient pier. I pointed it out to the captain, who smiled at my naivety and said, "There are families who live, grandson following grandsire, by sifting these ruins."

"So I've been told, but that cannot be one of their boats. It's too small to take much loot away in."

"Jewelry or coins. No one else goes ashore here. There's no law—the pillagers murder each other, and anyone else who lands."

"I must go there. Will you wait for me?"

He stared at me as though I were mad. "How long?"

"Until noon. No later."

"Look," he said, and pointed. "Ahead is the last big bend. Leave us here and meet us there, where the channel bows around again. It will be afternoon before we get there."

I agreed, and he had the *Samru*'s boat put into the water for me, and told four men to row me ashore. As we were about to cast off, he unbelted his craquemarte and handed it to me, saying solemnly, "It has stood by me in many a grim fight. Go for their heads, but be careful not to knick the edge on their belt buckles."

I accepted his sword with thanks, and told him I had always favored the neck. "That's good," he said, "if you don't have shipmates by that might be hurt when you swing it flat," and he pulled his mustache.

Sitting in the stern, I had ample opportunity to observe the faces of my rowers, and it was plain they were nearly as frightened of the shore as they were of me. They laid us alongside the small boat, then nearly capsized their own in their haste to be away. After determining that what I had seen from the rail was in fact what I had taken it to be, a wilted scarlet poppy left lying on the single seat, I watched them row back to the *Samru* and saw that though a light wind now favored the billowing mains'l, the sweeps had been brought out and were beating a quick-stroke. Presumably the captain planned to round the long meander as swiftly as he could; if I were not at the spot he had pointed out, he could proceed without me, telling himself (and others, should others inquire) that it was I who had failed our appointment and not he. By parting with the craquemarte he had further salved his conscience.

Stone steps very like those I had swum from as a boy had been cut into the sides of the pier. Its top was empty, nearly as lush as a lawn with the grass that had rooted between its stones. The ruined city, my own city of Nessus though it was the Nessus of a time now long past, lay quiet before me. A few birds wheeled overhead, but they were as silent as the sun-dimmed stars. Gyoll, whispering to itself in midstream, already seemed detached from me and the empty hulks of buildings among which I limped. As soon as I was out of sight of its waters, it fell silent, like some uncertain visitor who ceases to speak when we step into another room.

It seemed that this could hardly be the quarter from which (as Dorcas had told me) furniture and utensils were taken. At first I looked in often at doors and windows, but nothing had been left within but wrack and a few yellow leaves, drifted already from the young trees that were overturning the paving blocks. Nor did I see any sign of human pillagers, although there were animal droppings and a few feathers and scattered bones.

I do not know how far inland I walked. It seemed a league, though it may have been much less. Losing the transportation of the *Samru* did not much bother me. I had walked from Nessus most of the way to the mountain war, and although my steps were uneven still, my bare feet had been toughened on the deck. Because I had never really become accustomed to carrying a sword at my waist, I drew the craquemarte and put it on my shoulder, as I had often borne *Terminus Est*. The summer sunshine held that special, luxurious warmth it gains when a suggestion of chill has crept into the morning air. I enjoyed it, and would have enjoyed it more, and the silence and solitude too, if I had not been thinking of what I would say to Dorcas, if I found her, and what she might say to me.

Had I only known, I might have saved myself that concern; I came upon her sooner than I could reasonably have expected, and I did not speak to her—nor did she speak to me, or so far as I could judge, even see me.

The buildings, which had been large and solid near the river, had long since given way to lesser, fallen-in structures that must once have been houses and shops. I do not know what guided me to hers. There was no sound of weeping, though there may have been some small, unconscious noise, the creaking of a hinge or the scrape of a shoe. Perhaps it was no more than the perfume of the blossom she wore, because when I saw her she had an arum, freckled white and sweet as Dorcas herself had always been, thrust into her hair. No doubt she had brought it there for that purpose, and had taken out the wilted poppy and cast it down when she had tied up her boat. (But I have gotten ahead of my story.)

I tried to enter the building from the front, but the rotting floor was falling into the foundation in places as the arches under it collapsed. The storeroom at the rear was less open; the silent, shadowed walk, green with ferns, had been a dangerous alley once, and shopkeepers had put small windows there or none. Still, I found a narrow door hidden under ivy, a door whose iron had been eaten like sugar by the rain, whose oak was falling into mould. Stairs nearly sound led to the floor above.

She was kneeling with her back to me. She had always been slender; now her shoulders made me think of a wooden chair with a woman's jupe hung over it. Her hair, like the palest gold, was the same—unchanged since I had seen her first in the Garden of Endless Sleep. The body of the old man who had poled the skiff there lay on a bier before her, his back so straight, his face, in death, so youthful, that I hardly knew him. On the floor near her was a basket—not small yet not large either, and a corked water jar.

I said nothing, and when I had watched her for a time I went away. If she had been there long, I would have called to her and embraced her. But she had just arrived, and I saw that it was impossible. All the time I had spent in journeying from Thrax to Lake Diuturna, and from the lake to the war, and all the time I had spent as a prisoner of Vodalus, and in sailing up Gyoll, she had spent in returning here to her place, where she had lived forty years ago or more though it had now fallen into decay.

As I had myself, an ancient buzzing with antiquity as a corpse with flies. Not that the minds of Thecla and the old Autarch, or the hundred contained in his, had made me old. It was not their memories but my own that aged me, as I thought of Dorcas shivering beside me on the brown track of floating sedge, both of us cold and dripping, drinking together from Hildegrin's flask like two infants, which in fact we had been.

I paid no heed to where I walked after that. I went straight down a long street alive with silence, and when it ended at last I turned at random. After a time I reached Gyoll, and looking downstream saw the *Samru* riding at anchor at the meeting place. A basilosaur swimming up from the open sea would not have astounded me more.

In a few moments I was mobbed by smiling sailors. The captain wrung my hand, saying, "I was afraid we'd come too late. In my mind's eye I could see you struggling for your life in sight of the river, and us still half a league off."

The mate, a man so abysmally stupid that he thought the captain a leader, clapped me on the back and shouted, "He'd have given 'em a good fight!"

XXXIII

The Citadel of the Autarch

THOUGH EVERY LEAGUE that separated me from Dorcas tore my heart, it was better than I can tell you to be back on the *Samru* again after seeing the empty, silent south.

Her decks were of the impure but lovely white of new-cut wood, scrubbed daily with a great mat called a *bear*—a sort of scouring pad woven from old cordage and weighed with the gross bodies of our two cooks, whom the crew had to drag over the last span of planking before breakfast. The crevices between the planks were sealed with pitch, so that the decks seemed terraces paved in a bold, fantastic design.

She was high in the bow, with a stem that curled back upon her. Eyes, each with a pupil as big as a plate and a sky-blue iris of the brightest obtainable paint, stared out across the green waters to help find her way; her left eye wept the anchor.

Forward of her stem, held there by a triangular wooden brace itself carved, pierced, gilded, and painted, was her fig-urehead, the bird of immortality. Its head was a woman's, the face long and aristocratic, the eyes tiny and black, its expres-sionlessness a magnificent commentary on the somber tranquillity of those who will never know death. Painted wooden feathers grew from its wooden scalp to clothe its shoulders and cup its hemispherical breasts; its arms were wings lifted up and back, their tips reaching higher than the termination of the stem and their gold and crimson primary feathers partially obscuring the triangular brace. I would have thought it a creature wholly fabulous—as no doubt the sailors did—had I not seen the Autarch's anpiels.

A long bowsprit passed to starboard of the stem, between the wings of the samru. The foremast, only slightly longer than this bowsprit, rose from the forecastle. It was raked forward to give the foresail room, as though it had been pulled out of true by the forestay and the laboring jib. The mainmast stood as straight as the pine it had once been, but the mizzenmast was raked back, so the mastheads of the three masts were considerably more separated than their bases. Each mast held a slanting yard made by lashing together two tapering spars that had once been entire saplings, and each of these yards carried a single, triangular, rust-colored sail.

The hull itself was painted white below the water and black above it, save for the figurehead and eyes I have already mentioned, and the quarterdeck rail, where scarlet had been used to symbolize both the captain's high state and his sanguinary background. This quarterdeck actually occupied no more than a sixth of the *Samru*'s length, but the wheel and the binnacle were there, and it was there that one had the finest view, short of that provided by the rigging. The ship's only real armament, a swivel gun not much larger than Mamillian's, was there, ready alike for freebooters and mutineers. Just aft of the sternrail, two iron posts as delicately curved as the horns of a cricket lifted many-faceted lanterns, one of palest red, the other viridescent as moonlight.

I was standing by these lanterns the next evening, listening to the thudding of the drum, the soft splashing of the sweep-blades, and the rowers' chant, when I saw the first lights along the riverbank. Here was the dying edge of the city, the home of the poorest of the poorest of the poor—which only meant that the living edge of the city was here, that death's dominion ended here. Human beings were preparing to sleep here, perhaps still sharing the meal that marked the day's end. I saw a thousand kindnesses in each of those lights, and heard a thousand fireside stories. In some sense I was home again; and the same song that had urged me forth in the spring now bore me back:

> Row, brothers, row!
> The current is against us.
> Row, brothers, row!
> Yet God is for us.
> Row, brothers, row!
> The wind is against us.
> Row, brothers, row!
> Yet God is for us.

I could not help but wonder who was setting out that night.

Every long story, if it be told truly, will be found to contain all the elements that have contributed to the human drama since the first rude ship reached the strand of Lune: not only noble deeds and tender emotion, but grotesquerie, bathos, and so on. I have striven to set down the unembellished truth here, without the least worry that you, my reader, would find some parts improbable and others insipid; and if the mountain war was the scene of high deeds (belonging more to others than to me), and my imprisonment by Vodalus and the Ascians a time of horror, and my passage on the *Samru* an interlude of tranquillity, then we are come to the interval of comedy.

We approached that part of the city where the Citadel stands—which is southern but not the southernmost—under sail and by day. I watched the sun-gilt eastern bank with great care, and had the captain land me on those slimy steps where I had once swum and fought. I hoped to pass through the necropolis gate and so enter the Citadel through the breach in the curtain wall that was near the Matachin Tower; but the gate was closed and locked, and no convenient party of volunteers arrived to admit me. Thus I was forced instead to walk many chains along the margin of the necropolis, and several more along the curtain wall to the barbican.

There I encountered a numerous guard who carried me before their officer, who, when I told him I was a torturer, supposed me to be one of those wretches that, most often at the onset of winter, seek to gain admission to the guild. He decided (very properly, had he been correct) to have me whipped; and to prevent it I was forced to break the thumbs of two of his men, and then demand while I held him in the way called the *kitten and ball* that he take me to his superior, the castellan.

I admit I was somewhat awed at the thought of this official, whom I had seldom so much as seen in all the years I had been an apprentice in the fortress he commanded. I found him an old soldier, silver-haired and as lame as I. The officer stammered out his accusations while I stood by: I had assaulted and insulted (not true) his person, maimed two of his men, and so on. When he had finished, the castellan looked from me to him and back again, dismissed him, and offered me a seat.

"You are unarmed," he said. His voice was hoarse but soft, as though he had strained it shouting commands.

I admitted that I was.

"But you have seen fighting, and you have been in the jungle north of the mountains, where no battle has been since they turned our flank by crossing the Uroboros."

"That's true," I said. "But how can you know?"

"That wound in your thigh came from one of their spears. I've seen enough to recognize them. The beam flashed up through the muscle, reflected by the bone. You might have been up a tree and been stuck by a hastarus on the ground, I suppose, but the most likely thing is that you were mounted and charging infantry. Not a cataphract, or they wouldn't have got you so easily. The demilances?"

"Only the light irregulars."

"You'll have to tell me about that later, because you're a city man from your accent, and they're eclectics and suchlike for the most part. You have a double scar on your foot too, white and clean, with the marks half a span apart. That was a blood bat's bite, and they don't come that large except in the true jungle at the waist of the world. How did you get there?"

"Our flier crashed. I was taken prisoner."

"And escaped?"

In a moment more I would have been forced to talk of Agia and the green man, and of my journey from the jungle to the mouth of Gyoll, and those were high matters which I did not wish to disclose thus casually. Instead of an answer, I pronounced the words of authority applicable to the Citadel and its castellan.

Because he was lame, I would have had him remain seated if I could; but he sprang to his feet and saluted, then dropped to his knees to kiss my hand. He was thus, though he could not have known it, the first to pay me homage, a distinction that entitles him to a private audience once a year—an audience he has not yet requested and perhaps never will.

For me to proceed now, clothed as I was, was impossible. The old castellan would have died of a stroke had I demanded it, and he was so concerned for my safety that any incognito would have been accompanied by at least a platoon of lurking halberdiers. I soon found myself arrayed in lapis lazuli jazerant, cothurni, and a stephane, the whole set off by an ebony baculus and a voluminous damassin cape embroidered with rotting pearls. All these things were indescribably ancient, having been taken from a store preserved from the period when the Citadel was the residence of the autarchs.

Thus in place of entering our tower, as I had intended, in the same cloak in which I had left it, I returned as an unrecognizable being in ceremonial fancy dress, skeletally thin, lame, and hideously scarred. It was with this appearance that I entered Master Palaemon's study, and I am certain I must almost have frightened him to death, since he had been told only a few moments before that the Autarch was in the Citadel and wished to converse with him.

He seemed to me to have aged a great deal while I was gone. Perhaps it was simply that I recalled him not as he was when I was exiled, but as I had seen him in our little classroom when I was a boy. Still, I like to think he was concerned for me, and it is not really so unlikely that he was: I had always been his best pupil and his favorite; it was his vote, beyond doubt, that had countered Master Gurloes's and saved my life; he had given me his sword.

But whether he had worried much or little, his face seemed more deeply lined than it had been; and his scant hair, which I had thought gray, was now of that yellow hue seen in old ivory. He knelt and kissed my fingers, and was more than a little surprised when I helped him to rise and told him to seat himself behind his table again.

"You are too kind, Autarch," he said. Then, using an old formula, "Your mercy extends from sun to Sun."

"Do you not recall us?"

"Were you confined here?" He peered at me through the curious arrangement of lenses that alone permitted him to see at all, and I decided that his vision, exhausted long before I was born on the faded ink of the records of the guild, must have deteriorated further. "You have suffered torment, I see. But it is too crude, I hope, for our work."

"It was not your doing," I said, touching the scars on my cheek. "Nevertheless, we were confined for a time in the oubliette beneath this tower."

He sighed—an old man's shallow breath—and looked down at the gray litter of his papers. When he spoke I could not hear the words, and had to ask him to repeat them.

"It has come," he said. "I knew it would, but I hoped to be dead and forgotten. Will you dismiss us, Autarch? Or put us to some other task?"

"We have not yet decided what we will do with you and the guild you serve."

"It will not avail. If I offend you, Autarch, I ask your indulgence for my age . . . but still it will not avail. You will find in the end that you require men to do what we do. You may call it healing, if you wish. That has been done often. Or ritual, that has been done too. But you will find the thing itself grows more terrible in its disguise. Will you imprison those undeserving of death? You will find them a mighty army in chains. You will discover that you hold prisoners whose escape would be a catastrophe, and that you need servants who will wreak justice on those who have caused scores to die in agony. Who else will do that?"

"No one will wreak such justice as you. You say our mercy extends from sun to Sun, and we hope it is so. By our mercy we will grant even the foulest a quick death. Not because we pity them, but because it is intolerable that good men should spend a lifetime dispensing pain."

His head came up and the lenses flashed. For the only time in all the years I had known him, I was able to see the youth he had been. "It must be done by good men. You are badly advised, Autarch! What is intolerable is that it should be done by bad men."

I smiled. His face, as I had seen it then, had recalled something I had thrust from my mind months before. It was that this guild was my family, and all the home I should ever have. I would never find a friend in the world if I could not find friends here. "Between us, Master," I told him, "we have decided it should not be done at all."

He did not reply, and I saw from his expression that he had not even heard what I had said. He had been listening instead to my voice, and doubt and joy flickered over his worn, old face like shadow and firelight.

"Yes," I said. "It is Severian," and while he was struggling to regain possession of himself, I went to the door and got my sabretache, which I had ordered one of the officers of my guard to bring. I had wrapped it in what had been my fuligin guild cloak, now faded to mere rusty black. Spreading the cloak over Master Palaemon's table, I opened the sabretache and poured out its contents. "This is all we have brought back," I said.

He smiled as he used to in the schoolroom when he had caught me out in some minor matter. "That and the throne? Will you tell me about it?"

And so I did. It took a long while, and more than once my protectors rapped at the door to ascertain that I was unharmed, and at last I had a meal brought in to us; and when the pheasant was mere bones and the cakes were eaten and the wine drunk, we were still talking. It was then that I conceived the idea that has at last borne fruit in this record of my life. I had originally intended to begin it at the day I left our tower and to end it when I returned. But I soon saw that though such a construction would indeed supply the symmetry so valued by artists, it would be impossible for anyone to understand my adventures without knowing something of my adolescence. In the same way, some elements of my story would remain incomplete if I did not extend it (as I propose to do) a few days beyond my return. Perhaps I have contrived for someone *The Book of Gold*. Indeed, it may be that all my wanderings have been no more than a contrivance of the librarians to recruit their numbers; but perhaps even that is too much to hope.

XXXIV

The Key to the Universe

WHEN HE HAD HEARD everything, Master Palaemon went to my little heap of possessions and took up the grip, pommel, and silver guard that were all that remained of *Terminus Est*. "She was a good sword," he said. "Nearly I gave you your death, but she was a good sword."

"We were always proud to bear her, and never found reason to complain of her."

He sighed, and the breath seemed to catch in his throat. "She is gone. It is the blade that is the sword, not the sword furniture. The guild will preserve these somewhere, with your cloak and sabretache, because they have belonged to you. When you and I have been dead for centuries, old men like me will point them out to the apprentices. It's a pity we haven't the blade too. I used her for many years before you came to the guild, and never thought she would be destroyed fighting some diabolical weapon." He put down the opal pommel and frowned at me. "What's troubling you? I've seen men wince less when their eyes were torn out."

"There are many kinds of diabolical weapons, as you call them, that steel cannot withstand. We saw something of them when we were in Orithyia. And there are tens of thousands of our soldiers there holding them off with firework lances and javelins, and swords less well forged than *Terminus Est*. They succeed in so far as they do because the energy weapons of the Ascians are not numerous, and they are few because the Ascians lack the sources of power needed to produce them. What will happen if Urth is granted a New Sun? Won't the Ascians be better able to use its energy than we can?"

"Perhaps that may be," Master Palaemon acknowledged.

"We have been thinking with the autarchs who have gone before us—our guild brothers, as it were, in a new guild. Master Malrubius said that only our predecessor has dared the test in modern times. When we touch the minds of the others, we often find that they have refused it because they felt our enemies, who have retained so much more of the ancient sciences, would gain a greater advantage. Is it not possible they were right?"

Master Palaemon thought a long time before he answered. "I cannot say. You believe me wise because I taught you once, but I have not been north, as you have. You have seen armies of Ascians, and I have never seen one. You flatter me by asking my opinion. Still—from all you've said, they are rigid, cast hard in their ways. I would guess that very few among them think much."

I shrugged. "That is true in any aggregate, Master. But as you say, it is possibly more true among them. And what you call their rigidity is terrible—a deadness that surpasses belief. Individually they seem men and women, but together they are like a machine of wood and stone."

Master Palaemon rose and went to the port and looked out upon the thronging towers. "We are too rigid here," he said. "Too rigid in our guild, too rigid in the Citadel. It tells me a great deal that you, who were educated here, saw them as you did; they must be inflexible indeed. I think it may be that despite their science, which may amount to less than you suppose, the people of the Commonwealth will be better able to turn new circumstances to their benefit."

"We are not flexible or inflexible," I said. "Except for an unusually good memory, we are only an ordinary man."

"No, no!" Master Palaemon struck his table, and again the lenses flashed. "You are an extraordinary man in an ordinary time. When you were a little apprentice, I beat you once or twice—you will recall that, I know. But even when I beat you, I knew you would become an extraordinary personage, the greatest master our guild would ever have. And you will be a master. Even if you destroy our guild, we will elect you!"

"We have already told you we mean to reform the guild, not destroy it. We're not even sure we're competent to do that. You respect us because we've moved to the highest place. But we reached it by chance, and know it. Our predecessor reached it by chance too, and the minds he brought to us, which we touch only faintly even now, are not, with one or two exceptions, those of genius. Most are only common men and women, sailors and artisans, farmwives and wantons. Most of the rest are eccentric second-rate scholars of the sort Thecla used to laugh at."

"You have not just moved into the highest place," Master Palaemon said, "you have become it. You are the state."

"We are not. The state is everyone else—you, the castellan, those officers outside. We are the people, the Commonwealth." I had not known it myself until I spoke.

I picked up the brown book. "We are going to keep this. It was one of the good things, like your sword. The writing of books shall be encouraged again. There are no pockets in these clothes; but perhaps it will do good if we are seen to carry it when we leave."

"Carry it where?" Master Palaemon cocked his head like an old raven.

"To the House Absolute. We've been out of touch, or the Autarch has, if you wish to put it so, for over a month. We have to find out what's happening at the front, and perhaps dispatch reinforcements." I thought of Lomer and Nicarete, and the other prisoners in the antechamber. "We have other tasks there too," I said.

Master Palaemon stroked his chin. "Before you go, Severian—Autarch—would you like to tour the cells, for old times' sake? I doubt those fellows out there know of the door that opens to the western stair."

It is the least-used staircase in the tower, and perhaps the oldest. Certainly it is the one least altered from its original condition. The steps are narrow and steep, and wind down around a central column black with corrosion. The door to the room where I, as Thecla, had been subjected to the device called the Revolutionary stood half open, so that though we did not go inside, I nevertheless saw its ancient mechanisms: frightful, yet less hideous to me than the gleaming but far older things in Baldanders's castle.

Entering the oubliette meant returning to something I had, from the time I left for Thrax, assumed gone forever. Yet the metal corridors with their long rows of doors were unchanged, and when I peered through the tiny windows that pierced those doors I saw familiar faces, the faces of men and women I had fed and guarded as a journeyman.

"You are pale, Autarch," Master Palaemon said. "I feel your hand tremble." (I was supporting him a little with one hand on his arm.)

"You know that our memories never fade," I said. "For us the Chatelaine Thecla still sits in one of these cells, and the Journeyman Severian in another."

"I had forgotten. Yes, it must be terrible for you. I was going to take you to the Chatelaine's old one, but perhaps you would rather not see it."

I insisted that we visit it; but when we arrived, there was a new client inside, and the door was locked. I had Master Palaemon call the brother on duty to let us in, then stood for a moment looking at the cramped bed and the tiny table. At last I noticed the client, who sat upon the single chair, with wide eyes and an indescribable expression blended of hope and wonder. I asked him if he knew me.

"No, exultant."

"We are no exultant. We are your Autarch. Why are you here?"

He rose, then fell to his knees. "I am innocent! Believe me!"

"All right," I said. "We believe you. But we want you to tell us what you were accused of, and how you came to be convicted."

Shrilly, he began to pour forth one of the most complex and confused accounts I have ever heard. His sister-in-law had conspired with her mother against him. They said he had struck his wife, that he had neglected his ill wife, that he had stolen certain moneys from her that she had been entrusted with by her father, for purposes about which they disagreed. In explaining all this (and much more) he boasted of his own cleverness while decrying the frauds, tricks, and lies of the others that had sent him to the oubliette. He said that the gold in question had never existed, and also that his mother-in-law had used a part of it to bribe the judge. He said he had not known his wife was ill, and that he had procured the best physician he could afford for her.

When I left him, I went to the next call and heard the client there, and then to the next and the next, until I had visited fourteen. Eleven clients protested their innocence, some better than the first, some even worse; but I found none whose protestations convinced me. Three admitted that they were guilty (though one swore, I think sincerely, that though he had committed most of the crimes with which he had been charged, he had also been charged with several he had not committed). Two of these promised earnestly to do nothing that would return them to the oubliette if only I would release them; which I did. The third—a woman who had stolen children and forced them to serve as articles of furniture in a room she had set aside for the purpose, in one instance nailing the hands of a little girl to the underside of a small tabletop so that she became in effect its pedestal—told me with apparently equal frankness that she felt sure she would return to what she called her sport because it was the only activity that really interested her. She did not ask to be released, only to have her sentence commuted to simple imprisonment. I felt certain she was mad; yet nothing in her conversation or her clear blue eyes indicated it, and she told me she had been examined prior to her trial and pronounced sane. I touched her forehead with the New Claw, but it was as inert as the old Claw had been when I had attempted to use it to help Jolenta and Baldanders.

I cannot escape the thought that the power manifested in both Claws is drawn from myself, and that it is for this reason that their radiance, said by others to be warm, has always seemed cold to me. This thought is the psychological equivalent of that aching abyss in the sky into which I feared to fall when I slept in the mountains. I reject and fear it because I desire so fervently that it be true; and I feel that if there were the least echo of truth in it, I would detect it within myself. I do not.

Furthermore, there are profound objections to it besides this lack of internal resonance, the most important, convincing, and apparently inescapable being that the Claw unquestionably reanimated Dorcas after many decades of death—and did so before I knew I carried it.

That argument appears conclusive; and still I am not sure that it is so. Did I in fact know? What is meant by *know*, in an appropriate sense? I have assumed I was unconscious when Agia slipped the Claw into my sabretache; but I may have been merely dazed, and in any case, many have long believed that unconscious persons are aware of their surroundings and respond internally to speech and music. How else explain the dreams dictated by external sounds? What portion of the brain is unconscious, after all? Not the whole of it, or the heart would not beat and the lungs no longer breathe. Much of the memory is chemical. All that, in fact, I have from Thecla and the former Autarch is fundamentally so—the drugs serving only to permit the complex compounds of thought to enter my own brain as information. May it not be that certain information derived from external phenomena are chemically impressed on our brains even when the electrical activity on which we depend for conscious thought has temporarily ceased?

Besides, if the energy has its origins in me, why should it have been necessary for me to be aware of the presence of the Claw for them to operate, any more than it would be necessary if they had their origin in the Claw itself? A strong suggestion of another kind might be equally effective, and certainly our careening invasion of the sacred precincts of the Pelerines and the way in which Agia and I emerged unhurt from the accident that killed the animals might have furnished such a suggestion. From the cathedral we had gone to the Botanic Gardens, and there, before we entered the Garden of Endless Sleep, I had seen a bush covered with Claws. At that time I believed the Claw to be a gem, but may not they have suggested it nonetheless? Our minds often play such punning tricks. In the yellow house we had met three persons who believed us supernatural presences.

If the supernatural power is mine (and yet clearly it is not mine), how did I come to have it? I have devised two explanations, both wildly improbable. Dorcas and I talked once of the symbolic significance of real-world things, which by the teachings of the philosophers stand for things higher than themselves, and in a lower order are themselves symbolized. To take an absurdly simple example, suppose an artist in a garret limning a peach. If we put the poor artist in the place of the Increate, we may say that his picture symbolizes the peach, and thus the fruits of the soil, while the glowing curve of the peach itself symbolizes the ripe beauty of womanhood. Were such a woman to enter the artist's garret (an improbability we must entertain for the sake of the explanation), she would doubtless remain unaware that the fullness of her hip and the hardness of her heart found their echoes in a basket on the table by the window, though perhaps the artist might be able to think of nothing else.

But if the Increate is in actual fact in place of the artist, is it not possible that such connections as these, many of which must always be unguessable by human beings, may have profound effects on the structure of the world, just as the artist's obsession may color his picture? If I am he who is to renew the youth of the sun with the White Fountain of which I have been told, may it not be that I have been given, almost unconsciously (if that expression may be used), the attributes of life and light that will belong to the renewed sun?

The other explanation I mentioned is hardly more than a speculation. But if, as Master Malrubius told me, those who will judge me among the stars will take my manhood should I fail their judgment, is it not possible also that they will confirm me in some gift of equal worth should I, as Humanity's representative, conform to their desires? It seems to me that justice demands it. If that is the case, may it not be that their gift transcends time, as they do themselves? The Hierodules I met in Baldanders's castle said they interested themselves in me because I would gain the throne—but would their interest have been so great if I were to be no more than the embattled ruler of some part of this continent, one of many embattled rulers in the long history of Urth?

On the whole, I think the first explanation the most probable; but the second is not wholly unlikely. Either would seem to indicate that the mission I am about to set out on will succeed. I will go with good heart.

And yet there is a third explanation. No human being or near-human being can conceive of such minds as those of Abaia, Erebus, and the rest. Their power surpasses understanding, and I know now that they could crush us in a day if it were not that they count only enslavement, and not annihilation, as victory. The great undine I saw was their creature, and less than their slave: their toy. It is possible that the power of the Claw, the Claw taken from a growing thing so near their sea, comes ultimately from them. They knew my destiny as well as Ossipago, Barbatus, and Famulimus, and they saved me when I was a boy so that I might fulfill it. After I departed from the Citadel they found me again, and thereafter my course was twisted by the Claw. Perhaps they hope to triumph by raising a torturer to the Autarchy, or to that position that is higher than the Autarch's.

Now I think that it is time to record what Master Malrubius explained to me. I cannot vouch for its truth, but I believe it to be true. I know no more than I set down here.

Just as a flower blooms, throws down its seed, dies, and rises from its seed to bloom again, so the universe we know diffuses itself to nullity in the infinitude of space, gathers its fragments (which because of the curvature of that space meet at last where they began) and from that seed blooms again. Each such cycle of flowering and decay marks a divine year.

As the flower that comes is like the flower from which it came, so the universe that comes repeats the one whose ruin was its origin; and this is as true of its finer features as of its grosser ones: The worlds that arise are not unlike the worlds that perished, and are peopled by similar races, though just as the flower evolves from summer to summer, all things advance by some minute step.

In a certain divine year (a time truly inconceivable to us, though that cycle of the universes was but one in an endless succession), a race was born that was so like to ours that Master Malrubius did not scruple to call it human. It expanded among the galaxies of its universe even as we are said to have done in the remote past, when Urth was, for a time, the center, or at least the home and symbol, of an empire.

These men encountered many beings on other worlds who had intelligence to some degree, or at least the potential for intelligence, and from them—that they might have comrades in the loneliness between the galaxies and allies among their swarming worlds—they formed beings like themselves.

It was not done swiftly or easily. Uncountable billions suffered and died under their guiding hands, leaving ineradicable memories of pain and blood. When their universe was old, and galaxy so far separated from galaxy that the nearest could not be seen even as faint stars, and the ships were steered thence by ancient records alone, the thing was done. Completed, the work was greater than those who began it could have guessed. What had been made was not a new race like Humanity's, but a race such as Humanity wished its own to be: united, compassionate, just.

I was not told what became of the Humanity of that cycle. Perhaps it survived until the implosion of the universe, then perished with it. Perhaps it evolved beyond our recognition. But the beings Humanity had shaped into what men and women wished to be escaped, opening a passage to Yesod, the universe higher than our own, where they created worlds suited to what they had become.

From that vantage point they look both forward and back, and in so looking they have discovered us. Perhaps we are no more than a race like that who shaped them. Perhaps it was we who shaped them—or our sons—or our fathers. Malrubius said he did not know, and I believe he told the truth. However it may be, they shape us now as they themselves were shaped; it is at once their repayment and their revenge.

The Hierodules they have found too, and formed more quickly, to serve them in this universe. On their instructions, the Hierodules construct such ships as the one that bore me from the jungle to the sea, so that aquastors like Malrubius and Triskele may serve them also. With these tongs, we are held in the forge.

The hammer they wield is their ability to draw their servants back, down the corridors of time, and to send them hurtling forward to the future. (This power is in essence the same as that which permitted them to evade the death of their universe—to enter the corridors of time is to leave the universe.) On Urth at least, their anvil is the necessity of life: our need in this age to fight against an ever-more-hostile world with the resources of the depleted continents. Because it is as cruel as the means by which they themselves were shaped, there is a conservation of justice; but when the New Sun appears, it will be a signal that at least the earliest operations of the shaping are complete.

XXXV

Father Inire's Letter

THE QUARTERS ASSIGNED to me were in the most ancient part of the Citadel. The rooms had been empty so long that the old castellan and the steward charged with maintaining them supposed the keys to have been lost, and offered, with many apologies and much reticence, to break the locks for me. I did not permit myself the luxury of watching their faces, but I heard their indrawn breath as I pronounced the simple words that controlled the doors.

It was fascinating, that evening, to see how much the fashions of the period in which those chambers were furnished differed from our own. They did without chairs as we know them, having for seats only complex cushions; and their tables lacked drawers and that symmetry we have come to consider essential. By our standards too, there was too much fabric and not enough wood, leather, stone, and bone; I found the effect at once sybaritic and uncomfortable.

Yet it was impossible that I should occupy a suite other than that anciently set aside for the autarchs; and impossible too that I should have it refurnished to a degree that would imply criticism of my predecessors. And if the furniture had more to recommend it to the mind than to the body, what a delight it was to discover the treasures those same predecessors had left behind: There were papers relating to matters now utterly forgotten and not always identifiable; mechanical devices ingenious and enigmatic; a microcosm that stirred to life at the warmth of my hands, and whose minute inhabitants seemed to grow larger and more human as I watched them; a laboratory containing the fabled "emerald bench" and many other things, the most interesting of which was a mandragora in spirits.

The cucurbit in which it floated was about seven spans in height and half as wide; the homuncule itself no more than two spans tall. When I tapped the glass, it turned eyes like clouded beads toward me, eyes blinder far in appearance than Master Palaemon's. I heard no sound when its lips twitched, yet I knew at once what words they shaped—and in some inexplicable sense I felt the pale fluid in which the mandragora was immersed had become my own blood-tinged urine.

"Why have you called me, Autarch, from the contemplation of your world?"

I asked, "Is it truly mine? I know now that there are seven continents, and none but a part of this are obedient to the hallowed phrases."

"You are the heir," the wizened thing said and turned, I could not tell if by accident or design, until it no longer faced me.

I tapped the cucurbit again. "And who are you?"

"A being without parents, whose life is passed immersed in blood."

"Why, such have I been! We should be friends then, you and I, as two of similar background usually are."

"You jest."

"Not at all. I feel a real sympathy for you, and I think we are more alike than you believe."

The tiny figure turned again until its little face looked up into my own. *"I wish that I might credit you, Autarch."*

"I mean it. No one has ever accused me of being an honest man, and I've told lies enough when I thought they would serve my turn, but I'm quite sincere. If I can do anything for you, tell me what it is."

"Break the glass."

I hesitated. "Won't you die?"

"I have never lived. I will cease thinking. Break the glass."

"You do live."

"I neither grow, nor move, nor respond to any stimulus save thought, which is counted no response. I am incapable of propagating my kind, or any other. Break the glass."

"If you are indeed unliving, I would rather find some way to stir you to life."

"So much for brotherhood. When you were imprisoned here, Thecla, and that boy brought you the knife, why did not you look for more life then?"

The blood burned in my cheek, and I lifted the ebony baculus, but I did not strike. "Alive or dead, you have a penetrating intelligence. Thecla is that part of me most prone to anger."

"If you had inherited her glands with her memories, I would have succeeded."

"And you know that. How can you know so much, who are blind?"

"The acts of coarse minds create minute vibrations that stir the waters of this bottle. I hear your thoughts."

"I notice that I hear yours. How is it that I can hear them, and not others?"

Looking now directly into the pinched face, which was lit by the sun's last shaft penetrating a dusty port, I could not be sure the lips moved at all. *"You hear yourself, as ever. You cannot hear others because your mind shrieks always, like an infant crying in a basket. Ah, I see you remember that."*

"I remember a time very long ago when I was cold and hungry. I lay upon my back, encircled by brown walls, and heard the sound of my own screams. Yes, I must have been an infant. Not old enough to crawl, I think. You are very clever. What am I thinking now?"

"That I am but an unconscious exercise of your own power, as the Claw was. It is true, of course. I was deformed, and died before birth, and have been kept here since in white brandy. Break the glass."

"I would question you first," I said.

"Brother, there is an old man with a letter at your door."

I listened. It was strange, after having listened only to his words in my mind, to hear real noises again—the calling of the sleepy blackbirds among the towers and the tapping at the door.

The messenger was old Rudesind, who had guided me to the picture-room of the House Absolute. I motioned him in (to the surprise, I think, of the sentries) because I wanted to talk to him and knew that with him I had no need to stand upon my dignity.

"Never been in here in all my years," he said. "How can I help you, Autarch?"

"We're served already, just by the sight of you. You know who we are, don't you? You recognized us when we met before."

"If I didn't know your face, Autarch, I'd know a couple dozen times over anyhow. I've been told that often. Nobody here talks about anything else, seems like. How you was licked to shape right here. How they seen you this time and that time. How you looked, and what you said to them. There ain't one cook that didn't treat you to a pastry often. All them soldiers told you stories. Been a while now since I met a woman didn't kiss you and sew up a hole in your pants. You had a dog—"

"That's true enough," I said. "We did."

"And a cat and a bird and a coti that stole apples. And you climbed every wall in this place. And jumped off after, or else swung on a rope, or else hid and pretended you'd jumped. You're every boy that's ever been here, and I've heard stories put on you that belong to men that was old when I was just a boy, and I've heard about things I did myself, seventy years ago."

"We've already learned that the Autarch's face is always concealed behind the mask the people weave for him. No doubt it's a good thing; you can't become too proud once you understand how different you really are from the thing they bow to. But we want to hear about you. The old Autarch told us you were his sentinel in the House Absolute, and now we know you're a servant of Father Inire's."

"I am," the old man said. "I have that honor, and it's his letter I carry." He held up a small and somewhat smudged envelope.

"And we are Father Inire's master."

He made a countrified bow. "I know so, Autarch."

"Then we order you to sit down, and rest yourself. We've questions to ask you, and we don't want to keep a man your age standing. When we were that boy you say everyone's talking of, or at least not much older, you directed us to Master Ultan's stacks. Why did you do that?"

"Not because I knew something others didn't. Not because my master ordered it, either, if that's what you're thinking. Won't you read his letter?"

"In a moment. After an honest answer, in a few words."

The old man hung his head and pulled at his thin beard. I could see the dry skin of his face rise in hollow-sided, tiny cones as it sought to follow the white hairs. "Autarch, you think I guessed at something back then. Perhaps some did. Perhaps my master did, I don't know." His rheumy eyes rolled up under his brows to look at me, then fell again. "You were young, and seemed a likely-looking boy, so I wanted you to see."

"To see what?"

"I'm an old man. An old man then, and an old man now. You've grown up since. I see it in your face. I'm hardly any older, because that much time isn't anything to me. If you counted all the time I've spent just going up and down my ladder, it'd be longer than that. I wanted you to see there has been a lot come before you. That there was thousands and thousands that lived and died before you was ever thought of, some better than you. I mean, Autarch, the way you was then. You'd think anybody growing up here in the old Citadel would be born knowing all that, but I've found they're not. Being around it all the time, they don't see it. But going down there to Master Ultan brings it home to the cleverer ones."

"You are the advocate of the dead."

The old man nodded. "I am. People talk about being fair to this one and that one, but nobody I ever heard talks about doing right by them. We take everything they had, which is all right. And spit, most often, on their opinions, which I suppose is all right too. But we ought to remember now and then how much of what we have we got from them. I figure while I'm still here I ought to put a word in for them. And now, if you don't mind, Autarch, I'll just lay the letter here on this funny table—"

"Rudesind . . ."

"Yes, Autarch?"

"Are you going to clean your paintings?"

He nodded again. "That's one reason I'm eager to be gone, Autarch. I was at the House Absolute until my master—" here he paused and seemed to swallow, as men do when they feel they have perhaps said too much "—went away north. Got a Fechin to clean, and I'm behind."

"Rudesind, we already know the answers to the question you think we are going to ask. We know your master is what the people call a cacogen, and that for whatever reason, he is one of those few who have chosen to cast their lots entirely with humanity, remaining on Urth as a human being. The Cumaean is another such, though perhaps you did not know that. We even know that your master was with us in the jungles of the north, where he tried until it was too late to rescue my predecessor. We only want to say that if a young man with an errand comes past again while you are on your ladder, you are to send him to Master Ultan. That is our order."

When he had gone, I tore open the envelope. The sheet within was not large, but it was covered with tiny writing, as though a swarm of hatchling spiders had been pressed into its surface.

His servant Inire hails the bridegroom of the Urth, Master of Nessus and the House Absolute, Chief of his Race, Gold of his People, Messenger of Dawn, Helios, Hyperion, Surya, Savitar, and Autarch!

I hasten, and will reach you within two days.

It was a day and more ere I learned what had taken place. Much of my information came from the woman Agia, who at least by her own account was instrumental in freeing you. She told me also something of your past dealings with her, for I have, as you know, means of extracting information.

You will have learned from her that the Exultant Vodalus is dead by her act. His paramour, the Chatelaine Thea, at first attempted to gain control of those myrmidons who were about him at his death; but as she is by no means fitted to lead them, and still less to hold in check those in the south, I have contrived to set this woman Agia in her place. From your former mercy toward her, I trust that will meet with your approval. Certainly it is desirable to maintain in being a movement that has proved so useful in the past, and as long as the mirrors of the caller Hethor remain unbroken, she provides it with a plausible commander.

You will perhaps consider the ship I summoned to aid my master, the autarch of his day, inadequate—as for that matter do I—yet it was the best I could obtain, and I was hard pressed to get it. I myself have been forced to travel south otherwise, and much more slowly; the time may come soon when my cousins are ready to side not just with humankind but with *us*—but for the present they persist in viewing Urth as somewhat less significant than many of the colonized worlds, and ourselves on a par with the Ascians, and for that matter with the Xanthoderms and many others.

You will perhaps already have gained news both fresher and more precise than mine. On the chance that you have not: The war goes well and ill. Neither point of their envelopment penetrated far, and the southern thrust, particularly, suffered such losses that it may fairly be said to have been destroyed. I know the death of so many miserable slaves of Erebus will bring no joy to you, but at least our armies have a respite.

That they need badly. There is sedition among the Para-lians, which must be rooted out. The Tarentines, your Antrus-tiones, and the city legions—the three groups that bore the brunt of the fighting—having suffered almost as badly as the enemy. There are cohorts among them that could not muster a hundred able soldiers.

I need not tell you we should obtain more small arms and, particularly, artillery, if my cousins can be persuaded to part with them at a price we can pay. In the meanwhile, what can be done to raise fresh troops must be done, and in time for the recruits to be trained by spring. Light units capable of skirmishing without scattering are the present need; but if the Ascians break out next year, we will require piquenaires and pilani by the hundreds of thousands, and it might be well to bring at least a part of them under arms now.

Any news you have of Abaia's incursions will be fresher than mine; I have had none since I left our lines. Hormisdas has gone into the South, I believe, but Olaguer may be able to inform you.

In haste and reverence,
INIRE

XXXVI

Of Bad Gold and Burning

NOT MUCH REMAINS to be told. I knew I would have to leave the city in a few days, so all I hoped to do here would have to be done quickly. I had no friends in the guild I could be sure of beyond Master Palaemon, and he would be of little use in what I planned. I summoned Roche, knowing that he could not deceive me to my face for long. (I expected to see a man older than myself, but the red-haired journeyman who came at my command was hardly more than a boy; when he had gone, I studied my own face in a mirror, something I had not done before.)

He told me that he and several others who had been friends of mine more or less close had argued against my execution when the will of most of the guild was to kill me, and I believed him. He also admitted quite freely that he had proposed that I be maimed and expelled, though he said he had only done so because he had felt it to be the only way to save my life. I think he expected to be punished in some way—his cheeks and forehead, normally so ruddy, were white enough to make his freckles stand out like splatters of paint. His voice was steady, however, and he said nothing that seemed intended to excuse himself by throwing blame on someone else.

The fact was, of course, that I did intend to punish him, together with the rest of the guild. Not because I bore him or them any ill will, but because I felt that being locked below the tower for a time would arouse in them a sensitivity to that principle of justice of which Master Palaemon had spoken, and because it would be the best way to assure that the order forbidding torture I intended to issue would be carried out. Those who spend a few months in dread of that art are not likely to resent its being discontinued.

However, I said nothing about that to Roche but only asked him to bring me a journeyman's habit that evening, and to be ready with Drotte and Eata to aid me the next morning.

He returned with the clothing just after vespers. It was an indescribable pleasure to take off the stiff costume I had been wearing and put on fuligin again. By night, its dark embrace is the nearest approach to invisibility I know, and after I had slipped out of my chambers by one of the secret exits, I moved between tower and tower like a shadow until I reached the fallen section of the curtain wall.

Day had been warm; but the night was cool, and the necropolis filled with mist, just as it had been when I had come from behind the monument to save Vodalus. The mausoleum where I had played as a boy stood as I had left it, its jammed door three-quarters shut.

I had brought a candle, and I lit it when I was inside. The funeral brasses I had once kept polished were green again; drifted leaves lay uncrushed everywhere. A tree had flung a slender limb through the little, barred window.

> Where I put you, there you lie,
> Never let a stranger spy,
> Like grass grow to any eye,
> Not of me.

> Here be safe, never leave it,
> Should a hand come, deceive it,
> Let strange eyes not believe it,
> Till I see.

The stone was smaller and lighter than I remembered. The coin beneath it had grown dull with damp; but it was still there, and in a moment I held it again and recalled the boy I had been, walking shaken back to the torn wall through the fog.

Now I must ask you, you that have pardoned so many deviations and digressions from me, to excuse one more. It is the last.

A few days ago (which is to say, a long time after the real termination of the events I have set myself to narrate) I was told that a vagabond had come here to the House Absolute saying that he owed me money, and that he refused to pay it to anyone else. I suspected that I was about to see some old acquaintance, and told the chamberlain to bring him to me.

It was Dr. Talos. He appeared to be in funds, and he had dressed himself for the occasion in a capot of red velvet and a chechia of the same material. His face was still that of a stuffed fox; but it seemed to me at times that some hint of life crept into it, that something or someone now peered through the glass eyes.

"You have bettered yourself," he said, making such a low bow that the tassel of his cap swept the carpet. "You may recall that I invariably affirmed you would. Honesty, integrity, and intelligence cannot be kept down."

"We both know that nothing is easier to keep down," I said. "By my old guild, they were kept down every day. But it is good to see you again, even if you come as the emissary of your master."

For a moment the doctor looked blank. "Oh, Baldanders, you mean. No, he has dismissed me, I'm afraid. After the fight. After he dived into the lake."

"You believe he survived, then."

"Oh, I'm quite sure he survived. You didn't know him as I did, Severian. Breathing water would be nothing to him. Nothing! He had a marvelous mind. He was a supreme genius of a unique sort: everything turned inward. He combined the objectivity of the scholar with the self-absorption of the mystic."

I said, "By which you mean he carried out experiments on himself."

"Oh, no, not at all. He reversed that! Others experiment upon themselves in order to derive some rule they can apply to the world. Baldanders experimented on the world and spent the proceeds, if I can put it so bluntly, upon his person. They say—" here he looked about nervously to make sure no one but myself was in earshot "—they say I'm a monster, and so I am. But Baldanders was more monster than I. In some sense he was my father, but he had built himself. It's the law of nature, and of what is higher than nature, that each creature must have a creator. But Baldanders was his own creation; he stood behind himself, and cut himself off from the line linking the rest of us with the Increate. However, I stray from my subject." The doctor had a wallet of scarlet leather at his belt; he loosened the strings and began to rummage in it. I heard the chink of metal.

"Do you carry money now?" I asked. "You used to give everything to him."

His voice sank until I could hardly hear it. "Wouldn't you, in my present position, do the same thing? Now I leave coins, little stacks of aes and orichalks, near water." He spoke more loudly: "It does no harm, and reminds me of the great days. But I am honest, you see! He always demanded that of me. And he was honest too, after his fashion. Anyway, do you recall the morning before we came out the gate? I was handing round the receipts from the night before, and we were interrupted. There was a coin left, and it was to go to you. I saved it and meant to give it to you later, but I forgot, and then when you came to the castle. . . ." He gave me a side-long glance. "But fair trade ends paid, as they say, and I have it here."

The coin was precisely like the one I had taken from under the stone.

"You see now why I couldn't give it to your man—I'm sure he thought me mad."

I flipped the coin and caught it. It felt as though it had been lightly greased. "To tell the truth, Doctor, we don't."

"Because it's false, of course. I told you so that morning. How could I have told him I had come to pay the Autarch, and then given him a bad coin? They're terrified of you, and they'd have disemboweled me looking for a good one! Is it true you've an explosive that takes days to go up, so you can blow people apart slowly?"

I was looking at the two coins. They had the same brassy shine and appeared to have been struck in the same die.

But that little interview, as I have said, took place a long time after the proper close of my narrative. I returned to my chambers in the Flag Tower by the way I had come, and when I reached them again, took off the dripping cloak and hung it up. Master Gurloes used to say that not wearing a shirt was the hardest thing about belonging to the guild. Though he meant it ironically, it was in some sense true. I, who had gone through the mountains with a naked chest, had been softened sufficiently by a few days in the stifling autarchial vestments to shiver at a foggy autumn night.

There were fireplaces in all the rooms, and each was piled with wood so old and dry that I suspected it would fall to dust should I strike it against an andiron. I had never lit any of these fires; but I decided to do so now, and warm myself, and spread the clothes Roche had brought over the back of a chair to dry. When I looked for my firebox, however, I discovered that in my excitement I had left it in the mausoleum with the candle. Thinking vaguely that the autarch who had inhabited these rooms before me (a ruler far beyond the reach of my memory) must surely have kept some means of kindling his numerous fires close to hand, I began searching the drawers of the cabinets.

These were largely filled with the papers that had so fascinated me before; but instead of stopping to read them, as I had when I had made my original survey of the rooms, I lifted them from each drawer to see if there was not a steel, igniter, or syringe of amadou beneath them.

I found none; but instead, in the largest drawer of the largest cabinet, concealed under a filigree pen case, I discovered a small pistol.

I had seen such weapons before—the first time having been when Vodalus had given me the false coin I had just reclaimed. Yet I had never held one in my own hands, and I found now that it was a very different thing from seeing them in the hands of others. Once when Dorcas and I were riding north toward Thrax we had fallen in with a caravan of tinkers and peddlers. We still had most of the money Dr. Talos had shared out when we met him in the forest north of the House Absolute; but we were uncertain how far it might carry us and how far we had to go, and so I was plying my trade with the rest, inquiring at each little town if there were not some malefactor to be mutilated or beheaded. The vagrants considered us two of themselves, and though some accorded us more or less exalted rank because I labored only for the authorities, others affected to despise us as the instruments of tyranny.

One evening, a grinder who had been friendlier than most and had done us several trifling favors offered to sharpen *Terminus Est* for me. I told him I kept her quite sharp enough for the work and invited him to test her edge with a finger. After he had cut himself slightly (as I had known he would) he grew quite taken with her, admiring not only her blade but her soft sheath, her carven guard, and so on. When I had answered innumerable questions regarding her making, history, and mode of use, he asked if I would permit him to hold her. I cautioned him about the weight of the blade and the danger of striking its fine edge against something that might injure it, then handed her over. He smiled and gripped the hilt as I had instructed him; but as he began to lift that long and shining instrument of death, his face went pale and his arms began to tremble so that I snatched her away from him before he dropped her. Afterward all he would say was *I've sharpened soldiers' swords often,* over and over.

Now I learned how he had felt. I laid the pistol on the table so quickly I nearly lost hold of it, then walked around and around it as though it had been a snake coiled to strike.

It was shorter than my hand, and so prettily made that it might have been a piece of jewelry; yet every line of it told of an origin beyond the nearer stars. Its silver had not yellowed with time, but might have come fresh from the buffing wheel. It was covered with decorations that were, perhaps, writing—I could not really tell which, and to eyes like mine, accustomed to patterns of straight lines and curves, they sometimes appeared to be no more than complex or shimmering reflections, save that they were reflections of something not present. The grips were encrusted with black stones whose name I did not know, gems like tourmalines but brighter. After a time I noticed that one, the smallest of all, seemed to vanish unless I looked at it straight on, when it sparkled with four-rayed brilliancy. Examining it more closely, I found it was not a gem at all, but a minute lens through which some inner fire shone. The pistol retained its charge then, after so many centuries.

Illogical though it might be, the knowledge reassured me. A weapon may be dangerous to its user in two ways: by wounding him by accident, or by failing him. The first remained; but when I saw the brightness of that point of light, I knew the second could be dismissed.

There was a sliding stud under the barrel that seemed likely to control the intensity of the discharge. My first

thought was that whoever had last handled it would probably
have set it to maximum intensity, and that by reversing the
setting I would be able to experiment with some safety. But
it was not so—the stud was positioned at the center of its
range. At last I decided, by analogy with a bowstring, that
the pistol was likely to be least dangerous when the stud was
as far foward as possible. I put it there, pointed the weapon
at the fireplace, and pulled the trigger.

The sound of a shot is the most horrible in the world. It is
the scream of matter itself. Now the report was not loud, but
threatening, like distant thunder. For an instant—so brief a
time I might almost have believed I dreamed it—a narrow
cone of violet flashed between the muzzle of the pistol and
the heaped wood. Then it was gone, the wood was blazing,
and slabs of burned and twisted metal fell with the noise of
cracked bells from the back of the fireplace. A rivulet of silver
ran out onto the hearth to scorch the mat and send up nau-
seous smoke.

I put the pistol into the sabretache of my new journeyman's habit.

XXXVII

Across the River Again

BEFORE DAWN, Roche was at my door, with Drotte and Eata. Drotte was the oldest of us, yet his face and flashing eyes made him seem younger than Roche. He was still the very picture of wiry strength, but I could not help but notice that I was now taller than he by the width of two fingers. I must surely have been so already when I left the Citadel, though I had not been conscious of it. Eata was still the smallest, and not yet even a journeyman—so I had only been away one summer, after all. He seemed a bit dazed when he greeted me, and I suppose he was having trouble believing I was now Autarch, particularly since he had not seen me again until now, when I was once more dressed in the habit of the guild.

I had told Roche that the three of them were to be armed; he and Drotte carried swords similar in form (though vastly inferior in workmanship) to *Terminus Est*, and Eata a clava I recalled having seen displayed at our Masking Day festivities. Before I had seen the fighting in the north, I would have thought them well-enough equipped; now all three, not only Eata, seemed like boys burdened with sticks and pinecones, ready to play at war.

For the last time we went out through the rent in the wall

and threaded the paths of bone that wound among the cypresses and tombs. The death roses I had hesitated to pick for Thecla still showed a few autumnal blooms, and I found myself thinking of Morwenna, the only woman whose life I have ever taken, and of her enemy, Eusebia.

When we had passed the gate of the necropolis and entered the squalid city streets, my companions seemed to become almost lighthearted. I think they must have been subconsciously afraid they would be seen by Master Gurloes and punished in some way for having obeyed the Autarch.

"I hope you're not planning on going for a swim," Drotte said. "These choppers would sink us."

Roche chuckled. "Eata can float with his."

"We're going far to the north. We'll need a boat, but I think we'll be able to hire one if we walk along the embankment."

"If anybody will rent to us. And if we're not arrested. You know, Autarch—"

"Severian," I reminded him. "For as long as I wear these clothes."

"—Severian, we're only supposed to carry these things to the block, and it will take a lot of talking to make the peltasts think three of us are necessary. Will they know who you are? I don't—"

This time it was Eata who interrupted him, pointing toward the river. "Look, there's a boat!"

Roche bellowed, all three waved, and I held up one of the chrisos I had borrowed from the castellan, turning it so it would flash in the sunlight that was then just beginning to show over the towers behind us. The man at the tiller waved his cap, and what appeared to be a slender lad sprang forward to put the dipping lugsails on the other tack.

She was two-masted, rather narrow of beam and low of freeboard—an ideal craft, no doubt, for running untaxed merchandise past the patrol cutters that had suddenly become mine. The grizzled old moonraker of a steersman looked capable of much worse, and the slender "lad" was a girl with laughing eyes and a facility for looking from them sidelong.

"Well, this 'pears to be a day," the steersman said when he saw our habits. "I thought you was in mournin', I did, till I got up close. Eyes? I never heard of 'um, no more than a crow in court."

"We are," I told him as I got on board. It gave me a ridiculous pleasure to find I had not lost the sea legs I had acquired on the *Samru*, and to watch Drotte and Roche grab for the sheets when the lugger rocked beneath their weight.

"Mind if I've a look at that yellow boy? Just to see if he's good. I'll send him right home."

I tossed him the coin, which he rubbed and bit and at last surrendered with a respectful look.

"We may need your boat all day."

"For the yellow boy, you can have her all night too. We'll both be glad of the company, like the undertaker remarked to the ghost. There was things in the river up till first light, which I suppose might have something to do with you opti-mates being out on the water this mornin'?"

"Cast off," I said. "You can tell me, if you will, what these strange things were while we are under way."

Although he had broached the subject himself, the steersman seemed reluctant to go into much detail—perhaps only because he had difficulty in finding words to express what he had felt and to describe what he had seen and heard. There was a light west wind, so that with the lugger's batten-stiffened sails drawn taut we were able to run upstream handily. The brown girl had little to do but sit in the bow and trade glances with Eata. (It is possible she thought him, in his dirty gray shirt and trousers, only a paid attendant of ours.) The steersman, who called himself her uncle, kept a steady pressure on the tiller as he talked, to keep the lugger from flying off the wind.

"I'll tell you what I saw myself, like the carpenter did when he had the shutter up. We was eight or nine leagues north of where you hailed us. Clams was our cargo, you see, and there's no stoppin' with them, not when there's a chance of a warm afternoon. We goes down to the lower river and buys them off the diggers, do you see, then runs them up the channel quick so's they can be et before they goes bad. If they goes off you lose all, but you make double or better if you can sell them good.

"I've spent more nights on the river in my life than anywhere else—it's my bedroom, you might say, and this boat's my cradle, though I don't usually get to sleep until mornin'. But last night—sometimes I felt like I wasn't on old Gyoll at all, but on some other river, one that run up into the sky, or under the ground.

"I doubt you noticed unless you was out late, but it was a still night with just little breaths of wind that would blow for about as long as it takes a man to swear, then die down, then blow again. There was mist too, thick as cotton. It hung over the water the way mists always does, with about so much clear space as you could roll a keg through between it and the river. Most of the time we couldn't see the lights on either shore, just the mist. I used to have a horn I blowed for those that couldn't see our lights, but it went over the side last year, and being copper it sunk. So I shouted last night, whenever I felt like there was another boat or anything close by us.

"About a watch after the mist came I let Maxellindis go to sleep. Both sails was set, and when each puff of air come we would go up river a bit, and then I'd set out the anchor again. You maybe don't know it, optimates, but the rule of the river is that them that's goin' up keeps to the sides and them that's goin' down takes the middle. We was goin' up and ought to have been over to the east bank, but with the mist I couldn't tell.

"Then I heard sweeps. I looked in the mist, but I couldn't see lights, and I hollered so they'd sheer off. I leaned over the gunnel and put my ear close to the water so's to hear better. A mist soaks up noises, but the best hearin' you can ever have is when you gets your head under one, because the noise runs right along the water. Anyway, I did that, and she was a big one. You can't count how many sweeps there is with a good crew pullin', because they all go in and come up together, but when a big vessel goes fast you can hear water breakin' under her bow, and this was a big one. I got up on top of the deckhouse tryin' to see her, but there still wasn't any lights, though I knew she had to be close.

"Just when I was climbin' down I caught the sight of her—a galleass, four-masted and four-banked, no lights, comin' right up the channel, as near as I could judge. Pray for them that's comin' down, thinks I to myself, like the ox said when he fell out of the riggin'.

"Of course I only saw her for a minute before she was gone in the mist again, but I heard her a long while after. Seein' her like that made me feel so queer I yelled every once in a while even if no other craft was by. We had made another half league, I suppose, or maybe a little less, when I heard somebody yell back. Only it wasn't like answerin' my hail, but like somebody'd laid a rope end to him. I called again, and he called back regular, and it was a man I know named Trason what has his own boat just like I do. 'Is it you?' he called, and I said it was and asked if he was all right. 'Tie up!' he says.

"I told him I couldn't. I had clams, and even if the night was cool, I wanted to sell soon as I could. 'Tie up,' Trason calls again, 'Tie up and go ashore.' So I call back, 'Why don't you?' Just then he come in sight, and there was more on his boat than I would've thought it would hold—pandours, I'd have said, but every pandour ever I saw had a face brown as mine or nearly, and these was white as the mist. They had scorpions and voulges—I could see the heads of them stickin' up over the crests of their helmets."

I interrupted him to ask if the soldiers he had seen were starved looking and if they had large eyes.

He shook his head, one corner of his mouth twisting up.

"They was big men, bigger than you or me or anybody in this boat, a head taller than Trason. Anyway, they were gone in a moment, just like the galleass. That was the only other craft I saw till the mist lifted. But . . ."

I said, "But you saw something else. Or heard something."

He nodded. "I thought maybe you and your people here was out because of them. Yes, I saw and I heard things. There was things in this river I never saw before. Maxellindis, when she woke up and I told her about it, said it was the manatees. They're pale in moonlight and look human enough if you don't come too close. But I've seen 'em since I was a boy and never been fooled once. And there was women's voices, not loud but big. And something else. I couldn't understand what any of 'em was sayin', but I could hear the tone of it. You know how it is when you're listenin' to people over the water? They would say *so-and-so-and-so*. Then the deeper voice—I can't call it a man's because I don't think it was one—the deeper voice'd say *go-and-do-that-and-this-and-that*. I heard the women's voices three times and the other voice twice. You won't believe it, optimates, but sometimes it sounded like the voices was coming up out of the river."

With that he fell silent, looking out over the nenuphars. We were well above that part of Gyoll opposite the Citadel, but they were still packed more densely than wildflowers in any meadow this side of paradise.

The Citadel itself was visible now as a whole, and for all its vastness seemed a glittering flock fluttering upon the hill, its thousand metal towers ready to leap into the air at a word. Below them the necropolis spread an embroidery of mingled white and green. I know it is fashionable to speak in tones of faint disgust of the "unhealthy" growth of the lawns and trees in such places, but I have never observed that there is actually anything unhealthy about it. Green things die that men may live, and men die that green things may live, even that ignorant and innocent man I killed with his own ax there long ago. All our foliage is faded, so it is said, and no doubt it is so; and when the New Sun comes, his bride, the New Urth, will give glory to him with leaves like emeralds. But in the present day, the day of the old sun and old Urth, I have never seen any other green so deep as the great pines' in the necropolis when the wind swells their branches. They draw their strength from the departed generations of mankind, and the masts of argosies, that are built up of many trees, are not so high as they.

The Sanguinary Field stands far from the river. We four drew strange looks as we journeyed there, but no one halted us. The Inn of Lost Loves, which had ever seemed to me the least permanent of the houses of men, still stood as it had on the afternoon when I had come there with Agia and Dorcas. The fat innkeeper very nearly fainted when he saw us; I made him fetch Ouen, the waiter.

I had never really looked at him on that afternoon when he had carried in a tray for Dorcas, Agia, and me. I did so now. He was a balding man about as tall as Drotte, thin and somehow pinched looking; his eyes were deep blue, and there was a delicacy to the molding of his eyes and mouth that I recognized at once.

"Do you know who we are?" I asked him.

Slowly, he shook his head.

"Have you never had a torturer to serve?"

"Once this spring, sieur," he said. "And I know these two men in black are torturers. But you're no torturer, sieur, though you're dressed like one."

I let that pass. "You have never seen me?"

"No, sieur."

"Very well, perhaps you have not." (How strange it was to realize that I had changed so much.) "Ouen, since you do not know me, it might be well if I knew you. Tell me where you were born and who your parents were, and how you came to be employed at this inn."

"My father was a shopkeeper, sieur. We lived in Oldgate, on the west bank. When I was ten or so, I think, he sent me to an inn to be a potboy, and I've worked in one or another since."

"Your father was a shopkeeper. What of your mother?"

Ouen's face still held a waiter's deference, but his eyes were puzzled. "I never knew her, sieur. Cas they called her, but she died when I was young. In childbirth, my father said."

"But you know what she looked like."

He nodded. "My father had a locket with her likeness. Once when I was twenty or so I came to see him and found out he'd pledged it. I'd come into a bit of money then helping a certain optimate with his affairs—carrying messages to the ladies and standing watch outside doors and so on, and I went to the pawnbroker's and paid the pledge and took it. I still wear it, sieur. In a place like ours, where there's so many in 'n out all the time, it's best to keep your valuables about you."

He reached into his shirt and drew out a locket of cloisonné enamel. The pictures inside were of Dorcas in full face and profile, a Dorcas hardly younger than the Dorcas I had known.

"You say you became a potboy at ten, Ouen. But you can read and write."

"A bit, sieur." He looked embarrassed. "I've asked people, various times, what writing said. I don't forget much."

"You wrote something when the torturer was here this spring," I told him. "Do you recall what you wrote?"

Frightened, he shook his head. "Only a note to warn the girl."

"I do. It was, 'The woman with you has been here before. Do not trust her. Trudo says the man is a torturer. You are my mother come again.'"

Ouen tucked his locket under his shirt. "It was only that she was so much like her, sieur. When I was a younger man, I used to think that someday I'd find such a woman. I told myself, you know, that I was a better man than my father, and he had, after all. But I never did, and now I'm not so sure I'm a better man."

"At that time, you did not know what a torturer's habit looked like," I said. "But your friend Trudo, the ostler, knew. He knew a good deal more about torturers than you, and that was why he ran away."

"Yes, sieur. When he heard the torturer was asking for him, he did."

"But you saw the innocence of the girl and wanted to warn her against the torturer and the other woman. You were right about both of them, perhaps."

"If you say it, sieur."

"Do you know, Ouen, you look a bit like her."

The fat innkeeper had been listening more or less openly. Now he chuckled. "He looks more like you!"

I am afraid I turned to stare at him.

"No offense intended, sieur, but it's true. He's a bit older, but when you were talking I saw both your faces from the side, and there isn't a patch of difference."

I studied Ouen again. His hair and eyes were not dark like mine, but with that coloring aside, his face might almost have been my own.

"You said you never found a woman like Dorcas—like that one in your locket. Still you found a woman, I think."

His eyes would not meet mine. "Several, sieur."

"And fathered a child."

"No, sieur!" He was startled. "Never, sieur!"

"How interesting. Were you ever in difficulties with the law?"

"Several times, sieur."

"It is well to keep your voice low, but it need not be so low as that. And look at me when you speak to me. A woman you loved—or perhaps only one who loved you—a dark woman—was taken once?"

"Once, sieur," he said. "Yes, sieur. Catherine was her name. It's an old-fashioned name, they tell me." He paused and shrugged. "There was trouble, as you say, sieur. She'd run off from some order of monials. The law got her, and I never saw her again."

He did not want to come, but we brought him with us when we returned to the lugger.

When I had come upriver by night on the *Samru*, the line between the living and the dead city had been like that between the dark curve of the world and the celestial dome with its stars. Now, when there was so much more light, it had vanished. Half-ruinous structures lined the banks, but whether they were the homes of the most wretched of our citizens or mere deserted shells I could not determine until I saw a string on which three rags flapped.

"In the guild we have the ideal of poverty," I said to Drotte as we leaned on the gunnel. "But those people do not need the ideal; they have achieved it."

"I should think they'd need it most of all," he answered.

He was wrong. The Increate was there, a thing beyond the Hierodules and those they serve; even on the river, I could feel his presence as one feels that of the master of a great house, though he may be in an obscure room on another floor. When we went ashore, it seemed to me that if I were to step through any doorway there, I might surprise some shining figure; and that the commander of all such figures was everywhere invisible only because he was too large to be seen.

We found a man's sandal, worn but not old, lying in one of the grass-grown streets. I said, "I'm told there are looters wandering this place. That is one reason I asked you to come. If there were no one but myself involved, I would do it alone."

Roche nodded and drew his sword, but Drotte said, "There's no one here. You've become a great deal wiser than we are, Severian, but still, I think you've grown a little too accustomed to things that terrify ordinary people."

I asked what he meant.

"You knew what the boatman was talking about. I could see that in your face. You were afraid too, or at least concerned. But not frightened like he was in his boat last night, or like Roche or Ouen there or I would have been if we'd been close to the river and knew what was going on. The looters you're talking about were around last night, and they must keep a watch out for revenue boats. They won't be anywhere near water today, or for several days to come."

Eata touched my arm. "Do you think that girl—Maxellindis—is she in danger, back there on the boat?"

"She's not in as much danger as you are from her," I said. He did not know what I meant, but I did. His Maxellindis was not Thecla; his story could not be the same as my own. But I had seen the revolving corridors of Time behind the gamin face with the laughing brown eyes. Love is a long labor for torturers; and even if I were to dissolve the guild, Eata would become a torturer, as all men are, bound by the contempt for wealth without which a man is less than a man, inflicting pain by his nature, whether he willed it or not. I was sorry for him, and more sorry for Maxellindis the sailor girl.

Ouen and I went into the house, leaving Roche, Drotte, and Eata to keep watch from some distance away. As we stood at the door, I could hear the soft sound of Dorcas's steps inside.

"We will not tell you who you are," I said to Ouen. "And we cannot tell you what you may become. But we are your Autarch, and we tell you what you must do."

I had no words for him, but I discovered I did not need them. He knelt at once, as the castellan had.

"We brought the torturers with us so that you might know what was in store for you if you disobeyed us. But we do not wish you to disobey, and now, having met you, we doubt they were needed. There is a woman in this house. In a moment you will go in. You must tell her your story, as you told it to us, and you must remain with her and protect her, even if she tries to send you away."

"I will do my best, Autarch," Ouen said.

"When you can, you must persuade her to leave this city of death. Until then, we give you this." I took out the pistol and handed it to him. "It is worth a cartload of chrisos, but as long as you are here, it is far better for you to have than chrisos. When you and the woman are safe, we will buy it back from you, if you wish." I showed him how to operate the pistol and left him.

I was alone then, and I do not doubt that there are some who, reading this too-brief account of a summer more than normally turbulent, will say that I have usually been so. Jonas, my only real friend, was in his own eyes merely a machine; Dorcas, whom I yet love, is in her own eyes merely a kind of ghost.

I do not feel it is so. We choose—or choose not—to be alone when we decide whom we will accept as our fellows, and whom we will reject. Thus an eremite in a mountain cave is in company, because the birds and coneys, the initiates whose words live in his "forest books," and the winds—the messengers of the Increate—are his companions. Another man, living in the midst of millions, may be alone, because there are none but enemies and victims around him.

Agia, whom I might have loved, has chosen instead to become a female Vodalus, taking all that lives most fully in humanity as her opponent. I, who might have loved Agia, who loved Dorcas deeply but perhaps not deeply enough, was now alone because I had become a part of her past, which she loved better than she had ever (except, I think, at first) loved me.

XXXVIII

Resurrection

ALMOST NOTHING REMAINS to be told. Dawn has come, the red sun like a bloody eye. The wind blows cold through the window. In a few moments, a footman will carry in a steaming tray; with him, no doubt, will be old, twisted Father Inire, eager to confer during the last few moments that remain; old Father Inire, alive so long beyond the span of his short-lived kind; old Father Inire, who will not, I fear, long survive the red sun. How upset he will be to find I have been sitting up writing all night here in the clerestory.

Soon I must don robes of argent, the color that is more pure than white. Never mind.

There will be long, slow days on the ship. I will read. I still have so much to learn. I will sleep, dozing in my berth, listening to the centuries wash against the hull. This manuscript I shall send to Master Ultan; but while I am on the ship, when I cannot sleep and have tired of reading, I shall write it out again—I who forget nothing—every word, just as I have written it here. I shall call it *The Book of the New Sun*, for that book, lost now for so many ages, is said to have predicted his coming. And when it is finished again, I shall seal that second copy in a coffer of lead and set it adrift on the seas of space and time.

Have I told you all I promised? I am aware that at various places in my narrative I have pledged that this or that should be made clear in the knitting up of the story. I remember them all, I am sure, but then I remember so much else. Before you assume that I have cheated you, read again, as I will write again.

Two things are clear to me. The first is that I am not the first Severian. Those who walk the corridors of Time saw him gain the Phoenix Throne, and thus it was that the Autarch, having been told of me, smiled in the House Azure, and the undine thrust me up when it seemed I must drown. (Yet surely the first Severian did not; something had already begun to reshape my life.) Let me guess now, though it is only a guess, at the story of that first Severian.

He too was reared by the torturers, I think. He too was sent forth to Thrax. He too fled Thrax, and though he did not carry the Claw of the Conciliator, he must have been drawn to the fighting in the north—no doubt he hoped to escape the archon by hiding himself among the army. How he encountered the Autarch there I cannot say; but encounter him he did, and so, even as I, he (who in the final sense was and is myself) became Autarch in turn and sailed beyond the candles of night. Then those who walk the corridors walked back to the time when he was young, and my own story—as I have given it here in so many pages—began.

The second thing is this. He was not returned to his own time but became himself a walker of the corridors. I know now the identity of the man called the Head of Day, and why Hildegrin, who was too near, perished when we met, and why the witches fled. I know too in whose mausoleum I tarried as a child, that little building of stone with its rose, its fountain, and its flying ship all graven. I have disturbed my own tomb, and now I go to lie in it.

· · ·

When Drotte, Roche, Eata, and I returned to the Citadel, I received urgent messages from Father Inire and from the House Absolute, and yet I lingered. I asked the castellan for a map. After much searching he produced one, large and old, cracked in many places. It showed the curtain wall whole, but the names of the towers were not the names I knew—or that the castellan knew, for that matter—and there were towers on that map that are not in the Citadel, and towers in the Citadel that were not on that map.

I ordered a flier then, and for half a day soared among the towers. No doubt I saw the place I sought many times, but if so I did not recognize it.

At last, with a bright and unfailing lamp, I went down into our oubliette once more, down flight after flight of steps until I had reached the lowest level. What is it, I wonder, that has given so great a power to preserve the past to underground places? One of the bowls in which I had carried soup to Triskele was there still. (Triskele, who had stirred back to life beneath my hand two years before I bore the Claw.) I followed Triskele's footprints once more, as I had when still an apprentice, to the forgotten opening, and from there my own into the dark maze of tunnels.

Now in the steady light of my lamp I saw where I had lost the track, running straight on when Triskele had turned aside. I was tempted then to follow him instead of myself, so that I might see where he had emerged, and in that way perhaps discover who it was who had befriended him and to whom he used to return after greeting me, sometimes, in the byways of the Citadel. Possibly when I come back to Urth I shall do so, if indeed I do come back.

But once again, I did not turn aside. I followed the boy-man I had been, down a straight corridor floored with mud and pierced at rare intervals with forbidding vents and doors. The Severian I pursued wore ill-fitting shoes with run-down heels and worn soles; when I turned and flashed my light behind me, I observed that though the Severian who pursued him had excellent boots, his steps were of unequal length and the toe of one foot dragged at each. I thought, One Severian had good boots, the other good legs. And I laughed to myself, wondering who should come here in afteryears, and whether he would guess that the same feet left both tracks.

To what use these tunnels were once put, I cannot say. Several times I saw stairs that had once descended farther still, but always they led to dark, calm water. I found a skeleton, its bones scattered by the running feet of Severian, but it was only a skeleton, and told me nothing. In places there was writing on the walls, writing in faded orange or sturdy black; but it was in a character I could not read, as unintelligible as the scrawlings of the rats in Master Ultan's library. A few of the rooms into which I looked held walls in which there had once ticked a thousand or more clocks of various kinds, and though all were dead now, their chimes silenced and their hands corroded at hours that would never come again, I thought them good omens for one who sought the Atrium of Time.

And at last I found it. The little spot of sunshine was just as I had remembered it. No doubt I acted foolishly, but I extinguished my lamp and stood for a moment in the dark, looking at it. All was silence, and its bright, uneven square seemed at least as mysterious as it had before.

I had feared I would have difficulty in squeezing through its narrow crevice, but if the present Severian was somewhat larger of bone, he was also leaner, so that when I had worked my shoulders through the rest followed easily enough.

The snow I recalled was gone, but a chill had come into the air to say that it would soon return. A few dead leaves, which must have been carried in some updraft very high indeed, had come to rest here among the dying roses. The tilted dials still cast their crazy shadows, useless as the dead clocks beneath them, though not so unmoving. The carven animals stared at them, unwinking still.

I crossed to the door and tapped on it. The timorous old

woman who had served us appeared, and I, stepping into that musty room in which I had warmed myself before, told her to bring Valeria to me. She hurried away, but before she was out of sight, something had wakened in the time-worn walls, its disembodied voices, hundred-tongued, demanding that Valeria report to some antiquely titled personage who I realized with a start must be myself.

Here my pen shall halt, reader, though I do not. I have carried you from gate to gate—from the locked and fog-shrouded gate of the necropolis of Nessus to that cloud-racked gate we call the sky, the gate that shall lead me, as I hope, beyond the nearer stars.

My pen halts, though I do not. Reader, you will walk no more with me. It is time we both take up our lives.

————————

To this account, I, Severian the Lame, Autarch, do set my hand in what shall be called the last year of the old sun.

————————

APPENDIX

The Arms of the Autarch and the Ships of the Hierodules

NOWHERE ARE THE manuscripts of *The Book of the New Sun* more obscure than in their treatment of weapons and military organization.

The confusion concerning the equipment of Severian's allies and adversaries appears to derive from two sources, of which the first is his marked tendency to label every variation in design or purpose with a separate name. In translating these, I have endeavored to bear in mind the radical meaning of the words employed as well as what I take to be the appearance and function of the weapons themselves. Thus *falchion, fuscina,* and many others. At one point I have put the *athame,* the warlock's sword, into Agia's hands.

The second source of difficulty seems to be that three quite different gradations of technology are involved. The lowest of these could be termed the smith level. The arms produced by it appear to consist of swords, knives, axes, and pikes, such as might have been forged by any skilled metalworker of, say, the fifteenth century. These appear to be readily obtained by the average citizen and to represent the technological ability of the society as a whole.

The second gradation might be called the Urth level. The

long cavalry weapons I have chosen to call *lances, conti,* and so on undoubtedly belong to this group, as do the "spears" with which the hastarii menaced Severian outside the door of the antechamber and other arms used by infantry. How widely available such weapons were is not clear from the text, which at one point speaks of "arrows" and "long-shafted khetens" being offered for sale in Nessus. It seems certain that Guasacht's irregulars were issued their conti before battle and that these were collected and stored somewhere (possibly in his tent) afterward. Perhaps it should be noted that small arms were issued and collected in this way in the navies of the eighteenth and nineteenth centuries, although cutlasses and firearms could be freely purchased ashore. The arbalests used by Agia's assassins outside the mine are surely what I have called Urth weapons, but it is likely these men were deserters.

The Urth weapons, then, appear to represent the highest technology to be found on the planet, and perhaps in its solar system. How efficient they would be in comparison with our own arms is difficult to say. Armor appears to be not wholly ineffective against them, but precisely this is true with regard to our rifles, carbines, and submachine guns.

The third gradation I would call the stellar level. The pistol given Thea by Vodalus and the one given Ouen by Severian are unquestionably stellar weapons, but about many other arms mentioned in the manuscript we cannot be so sure. Some, or even all, of the artillery used in the mountain war may be stellar. The *fusils* and *jezails* carried by special troops on both sides may or may not belong to this gradation, though I am inclined to think they do.

It seems fairly clear that stellar weapons could not be produced on Urth and had to be obtained from the Hierodules at great cost. An interesting question—to which I can offer no certain answer—concerns the goods given in exchange. The Urth of the old sun seems, by our standards, destitute of raw materials; when Severian speaks of mining, he appears to mean what we should call archaeological pillaging, and the new continents said (in Dr. Talos's play) to be ready to rise with the coming of the New Sun have among their attractions "gold, silver, *iron,* and *copper* . . ." (Italics added.) Slaves—some slavery certainly exists in Severian's society—furs, meat and other foodstuffs, and labor-intensive items such as handmade jewelry would appear to be among the possibilities.

We would like to know more about almost everything mentioned in these manuscripts; but most of all, certainly, we would like to know more about the ships that sail between the stars, commanded by the Hierodules but sometimes crewed by human beings. (Two of the most enigmatic figures in the manuscripts, Jonas and Hethor, seem once to have been such crewmen.) But here the translater is forced against one of the most maddening of all his difficulties—Severian's failure to distinguish clearly between space-going and ocean-going craft.

Irritating though it is, it seems quite natural, given his circumstances. If a distant continent is as remote as the moon, then the moon is no more remote than a distant continent. Furthermore, the star-traveling ships appear to be propelled by light pressure on immense sails of metal foil, so that an applied science of masts, cables, and spars is common to ships of both kinds. Presumably, since many skills (and perhaps most of all that of enduring long periods of isolation) would be required equally on both types of craft, crewmen from vessels that would only excite our contempt may sign aboard others whose capabilities would astonish us. One notes that the captain of Severian's lugger shares some of Jonas's habits of speech.

And now, a final comment. In my translations and in these appendixes I have attached to them, I have attempted to eschew all speculations; it seems to me that now, near the close of seven years' labor, I may be permitted one. It is that the ability to traverse hours and aeons possessed by these ships may be no more than the natural consequence of their ability to penetrate interstellar and even intergalactic space, and to escape the death throes of the universe; and that to travel thus in time may not be so complex and difficult an affair as we are prone to suppose. It is possible that from the beginning Severian had some presentiment of his future.

G.W.

Gene Wolfe was born in 1931. He served in the Korean War and afterwards studied mechanical engineering. In 1972 he became editor of an engineering periodical. His first story ('The Dead Man') appeared in 1965, after he had already been writing for some time. During the 60s and the 70s Wolfe wrote a large number of short stories, many of which were published in Damon Knight's *Orbit* anthologies. In 1973 'The Death of Doctor Island', part of a quartet of stories later collected as *The Wolfe Archipelago* in 1983, won a Nebula award. His first novel (*Operation Ares*) was published in 1970, but was heavily cut by the publisher. His second novel was *The Fifth Head of Cerberus*, published in 1972. In 1980, he started to publish a long sequence of novels called The Book of The New Sun, beginning with *The Shadow of the Torturer* (1980). The final book in the sequence was *The Citadel of the Autarch* (1983), although there followed a sequel in 1987 (*The Urth of the New Sun*). Of these books, *The Shadow of the Torturer* won a World Fantasy Award and *The Claw of the Conciliator* (1981) won a Nebula. He wrote several more novels before starting on a new sequence in 1993 called The Book of The Long Sun.